BAD
LAWYER

OTHER BOOKS
BY DAVID CRAY

Keeplock

BAD LAWYER

David Cray

An Otto Penzler Book

CARROLL & GRAF PUBLISHERS, INC.
NEW YORK

First Carroll & Graf edition 2001

Carroll & Graf Publishers, Inc.
A Division of Avalon Publishing Group
19 West 21st Street
New York, NY 10010-6805

Library of Congress Cataloging-in-Publication Data is available.
ISBN: 0-7867-0825-5

Manufactured in the United States of America

For Otto Penzler
who came looking, twice

Prologue

This is a book about love. Ferocious love, jealous love; love that excluded all but the lovers, love that reserved the traditional virtues of duty and honor to itself alone. I know I'm putting the cart before the horse, beginning my final argument before presenting the evidence, but questions of guilt or innocence are without meaning here, a point that needs to be made early on by a man already judged.

There were three lovers in this triangle, a curiously asexual *menage à trois* that maintained itself through a tyranny of memory, a pure terror of the past. We had no real leader, though I, with my personal narcissism (not to mention my fuck-you attitude) was the most obviously visible. But I was never, as some have suggested, the puppet-master, not with coconspirators as tough and powerful as Caleb Talbot and Julia Gill.

I begin, naturally, with myself, Sidney Itzhak Kaplan, third generation American Jew, born in Williamsburg, Brooklyn, in the year 1944, raised in Sheepshead Bay, also Brooklyn. My paternal great-grandfather, Hyman Baruch, hit these shores in 1879, along with his young wife, Esther, and quickly set up housekeeping in a basement room on Norfolk Street in Manhattan. Unable to find steady work, Hymie became the proverbial wandering Jew, loading his rented wagon with everything from pots to perfume to spectacles, working the towns of New Jersey and Pennsylvania, absent (so I was told again and again) for months at a time.

My grandfather, Itzhak (who lived in our house after his wife, Ethyl, died) was born in 1898, the last of nine children. By that time, Hyman had moved his family to the relative splendor of an old-law tenement on Hester Street. The family—mother, father, and six surviving kids—lived in the second and third of four rooms. The last room, the windowless cube at the end of the line, was reserved for the cutting and sewing of shirtwaists. Summer and winter, a huge stove in the front room glowed red-hot to keep the pressing irons heated. My grandfather carried a thick, rubbery scar on his left arm, a souvenir of that stove.

In 1899, a year after my Grampa Itzy's birth, his father disappeared. Itzy's brother, Nathan, the oldest at sixteen, was dispatched to find him. What Nathan found was a grave outside the town of Tranquility in northwestern New Jersey, and a story about a Jew kicked in the chest by his horse. Nathan, ever the good son, dug up the body in an effort to make an identification.

"Sidney," Grampa Itzy told me six decades later, "the stiff's shirt was made by my own *hands*."

Grampa Itzy, who'd been less than a year old when his father disappeared, had tiny, black eyes that glowed whenever he leaped into hyperbole. The next part of it, though, had passed into history; it was believed absolutely by dozens of assorted aunts, uncles, and cousins. "Even with all the decay, Nathan could see they had shaved our father's head. Also the beard. The beard was missing."

As time went on, the children married and moved out. Grampa Itzy was the last to go, marrying Ethyl Pearlman in 1920. By that time he was already the proud owner of a men's clothing store on Grand Street between Orchard and Ludlow.

"I was famous up and down the Lower East Side. A *macher*, yes, but also a *mavin* with a needle." At this point he would raise his teaglass to his lips, the gesture at once coy and calculating. "For Meyer Lansky, I made all his suits. Also for Albert Anastasia." Then he'd sip, swallow, lower the glass to his lap. "In them days we was all the same. The Jews, the Italians, it didn't make no difference. You got a little money, you wanted to look good."

My father, David Baruch Kaplan, was born in 1921, the first of three children, the others girls and married off just after Pearl Harbor. David Baruch, in the great patriarchal tradition, was given the family business on a platter. He was brought into the store at age ten, his fortune supposedly made, only to crash, head-on, into the Great Depression, his patrimony amounting to a decade of twelve-hour days in a nearly empty store.

The experience soured him, left him bitter and cynical, unable to enjoy the lucky accident that finally brought prosperity. Drafted into the army shortly after Pearl Harbor, David broke his leg in basic training, a piece of good fortune that left him with a slight limp and a jump start on the rest of his generation.

My father and grandfather were angry, belligerent men, as am I. They had excuses; I don't. Yet, in what was fast becoming the family tradition, I fought my way through high school, psychologically as well as physically, a touchy kid left to stand alone by the schoolyard fence. My best (and only) friend was a Catholic school boy named Vinnie Barrone who spoke out of the side of his mouth, an act of homage to his convict father.

My summers were spent in the store, sweeping the floors, dusting the mannequins, stocking the shelves, though my father made it clear that I would never walk in his shoes. Or sell them, either. "Sidney," he told me on the day after my *bar mitzvah*, "the Lower East Side is going to the dogs." By which he meant the Puerto Ricans. "And I don't have the energy to move the business. Besides which, the department stores'll ruin us in the long run no matter what." He shook his head, leaned back against a free-standing counter piled with shirts. "What I'm gonna do is put away enough money so that me and your mother should be comfortable in our old age. But you, Sidney, you gotta find another way."

My way, though I couldn't have spelled it out even while it was happening, was Brooklyn College (at the time free and predominantly Jewish), then Brooklyn Law School on a scholarship. I graduated third in my class, a lanky, scowling young man who yearned for the courtroom, for combat, for a test of wills that could be measured by words like guilty and innocent.

Two weeks after being admitted to the bar, I went to work in the Manhattan D.A.'s office, passing from gofer to the elite Homicide Unit to private practice in less than seven years. Over the next twenty-plus years, I represented some of the worst criminals in New York, low- and high-level mob figures, drug dealers with briefcases full of banded hundreds. I had the Rolex, the pinky ring, the 450SL, the co-op on Central Park West, the summer house on Fire Island. I had a suite of offices on Broad Street in lower Manhattan, a stable of hard working subordinates who didn't object to my stealing the glory, the kind of celebrity that brought a table at the Four Seasons without suffering the indignity of phoning ahead for a reservation.

Then it all went bad, seemingly overnight, though I now realize the process took several years. From my clients' point of view, the decline meant no more than Sid Kaplan loses cases, that defendants defended by Sid Kaplan not only go to prison, but (as Sid Kaplan is personally hated by sentencing judges) routinely feel the weight of the proverbial thrown book. From my point of view, it was a soul and body destroying combination of alcohol and cocaine that allowed my fifty-plus body to work sixteen-hour days, seven days a week, that left me befuddled by the complexities of courtroom procedure. By the time I gave it up and went into rehab for a year, I was buying cocaine by the ounce, consuming it (along with quarts of Chivas) as fast as I could put it into my body, floating half the time, as high from the fatigue as from the drugs.

At first glance, Caleb Jesse Talbot, born in the town of Brantley, Alabama, in the year 1941, the only child of Zacariah and Rose Talbot, seemed an utterly harmless man. Under five-ten, more than three hundred pounds, the starched collars of his white shirts cut into his jowls, the edges disappearing under a wave of ebony flesh. He had eyes, Caleb did, that protruded (the result of a thyroid condition, so he insisted) as if pushed from inside by the double whammy of his collar and his tightly knotted tie.

I don't know where Caleb went for the jackets he inevitably wore, but unlike his shirts, they somehow managed to accommodate his enormous shoulders and back, his equally enormous belly and ass, without buttons flying like sprinkled corn in a microwave. Similarly, his sharply creased black trousers fell smoothly over his buttocks and thighs, then dropped in a straight line to brush the tops of his tasseled loafers. Caleb had tiny feet and hands; his fingers were thick and of equal length, his square, pink palms curiously unlined. His face was unlined as well, the skin puffed out in a smooth, often rippling sheet that overpowered his small nose and pursed mouth.

Caleb liked to play the "good cop" to my "bad cop" whenever I needed to get the truth from my lying clients and their lying witnesses. He had a name for the persona he adopted at these times, calling it Uncle Zeke, after a Brantley relative with a special talent for the bow and scrape.

Caleb could summon Uncle Zeke at will. I use the word "summon" because Uncle Zeke was not what Caleb Talbot's life had been about.

The Talbot family rode north on the great wave of black immigration that followed WWII, settling on 168th Street near Amsterdam Avenue in the winter of 1951. Zacariah found work driving a bus for the Transit Authority while Rose hiked across the Alexander Hamilton Bridge each day to clean apartments in nearby Morris Heights. Caleb did well at school, excelled in athletics, had numerous girlfriends, managed to resist the temptations of the street. When he applied for the NYPD after a two year stint in the army, his record was squeaky clean. This was an absolute necessity, or so Caleb assured me, for a black recruit in 1963.

"They checked me good. Checked my record, in the Army and out, visited my neighbors, my high school teachers, lookin' to sniff out any hint of a reason to dump my application." A pause, then, followed by a grim smile. "Course, they missed the stranger. In those days, I never showed nobody the stranger."

The stranger was Caleb Talbot's name for the part of his being that craved alcohol, a specter that first came to perch on his shoulders after a high school party. Caleb had very broad shoulders, but the stranger was insatiable.

"It was like findin' myself, that first time I tossed down a shot. You know, finding out who I really was. By the time I graduated, I was drinkin' hard most every day."

His capacity was apparently as great as his body, then a relatively svelte 220 pounds, because he survived the Academy, graduating third in his class, and was put out on the street a confirmed drunk. The NYPD sent him up to the big Three-O, the Thirtieth Precinct in Harlem, where he proceeded to run through his old neighborhood like typhus through a refugee camp.

"I liked to hurt," he explained, "liked to use the stick, a sap, my hands, whatever there was. Nobody minded, my partners maybe thinkin' I had a right, being as these were my own people I was hurtin'."

Years later, while detoxing for the tenth and final time, Caleb finally realized that he was beating himself, that each blow he'd struck was a measure of just how much he hated the popeyed man he encountered each morning in his bathroom mirror. He described the intensity of the experience as "a blind man opening his eyes to see the sky, saying, 'Hey, shit, man, the motherfucker really *is* blue.'"

Unfortunately, the vision that ultimately kept him sober didn't show itself until Caleb was summarily dumped by the NYPD for assaulting a street mutt in full view of a community activist, the Reverend Casper Lewis. In retrospect, it could have been worse. Caleb might have assaulted Reverend Lewis; he was that drunk at the time. Still, he came within an eyelash of being indicted, saved only by yours truly after a long lunch with an ADA named Adrienne Paskit just before she went to the Grand Jury. I reminded her of the victim's extensive criminal record, my client's unblemished career, my intention to fight to the death if Caleb Talbot was formally charged.

It was a bluff. I was representing Officer Talbot pro bono (not through the goodness of my heart, let me assure you, but only because the court expected a certain number of freebies) and wanted him out of my career path as quickly as possible. So when the Grand Jury failed to return an indictment, I assumed it was a done deal, that Caleb and I were quits forever, but a year later, when he showed up at my office and asked for a job, I gave it to him.

At the time I had four lawyers and a gaggle of attractively turned-out paralegals and secretaries laboring in my offices. Being of a theatrical turn of mind, I loved to play the *patron* (when I wasn't playing the tyrant). How better to exhibit the benevolence of my dictatorship than hire a fat, black, ex-cop/ex-lush to be my personal investigator?

I know little more of Julia Gill's pre-Kaplan history than a single sentence uttered on a February night two years before this story begins.

Caleb was there, perched on the edge of a club chair, his feet, like the skirt around the chair's base, gently brushing the carpet. I was fiddling with the radio (our Trinitron was in the shop, awaiting the next inflow of cash), running through the stations in search of something vaguely resembling *Monday Night Football*. Julia was sitting on our leather sofa, feet tucked beneath her buttocks, arms crossed over a narrow chest. She seemed unusually tense, lighting one cigarette after another, but neither I nor Caleb chose to comment. There were times when Julia smoldered, when she seemed about to burst into flame, and we accepted her moods, as she accepted ours.

But this time she chose to speak, to give momentary voice to the demons flitting through her soul. "My father," she intoned, raising her head, "began to pimp me off when I was eleven." Then she looked from me to Caleb as if demanding the answer to a riddle.

I do know that Julia Gill was a heroin addict and a prostitute. I know that the veins running along the insides of both arms were brown ribbons of scar tissue, that she almost died in jail because she refused to accept methadone. She was my client at the time, my *paying* client. Her pimp, resplendent in a fur-lined satin coat that dropped to his ankles, had hired my firm because, as he openly expressed it, "I'll get my money back five times over before I burn the bitch out."

It was a nothing case and ordinarily I would have tossed it to one of the hirelings, but something in the pimp's attitude ruffled my macho feathers. Julia had made two mistakes. First, she'd stolen a small statue from a trick's limousine, a pre-Columbian statue of Aztec origin worth $35,000. Second, the victim was a bachelor, childless, and willing (even eager) to admit to his peccadilloes.

Two detectives had taken him on a tour of the various New York strolls and he'd identified Julia Gill as she walked a beat near the 59th Street Bridge. This after viewing hundreds of prostitutes in a half-dozen locations, thus rendering his identification truly impressive. Add his memory of a scorpion tattooed on the perpetrator's left buttock that nicely matched the tattoo on my client's left buttock and you have a case that *cannot* go to trial. Julia had been charged with grand larceny in the third degree, a class D felony punishable by up to seven years in prison, every day of which, the prosecutor assured me, she would receive if . . .

The rule is three strikes and you're out. Julia had whiffed at two fastballs, but she'd gotten a hit on the final pitch. Instead of turning the statue over to her pimp or trying to sell it, she'd stashed it in the basement of a neighboring tenement. The insurance company, Manhattan Life, the largest in the city, wanted that statue much more than it wanted to avenge itself on a junkie-whore named Julia Gill. It was that simple.

Without consulting my client, I worked out two deals, both contingent upon restitution: six months on Rikers Island followed by probation; or successful completion of a drug treatment program at a residential treatment center followed by probation. The second offer seemed the obvious choice, but "successful completion," as defined by the RTCs themselves, meant at least a year of wall-to-wall group therapy sessions under conditions equivalent to medium-security incarceration. And Julia Gill had been around long enough to know it.

Nevertheless, after a week of considering the alternatives (including going to trial), Julia took the RTC. I remember her as she appeared before the sentencing judge, spectral thin, her cheeks bruised gray by the pain of cold-turkey withdrawal.

"Your Honor, I'm sorry for what happened." She'd drawn herself up to her full height, though her voice quavered. "I didn't know the statue was valuable when I took it. It was just supposed to be . . ." Julia's lashes were long and so blond as to be nearly invisible. They'd whisked over her slanted green eyes like feathers. "Just something to have, I guess. Something to take with me when I left."

I remember willing her eyes to drop to the toes of her shoes. I remember whispering, "Bow your head." I remember Julia's sharp chin slowly falling onto her chest, the bemused smile she hid from the judge.

It was a performance worthy of the Little Match Girl, a masterful performance, even if a bit on the *pro forma* side. Julia knew the statue was valuable (as she knew the exact nature of her sentence), that's why she'd hidden it away instead of displaying it on a shelf. Nevertheless, this was her chance (her *only* chance) to rise above the back-room plea bargaining, to assert an individual self, and she took it.

Fourteen months later, Julia Gill (encouraged by Caleb Talbot, who'd worked on her case) returned in search of a job. Again, *noblesse oblige* ruled the day and I took her (and her recently acquired secretarial skills) into my corporate bosom.

I date the beginning of my personal demise from the day of my mother's death.

Magda Leibovits, eighteen years old, came to America in 1938 from Budapest, Hungary, shortly after Germany's invasion of that country. Her escape was neither miraculous nor complicated. Magda's family, after marshalling its resources, found it had a bankroll sufficient to secure passage out for a single member. Magda was chosen and packed off to distant New York.

When I was very young, I remember her passing her mornings at the kitchen table, writing letters to one organization after another, seeking information on the fate of the family she'd left behind in Hungary. She corresponded with groups, official and unofficial, in the United States, in Israel, in Budapest, Kraków, Prague, Bonn, Paris, Amsterdam, Brussels. A ghost searching for ghosts.

She was always standing by the door when the postman arrived, and I, before I started school, stood with her. I loved the foreign stamps, the spidery handwriting, the odd return addresses. The letters seemed exotic and mysterious, an adventure in the making. They were, in fact, the only life my mother had.

I lost a big case on the day Magda died, one of my biggest. My father was long gone by then, and I'd seen so little of my mother in the intervening years that my secretary (not Julia Gill) decided to hold back the news until after the jury came in with its verdict. I recall being angry, though whether at losing the case or my secretary's oh-so-accurate reading of my priorities, I can't say. Perhaps anger was my substitute for grief, as it was my substitute for every other emotion.

For some reason, I went to Magda's house, the house of my childhood, instead of the funeral home, and let myself in. It wasn't a very big house, three small bedrooms upstairs, the last tiny enough to qualify as a closet. Downstairs, a living room with a little nook for the dinner table, a half-bath, a kitchen. The unfinished basement, too damp for storage, held the furnace, the washer and dryer, a few rusted tools, their handles gray and moldy.

I went through the house like a burglar, from room to room, touching the odds and ends of Magda's life—knives and forks, a lace doily on a chair back, the ceramic butterfly I'd given to her on a long-forgotten birthday—holding these objects in my palm as if trying to gauge their weight. My mood was speculative, curious, almost wondering; my progress stately, careful, punctuated only by the occasional snort of first-cut cocaine.

Inevitably, I came to Magda's bedroom, opened the closets, the drawers in her bureau, feasted on a row of faded housecoats, a pile of neatly mended cotton underwear. Then, beneath a stack of flat white boxes, each containing a pair of nylon stockings, I found a book.

Though kept chronologically, the book was more ledger than diary. In it, my mother had fashioned a record of her correspondence, entering the date and the contents of each letter she'd sent or received. At the very end, after filling more than a hundred pages, she'd listed the names of her immediate and extended families, and their ultimate destinations: Auschwitz, Birkenau, Sobibor, Treblinka, Belzec . . .

Half the names bore the tag *unknown*, but I think it's safe to assume that Magda had given up on these, because underneath the list she'd printed two lines in crude block letters:

TOD MACHT FREI

DEATH MAKES FREE

The date of this final entry: October 16, 1963.

I twisted as I fell, like a burning sheet of paper tossed from a high window. Pieces of my life, charred black, flew away as I dropped. My wife, Iris, first, taking my son, David, and what was left of the family fortune to sunny Los Angeles. The hirelings, except for Caleb and Julie, came next. Sharp enough to read the graffiti on the wall (where it was, indeed, writ large), they left for more promising situations. Then I arrived at work one morning to find my office padlocked, my landlord's attorney standing next to a city marshall, the marshall holding an order to evict.

The Mercedes was gone by then, likewise the Rolex and the pinky ring, the antiques and the co-op overlooking Central Park, and I remember feeling distinctly relieved when I caught sight of the marshall standing in front of the door. He was a short, dumpy man with a ratty mustache, the kind of bureaucrat I routinely bullied in my prime, but I simply turned and walked away, walked directly to the men's room where I began a monumental binge by filling my nose with cocaine.

By the time I reached Bellevue's crowded emergency room three days later, my heart was pounding in my chest like a trapped animal. My clothes were drenched with sweat; blood dripped from both nostrils. My eyes were rolling in their sockets, while my arms and legs jerked like the limbs of a puppet in the hands of an epileptic puppeteer. I fully expected to die, felt that I deserved nothing less, was ecstatic and terrified at the same time, a mental state that left the emergency room staff profoundly unimpressed.

They'd seen it all before, of course; they saw it every day. I was given the requisite medication, trundled off to a bed on the third floor, assured that I would live to fight another day.

But I had no fight left. And in the dim, sedated light of the following dawn, I felt my life close around me, as dark and confining as a shroud. The routine of the hospital flowed defiantly: a nurse took my vitals, a doctor repeated the process an hour later, breakfast was laid on the rolling table next to my bed, an orderly tugged me into a chair and fussed with a set of clean sheets. My three neighbors rose, took walks, watched television, received guests, chatted among themselves. I seemed, by comparison, utterly irrelevant, a non-being, devoid of either force or substance.

It was in the middle of this orgy of self-pity that Julia Gill and Caleb Talbot showed up. I remember they were carrying green visitor's cards and that Julia held hers against her breasts while Caleb let his dangle from his clubby fingers. At another time—and I realized this as they approached my bed, each flashing a thin, unsure smile—I might have been angry at their presumption, but at that moment I would have welcomed my executioner.

"You hit bottom yet?" Caleb asked without preamble. "You ready, boss?"

I remember nodding quickly, then wishing I could take it back, that there was something still within me able to summon a hint of defiance.

On the following day I went, by cab, from Bellevue Hospital to the Rushmore Institute on East 83rd Street and spent the next year in one of two modes. Either I endured the vicious attacks of eight group members or I joined eight group members in attacking some other unfortunate. The experience was hellish by design. You had to be open, to reveal some new awful truth at every turn, a sore wound on which your brothers and sisters would feast. Nor could you back off when it came time to score the others. Pain was to be given, as well as received; one was expected to do one's bit, to make the sado-masochistic sacrifice.

At the end of each session we joined hands to form a ring and begged some obscure, beneficent (and almost certainly Christian) deity for the strength to get through the night.

The question that leaps out is simple enough: Why didn't I just leave, especially during those first few months when the urge for cocaine had me terrified by my own dreams? The simplest answer is that I was afraid of the world, that within the Institute (we referred to it, one and all, as the *Institution*) I felt safe. At least I knew from which direction the blows would come. But beyond that, as I recovered my physical strength and my bad attitude, I realized that the pure will to survive (which precluded the use of any mind-altering substance) was reasserting itself. If I remained in the Institution, it would grow; if I left, it would shrink, perhaps die.

Eventually, when the staff pronounced me fit to entertain, Julie and Caleb came to see me. I had no other visitors. My son phoned from time to time, but I had little to say to him. David was a good boy, a graduate student in archeology at UCLA who neither smoked nor drank. His calls reeked of perfunctory obligation, as if he, too, realized that we had no common ground, not even that of his childhood.

It was Julie who provided me with the last piece of the addiction puzzle. We were in the dayroom, the two of us, and I was sitting by the window in a deep funk. After eight months of voluntary incarceration I'd come to the point where I didn't give a damn about sobriety *or* drugs. My general mood flicked, almost from moment to moment, between unfocused rage and profound despair.

"Sid, you look like shit." Julie was quite slender, with prominent bones that remained somehow delicate, as if the contours of her brow, cheeks and jaw had been shaded in by an artist.

I remember shrugging my shoulders, unable to summon the energy for actual speech.

"What it is," she said after a minute, "is grief. You're in mourning." She lit two cigarettes, put one in my hand. "And it'll never go away. That's the important part, Sid. The grieving will never end because your lover isn't dead and buried. She's right across the street, in the parks, the bars, even the supermarkets."

I turned to face her. "You're talking resurrection here? Reanimation?"

"No, Sid, not resurrection. Possession. Possession and death."

I came out of the Institution in 1995, older, wiser, and destitute. Caleb and Julie, both working for other lawyers, met me at the door and took me into the apartment they shared on East 25th Street. I believe, at the time, I was bewildered by the arrangement; there was no physical relationship, and the exact nature of the emotional transactions somehow eluded me. Then one night I dreamed that Julie and Caleb had left me, that I made one sarcastic remark too many and they'd packed their bags and walked away.

I leaped out of the bed, my body soaked with sweat, and charged into the hallway, getting as far as Julie's door before coming to myself. Julie slept with her door cracked open, a sop to her fear of entrapment, and I could clearly see the long line of her body under the sheets. Still, I waited, my fingers resting on the brass knob, until her chest rose and fell, until I was sure I still had her with me.

I went into the living room and sat on a hump-backed chair by the window and began to sob uncontrollably. A moment later, I felt a presence and turned to find Caleb kneeling beside the chair. Behind him, Julie stood in the doorway, one hand raised to her lips. Their eyes were invisible in the darkness, but I didn't need a lamp to read the message. I was home and that was all there was to it. I'd found my ghosts.

Part I

One

The minute I laid eyes on the old woman, I knew she was going to lie to me. Posed there in my office, she gave me a long moment to absorb the extent of her misery. To admire the mousey hair dribbling over the back of her collar, the dark pouches beneath her swollen eyes. Her narrow lips were greasy with dark red lipstick, the only sign of color in her white-on-gray face.

"Mr. Kaplan?" She wore a faded cloth coat (threadbare, naturally) buttoned up to her throat and she clutched it with her right hand like it was the only thing between her bony frame and the wicked January wind. "My name is Thelma Barrow."

"Call me Sid. And take a seat, Mrs. Barrow."

"Please, my . . ."

First, she was going to tell me how her little buddykins was sitting (right now, even as we speak) in the Tombs, or in Rikers, or the Brooklyn House of Detention, how his miserable mutt existence (not to mention his sexual identity) was being threatened by the element dwelling therein. Then she was going to ask me to please save the darling boy who'd once suckled at her milk-swollen breasts.

". . . my little girl has been arrested and I don't know what to do."

For once, I didn't mind getting it wrong. A little girl instead of a little boy. It made the sexual identity part much more interesting.

"Is this the first time?" I looked at her looking at me through small, almost perfectly round eyes. "That your daughter's been arrested I mean."

For a minute I thought she was going to show me how angry the question made her. Then she sighed and clutched her purse to her belly. "No," she admitted, "not the first time. But now it's different. Now it's murder."

"Murder?"

"Second degree murder, yes."

Once she'd gotten it out, revealed the family shame, she seemed to relax a little, but her sharp knees were still pressed together, her torso rigid against the back of the chair. Personally, I thought it was a nice touch, the stiff upper lip and the wet swollen eyes. Tough love personified.

"All right, Mrs. Barrow, I'm going to ask you some questions and I want you to give me short, clear answers. Right to the point, okay?"

"I understand," she said, her mouth tightening down.

"Good, what's your daughter's name?"

"Priscilla Sweet. I call her Prissy."

"When was she arrested?"

"Two days ago. She . . ."

"Please don't volunteer anything." I slid my chair back a few feet, stood up and began to pace. "Where are they holding her?"

"Rikers Island."

"No bail?"

That brought a single tear. It ran along the left side of her nose, then caught a deep groove running from her nostril to the outside of her mouth. "No." She shook her head.

"Her priors, what were they for?"

"Drugs." She glanced to the left and shrugged. "Of course."

"And the sentences?"

"Probation twice, then two years in prison."

"The victim, the person she's alleged to have killed, did she know this individual?"

"Her husband, Byron." She snatched her bag up into her chest and pursed her lips as if about to spit. "The black bastard."

Knowing full well that within a week or two I'd be the *Jew lawyer* (that is, if I hadn't already earned the appellation), I grunted my appreciation of her comment and hardened my heart.

"How long were they married, Mrs. Barrow? Prissy and Byron?"

"Ten years." Her lips tightened. "He beat her, Mr. Kaplan. He got her into the drugs."

"I believe you, Thelma. Now tell me, were there any witnesses to the alleged homicide?"

"No, they were by themselves in their apartment when it . . . ." She was back to the suffering senior. ". . . when it happened."

"The cops arrest her at the scene?"

A nod, then another tear.

"What about children?"

She looked up at me, shook her head. "None. Thank God."

I thought of Caleb, with his ebony skin and goggle eyes, how much he wanted to have children, what a good father he'd make. "The husband, Mrs. Barrow, he ever been arrested?"

That brought a short, bitter laugh.

"And your daughter, she have any bruises? I mean right now."

"Prissy's got an eye like *this*."

I stopped pacing and sat behind my desk. It was time for the lie. I rubbed the ball of my thumb in a slow circle across the tips of my middle and fore fingers. "Money," I said, "the root of all freedom."

"I'm not a rich woman." The standard opening line. "I've been working all my life. I'm a widow."

"Mrs. Barrow, let me be frank. If you want it pro bono, try Legal Aid. Everything else costs money. Especially me."

"Well," she said, after a moment's reflection, "I have five thousand dollars in the bank."

I stared at her for a moment, until her expression hardened and I was sure five grand was all I was going to get. For now.

"That'll be a start," I said, knowing I couldn't do a decent job for ten times that amount. "If you'll write me a check, I'll be down to see your daughter this afternoon."

"The money's in a certificate of deposit. I'd have to pay a penalty."

"You want me to wait until it matures?" When she didn't respond, I continued. "Today's Friday. Postdate the check and I'll make the deposit on Monday."

She frowned, but her hands went down into her purse. "You're willing to trust me until Monday? I'm surprised." Her small mouth lifted into a coy smile.

"You look like an honest woman." Meanwhile, the law provided for triple damages on a bad check and I was fully prepared to sue for every penny if it bounced. That's how broke I was.

I opened my once-elegant attache case, tossed in some paperwork, added a tiny 35mm camera loaded with high-speed film. "Wait here, Mrs. Barrow. My secretary will be in to get some basic information. Names, addresses, phone numbers, like that. I'll call you in the morning."

She stared up at me, her expression wary, but didn't say anything as I left the room, closing the door behind me. Julie was sitting on the edge of her desk in my outer office. She looked at me expectantly.

"Get her signature on a retainer agreement," I said, "then have Caleb check her vitals. Mortgages, bank accounts. . . . You know the drill."

The jail on Rikers Island was the sole reason I owned a car. Stuck out in the East River between Queens and the Bronx, it could only be reached via a bridge at the foot of Hazen Street in Astoria, an impossibly long subway–bus ride from my office in Manhattan. When I first broke into the business, back in the late '60s, Rikers Island housed fewer than five thousand prisoners. Now it held more than twenty thousand and the city fathers, despite a stunning drop in the crime rate, were expecting a twenty percent increase in the coming decade.

Rikers was a place of limitless misery and violence, a hell on earth for everyone, including (and especially) the men and women who worked there. Lawyers often referred to the Rikers complex as the House of Pain; suffering ran through it like flu virus through a fourth grade classroom. Usually, that was good for business, the misery, violence, suffering, and pain, but in this case it was going to present me with a problem. It would be a long time before Priscilla Sweet got her day in court and I needed to know if she could deal with incarceration. There are no activities for detainees; those who can't make bail remain in their cells or in open housing units day after day after day. Many take the first plea bargain offered by the state, preferring a New York prison to a long series of empty days punctuated by the occasional sexual assault. If little white Prissy was among this group, I needed to know it before I spent her mama's five grand.

I caught a break at the reception area of the Rose Singer Center, the women's jail. A black corrections officer named McCoy was working the desk. McCoy was sharp-eyed and polite to a fault, a veteran's veteran who'd been around long enough to know the difference between honest and dishonest graft.

"Officer McCoy," I said, slapping my unzipped case on the desk, "how goes it?"

He glanced at his watch. "Slowly, Kaplan. Very, very slowly." Opening my case for inspection, he deftly palmed the twenty tucked beneath a small strap. "Who's the lucky victim?"

"Woman named Priscilla Sweet."

"No kidding?" McCoy raised an eyebrow. "Looks like you got yourself a celebrity. Made the *Post* and the *News*."

I started to ask him what the papers were saying, then changed my mind, figuring I could count on him for anything but an unbiased report. "You know, I'm in a bit of a hurry here, being as it's getting on to five o'clock." That was part of what the twenty was all about.

"No problem. I'll have her down in fifteen minutes." He held up my camera. "What's this?"

"The mother claims the daughter's bruised and I need to take a few pictures." That was the other part of the twenty. Theoretically, I was supposed to get permission to shoot pictures or have a doctor examine my client. Permission that could be easily postponed until all visible trace of Ms. Sweet's injuries disappeared.

McCoy nodded thoughtfully and picked up the phone. "Fifteen minutes," he repeated.

Thirty minutes later he called my name. "Kaplan," he said, his voice indifferent, "room eight."

One look at Priscilla Sweet erased any concern I had for her fragility. Despite a fading bruise that covered half her face and a swollen right brow, eyes as gray and hard as a sheet of stainless steel met and held my own as I came through the door. "You bring any cigarettes?" she asked.

I laid my briefcase on the table, opened the snaps, took out an untouched pack of Winstons, tossed them over. She snapped the cellophane off and popped one into her mouth. "Appreciate it," she said when I offered a light. "I won't get my commissary till tomorrow."

She leaned back in the chair and let her head fall back slightly as she filled her lungs with smoke. I watched her carefully, thinking how little she resembled her mother. Priscilla Sweet's eyes were narrow and set far apart, her mouth was full and generous, her nose was small and sharp at the tip.

"You know who I am?" I asked.

"Sid Kaplan," she responded promptly. "I asked for you."

"That right?"

"You represented a buddy of mine, about seven years ago. Guy named Peter Howard." She raised her eyes to meet mine. "He did okay."

I nodded thoughtfully, just as if I actually remembered Peter Howard. "I spoke to your mother briefly, Priscilla, and I'm going to speak to the A.D.A. as soon as we're finished here."

"She tell you what happened?"

"She told me as much as I need to know, at least for now." I crossed my legs, unbuttoned my jacket. "What I wanna do today is explain self-defense and the law, let you think about it for a while before you tell me exactly what happened. *Comprende?*"

Her smile was understanding in the extreme, the knowing grimace of a woman who'd been there often enough to have the drill memorized.

"Your mother tells me your old man liked to use his hands. That right?"

"That's right." She folded her arms across her chest.

"Can you prove it? You ever go to the cops, get an order of protection? You got witnesses?"

"All of the above."

"Good, now here's the reality. According to the law, you had an obligation to retreat. If you shot your husband *as* he was attacking you, and you can prove it . . ."

"I thought proving was up to the prosecution."

"That's the theory, Priscilla. But in the absence of independent witnesses, the only way to prove self-defense is to have you testify. And if you testify, the judge will instruct the jury that you have a vested interest in the outcome of the case and therefore your testimony should be carefully scrutinized. You get the picture?"

She let her arms drop into her lap and crossed her legs, apparently unconcerned with the possibility of prison. "Thank God for O.J. Simpson."

I winked at her, flashed a genuine smile. "O.J. made it a lot easier for battered women," I admitted, "but acquittal's still not a given. Let me explain the rest of it. The law expects you to take advantage of any reasonable opportunity to retreat. That means if you shot your husband *after* an attack, when you could have gotten out, you're technically guilty of a homicide, though not necessarily murder. If that's the case, my defense will be two-fold: battered wife syndrome combined with 'give the woman a medal for ridding the planet of this scumbag.' "

That brought a peal of laughter. "I think we're gonna get along," she said.

"If we do, it'll be a first for me." I paused to retrieve the camera. "Because I'm not here to make friends."

"You're here to take pictures?"

I pointed to her eye. "I want to document the damage before it disappears."

She rose, stepped back away from the window and the guard on the other side, unzipped her city-issued orange jumpsuit, and let it fall to her waist. There were (again, fading) bruises on her ribs, chest, and thighs.

"Something else you might want to think about," I said as I focused the camera, "I don't believe we'll get a doctor to say those bruises are forty-eight hours old." She started to respond, but I waved her off. "Something else to think about," I insisted, "before we get to the nuts and bolts." I stood up, prepared to leave. "At the arraignment, who represented you?"

"A Legal Aid lawyer named Rothstein. Carol Rothstein. You know her?"

I shook my head. "How 'bout the cops? You give them a statement?"

She answered me with a sneer.

Two

The pay phones in the reception area were taken up by mutt relatives trying to arrange some kind of justice for their loved ones, so I drove to a diner on 21st Street between the Triboro and 59th Street Bridges to make my phone calls. Once upon a time, when I was flying high, I'd gotten the owner's daughter off on a drug possession charge. The search of her vehicle having been blatantly unconstitutional (at least by 1982 standards), the effort on my part had been minimal, but Georgie Petrarkis had been impressed enough to spring for the occasional coffee and danish when I happened by.

"Counselor, how are you doing?" He was standing behind the register, a thick, swarthy man with an enormous fleshy nose.

"In a rush, Georgie." I flipped a sawbuck on the counter and he handed me a roll of quarters. There was a time when I had a calling card. Not to mention a cellular phone. "Anything fresh out of the oven?"

"Anna-Marie," he called to his wife, "for the counselor, coffee and an almond horn."

I walked back to the pay phones, dropped in the obligatory quarters, punched out my office number. "Julie," I said when she answered on the second ring, "it's Sid."

"Really?"

"Get hold of Caleb . . ."

"He's sitting right here. You wanna talk to him?"

"No, I don't have the time. Tell him to poke around, see what his cop friends have on our client. Her name's Priscilla Sweet. Also get her yellow sheet, the victim's, too. His name is Byron Sweet."

"That's it?" Somehow, Julia always found my sense of urgency amusing. Probably because I spent most of my waking life in a panic. Meanwhile, I slept like a baby while she spent the wee hours watching C-SPAN rebroadcasts.

"Yeah, I'll be back to the office as soon as I can." I hesitated, not wanting to get anyone's hopes up, then softened. "It could be we have something big here. Assuming we play it right and don't run out of money. You do a credit check on the mother?"

"I'll have it in an hour or so. If I can scrape the two hundred together."

I hung up the phone, shoved another quarter into the slot, dialed Legal Aid in Manhattan. After only two wrong connections, I found Carol Rothstein at her desk. She seemed a little disappointed when I told her I was taking over Ms. Sweet's defense, though she must have been expecting it. "The state's case," she told me, "is being prepared by an A.D.A. named Buscetta."

Though I rang off without comment, the name, Carlo Buscetta, warmed my frozen heart. (Not to the point of melting, mind you, just enough to start a colony of bacteria growing on the surface.) Buscetta had a reputation as the hardest hard-ass in the D.A.'s office. I'd been up against him three times, losing once. On that occasion, when the clerk read the verdict, he'd tossed my client (a run-of-the-mill thief, by the way) a triumphant glare that reeked of pure lust.

Buscetta wasn't in his office, so I introduced myself to one of his sycophants and left the number on the pay phone. Then I called a *Newsday* reporter named Phoebe Morris on her cellular phone. She answered on the fourth ring, took my number, said she'd call back in ten minutes.

I returned to the counter, unbuttoned my jacket, shifted my little .32 automatic (which had remained in the glove compartment of the car while I was inside the Rikers jail) to the left before sitting down. My carry permit had come by way of a threatening client who'd escaped from a Corrections Department bus on his way to Attica. As it turned out, the client headed north after his escape, trying for Canada and not a piece of my hide, but I'd held onto the permit afterwards. That was because the gun made me feel powerful.

A few minutes later, the phone rang in the back. I caught it on the third ring.

"Kaplan."

"Buscetta. You called me."

Carlo Buscetta was reputed to hate all defense lawyers, and Jewish defense lawyers especially. I'd never been able to resist needling him about our respective ethnicities. "Hey, *paisan*, how goes it?"

"I'm very busy, *Sid*ney." He put a heavy emphasis on the first syllable of my name, put a little sneer into it, too.

"Carlo, don't be a *putz*, we're gonna be up against it again. With Priscilla Sweet. It'll be just like the good old days."

"Duly noted. Is that all?"

"That means she talks to nobody. No prosecutors, no cops without me being present. You get that, *boychick*?" When he didn't answer, I pushed ahead with the main point. "Personally, I can't believe the D.A. wants to prosecute this poor, battered woman. Carlo, she's been beaten to within an inch of her life."

He laughed, apparently familiar with Ms. Sweet's physical condition. "Forget about it, Sidney. The victim was sitting down when she blew him away."

"She told you that?" I held my breath, waiting for the axe to fall. In this business, everybody lies to everybody.

"I can't talk about . . ."

"First you say my client made a statement, which she denies, then you say you can't *talk* about it?" My voice was up a full octave.

He sighed. "Your client did not make a statement. And that's all I have to say at this time."

"Good, call me when you're ready to cut a deal."

"Oh, I can make you an offer right now."

It was my turn to sigh. His tone was much too confident. "Let's hear it."

"If your client pleads to the top count, we'll forget about the quarter pound of cocaine we found in her apartment."

"You're saying the cocaine was in plain view?" The cocaine which neither Priscilla, nor her sainted mother, had bothered to mention.

"Let me know if your client wants the deal, *Sid*ney."

I finished my coffee at the counter, raised the cup for a refill, shoved a chunk of warm pastry into my mouth. Anna-Marie was coming toward me with the carafe when the phone rang again.

"Kaplan."

"Sid? It's Phoebe Morris."

"Phoebe." I dry-swallowed a mass of almond paste the size of a golf ball. "How are you?"

"Busy. What's up?"

Phoebe Morris didn't like me and wasn't afraid to tell me so. Perhaps because she knew I wouldn't be offended. Her dislike did not, of course, affect our business relationship. In the past, I'd leaked information to her whenever I had a media-worthy client.

"I'm representing Priscilla Sweet."

She hesitated for a moment, then said, "Oh, yes, I recall. The woman who killed her husband."

"The *battered* woman who killed her husband," I corrected. "With a *documented* history, proof of which I am prepared to supply at a later date."

"The cops are saying she was a drug dealer, that she has a record."

"Look, she had a troubled life. I mean what are we saying here, Phoebe? If you're not a good citizen it's okay for your husband to kick your ass?"

That was the angle I hoped Phoebe Morris would play up: justice for *all* women, even dope dealers.

"Her husband was black," I continued. "Maybe we oughta condemn her for that alone. You know, if she spread her legs for one of *them*, she's capable of anything."

"Enough, Sid, I get the point."

"There's lots of people out there, Phoebe, who are gonna be thinking along those very prejudiced lines. If liberals like yourself refuse to demand justice for Priscilla Sweet, she'll be all but convicted before the trial begins."

She paused briefly, then, apparently unimpressed by my rhetoric, said, "Let's stay in touch."

An hour and a half later, I was back in my Union Square offices, whining about the cocaine charge and my lying client while Julie sat behind her desk, typing away at a computer keyboard. More than likely, she was simply waiting me out, knowing I'd run down sooner or later. In this case, with other things on my hand, it was sooner. "All right," I finally said, "so what'd you get on mama?"

"What I got, in addition to the information you wanted, was a bill for two hundred dollars payable immediately in cash." She backed her chair away from the desk and swiveled toward me. "Right now, this minute, we don't have enough money for Chinese takeout."

"The old lady gave me a check for five large. It goes in the bank on Monday."

"Today's Friday, Sid. In case nobody told you. That check you got won't clear until Wednesday, at the earliest."

I stopped pacing and sat down again. Time to face the reality of the flesh. "Go over to the Slipper, see Benny. Tell him I'll make good the end of next week."

"How much?"

"Make it five bills."

"That's six coming back, right?"

"If the check doesn't clear until Thursday, it's seven," I corrected. "So what's the story on Barrow? She got any money?"

"Not to speak of." Her mouth expanded into a narrow smile. "A five thousand dollar CD, which you know about, a few thousand dollars in a money market, a few hundred more in a checking account. No stocks, no bonds."

"What about property?"

"Oh, you mean the house?"

I had to return Julie's smile, despite myself. Julie loved to set me up, to put a pin to my very swollen head. "C'mon, Julie, don't bust what little balls I have left."

"Barrow owns and lives in a single-family home on 73rd Avenue just off 164th Street in Queens. Been there since 1959. Judging from the assessed valuation, I'd say it's worth maybe $260,000."

"And the mortgage? How much does she owe?"

"*Nada*, Sid. As in not a goddamned penny."

Three

On the morning after my consultation with Priscilla Sweet, I popped out of bed full of piss and vinegar. The piss went quickly, preceding a thorough brushing, washing, and blow-drying, but the vinegar remained. For the first time in years, I was ready and eager for the battle, a realization that seized me as I peered into the fogged mirror. I had a thick head of salt-and-pepper hair, my pride and joy, and I slowly ran a comb through it, watched the hairs unroll momentarily, then twist back into their customary curl.

"Priscilla, my sweet," I muttered as I put the comb into my back pocket, "will you be my guardian angel? Or just another beckoning siren?"

Siren or not, I was, like Ulysses, determined to hear Priscilla's tune. To that effect, I carefully trimmed the forest of hairs growing inside my ears, adding those in my nostrils for good measure. Just in case I needed to smell a rat.

I came out into the living a room a few minutes later, whistling tunelessly. Julie was bent over a prayer plant by the window, snipping dried leaves with a tiny pair of scissors.

"Morning, Sid," she called without turning around. "What's for breakfast?"

"First things first." Breakfast before coffee is not a possibility for me. "Is Caleb back yet?"

Julie turned and glanced at the clock on the wall, a Regulator knock-off she'd picked up at a Canal Street flea market. "It's not even eight o'clock. The tour's just ending." When Caleb needed favors from ex-buddies still on the force, he liked to catch them as they came off the late tour, figuring they'd be too tired to argue. "I wouldn't look for Caleb before nine."

I walked into the kitchen, poured myself a cup of coffee, then returned to the living room and took my customary seat on an overstuffed chair against the wall. The furniture in our home may have come by way of R. H. Macy's instead of Roche Bobois, but it matched nicely and was uniformly comfortable. A high-backed sofa and two chairs, cherry tables with brass lamps, a tough, springy carpet, even a cushioned rocker near the window. All by way of a foolish credit officer approached on a very busy Labor Day weekend. Before that it'd been Salvation Army thrift stores and broken springs in the butt.

The wall behind me was covered with old photographs, stiff portraits of men, women and children, of marriages, funerals, engagements. These were my maternal relatives, the photos discovered among Magda's things when I closed the house in Sheepshead Bay. I'd taken them out, put them in a box on the top shelf of the linen closet where Julie had found them several years later.

"This is your life, your past," she'd explained as she tapped picture hooks into the plasterboard. "You should be proud of it."

At the time, I didn't see the point, since I had dozens of cousins, aunts, and uncles living in the New York suburbs, and rarely saw them. But I wasn't stupid enough to stop her and I eventually figured it out. In some ways, like my mother, I was more tied to the dead than the living.

Caleb's Alabama family surrounded the door on the far wall. Some of the figures were formally posed, but most of the photos had been snapped with an ancient Brownie. An old white church, its steeple canted to the left, formed the background for half the photographs.

"Sid?"

I looked up to find Julie standing in front of me, a quizzical smile playing with the edges of her mouth. She was holding one hand out, as if offering me the brown-edged leaves that lay in her palm.

"Yeah?"

"Don't get your hopes up too high."

I crossed my legs, pulled at my coffee, silently conceded the insight. "I'll admit it looks too much like a big break to be true. Carlo Buscetta for a prosecutor, the story already in the papers, fresh bruises on the client, a history of abuse . . ."

"And a quarter pound of cocaine." Julie crumpled the leaves in her hand, dropped them into an ashtray, lit a Newport. "You can't make Priscilla Sweet into a virgin martyr."

"I can't? Julie, give me a bank of video cameras and I'll revise her image. Hell, I'll make her into Joan of Arc."

"Not with five thousand dollars."

She turned and strolled into the kitchen, her movements graceful, almost languid. As if despite four years of sobriety, she still carried a full load of heroin somewhere in her flesh. Maybe that was why she liked plants so much.

I was in the kitchen, folding blueberries into a bowl of pancake batter when Caleb came in thirty minutes later. "Where you at, boss?" he called.

"In the kitchen. Making your breakfast."

His head appeared in the doorway a moment later. "Julie here?"

"She's taking a shower."

"Yeah?" Caleb looked around as if checking to make sure I wasn't lying. "Well, I got Byron's yellow sheet. Priscilla's, too." He tossed an envelope onto the desk and took a seat. "Cost me fifty bucks. Shit, I can remember when I was able to open doors with just a smile."

I filled a mug with coffee and set it on the table in front of him. "So, what's the bad news?"

"Byron got out of prison thirteen months ago. Coming off a two year mandatory for selling a half ounce to a narc."

"Seems to run in the family." I began to drop pancake batter into a hot frying pan. "And the good news?"

"In 1994, Byron was charged with first degree assault after he attacked his wife in public. Eventually, he pled guilty to third degree assault and spent eight months at Rikers. Improving his attitude, no doubt."

I slid a spatula under the edge of a pancake, began to work it in a circle. "Any other violence on the sheet?"

"Nothing."

Julie, her coarse blond hair flying in all directions, picked that moment to come into the kitchen. Later, she would mousse her hair into submission, but for now, in our company, she was content to look like an owl clipped with a pair of hedge shears.

I flipped the pancakes, took down three plates, went to the refrigerator for syrup and butter while Caleb filled Julie in. When he was finished, she put her finger directly on the essential point.

"Priscilla was outside while her husband was in prison? That's the way it went?"

"Right," Caleb said, "by the time she finished her sentence, Byron was already in prison."

"And the assault. That took place before either one of them went upstate?"

"Right again."

"And she took him back when he got out?"

I dropped a plate in front of Caleb, another in front of Julie. "Enough negativity. It's time to eat."

Caleb folded his hands and bowed his head. "Thank you Lord Jesus for the food on my plate and for all the good things that come my way."

I think he did it to irritate me, but if so, I didn't give him the satisfaction of a response. "The both of you, you're missing something important. Priscilla Sweet has no drug busts, no busts of any kind, after her release from prison. It was Byron who brought drugs into the household." I put my hand over my heart. "Yes, Byron the Beater, who forced my poor, brutalized client back into a life of crime."

"You're really worried about the cocaine?"

"I'm worried a jury will want to convict her for *something*, that they'll work out a compromise and go with drug possession."

Caleb held up a loaded fork, looked at it for a moment, popped it into his mouth. "I couldn't get to Shawn McLearry or any of the other suits working the case. They were gone for the weekend. But I did speak with one of the uniforms who responded to the 911 call, a Spanish boy name of Alfonso Rodriguez. He told me the wound was through-and-through, that forensics pulled a slug out of the chair. He said Byron was definitely in that chair when she blew him away."

"Maybe he was getting up," Julie mused. "Maybe he threatened her and was coming out of the chair. I'd say Priscilla had reason to believe he'd carry through."

"Whatta ya say we get to work?" I said. "See what the day brings?"

"I was hopin' the day would bring me a little sleep, boss," Caleb responded. "Seein' as I been up since three o'clock this morning."

"Fine, take a nap. But I want you to be there when I visit my client this afternoon, use some of that cop radar to pick out the lies. Also, I'm gonna ask for a list of potential witnesses to Byron's abuse. Better if you should put the list together yourself, since you'll most likely be interviewing them."

He nodded once, then went back to his breakfast.

"Julie, I want you to get the film developed, then call Phoebe Morris, see if she's interested in a set of photos and a copy of Byron Sweet's bona fides."

"You're not gonna meet with her personally?"

I shook my head. "What I'm thinking is that you'll get along with her better than I can." That was another thing about Julie. Caleb as well. They were, the both of them, absolutely reliable. The media war to come would be vicious, with both sides leaking information. We needed to get it right the first time, and I handed the job to Julie without a second thought. "If Phoebe runs those photographs in *Newsday*, the other papers will follow along. Ditto for the networks." I waved my fork in a rising spiral. "Remember, it's up to us to keep the story alive until we go to trial. We do that, we're not gonna have to worry about paying the rent. Ever again. This I promise you."

Four

Caleb went off to catch his nap almost as soon as he'd shoveled the last of his breakfast into his mouth. He had a knack for falling asleep at will, a knack Julie would have killed to possess. Fortunately for Caleb, it was Julie's turn to do the dishes and as she chose obligation over jealousy, he went to his rest unscathed. I sat at the table, watched her work for a few minutes while I finished my second mug of coffee, then went back to an office consisting of a scarred wooden desk, a three-drawer file cabinet, a telephone-answering machine with a mind of its own, and a manual Smith-Corona typewriter. All squeezed into a windowless corner of my bedroom.

I sat down at the desk, picked up the phone, punched out Thelma Barrow's number.

"Hello?" Her voice was thin, wavering slightly in pitch, the voice of someone (or so I thought at the time) perpetually expecting bad news.

"Sid Kaplan here."

"Did you see Priscilla?"

"As I said I would, Mrs. Barrow."

"She's being punished for something. She couldn't call me. That's why I didn't know."

I pushed the chair back, put my feet on the desk, stared at a photo of my son, David. "Well, I did see Priscilla, but I haven't decided to take the case."

"Mr. Kaplan, please . . ."

"See, I've got this big problem. It seems my client and her mother began our relationship by lying to me."

"I never . . ."

"Yeah, you *did*, you did lie to me. I asked you what Priscilla was charged with, remember?"

"Yes." She sounded genuinely puzzled.

"And you never mentioned the cocaine. That's called a lie of omission." She started to mumble some excuse, but I cut her off. "Don't tell me you forgot, or you didn't think it was important. Nobody forgets ten-to-life. Or feels it doesn't matter."

She was silent for a moment, as if trying to make a decision, then said, "You're very rude, Mr. Kaplan."

"Please, call me Sid."

That brought another pause. "I don't . . ."

"My problem is that your daughter *also* lied to me. My problem is that you both lied about something you both knew I'd discover. My problem is that you lied about money."

"Money?" Her voice contained equal measures of outrage and surprise.

"Drug cases are won or lost at preliminary hearings, Mrs. Barrow, and your daughter knows it. The evidence has to be excluded or the jury convicts." I dropped my feet to the carpet and leaned forward. "That means I'll have to make appearances in court, write and file briefs, do research or hire someone else to do it." I let my voice drop. "Five thousand doesn't begin to cover my time and expenses. Doesn't even *begin*."

"Mr. Kaplan . . ."

"Sid."

"Look, Sid, if you think I was trying to . . ." She hesitated long enough for me to wonder if she'd been about to use the phrase *Jew you down*. ". . . chisel, you're wrong. I don't know anything about cases or trials. For goodness sake, I'm a widow from Queens. My husband, Joe, owned a hardware store in Middle Village."

"So you're saying, the other times Priscilla was busted, you didn't get involved?"

"No, I'm not saying that."

"Then you know." I kept my voice flat. It was time to move on, give her something to play with. "Mrs. Barrow, did you ever witness Byron's abuse? Personally?"

"Call me Thelma." She giggled, the sound remote, like the release of a held breath. "And, yes, I did. It happened shortly before my husband died. Priscilla came to the house one night, beaten so badly I couldn't look her in the face. The next morning, while we were eating breakfast, Byron appeared out of nowhere. He knocked Prissy off her chair, then dragged her out. I mean literally, Sid. He dragged her out by the hair and forced her into his car."

She was angry now, and I could easily imagine her sitting in the witness box, her eyes overflowing, her lower jaw trembling.

"Did anybody else see this happen?"

"My husband, like I just told you."

I started to say, "Anybody *alive*," but caught myself in time. "Someone else who can testify, Thelma."

"Only my neighbor, Gennaro Cassadina. But I don't think . . . See, Mister Cassadina's eighty-five and he doesn't always remember everything."

"That's all right. I'll definitely be out to see him. Now . . ." Sudden changes of topic are part and parcel of every courtroom lawyer's technique. Cop interrogators, incidentally, employ the same device, especially when circumstances preclude the use of balled fists. "Now, there *is* something I wanted to ask you about, Thelma."

"Yes?" Her voice hardened, as if she'd decided not to go down without a fight.

"Do you remember when your daughter came out on parole?"

"Of course."

"Well, I don't know if I've got this right, but I'm looking at Byron's rap sheet and it seems like he was in prison at the time." I hesitated, but when she didn't jump at the bait, I decided to make it as plain as I could. "See, the jury's gonna want to know why she took him back after three years of living apart. And the prosecutor's gonna say they were two drug dealers who had a falling out."

"Maybe he forced her."

"Maybe?" I swiveled the chair in a half-circle and looked out the window. Drops of cold January rain speckled the glass. The gray spongy mist beyond was so dense I couldn't see the building across the street. "Mrs. Barrow, are you going to visit your daughter today?"

"Yes, in about an hour." She paused, then asked, "Will you be seeing Priscilla?" Her voice was tentative, like she wasn't certain she had a right to ask questions.

"I'll be over this afternoon. What I want you to do in the meantime is bring up this question of Byron's parole and why your daughter let him back into her life. Give her a chance to think about it before I get there."

I hung up a moment later, went into the kitchen, filled a mug with coffee, then returned to my office. The next job, as I saw it, was to clear the deck. I had three clients at the time, mutts, one and all, who'd somehow managed to scrape up the cost of an informed plea bargain. Or, at least, that's what I'd thought when I'd taken them on. Unfortunately, one of the bunch, a Hell's Kitchen drug dealer named Owen Shaughnessy, was making noises like he wanted to go to trial. Never mind the fact that he'd sold three ounces of heroin to an undercover cop. Never mind the fact that the transaction had been recorded on both video and audio tape. Never mind the fact that, given his record, he'd get an extra ten years in prison for his refusal to accept the state's more-than-generous offer of two-to-six. Owen Shaughnessy felt he'd purchased the right to jury trial with his lousy two grand, that he was entitled.

My problem was that I'd already pulled out all the stops; I'd cursed his stupidity, screamed in his face, banged my chair on the floor. His response: "Hey, somethin' could happen. You don't know the fuckin' future."

I decided to meet with my clients that afternoon, to ferret out their respective prosecutors on Monday morning. If I couldn't talk Mister Shaughnessy into a sane course of action, I'd do everything I could to have his trial postponed until after Priscilla Sweet had been judged. As for the other two, I intended to make an appearance at their sentencings (hopefully in the same courtroom on the same day), wish them good luck, and be on my way to bigger and better things.

Two hours later, I strolled into the kitchen to find Caleb busy with his lunch. He had a plate of cold cuts—ham, swiss, and turkey—spread before him, another plate with slices of onion, tomato, and hot pepper to his left. A basket of heated rolls in the middle of the table steamed lightly.

"You ready for lunch, boss?"

"It's a little early for me. You didn't make fresh coffee by any chance?"

"Your favorite: chocolate, raspberry, almond supreme."

I shuddered. "I take it this is Julie's work?"

"My work, Julie's orders. Siddown." He got up, filled a mug with coffee, and set it in front of me. "Try holding your nose," he instructed.

Being, at heart, a charitable man, I waited until Caleb constructed his sandwich, blessed it, and brought it to his mouth before raising the essential question.

"That cop, Rodriguez, he was first on the scene, right?"

Caleb nodded, then bit into his sandwich. His eyelids drooped slightly and his nostrils flared as he began to chew.

"Rodriguez say anything about cocaine?"

"Uh-uh."

"You ask?"

He looked at me for a moment, then bit into his sandwich again. "Man told me he went through the rooms, made sure there wasn't no killer hidin' in the closet, then went into the hall and waited for the suits."

"Caleb, did you *ask* him if he saw the cocaine?"

"It's too early to get nervous, boss." He laid his sandwich on the plate. "And what Officer Rodriguez saw don't amount to a hill of shit. If the sergeant running the case, Sergeant what's-his-name . . ."

"Shawn McLearry . . ."

"Yeah, if Sergeant McLearry says he found the coke in plain view, Rodriguez won't be the one to call him a liar." Caleb jabbed a dripping sandwich in my direction and smiled. "That ain't the way the job works."

I nodded agreement and settled down to my coffee. Though cops ordinarily need a warrant to conduct a search, an exception allows them to seize evidence of a crime if said evidence is lying in plain view and they have a legitimate reason for being there. Looking through the rooms for a perpetrator or other victims was, of course, legitimate police business.

A few minutes later, Julie came into the apartment. I heard her shake out her raincoat in the hallway, then slam and lock the door. "I hate gray days," she called as she walked into the kitchen. Drops of rain glistened in her hair. "You see this?" She dropped a soggy *Newsday* in my lap.

I thumbed through it quickly, finding Phoebe Morris's column on page five. It ran under the headline, *Justice For The Undeserving?*, and first examined several cases in which poor women with a criminal background and a proven history of abuse had been convicted of murdering their husbands, then contrasted their treatment with that of several middle-class women who'd either been exonerated by a jury or never been charged. Priscilla Sweet's name, along with a detailed history of her criminal activities, appeared near the end of the column.

"Does the fact," Phoebe concluded, "that Priscilla Sweet doesn't live in a Long Island bedroom community, that she doesn't have 1.5 children, or attend PTA meetings or church socials, mean that she has lost the right to defend herself? The question begs an answer."

I passed the newspaper to Caleb, then turned to Julie. "Phoebe took me at my word."

"I guess there's something about you that inspires trust." Julie picked up a roll and deftly split it. "Looks like the other side's been busy, too."

Julie was referring to Priscilla's criminal background which Phoebe Morris could only have gotten from the prosecution or the cops.

"Anyway," Julie continued, "the photos came out okay." She tossed an envelope onto the table. "Your client looks good in yellow-green."

I laid the prints on the table and examined them closely. The fading bruises, especially one on the right side of her back which looked like an enormous birthmark, were still prominent.

"Did you make an appointment with Ms. Morris?" I asked.

"I'm meeting her this afternoon. She seemed eager."

I nodded my appreciation. "Caleb, whatta ya say we get ready to visit our client?"

Caleb dropped the photos and began to make another sandwich. "For the ride," he explained. As if explanations were necessary.

Five

It took a good part of the afternoon, not to convince Owen Shaughnessy that a trial would be a disaster, but to uncover the reason why he was determined to remain at Rikers. Owen, it seemed, was in love with another prisoner, a prostitute-junkie named Mario Cassano, and was prepared to risk ten years of his life in order to spend a few additional months with his paramour. Or, at least, he was willing until Caleb explained (for the fourth or fifth time) that if Owen took the state's offer, he'd do his time at a minimum security joint. If he went to trial and lost, on the other hand, the length of his sentence would guarantee incarceration at a maximum security prison.

"Southport," Caleb intoned, "Green Haven, Clinton, Attica."

"But I love him," Owen replied.

"Southport," Caleb repeated, "Green Haven, Clinton, Attica."

From Owen Shaughnessy, Caleb and I made our way to the reception desk at the Rose Singer Jail, where I submitted to a search of my briefcase. I didn't know the officer who fumbled through my papers—a man named Robinson, according to his nameplate—but as he took the twenty I'd tucked behind the inside strap, I figured we'd get along. Sure enough, it being late in the afternoon and most of the visitors departed, twenty minutes later I was saying hello to my client.

"Sidney." Her greeting was as self-contained as her bland expression, but the intelligence in her cold sharp eyes betrayed her concern. She'd been expecting me all afternoon. "I thought you weren't coming." Her gaze jumped from me to Caleb.

"Priscilla," I said rather formally, "this is my investigator, Caleb Talbot." I waited for them to exchange a nod before continuing. "Caleb is going to be important to your defense. He's the one who'll be out there contacting witnesses to your husband's abuse. I brought him here so the two of you could start working on a list of names. Meanwhile, I've got a phone call to make. I'll be back in a few minutes."

I half-ran to the only unused pay phone in the waiting room, dropped in a quarter, and punched out my own number. Julie answered on the third ring.

"Julie, did you see Phoebe Morris yet?"

"No. She called earlier, said she'd be tied up most of the afternoon. I'm meeting her in a couple of hours."

"Good, good. Now, look, I want you to make sure you give her photos that show Priscilla's Rikers Island jumpsuit. At some point, I might have to prove the pictures were taken after Priscilla shot her husband."

"Sid, we got a problem here?"

"No, no. But I'm sure Carlo's gonna stall us on getting a doctor in to see our client. Once the bruises fade . . ." I didn't bother with the rest of it. "By the way, Caleb pulled off one of his miracles. Owen Shaughnessy decided to plead guilty. It's a good story. I'll tell you about it when I get home." I paused for a moment, afraid to ask the next question, afraid of Julie's answer. It was funny, in a way, and ridiculous. After decades of driving people out of my life, the only thing I really feared was solitude. "You gonna be home tonight?"

"Yeah, Sid, I'll be around." Her voice was suffused with understanding. Reminding me of how much I hated to be understood, and of how much I'd opened myself up to her, how hard it was for me to be known.

"Great. Well, I'm going back to my client. Be nice to Phoebe."

But I didn't return immediately. Instead, I lit a cigarette and

watched the parade of the wretched while I thought about my life
with Julie and Caleb.

Some time before, I'd come to realize that our asexual *menage à
trois* couldn't last. It couldn't last precisely because it was asexual.
Sooner or later, the way I saw it, one of us would develop a relationship that satisfied emotionally while stimulating sexually and
that would be the end of that.

One day at a time. That's the credo of the recovering addict, and
that's the way I was trying to play it with Julie and Caleb. This
despite knowing how much it would hurt to lose either. I'd had
affairs from time to time, but the women I chose had refused to
accept my lifestyle, a decision for which I was mostly grateful and
didn't blame them in the least.

It was Caleb, of course, who'd developed the most rational solution to the basic problem, a solution named Ettamae Harris.
Ettamae, a widow with two grown children, lived uptown, in
Harlem. She was as thin as Caleb was fat and she loved to cook,
virtues that went to the core of Caleb's personal need. They spent
most weekends and occasional weeknights together, making love on
Saturday night, going to church services on Sunday morning.

We had Ettamae to dinner in our apartment from time to time,
and I can vividly recall a Sunday afternoon when she'd brought
along two of her grandchildren. Ray and Jake, twins and toddlers,
had pulled Caleb down to the floor and used him for a beach ball. A
very willing beach ball who'd obviously played the role many times
before. But that was the thing about Caleb. You took away the
booze, he was a nice, slightly nerdy guy. He didn't have to *play* the
good cop, because he *was* the good cop.

Julie was in an entirely different position, not surprising when you
consider that Caleb and I had spent our lives abusing while she'd
spent hers being abused. In Julie's world, sex had always been about
exploitation, power, and money. She did have occasional partners,
always women, but these encounters were much closer to one night
stands than genuine relationships. And, I suspect, more depressing
than satisfying, even on the most physical level.

We never spoke openly about any of this; our messages were
always disguised. Caleb returning on Sunday evening with one of

Etta's pecan pies; Julie's worried gaze when I indulged my bad temper (trust me, a common occurrence); my own stubborn refusal to think of myself as anything but us.

I put out my cigarette and walked back to the interview room. Caleb was writing in a small notebook, his left hand moving awkwardly over the page while Priscilla recited a list of names, dates, and places. I sat down without speaking and took the opportunity to observe my client. On the previous day, I'd mentioned the need of witnesses to Byron's abuse, so I'd expected a certain amount of preparation, but Priscilla's organized presentation, delivered with no sign of emotion, indicated that she'd spent a lot more than twenty-four hours getting ready. Priscilla not only named individuals, supplying exact dates when possible, approximations when she wasn't sure, she delivered capsule evaluations of each person named.

Evidence of premeditation? Of a guilty mind? The truth was that guilt or innocence (except as pronounced by a jury) didn't particularly interest me. What I wondered, as I sat there watching my client light one cigarette after another, was if sending me a message was part of her calculations. Maybe she wanted me to know she'd been thinking about violent death for a long time, that she was prepared. The cops had undoubtedly pressed her for some kind of a statement, but Priscilla hadn't risen to whatever bait they'd dangled. And she hadn't left a quarter pound of cocaine laying out where the cops could find it, either.

Ten minutes later, after Caleb folded his notebook and stuck it inside his jacket, it was finally my turn.

"I'm sitting here," I said with a casual wave of my hand, "listening to you recite your tale of woe and I gotta give it to you. Any doubt I might have had about your husband abusing you has been permanently erased." I smiled, leaned forward in the chair, let my smile dissolve. "So why'd you take him back?"

Priscilla dropped her elbow to the top of the table, laid her chin in her palm. "You gave my mother a very hard time this morning," she said.

"That's what mothers are for."

She laughed, the sound oddly musical in the small room. "Maybe so," she conceded. "But if she has a heart attack, we've lost an important witness."

"Priscilla, your mother's as tough as you are." I meant the remark to be disarming, but Priscilla took it quite seriously.

"I hope you're right," she said, "but there's something you need to understand. I love my mother and I don't want her to be hurt any more than she's already hurt."

More than pleased, I nodded agreement. The closer Priscilla to her mother, the more likely Thelma to take out a little mortgage when we were desperate for cash. "So, why'd you take him back, Priscilla? This scumbag who beat your ass from morning till night."

Instead of answering, she glanced through the window at a female corrections officer seated on a stool outside. The guard, severely overweight, was staring off into space.

"I don't think she has the answer," I said.

"Patience, Sid." Priscilla slid her chair a little closer to the table and opened my briefcase. She picked up a yellow pad and a pen with her right hand, looked up at me, then dropped a small key into the case. I started to ask her how she managed to hang onto the key through successive strip-searches by the cops and the D.O.C., but the question would have been strictly rhetorical. There was only one way it could have been accomplished: she must have swallowed it, crapped it out, then retrieved it. Drug smugglers use the same technique.

Priscilla pulled the pad close to her, wrote *Citibank 1st Ave and 15th Street Box 2071.*

"Very nice, my dear. Very, very nice."

I pulled a standard Power of Attorney form out of my briefcase, slipped the key into my pocket, and pushed the form across the table. Without hesitating, Priscilla bent her head and began to fill it out. "I loved Byron," she said. "Or I loved some of him, bits and pieces. Or I maybe I just liked getting beat down." Her voice was as matter-of-fact as the pen moving from space to space on the form. "The thing with Byron was that he was doing too much coke, staying awake for days at a time. The whole thing got out of hand."

I glanced at Caleb out of the corner of my eye. He was clipping his fingernails with a little clipper attached to his key ring, his studied indifference a clear indication that his gentle ministrations weren't needed.

"You'll forgive me, Priscilla, if I say you don't appear to be in mourning."

She curled the right side of her lip into a bow, tilted her head slightly as she looked up at me. It was a smile, one I would become thoroughly familiar with, that held back more than it revealed.

"This is Rikers Island, Sid. It doesn't pay to be soft."

I stood up and began to pace. "Is that what you're gonna tell the jury? That it only *looks* like punching a hole through Byron's chest means less to you than stepping on a cockroach? That deep down you still love him?"

"It's the cocaine that really frightens you, isn't it?"

I ignored the question. "Remember, it's up to us to prove you killed Byron in self-defense. The prosecutor will be the one trying to supply reasonable doubt. Plus, juries are mostly too stupid to follow what witnesses actually say. They rely on manner, like they were at home watching television. If you come off as the ice princess, it makes our job a lot harder."

"Then I guess I'll have to practice crying." She took out a Newport, lit it up. "Maybe I can find a sympathetic bull dyke to let me lean on her shoulder."

Caleb cleared his throat, the sound bursting into the little capsule Priscilla and I had created, startling us both. "Speakin' of that cocaine, Priscilla," he said. "Where was it when the cops came in?"

"In a suitcase in the bedroom closet." She tapped the ash from her cigarette loose, watched it drop to the dirty tiles on the floor.

"Now, see . . ." Caleb began.

"Wait a second." I cut him off with a shake of my head. "The apartment was leased in your name, right?" I stopped, waited for her to nod. "That's presumptive evidence that you, in fact, possessed the cocaine. The jury hears that, they're gonna convict unless *we* prove it belonged to your husband, that you were a virtual prisoner in that apartment, that . . ."

She jerked her head to the left, exposing the bruise covering the right side of her face. "It *was* Byron's cocaine and I *was* a prisoner."

I reversed my chair and sat down, straddling the seat. "Tell me about the period between your leaving prison and Byron's parole. You report to your parole officer?"

"The first Monday of every month."

"Ever miss an appointment?"

"Never."

"You have a job?"

"Yeah." She took a hit on her Newport, curled her lip into a smile, the quick flash of anger disappearing as if it had dropped into a bottomless well. "Tucker Trucking in Maspeth. The owner's a guy named Paulie Gullo. I worked in the office."

"And what did you do there?"

"A small business like that, you do a little bit of everything, from payroll to bullshitting creditors about the check being in the mail. And you're always four jobs behind."

"Think you could make me a list?"

"Sure. I'll do it tonight."

"Okay," Caleb broke in. "Let's get back to the . . ." He chuckled manfully. ". . . the scene of the crime. How long did it take the cops to get there? After the shooting I mean."

"About twenty minutes."

"And the first cops to arrive, they were in uniform?"

"That's right."

"Tell me what they did, as best you can remember."

She dropped her cigarette to the floor and ground it out. "The first thing they did, when I answered the door, was push their way inside. I can't say I offered much resistance, but they definitely didn't ask permission. Then they saw Byron and one of them—the white cop—pulled out his gun while the other one checked Byron's pulse. When they were sure he was dead, they asked me what happened. I told them I wanted to exercise my right to speak with an attorney before questioning."

"Bet that made 'em happy." Caleb was nodding and grinning at the same time.

"One of them, the one with the crewcut, I don't remember his name. He said, 'If it was self-defense, there's a possibility you could walk away from all this. But you gotta tell us what happened.' "

"And what'd you say?"

"I told him he should take his possibilities and stick 'em up his ass. That's when they cuffed me and took me into the hallway."

"They didn't search the apartment?"

"The skinny one, his name was Rodriguez, he went back in."

"How long did he stay inside?"

"A few minutes, then he came back to wait for the detectives."

"And the detectives? Did they ask you questions?"

"Not at first. They spoke to Rodriguez, then went into the apartment. About a half hour later, they came out with the coke."

I laid my arms on the back of the chair and leaned forward. "Lemme see if I've got this right. The cocaine was in a suitcase in the bedroom closet. The uniforms didn't find it. The detectives searched immediately upon arrival, without getting a warrant. That about it?"

"Yeah." She lit another cigarette. "Is that good for us?"

Actually, it was good and bad. Good because the search was patently unconstitutional, bad because any effort to have the cocaine suppressed would amount to a trial in itself.

"It depends on whether or not the cops tell the truth," Caleb explained. "Most likely, they're gonna lie and say the cocaine was out in the open, which makes it admissible. And the judge is gonna take their word for it."

The news didn't seem to bother my client. Priscilla nodded thoughtfully, as if she'd already considered the possibility.

"It's no joke, Priscilla." I dropped my bully persona (just for a moment, of course) and spread my hands. "What a jury's likely to do is acquit on the top charge, convict on the lesser, and think they're doing you a favor. Meanwhile, if the judge is in a bad mood on sentencing day, you can spend almost as much time in prison for the coke as you can for the murder."

I don't know what I expected—fear, maybe, or outrage—but Priscilla's expression didn't change. I remember thinking, at the time, that her eyes were pewter coins, that they betrayed nothing at all. Even as they probed the fuzzy matter inside my skull.

"Then you'll have to get me acquitted." She dropped her hand down onto her lap, the smoke rising from her cigarette to momentarily veil her features. "Why don't we talk about bail? Is bail a possibility?"

"A possibility, sure. It depends on how much and what kind of publicity we get between now and when you're arraigned." I stood up, my bad attitude back in place. "But the thing is, Priscilla, I don't see what good it's gonna do you. I mean, where will the money come from? Being as your sainted mother told me five grand was all she had in the world."

This time, Priscilla's smile was genuine, an appreciation of the trap she'd sprung on herself. "I love you, Sid," she said. "I love you to pieces."

"That's fine, just *fine*," Caleb said, "but will you still love him tomorrow? When some women's organization with deep pockets offers to represent you?"

"It's already happened. The New York Women's Council spoke to my mother right after . . ." She paused for a moment. "Right after I was arrested. They offered me a lawyer, but I turned them down. The last thing I need to worry about is my attorney confusing the issues."

I began to close my briefcase. "Couldn't agree more. Anything else I should know?"

She stepped back, out of the guard's view. Her left hand rose to the zipper at the top of her jumpsuit and pulled it down to her waist. Then she unhooked her brassiere, allowing her breasts to fall into their natural set. Between her breasts, two raised weals, each the approximate diameter of a lit cigarette, leaped into focus, as glaring as headlights. "Ace in the hole, Sid," she said. "Ace in the hole."

Six

The rain had stopped by the time Julie and I got on the road the following morning, a Sunday, but the clouds still hung just above the tops of the tallest buildings, a solid gray mass echoing the concrete and stone below. The roads and sidewalks were almost deserted at eleven o'clock in the morning, typical of January in New York when the good citizens, after the Christmas–New Year frenzy, seem to draw back into their shells, adopting a puritanical work ethic punctuated by the occasional televised basketball game and the *New York Times* crossword puzzle.

We were heading for an interview with Thelma Barrow and her neighbor, Gennaro Cassadina, after a stop at Mount Hebron Cemetery to visit the graves of my parents. We drove out to Mount Hebron, Julie and I, at least once a month and I know Julie enjoyed these trips. With no positive family experience of her own, she accepted (and, to an extent, envied) the obvious bond. Me, I had my doubts. At times I entered that graveyard with my heart pounding in my chest. As if David and Magda Kaplan might rise up through the earth, point accusing skeletal fingers: "Where were you when we needed you?"

The literal answer—I was filling my nose with cocaine—was at least obvious. Not so obvious (to me, at least) was why I went to

Mount Hebron in the first place. Maybe my visits were inspired by
Magda's search for her family, a case of the mother's sin being visited upon the son. Maybe I was also destined to chase ghosts.

That was my favorite rationale. It had a poetic ring to it and at
least a grain of truth. But the answer was probably much simpler.
Like every out-of-control addict, I'd spent my life filling the empty
spaces with drugs; like every sober addict, I needed to fill those
spaces with something else. And I needed to recover the past as well.

The word repentance is too Christian for my taste. The guilt I
felt was grasping and greedy. I knew there was a debt to be paid,
knew also that I hadn't even managed a down payment. I couldn't,
of course, make things right with my parents; they were dead and
I'd missed my chance. But I hadn't had any luck with my son either,
despite the fumbling attempts I'd very self-consciously made to
bridge the gap between us. That was because, unlike my partner
Caleb, withdrawal from cocaine and alcohol hadn't affected my
basic personality. As competitive, opinionated, and generally
unlikeable as ever, I was only at home in the company of survivors,
like Caleb and Julie, who'd been so far down it required no more
than a slight tilt of the mind to drop over the edge into oblivion.
Who'd somehow decided to fight their way back to life, to resur-
rect themselves.

Mount Hebron Cemetery, in Flushing, is relatively small by New
York City standards, and the graves are set close together. Bounded
on the west by the Van Wyck Expressway and the Grand Central
Parkway, the relentless whine of rubber on asphalt overlays the
headstones like an auditory shroud. Still, despite the lack of atmosphere, I never found it empty of mourners. Unlike many Jewish
cemeteries, set in pockets of the city long deserted by the communi-
ties that built them, Mount Hebron lies on the western edge of a
thriving, mostly orthodox, Jewish neighborhood.

My parents' shared grave was set in the middle of the cemetery,
and Julie and I walked to it without hesitation. The first thing I did
was pick a small rock off the pathway and lay it on the footstone, an
old Jewish custom the meaning of which I'd long ago forgotten. I
remember Julie, as she came to stand alongside me, silhouetted
against the gray sky in a hooded coat that fell almost to her ankles.
Her gloved hands were curled into black crescents as she knelt, then

ran a finger along the Hebrew letters that spelled out my parents' names.

"My father loved my mother," I told Julie after a brief silence. "He pursued her relentlessly. I think he wanted to fill the empty spaces in her heart, but, of course. . . . Anyway, in David's life there was Magda and there was work. And not the store, either. He didn't give a damn about the store. For the generation that came of age in the Depression, work was sacred, an obligation, a rite. And my father was good at it, Julie. He survived the Depression, survived the post-war exodus of Lower East Side Jews. He survived long enough to die in his store, at age fifty-three, as he was marking down a rack of sport jackets."

Julie rose to her feet. "What's the point?" she asked.

"The point is that it's time to go to work." I took Julie's arm and began to walk back toward the car. It wasn't really cold, but the air was damp enough to produce a semicircle of drops on the edge of her hood. We passed a group of Hasidic men as we came out onto Main Street. They strode by us, their manner purposeful and certain, their beards seeming to float in the light breeze.

"Your mother outlasted him," Julie observed as he got into the car. "He wanted to protect her, but she outlived him by fifteen years."

"I said he *wanted* to fill her heart. I didn't say that he succeeded." I slid behind the wheel, started the car. "The truth is that she froze him out. He tried, but she froze him out. After that, the store was the only thing he had left."

Julie leaned over to kiss me on the cheek. "You're forgetting somebody," she told me, "and you know it."

"Yeah," I admitted. "I know it." The somebody, of course, was the boy who'd worked summers and weekends in the store. The somebody was David Kaplan's son. The somebody was me.

"Home sweet home," Julie said as I pulled to the curb in front of a two-story frame house on the south side of the road and shut down the ignition.

"Does have that look to it," I admitted. Though it was the middle of winter, it was easy to imagine Thelma's small yard in bloom. Azaleas and rhododendrons ran along the front of the house, skipping over a red brick stoop. The azaleas, low-growing and well-trimmed, were set beneath the windows, while the taller rhododendrons stood with their backs to the white vinyl siding that covered the house. A trellis, interlaced with the green, fingerlike stems of a climbing rose, framed the walkway between the sidewalk and the front door.

Inside, in the living room where Thelma led us, it was much the same. The furniture was strictly department store, Macy's by way of A&S; it looked to have been purchased in the fifties and as carefully maintained as the family heirlooms of a tenth-generation WASP.

"I baked cookies." A wide smile elevated the two deep lines that ran from the top of Thelma's nose to the corners of her mouth, revealing what had once been a pair of fetching dimples. "Butter cookies. They're still warm."

She set a tray on the table and began to pour coffee into gold-rimmed cups. "Help yourself."

After a sip at the coffee, I dutifully bit into one of the cookies. It tasted like a dog biscuit.

"Of course, I don't use sugar," Thelma said. "Not with my diabetes. And I don't believe in those chemical sweeteners, either." She was wearing a cashmere sweater over a wool skirt, the outfit considerably more valuable than the raggedy coat she'd worn to my office.

I swallowed manfully and nodded my head in agreement. "The cookies are . . . unique."

Julie dipped the one she held into the coffee, the act carrying a certain desperate quality that had me smiling as I set down my cup.

"Thelma, I want you to tell us what Priscilla's life was like before she met Byron. And I don't want you to exaggerate." I crossed my legs, raised a lecturing finger. "Remember this—if you get up on the witness stand, say Priscilla graduated first in her class, you *must* have report cards to back it up. If you don't, the jury won't believe you. They'll think you're lying to protect your daughter. And if they think you'd lie about something small, they'll decide you're lying about everything else, too."

Thelma sniffed once, her bird-bright eyes all but closing, then muttered, "Okay, I understand," before getting down to business.

The Priscilla Sweet who emerged seemed a fairly ordinary child, neither Queen of the Prom nor Ugly Duckling. Her strengths were a quick, vivacious smile (demonstrated in a half-dozen snapshots) and a general enthusiasm for life. She'd done well at school, had various boyfriends, spent her summer vacations flipping hamburgers at the local McDonald's. After high school, she'd gone on to Columbia University and was holding her own when she met Byron Sweet. Byron, according to Thelma, had filled Priscilla's head with "black communist ideas," telling her the university was a tool of the oppressor class, that the revolution was on the way and she'd better get her act together.

"It came so fast," Thelma explained, "so fast. They were married and living in a slum before Joe and I could do anything about it. Then came the drugs and . . . and the rest."

The rest, which I had to force out of her, was cocaine and marijuana dealing and a prematurely born child who died within a week of his birth.

"Byron blamed it all on the system. He thought being black gave him the right to do any damn thing he wanted. And that included beating his wife. The time he took Priscilla out of the house, he kept saying, 'White bitch, white bitch.' Over and over again."

I interrupted before Thelma's recitation descended into pure diatribe, reminding myself that there would almost certainly be blacks on the jury, that race would be an issue, that a hung jury would result in a second trial and we couldn't afford the first.

"Okay, why don't we cut to the confrontation between Priscilla and Byron, the one you witnessed. You can begin with the time and day she knocked on the door."

As Thelma described the incident in detail, her angry facade began to peel away. For the first time, I was able to see her pain, to see the helpless, bewildered mother unable to protect her child. That was the side she was going to have to show to the jury and I was more than pleased to know it existed.

Byron's assault had taken place about a year before. Priscilla, who'd showed up on Thelma's doorstep one night, had been so badly beaten (according to Thelma) that she couldn't speak above a whisper. Not that Thelma needed to hear an explanation.

"Well, I guess I knew what happened, didn't I? Priscilla wouldn't go to the hospital, wouldn't let us call the police. I made up an ice pack with a plastic bag and some towels, then Joe and me, we put our daughter to bed. It feels funny to say it like that—she was thirty-three years old, after all, and not a little girl—but that was the way it felt. Like she was a two-year-old and needed tucking-in so the monster in the closet wouldn't get her."

"But the monster did get her." Julie's voice was flat. She was looking down, watching the palms of her hands make slow circles, one against the other.

"Byron got in through a bedroom window. I'm sure it was locked because Joe was very careful about locking the windows at night, but somehow. . . . Anyway, Byron marched into the kitchen, and knocked Priscilla off the chair. 'White bitch, white bitch.' I couldn't believe what I was hearing."

Thelma's faucets were full on, now, the tears running almost continually as she dropped her face to her hands. "Joe tried to help her. He picked up a chair and was holding it over his head. I had the phone in my hand, ready to call 911. Byron was standing behind Priscilla with his right arm around her throat, shouting, 'I'll kill the bitch. I swear I'll kill the bitch.' He was crazy, out of his mind. His eyes were rolling in his head like he was having a fit."

She sniffed up her tears, her lips tightening as she pulled herself together. "It was chaos," she continued, "and so unexpected. Byron appeared out of nowhere and we didn't understand about violence." Her eyes flicked from mine to Julie's. "Joe had a heart attack two months later. From what happened is what I think. Byron took his daughter, and Joe couldn't stop him. That's all Joe ever talked about."

The only response I could think of—don't worry, your daughter got even—seemed inappropriate, so I changed the subject. "Did Priscilla say anything to you? Did she ask for help?"

"She couldn't. He was choking her."

"So you just let him go?" I waited for her to nod, then continued. "Where does the neighbor come in, Mister Cassadina?"

"Byron dragged her out through the front door. She was fighting him, but he was too strong. Gennaro was walking his dog near Byron's car. He saw it all."

"Did he try to do something? Try to intervene?"

"I think he wanted to, but there's not much you can do when

you're eighty. And you know how those people are built. Byron looked like a . . ." She took a deep breath as she censored herself, then gave me a defiant look that bordered on triumph, as if she'd won some important point. "Like a bear. He looked like a bear."

"Did you report this incident to the police?" Not for the first time that afternoon, I congratulated myself on leaving Caleb at home.

"I certainly did. I went down to the 107th Precinct that very day and spoke to Sergeant Shannahan. He works in the Domestic Violence Unit."

"And he said . . ."

"He said he'd make a report, but unless Priscilla filed a complaint there wasn't much he could do. Not with Byron living in Manhattan."

"What about the burglary?"

"The what?"

"You said Byron broke in through a window."

"I said, *probably*. Nothing was actually broken."

"All right." I looked around for an ashtray, found none, considered using the cookie dish, but settled for drumming my fingers on my knee. "I take it Priscilla didn't want to file a complaint. Is that the way it went?"

Thelma began a complicated explanation of the phone calls that flew back and forth in the week following the assault. Myself, I tuned out after the second sentence. Given sufficient preparation, Thelma would make a powerful witness, especially if Shannahan had filed a report that substantiated her account. That would be true even if Gennaro turned out to be an incontinent drooler.

"Thelma," I said when she paused for breath, "there's two things I want you to do now. I want you to call Gennaro, ask him to meet me outside, show me where he was standing when Byron dragged your daughter to the car. Then I'd like you to get some of Priscilla's things together. Report cards, if you have them, graduation pictures, preschool finger paintings . . ."

"I understand, Sid."

"Good." I waited until she was standing, before springing the bad news. "But there is one other thing we need to talk about. You remember our conversation yesterday? When I asked you why Priscilla took her husband back after he was released from prison?"

"Yes." Her tone was wary, as if she'd been ambushed once too often.

"Well, the problem is that unless we get a woman on the jury who's been abused by her husband—and the prosecutor's going to do everything in his power to see that doesn't happen—there's only one way to make the individuals charged with judging your daughter's guilt or innocence understand." I stopped, smiled, waited for a grudging nod. "We're going to have to find a psychologist, preferably a woman, to take the stand and explain it. It doesn't really matter what she says. Her purpose is to give the jury an out."

Thelma rose to her full height and folded a pair of thin arms across a narrow chest. "And this psychologist? How much will she cost?"

"Very good, Thelma." I bowed in respect. "Figure thirty-five hundred for a hired gun with minimum credentials. Ten grand for a tenured Harvard Medical School professor with six or seven volumes to her credit." She started to say something, but I waved her off. "We're a long way from trial. For now, it's just something else to think about."

I watched Thelma cross the room, disappear into the kitchen. Then I turned to Julie.

"Thelma's your witness from now on. It's up to you to get her ready. I don't want to see her until a few days before the trial. Assuming it comes to that."

Julie took a second to think it over, then nodded. "I don't see a problem."

"What about the way she pronounces the word *black*?"

"That's for our benefit, Sid. Thelma's too smart to think she can get away with it in front of a jury. By the time we go to trial, she'll be ready to swear that she and her husband welcomed Byron into the family, that they were looking forward to grandchildren. This I promise you."

I got up and pulled on my coat. "Good enough. I'm going to interview the neighbor. Maybe I'll have a smoke at the same time."

The air outside had the texture of borscht. I pulled up the collar of my Burberry trench coat (mine, like the rest of my wardrobe, only because secondhand clothing had no resale value) and lit up a

Camel. The smoke I blew out hovered in front of my face for a moment, as if trying to decide whether to rise or fall.

A few minutes later, Gennaro Cassadina stumbled out of his house. Tall and gaunt, the mottled skin of his cheeks was broken by tufts of inch-long gray stubble. He wore a yellow slicker, a matching yellow hat that fell back over his collar like a fireman's helmet, and a pair of unbuckled galoshes that rose to his knees. The enormous red umbrella he held above his head seemed almost obscene against the gray landscape. Especially in light of the fact that it wasn't raining.

I watched him stagger across the lawn, arms and legs flapping against the slicker like trapped snakes, and felt a moment's sympathy. Then he got within ten feet and the distinct odor of almonds washed over my face. It took me a second to realize that I was smelling his breath and the first thing I thought of was cyanide. But Gennaro wasn't poisoned, he was pickled, the smell of almonds not derived from cyanide, but Amaretto.

"I'ma niney-faw year old," my witness shouted after bringing his raggedy bones under control. "And I'ma still getta laid. Fucka you."

Seven

Julie and I were sitting in the living room, watching *60 Minutes* when Caleb returned just before eight o'clock that evening. He was carrying a doggie bag filled with Ettamae's peppered short ribs (thus saving us from our third pizza that week) and a carefully folded newspaper.

"You read the *Sun* this afternoon?" he asked without preamble.

"I was going to," I replied, "but I couldn't see the print through the clouds."

"Never met a lawyer who could resist a bad joke," Caleb said, depositing the newspaper in my hands before heading off to the kitchen. Julie and I, already salivating, followed closely behind. I sat down at our tiny breakfast table and spread out the *The Harlem Sun*, New York's largest black-owned newspaper, while Julie went for a jug of lemonade and three glasses.

The prevailing mood was clearly one of celebration and there was a time when the lemonade might have been champagne or bourbon, preceded (and followed) by several lines of white powder. One day at a time, that's the theory, but some days are much easier than others. At that moment, I felt a rush of fierce desire, felt it roar up through my arms and into my face. It was a sensation I'd experienced many times, usually in dreams, and I knew (or hoped) that if I waited a few minutes, it'd go away.

Julie filled a glass and set it down in front of me. Then her fingers rose from the glass in a languid arc to caress my cheek.

"Ya know, Julie," I said, "I really hate it when you read my mind."

She sat down next to me and jabbed a fingernail into my ribs. "Macho Sid. Gonna do it all by himself. You ever stop to consider that someone else in the room might be feeling the same thing?"

Caleb dumped the ribs into a glass pie dish, shoved the dish in the microwave, and shut the door. "Forget that AA bullshit for a minute." He was clearly annoyed, his small mouth a black line between walrus cheeks. "Read the goddamned paper, Sid. Page four."

I dutifully opened the tabloid, finding the story in question at the bottom half of the page. It bore the clever headline: NO JUSTICE, NO PEACE FOR BYRON SWEET.

"Read it out loud." Julie was leaning into the refrigerator, gathering the ingredients for a Caesar salad.

The story, an interview with Reverend Mathias Silverstone, an ordained Presbyterian minister whose flock included Sebastian and Rose Sweet, parents of Byron Sweet, was straightforward enough. Mathias intended to preach a sermon denouncing the fact that a black man had been shot down in the prime of life and the white-owned media were preparing to exonerate his killer before the trial had even begun.

If Byron Sweet had been white and his wife black, Reverend Silverstone was quoted as saying, *these same people would call for a lynching. It's got to stop.*

The reporter, Rachman Cousins, whose byline headed the story, stopped short of actually canonizing the dearly departed Byron, but he did list the names of four black women, battered one and all, whose claims of self-defense had been ignored by the media and rejected by a jury.

"That reporter ain't lyin'," Caleb said.

"If Byron's a choirboy," I insisted, "then Priscilla's the Virgin Mary."

Julie turned away from the counter by the sink and began to set the table. "What is it you want, Sid? You want to grab the brass ring, fly off into that madness? It didn't do much for you the first time around."

I think the question was supposed to catch me off-guard, but the truth was that I'd been considering the question all day. I got up and went to the refrigerator for a bottle of Louisiana Hot Sauce and a jar of salad dressing. Blue Cheese, if I remember right. "It isn't the money," I said, then looked defiantly from Julie to Caleb, daring them to contradict me.

"We know that," Caleb said. "Julie wasn't talking about the money. More like the thrill of it all." He took the ribs out of the microwave and set them on the table.

"The thrill? Why not the *high* of it all?"

"Forget it, Sid," Julie said. "Nobody's trying to put you on the spot."

I sprinkled hot sauce onto my ribs, took a bite, then wiped my fingers on a paper napkin. "I understand Caleb's point, and he's got it right. I'm never more alive than when I'm in that courtroom. Plagues? Riots? Wars? Julie, as far as I'm concerned, the only endangered human being in the entire universe is my client. The only war is in that room."

Twenty minutes later, I was getting up to do the dishes when the phone rang. Julie answered, mouthed *Phoebe Morris*, and listened for a moment. "I don't think that's a problem. You wanna talk to Sid?"

I took the call in my bedroom. "Phoebe, it's Sid. How goes it?"

"It's deadline time. And *it* goes very slowly. Look, we're running the photos in tomorrow's edition. That's the good news. The bad news is that we're running your client's rap sheet as well. Any comment?"

"I thought you already catalogued my client's sins?"

"Well, we're doing it again."

"Did Buscetta give you an exclusive or did he mail a little package to every journalist on the east coast?"

"For the record, Sid."

"For the record, I resent this effort to influence the course of justice before a single piece of evidence has been presented against my client in a court of law." I could hear Phoebe's fingers pound away at a keyboard. It'd been a long time since anyone had thought enough of my bullshit to actually write it down. "Off the record, are you going with *Byron's* rap sheet, too? The one you received this afternoon from a protected source?"

"We're saving it. In case the story has legs."

"Does that mean your editors think it *will* have legs?"

"That means, Sid, that it's up to you."

I began the following day with a shower, four cups of coffee, and a brace of extremely productive calls. The first went to Carlo Buscetta, who referred me, after I asked permission to have my client examined by a doctor, to the Department of Corrections. The DOC, after shuttling me from clerk to clerk for thirty minutes, finally transferred me to a supervisor who announced that my request would be taken under advisement. With Priscilla's bruises already fading, postponement was tantamount to refusal.

Satisfied, I hung up and redialed Carlo Buscetta's number, hoping to catch him before he headed off to court. To my surprise, he picked up on the first ring.

"State your business, *Sid*ney," he said as soon as he heard my voice. "I don't have time for any more bullshit this morning."

"Then I'll make it simple. I need to examine the crime scene."

"So sorry, Mr. Kaplan, no can do. Priscilla Sweet's apartment was burglarized last night. I'm told the place was torn to pieces."

"And the chair? The one Byron was sitting in when he was shot?" I was hoping the chair had been damaged in some way that would make it inadmissible in a court of law. No such luck.

"The chair's in an evidence locker, *Sid*ney. Where it belongs."

Ten minutes later, I was in a cab heading for a safe deposit box at Citibank's First Avenue and Fifteenth Street branch. The key my client had given me was no longer burning a hole in my pocket. That's because it was burning a hole in my right palm.

The clerk in charge of the safe deposit vault was suspicious enough to take my Power of Attorney form to a supervisor who was suspicious enough to ask for identification. I think the supervisor, Annette Robbins, might have enjoyed refusing me, especially after I announced that the owner of the box was sitting in the Rose Singer

Jail on Rikers Island. But when I promised her that if my client's interests were in any way compromised by her refusal to allow me access, I'd respond with an aggressive, mean-spirited lawsuit, her managerial heart softened and she instructed the clerk to give me the box and show me to a "privacy cubicle."

I suppose I should have opened the box slowly, savoring the mystery the way a bibliophile might savor a rare first edition. Instead, ever the *gourmand*, I tore the lid open, turned the box over, and dumped the contents onto the table. Two items tumbled out, a passport and a stack of letters tied with a white ribbon. I remember thinking, even as I opened the passport, that the ribbon was a nice touch.

The individual named on the passport was Morgan Paxton; the face in the small, ugly photograph belonged to Byron Sweet. Both of them had taken a trip to Panama a short time after Byron was released from prison.

I put the passport on the table and untied the letters. They were in sequence, with the earliest dates on top, written by Byron on prison stationary. For the next hour, I kept reminding myself that I was reading Priscilla's version of her reconciliation with Byron. I had no way of knowing, for instance, if there weren't other letters, perhaps dealing with the sale and distribution of drugs, that she'd chosen to keep to herself.

Despite my suspicions, a quick scan told me that Byron Sweet's literary self-portrait, assuming I could have it put into evidence, would shed the best possible light on his and his wife's post-prison reunion. Carlo would challenge any attempt to show the letters to the jury on two grounds. First, that they were hearsay, which, in fact, they were. Second, and more importantly, that they were irrelevant. I could overcome the hearsay problem by offering the letters as proof, not of the statements they contained, but of Priscilla's state of mind when she received them. But how were they relevant to Priscilla's claim of self-defense?

Nevertheless, the letters were my first real glimpse of Byron as human instead of monster. Previously, in a typical act of unconscious bias, I'd been imagining him as a hulking brute, had him alternately adding the words *bitch* and *whore* to every guttural command. Meanwhile, Byron Sweet's letters were witty and sophisticated.

There were long passages describing his efforts to gain control of his temper and his life. He wrote of "adjustment therapy" sessions and the "need to repair the unalterable past." Whole letters were devoted to the small pleasures he and Priscilla had once shared—foreign movies, a trip to Baja California, a sunset viewed from a Long Island City pier. Others remembered their shared sorrows. Their premature son, Jason, who'd died in an incubator four days after his birth. Byron's twin sister who'd been killed in a wreck on the Cross Bronx Expressway, run off the road by a fifteen-year-old in a stolen car.

It wasn't until I walked out of the bank, letters and passport tucked into my briefcase, that I fully understood the obvious fact that my client had begun preparing her defense long before the day she murdered her husband. Moreover, she'd had that key with her when she pulled the trigger, had taken the time to swallow it before the cops turned up. Looking back, I know the proper response on my part should have been fear, but what I actually felt at the time was admiration.

The air outside the overheated bank was sharp and cold. Overnight, a piercing north wind had pushed the rain out into the Atlantic, replacing it with a glaring winter sun that hung just above the roof lines on the southern side of Fourteenth Street. I was looking for a diner and lunch, but the first place to catch my eye was a small dark bar with a hand-lettered sign in the window extolling the virtues of its half-pound hamburgers. It beckoned to me like a whore from the mouth of a dark alley and I had a quick vision of myself holding a schooner of Bass Ale in one hand, a half-eaten burger in the other while a tenor sax, playing in the low registers, purred from the jukebox.

I listened to that sax for a moment, imagined Ben Webster's lips curled around the mouthpiece; I heard it filter through the casual chatter of the pedestrians who moved around me, persistent and implacable. Then I moved on.

Eight

I drove from Citibank out to the Tucker Trucking warehouse on 56th Avenue in Maspeth. There I found Priscilla Sweet's former employer, Paulie Gullo, and his two office workers, Iris Sanchez and Miriam Konig. They were, the three of them, pure New York, an Italian, a Jew, and a second generation Puerto Rican. Better yet, each of them confirmed my client's story. After coming out of prison, she'd given every indication that she'd pulled her life together.

"Priscilla was never late," Miriam Konig declared as she searched a file cabinet for Priscilla's time cards. "And she never took a day off. Not until Byron came back into her life."

"And she didn't have an attitude, neither," Paulie Gullo told me. "In this line of work, you gotta be ready to jump from one job to another. Routing, payroll, customers and creditors, vehicle maintenance. Priscilla could do it all, and she did." He tossed Iris Sanchez a nasty look, then added, "Without whining."

It was only after Byron's release from prison that Priscilla began to change. "At first," Miriam Konig told me, "it was okay. Byron, he was a funny guy, loved to joke around, and Priscilla, she was real quiet. It was like they just fit together." Miriam was wearing a knit, chocolate-brown suit and a yellow blouse. No jewelry, no makeup.

"But then, a couple months in, Priscilla showed up with a shiner and from there it was all downhill."

I listened to this recitation of Priscilla's fall from grace until Gullo and his workers began to repeat themselves. Then I took Paulie Gullo outside and braced him. "Paulie," I asked, "did you grow up in Brooklyn?"

"Yeah," he grinned. "How'd you know?" His head was completely bald on top, but he'd let his hair grow long on the right side, his intention, undoubtedly, to comb it back over his naked scalp. Unfortunately, the breeze had pulled the fringe loose and it hung over his right ear like the edges of a feather duster.

"Because it takes one to know one. I grew up in Sheepshead Bay."

A sparkling green truck pulled up as we spoke. Gullo eyed it, then nodded. "Look, I gotta cut this short, get that load off."

"Then I'll make it simple. Were you fucking Priscilla Sweet?"

He tossed me a look of pure astonishment, then burst out laughing. "What're you, a mind reader?"

"Something about your protective attitude led me to draw the obvious conclusion." I waited until he shrugged, then asked, "Are you married, Paulie? You have kids?"

"All right, I get the picture."

"You still want to testify?" Actually, I intended to call him no matter what he wanted.

"Will I be asked about . . ."

"Not by me."

To his credit, Gullo considered the ramifications before he replied. "Yeah," he finally said, "I'll do it for Priscilla. I was crazy about her. She's the only woman I ever met who knew anything about anything."

My good mood carried me through the heart of Queens, from Paul Gullo's warehouse to the far side of the Hazen Street Bridge where I popped the trunk as I slowed for the mandatory car search. A beefy corrections officer leaned into the window and looked the car over. "I know you," he said after a moment. "I recognize you."

"Yeah, I'm the guy who escaped last week. I miss the place and I'm trying to get back inside."

I expected him to catch an attitude, which would have pleased me immensely, but he shook his head. "Uh-uh. You're in the paper. Wait a minute." He turned back to his kiosk, snatched a copy of the *New York Post* off the counter, began to thumb through the pages. "In Jay Harrison's column. Your picture. Here."

Sure enough, there I was, looking more than a little shifty, as I pushed my way through a mob of reporters. The photo appeared to be at least ten years old.

"You wouldn't want to part with that?" I asked, gesturing at the paper. "Save me a stop on the way home?"

Jay Harrison, a columnist with the *Post* for as long as I could remember, had a dual reputation as a thinly disguised racist and a rabid law-and-order fanatic. I remember wondering which way he'd come down on this one. Would he take up the cause of a black wife beater? It didn't seem likely. No more likely than his taking up the cause of the woman who killed the black wife beater.

When I finally got a chance to read Harrison's column, fifteen minutes later after sending up for my client, I found that Harrison had a third predilection that I hadn't considered. He simply *hated* defense lawyers.

The column was about Sid Kaplan. It named my famous (and notorious) clients, detailed their crimes without bothering to add the word *alleged*, revealed my problems with drugs, alcohol, and divorce without including my year of rehab.

> Sid Kaplan reminds me of all those washed-up fighters I covered during my years on the sports beat. Dreaming of glories won and lost, of riding that roller coaster one last time. I, for one, hope Sid lacks the price of admission. He was that good in his prime.

Some people are inspired by competition, but I've always needed out-and-out enemies. I suppose it runs in the family, because I can clearly remember my Grampa Itzy describing himself as a "belligerent Jew."

"Do I look like a turtle I should pull in my head?" he'd asked his ten-year-old grandson. "Am I a chicken I should hold out my neck for the butcher's knife?"

The questions had been strictly rhetorical, but the message, which I'd already adopted, was that you define yourself by your choice of enemies, and by your victories over them. That was why I'd made a career of battling with police, prosecutors, judges, the New York State Bar Association . . . anyone or anything that stood between my client and acquittal.

Fifteen minutes later, I was sitting across from Priscilla Sweet, puzzling over the sudden change in her expression. That sardonic twist I was used to seeing at the corner of her mouth was gone and her eyes had shed their cold glitter.

"Problem here?" I asked. "You don't look so good."

"I took PC this morning."

PC is prison shorthand for protective custody. In theory, it's an option for prisoners threatened by other prisoners. In practice, it means twenty-three hours a day in a six-by-ten foot cell.

"Somebody's after you?"

Priscilla shrugged, lit a cigarette. "It's a racial thing. I should have seen it coming." She glanced down at her lap for a moment, then sucked in a deep breath. "Look, Sid, my mother's not coming up with any bail money. She'd have to use her house for collateral and the way she sees it, I fucked up too many times in the past for her to take the risk. Me, I can't say as I really blame her, but what it means is we have to go for a speedy trial. I'm doing hard time now."

I stood up and began to pace. A speedy trial benefited me in two very important ways. First, it'd be a lot easier to hold the media's interest for six months than for the standard eighteen. Second, and more importantly, if I went forward with all due constitutional speed, we might actually get a jury verdict before being evicted from our offices and our apartment. But there were drawbacks as well.

"Look, Priscilla, a quick trial is fine for O.J. Simpson. Or anybody else with enough money to hire an army of lawyers, paralegals, and investigators. That's not the case here." Not unless I let the pressure build, then squeezed Thelma.

Priscilla took my hand and held it against her cheek. Her eyes were brimming. "My whole life has been hell. My father . . ." She choked back the next words. "I just can't take any more. That's what it boils down to. I sit in that cell, listen to the psychos on the block.

They rant and rave all day; at night, they scream." As she went on, her mouth firmed and her eyes narrowed slightly. "And what I think is that if I stay in isolation long enough, I'll be screaming, too."

"I know how you feel, but . . ."

She let my hand drop and pulled away. "It's no good, Sid. I want you to represent me, but if you can't get me to trial within six months, I'll have to find somebody else." Her eyes were cold again. Cold and flat. "Christ knows I don't want to."

I turned away for a moment. Priscilla had put me in my place and I didn't want her to catch a glimpse of my wounded vanity. "You have a right to a trial within six months. If you want me to go forward, of course I'll do it." I walked over to the cubicle's window, stared at the bored corrections officer perched on his stool. "Meanwhile, you're being indicted today," I said without turning around. "You could be arraigned as early as Friday. The court will expect me to make a request for bail and what I need to know is if you made all your appearances."

"On my other busts?"

"Yeah."

"Every one."

"That's good, Priscilla. Makes you look like an honest mutt."

She came over to me, linked her arm through mine. "Don't be mad at me, Sid. You know I love you."

I remember her breast pushing against the back of my arm, a sudden rush of excitement that rippled down through the hairs on my chest and belly as I led her back to the table. "I had a conversation with your boss," I said without removing my arm, "and your coworkers. Those people over there in Maspeth, they're on your side and they're gonna make great witnesses. Even if the prosecutor picks up on the fact that you were sleeping with your boss. And the fact that he's married."

Her customary half-smirk blossomed into a pair of fetching dimples. They looked a good deal better on her than they did on her mother.

"I hadn't been with a man in almost four years." She shook her head. "At the time, it didn't seem like a big deal."

"You want to tell a jury that a married man is no more than a roll in the hay for you?" I flicked my ashes onto the floor. "You know,

I'm tempted to ask you how long Byron lived after you shot him and whether or not you tried to get help, but I'm not going to do it. No, I think it's something you should think about. I mean it's possible that you were in shock, right? The explosion must have been unbelievably loud in that small room, especially for someone unfamiliar with handguns. Or maybe you tried to call, maybe 911 was busy." I took a notebook out of my briefcase, laid it on the table, dropped a pen onto the notebook. "You can tell me the *whole* story after the arraignment, but for now I'll settle for a list of unfriendly witnesses. Byron's friends, the people he did business with, anybody likely to advance the prosecution's case."

Priscilla tapped a blunt nail on the edge of the table. "I don't want you to hate me." She was staring up, her eyes as gray (and as opaque) as the surface of a calm lake on a cloudy day. "I know I'm not a good citizen—I'm not trying to get away from that—but I don't want *you* to hate me."

Nine

Within twenty-four hours, Priscilla's demand for a speedy trial, which I carried home and presented to Caleb and Julie that evening, had us hopping like laboratory rats on an electrified grid. I was used to this mode, had been through it any number of times in the past, but for my associates, who'd joined me when I was already on the decline, the experience was entirely new. What it meant, in terms of their personal lives, was that they wouldn't have any personal lives. It was that simple and I put the reality to them with enough force to prevent any misinterpretation.

It was seven o'clock, half an hour after the start of the Knicks game which I hadn't turned on, when Caleb came into the apartment and we sat down to dinner. Halfway through, I pointed to the skeletal remains of a baked chicken and said, "Best enjoy this. You may not see another home-cooked meal until the trial's over. Starting tomorrow, we meet in the office every night, report progress, plan our next moves. We'll always be two steps behind, always in crisis. By the time we get a verdict, you'll think you've been through a war." I remember being so consumed with self-love that I actually tapped the edge of my plate with a fork before delivering the punch line. "And what you should think about, when you're so tired you can't focus your attention long enough to wipe your ass, is how you'll feel if you *lose* the war."

Caleb and Julie looked at each other for a moment, then burst into applause.

" 'Into the Valley of Death,' " Julie quoted.

"If those six hundred were lawyers," Caleb announced, "then I'm personally rooting for the cannon to the right and left."

"You can laugh if you want," I said, "but you won't be laughing if your personal failures result in Priscilla Sweet's passing the next twenty-five years in a maximum security prison."

I pushed the remains of my dinner to one side and got down to business, presenting Caleb with Priscilla's list of hostile witnesses and a curt order to check them out.

"You want what, boss? Rap sheets, interviews . . ."

"Both."

"You know I gotta buy the rap sheets." He glanced at the list. "Number of people you got down, we're lookin' at a grand. At least."

"Thelma's check'll clear in a couple of days."

Julie waved a stripped chicken wing in my direction. "Don't forget, we've got rent to pay on both places. Not to mention the note on the furniture."

"Thank you for sharing that," I said. "Let's hope you're paying as much attention to the solutions as you are to the problems."

It was Julie's task to prepare rough drafts of the various written documents we'd file within fifteen days after Priscilla's arraignment. These included a demand letter asking for the prosecution's witness list as well as police reports, autopsy results, and forensic analyses.

The process is called discovery and every accused citizen is theoretically entitled to this material as soon as it's available. In practice, the prosecution stalls, claiming the paperwork has not been completed and/or compiled (a lie that virtually all New York judges accept without question), until after the trial, or the hearing in which the evidence is to be presented actually begins. The overwhelming majority of defendants, represented by Legal Aid attorneys, are allowed no more than a *pro forma* objection. I, on the other hand, had Phoebe Morris. And what I hoped would become an army of outraged feminists.

In addition to the demand letter, Julie was drafting several pretrial motions requesting that all of the evidence found inside Priscilla Sweet's apartment be excluded. Our theory was simple enough. First, the cops who responded to the 911 call entered the premises without benefit of a warrant, thus violating the Payton Rule. As a result, every subsequent action was in violation of the 14th Amendment to the Federal Constitution, as well as Article 1, Section 6 of the New York State Constitution. Second, even if the 911 call had been specific enough to justify the initial entry by the responding patrolmen, the detectives had no right to search a suitcase in the back of a closet without first obtaining a search warrant.

There would be a Mapp hearing on these issues just before the actual trial, at which time I would have an opportunity to call and examine witnesses. Meanwhile, it was important to submit a motion that cited every conceivable legal argument because we had no idea what evidence, besides the coke and the gun, the prosecution intended to present.

"I found the doctor," Caleb said as he stacked the dinner plates, "who treated Priscilla four years ago, after Byron attacked her in a joint called Pentangles Bar and Grill. He's still at Bellevue. Dr. Grace says that he has no specific memory of Priscilla Sweet and doesn't feel he has to testify. I found the social worker, Miriam Farber, too. The one who talked Priscilla into prosecuting Byron. It was Farber who took the photos that eventually sent Byron to Rikers."

I leaned back to light a cigarette. As I'd cooked dinner, cleaning up was not my chore. "Don't worry about Grace, Caleb. He'll change his mind when he's served with a subpoena. Anything else?"

"Yeah," Caleb said. "Something I heard this afternoon. I don't know how good it is, but there's a rumor going around that Byron's blood-alcohol level was .42 when his wife pulled the trigger. That maybe he was too drunk to be a threat."

"What about cocaine? He have cocaine in his system?"

"Don't know." Caleb got up, took a dish towel, began to dry the dishes. "We're talkin' about a rumor, boss. And what I'm gonna do, as I go along, is ask about Byron's capacity. See if he could hold his booze."

I slid my chair away from the table, stood up, and cleared my throat. "You guys wanna hold off for a minute. I have a little speech to make." Folding my arms across my chest, I waited for their full attention. "Julie, yesterday you asked me what I wanted from this case. Besides enough new business to pay the rent. Well, what I've decided to do is form a corporation, distribute the shares a third to each of us. Then I'm going to sign a personal services contract binding myself to the corporation for the next ten years. You hear what I'm saying? It's not about the money. It's about us and what we've done together." Thoroughly embarrassed, I huffed and puffed for a moment, then added, "If it wasn't for the two of you, the best I could hope to be, at this point in my life, is dead."

Caleb was first to react. He walked across the kitchen, dragged me into a bear hug, kissed me on both cheeks. "Partner," he said, stepping away, "you're the greatest. Ain't that right, Julie?"

"Yeah." She was standing by the sink, holding a soapy dish. I remember the soap running along her fingers, onto her wrist, dripping to the floor. "Sid's the greatest, all right." She crossed the kitchen to place a wet hand against my cheek. "But it's not like we didn't already know it."

I put my arm around her waist, drew her to me, held her for a long moment before pulling away. There was no sexual element to our hug. Julie was my sister, my family; I would protect her with my life, protect her as I'd never protected my parents, my wife, my son. There was something wrong with that, and I knew it. I knew it and I didn't care.

A few minutes later, we acknowledged the fact that our new partnership wouldn't be worth much if we didn't get Priscilla acquitted by returning to work. I went into my bedroom-office in search of my Rolodex. I'd been hoping to leave the forensic evidence (assuming it was admitted) unchallenged. After all, we weren't going to argue that somebody else pulled the trigger. But if Byron, in fact, had a .42 blood-alcohol and the prosecution was, in fact, going to contend that he was comatose when shot, we'd have to offer some evidence to the contrary. Evidence that could only come through an expert witness.

I thumbed through the Rolodex until I came to the number of Dr. Kim Park. Park, a naturalized citizen by way of Seoul, Korea, was a forensic pathologist with impeccable credentials and a love of the spotlight. He was small, almost elfin, with sharp, animated features that projected passionate belief in his own testimony. Jurors loved him.

In my prime, I'd used Park several times and what I remembered most about him, as I punched out his Chicago phone number, was that he liked four-star hotels as much as he liked testifying in a courtroom packed with reporters. I was calling him at the small office he maintained in his home and, given his workaholic reputation, wasn't surprised when he picked up on the second ring.

"Dr. Park," he said, his enunciation precise, his voice pitched high enough to thoroughly disguise the steel trap between his ears.

"Sid Kaplan, Kim. How's it hangin'?"

"Well, Sidney, according to the inside dope on Asians, not very far."

I dredged up an appreciative chuckle. "Look . . ."

"Over the weekend, while I was in New York, I read something about your case in *Newsday*. It sounds quite interesting."

"It's hot, Kim. Definitely hot."

I quickly outlined the case and the strategy we intended to pursue, both in the courtroom and through the media, ending with the blood-alcohol rumor. Kim took a moment to think it over, then asked the inevitable question.

"Did the . . . the deceased have cocaine in his system?" He'd been about to use the word *victim*.

"Don't know." I paused, took a deep breath. "What I'd like to do, Kim, is send you the autopsy material as soon as I get my hands on it."

"No problem. I'd love to see it."

"Oh, there's a problem, all right, and it's called money. As in we don't have dime number one."

"Well . . ."

"But what you gotta think about is your value on the lecture circuit." I knew that Kim worked the circuit for all it was worth, knocking down between seven and ten grand per speech. "We're looking at a *New York* trial here. With *New York* publicity." I ran on before he could interrupt. "Don't give me an answer now. What I'll do is fax the forensic material out to you as soon as I get it. You don't like what you see, I can always find some pro bono jerk to say Byron was about to run the hundred yard dash. Maybe the jury'll believe it. And maybe they won't care."

Ever the entrepreneur, Kim responded without hesitation. "And maybe," he reminded, "they'll convict an innocent woman."

The mid-week period went by in a blur. I got the details of Priscilla's indictment early Tuesday morning. Her crime having lacked any of the special circumstances necessary for a charge of murder in the first degree (and a possible death sentence), she'd been charged with second degree murder. This in addition to drug possession in the first degree, criminal use of a firearm in the first degree, and criminal possession of a weapon in the first degree. The homicide and drug possession charges, both A1 felonies, each carried a maximum penalty of twenty-five years to life. The others were all B felonies and, given Priscilla's repeat offender status, carried seven year minimums.

I remember gathering my troops that evening and reading the charges and penalties out loud, adding, "If the sentencing judge strings them out consecutively, Priscilla Sweet's gonna go from prison directly into the ground." This time there were no wise guy remarks. Caleb went back to his desk and continued to laboriously enter his interview notes. Julie returned to the motion she was writing while I pored over a rough draft of our demand letter.

We were riding a high generated by the evening news. All three networks had run with a press conference held by the Sweet family. Sebastian, Rose, and son William, along with Reverend Mathias Silverstone, had been perched on stiff, high-backed chairs that looked to have been dragged out of somebody's dining room. Their attorney, on the other hand, Henry Lee Thompson, had been seated just off to the left on a cushioned armchair. Thompson, tall and impossibly wide-shouldered, had delivered a passionate, rapid-fire speech on the vilification of black males, adding a homily on victim's rights that contradicted every other speech he'd given in the course of a long, successful career. Then he'd ducked the matter of Byron's abuse by accusing a reporter (black, by the way) of harboring racist sentiments. Thompson's face was all forehead, cheekbones, and jaw. His nose and lips, small anyway, seemed to fade away beneath a pair of black eyes angry enough to loosen the bowels of judges, jurors, and hostile journalists alike.

Thompson and I shared a number of traits. We were, the both of us, mindless advocates, belligerent to a fault and as committed to personal victory as champion pit bulls. The difference was that Henry Lee's advocacy extended beyond himself and his client to a political agenda that interested me not at all.

On the other hand, what did interest me was that Henry Lee's diatribe was certain to provoke a response from members of the community with political agendas of their own. That response wasn't long in coming. The phone rang about 8:30 and I picked it up without thinking.

"Kaplan."

The woman on the other end identified herself as Rebecca Barthelme, chairwoman of the New York Women's Council's advisory board.

"Oh, right," I said, interrupting. "I believe you've already been in touch with my client."

"That's correct." Her delivery was tight, her voice almost breathless with tension. "Before you came into the picture."

"I see. Well, what can I do for you?"

"The Council is considering an offer of aid to Priscilla. But we need a little more information before we can proceed."

"Is that right?"

"Mr. Kaplan, let's not make this any harder . . ."

"Call me, Sid. Please."

She took a deep breath, finally said, "Tell me what we can do for Priscilla."

"Okay, Priscilla needs two things from the Council. First and foremost, an expert on battered spouse syndrome. There's no money here, so I can't, much as I'd like to, simply go out and buy one. Second, a quiet, competent lawyer to act as my assistant."

"That's certainly possible," she replied. "Assuming Priscilla's circumstances . . ."

"Her circumstances? Rebecca, what you wanna do is take the following back to your governing board: that my client is innocent; that we have a legitimate claim of self-defense; that we have a documented history of abuse; that we have more witnesses than we can use at trial; that my client maintained a spotless record, both with her employer and with her parole officer, from the time she was released from prison until she went back to her husband."

"And you're prepared to prove these assertions?"

"One hand washes the other, Rebecca. Let me know what the board decides. Maybe we can get together when I give my press conference after Friday's arraignment."

I hung up a minute later, then turned to Caleb and Julie with a big smile on my face. "That was Rebecca Barthelme from the New York Women's Council. Looks like she wants a piece of the action."

"You gonna give it to her?" Julie asked.

"What I'll do, Julie, is put it to Priscilla, see what she thinks. But I'll tell ya, given the state of our finances, it feels like manna from heaven to me."

Priscilla, after I detailed the Council's generous offer, accepted without hesitation. "Now that you have some help," she told me, "maybe there won't be so much pressure about money. My mother's a nervous wreck."

The news kept getting better. On Thursday evening, the day before Priscilla's arraignment, as we awaited a delivery from a Thai restaurant on Fourteenth Street, Caleb proudly declared, "The Bellevue incident is in the bag."

He was talking about the confrontation that led to Priscilla's visit to the emergency room, then to her husband's incarceration.

"I've got three witnesses lined up and they're telling the same basic story. Priscilla's in Pentangles, the restaurant on Avenue B, having a quiet drink with a female friend. Byron shows up, rips her off the bar stool, and slaps her in the face. Priscilla makes the mistake of fighting back and he beats her into unconsciousness."

Caleb looked from Julie to me, tossed each of us a hard cop glare. "You hear what I'm sayin'? He got her down on the floor, sat on her chest, smashed her in the face with both hands. The bartender had to pull him off."

"This bartender," I asked after giving him a minute to calm down, "he available?"

"Yeah. His name's Lance McCormack, a would-be actor. I tracked him down at his apartment in Astoria. He remembers the incident and he's eager to testify. A waitress, too." Caleb glanced at his spiral notebook. "Amelia Green. She still works at the restaurant."

"Are either of them," Julie asked, "close friends of Priscilla's?"

"Never met her before and haven't seen her since. Mr.

McCormack and Ms. Green are just two good citizens out to perform their civic duty. Why, I'll bet, between 'em they don't do more than four grams of coke a week." When neither Julie nor I responded he went on. "Seriously, partners, we get these folks on the stand, nobody on the jury's gonna have any doubts about the abuse. The deal in the restaurant leads directly to the Bellevue emergency room visit which leads directly to Byron's stint on Rikers Island."

"And the order of protection," Julie said, "which was still in effect when Priscilla went to prison."

Ten

Part 81 of the New York Criminal Court, the fiefdom of Judge Rob Winokur, was one of two Parts dedicated to Supreme Court arraignments. Arraignment, in theory, is a simple procedure: the charges in the Grand Jury indictment are read to the defendant, a formal plea is taken, a brief appeal for bail (or the lack thereof) is considered, then the gavel bangs down. On a productive day, Judge Winokur processed as many as a hundred defendants.

In the early days of my private practice, I spent many an hour waiting in Judge Winokur's courtroom for my client's name to be called. Later on, at the height of my career, unless the client was very famous, I sent one of the flunkies to handle the dirty work. Then, after my career nosedived, I turned full circle and became just another *schmucko* lawyer reading a newspaper on the front row of benches because I didn't have other clients in need of my attention.

In a way, it had been comforting, like anything else that seems immutable. Part 81, a large room on the fifteenth floor of the Criminal Court Building at 100 Centre Street, was virtually devoid of ornamentation. It reeked of shabbiness, of surrendered irretrievable gentility. At one time, for example, though not within my memory, the floor tiles with their brown swirls probably resembled marble. Now they were scuffed and scratched and dusty. As if during some budget crunch, decades before, the maintenance staff had decided to sacrifice mops and polish.

The room was lined with wood paneling that ran a third of the way up each wall. The panels may originally have been of some attractive, valuable wood—maple, perhaps, or walnut, or even mahogany. But over the years they'd received so many coats of chocolate-brown paint, they now had the color and consistency of dried mud.

The seats in the jury box were in even worse shape, their brown leather covers torn and cracked. The excuse, I suppose, if anyone cared to ask, was that juries played no role in the arraignment proceedings. Just as well, because there was no way they could have followed the action. Not only were there no cameras in Judge Winokur's courtroom, there were no microphones either. The attorneys on the front bench talked among themselves, as did the four armed court officers and the spectators, a mix of defendants on bail, the families of the incarcerated accused, and assorted court buffs.

The din reduced the pleadings of the prosecutor and the defense attorney, who stood with their backs to the courtroom, to a vague murmur. Even Judge Winokur, who faced the spectators, could only be understood when he shouted at the attorneys in front of him. Winokur was halfway through his third, ten-year term of office, and had long ago mastered the art of attorney abuse. He was short and bald, with an ordinarily florid complexion that brightened to scarlet whenever the process of arraignment lasted longer than the three minutes it took the sand in a tiny hourglass sitting on the forward edge of his desk to run out.

Winokur had just taken his seat on the bench when I entered Part 81 on that Friday morning to discover a half dozen reporters gathered at the bar. They were almost certainly asking where Priscilla Sweet's name stood on the court calendar. If her case wouldn't be called until after lunch, they didn't want to waste the morning sitting in a courtroom. I started forward to clock in, looking for an answer to the same question, when a court officer named Moscowitz tapped me on the arm.

"Forget the mob, *boychick*," he said as he pulled me back into the hall. "Today you're a star."

Ira Moscowitz was the only Jewish court officer I'd ever met. He was short and burly, with arms as thick as my skull.

"Your client's gonna be called first in the afternoon session. Meanwhile, the guinea wants you downstairs in his office."

I was about to ask for the identity of "the guinea," though I knew he was talking about Carlo Buscetta, when the door burst open and the reporters charged into the hallway. They literally surrounded me, despite my verbal assurance that all of their questions would be answered after Priscilla's arraignment. I think they would have followed me onto the elevator if Ira hadn't barred their way.

Carl Buscetta's crowded office was just about the size of a prison cell. A fine layer of dust covered the window frame, the top of the filing cabinet, the seat of the visitor's chair. I wiped the seat with my handkerchief, then dropped the handkerchief in the wastebasket before I sat down.

"Big day, right *Sid*ney?" Everything about Carlo Buscetta was tight, from the black, vested suits he habitually wore to the acne-pitted skin stretched across his prominent cheekbones.

"Medium day, Carlo. If that."

Carlo stared at me for a moment, his little acne pits glowing red. "The plea board," he finally said, "has *ordered* me to make the following offer. If your client pleads guilty to the top charge, all lesser charges will be dismissed and the minimum sentence recommended."

I watched him straighten in the chair, his equanimity recovered, and tilt his head back to stare at me along the length of a prodigious nose. "So what you're saying here," I declared, "is that if my innocent client pleads guilty she can look forward to spending the next dozen or so years in Bedford Hills? You want me to recommend this travesty?"

Carlo responded by leaning over the edge of the desk. His mouth curved into a thin white crescent. "Your client," he snarled, "is a sleazebag dope dealer who got her ass kicked because she was skimming her partner's share of the profits."

I waited patiently for him to continue, but that, apparently, was as much as he was prepared to say. "And how long," I finally asked, "does my client get to consider the state's generous offer?"

"If she doesn't take the plea before arraignment, the deal is off."

"Carlo, you *goyishe* bastard, if you think I'm gonna go down to the holding pens, talk to my client through the bars with every mutt in the system listening, you must be living in a dream."

The epithet seemed to ripple through his short black hair. For a moment, I thought he was going to come over the desk, settle the issue of guilt or innocence with his fists, but he finally calmed. "I've arranged to have the defendant brought into the empty courtroom next to Part 81. You can talk to her there. If that's all right, *Sid*ney."

Ten minutes later, I was sitting next to Priscilla on a bench in the center of room 1545. An armed court officer stood at the exit to the judge's chambers, another lounged against the door leading to the hall. Priscilla slipped her finger around my palm and gripped tightly.

"It almost feels like freedom. I haven't seen this much empty space in a long time." She was wearing a standard orange jumpsuit, though she could have appeared in street clothes. The decision had been made at the last minute over the telephone; it fit nicely into my warts-and-all defense, and made her seem more like a victim.

"Priscilla, the one thing that *isn't* on today's agenda is freedom. Buscetta offered me a deal. If you plead to the top count, you get the minimum, fifteen-to-life."

"Sounds like the same deal he offered a week ago."

"Last week it would have been the maximum on the homicide, twenty-five years." I fumbled a pack of cigarettes out of my jacket.

"No smoking," the officer by the judge's chamber called out. "No smoking anywhere in this building."

"That a joke?" I shouted back to him. The no smoking signs in the hallways of justice were universally ignored, but if he wanted to be a prick, there was nothing I could do about it.

"No smoking," he repeated.

I put the pack away, let go of Priscilla's hand, stared into her gray eyes. "The way Buscetta tells it, Byron attacked you because you were skimming drug profits."

"That's bullshit. I . . ."

"The thing about Buscetta," I interrupted, "is that he's got the personality of a wolverine. Juries sense it and they don't like him. So what he does is compensate with a thorough presentation of his case. That means he's got at least two individuals willing to swear you were stealing from Byron. And don't be surprised if one of them comes out of Rikers. Jailhouse informants are a Buscetta specialty."

She flushed, the sudden burst of color accenting the faded bruises on the side of her face. "Do you really believe that I spoke about my case to anyone but you?"

"How is that relevant?"

"I guess it isn't." Priscilla curled one edge of her mouth into a half smile. "I guess it isn't. She crossed her legs, tucked her fingers between her thighs. "So tell me what I'm supposed to do about the plea."

"My advice is not to take it, that the deal will get better as we get closer to trial. Buscetta's not running the show here. There's a plea board in the D.A.'s office made up of supervisors. Buscetta has input, but the board makes the final decision. I think what they'll finally offer is manslaughter with a seven year minimum."

"Seven years?" Priscilla glanced around the courtroom. "Christ, I could use a cigarette." She pulled her hands free, looked at them for a moment, then folded her arms across her chest. "I can't wait seven years to start my life. Just can't. No, what I want to do is throw the dice. All or nothing."

Her eyes betrayed neither fear nor defiance. They were dead, flat, as if she was looking at something or somebody invisible to the rest of the world.

"I think it's time I told my story," she said. "Such as it is."

Eleven

"It took me a long time to understand that Byron was two people, one who loved me and one who hated me. It sounds trite when I say it out loud. Like I should have understood it in tenth grade when I read *Dr. Jekyll and Mr. Hyde*. I can remember Mrs. Kaufman explaining the part about Mr. Hyde being in there all the time. Invisible—or at least unacknowledged—but definitely there, like an evil genie waiting for Aladdin to rub the lamp.

"But I never got it. Not until the very end, until I was holding the gun in my hand. It was heavy and hard, that gun. There was no give to it, nothing to let you off the hook. No lie you could tell yourself.

"I'd heard somewhere that guns have safeties on them. That you have to do something to make them fire. So I pushed this little bar on the side of the gun and the cylinder popped out. Byron thought it was funny. The way I jumped.

"He said, 'Poor little Prissy. Life don't wanna work for you. Must be something you did in a prior incarnation. Somethin' you gotta work out.'"

"I remember the first time Byron hit me. The two of us were living on the Lower East Side and we didn't have shit for money. Or maybe shit was *all* we had. The toilet in that apartment backed up every other day. I thought poverty was virtuous back then, but this place was really unlivable. There were shooting galleries on every floor, dopers nodding in the halls. The local winos used the lobby for a toilet.

"What I did was get on Byron's case about moving out. I was waiting tables in Leshko's, the Polish hashhouse on Avenue B, and Byron was putting my wages up his nose. Chasing the coke with pints of apricot brandy. Me, I was very young, and very clean, and very stupid.

"I said, 'Byron, I have to get out of here. The junkies are grabbing me on the stairs.'

" 'Yeah, baby, we're gonna get out. Just give it a little time.'

"I said, 'We've been talking about it for six months.'

"Byron put the bottle in his mouth, finished it off real slow. Then he licked the last drops off his mouth and grinned at me.

"I said, 'I'm not joking this time. My folks are willing to let me stay with them, at least temporarily, and that's what I'm gonna do.'

"Byron came off that chair like he was spring-loaded. Punched me full force in the head. When I woke up a few minutes later, he was pressing a cold towel against my face. 'Baby, baby, baby, baby. . . .' There were tears on the ends of his mustache. I could feel them dropping onto my throat."

"I did my first lines of coke that night. It was wonderful, perfect; I've never felt as good, before or since. Byron loved me completely and I wanted him just as much as I wanted the next line. As if we were now joined forever, united by his fists and his dope."

"Two months later I was running into Leshko's bathroom every half hour for a little snort. You know, just to keep my head up so I could finish my shift. A month after that, I stopped going to work altogether. What was the point? I hadn't been making enough money to support Byron's habit and now I was matching him line for line.

"So we did what every middle-class coke junkie does. We started dealing to our friends. Buy a quality half, shave a few grams, make it up with cut, pass it on. It worked for almost a year, until our habits outgrew our customer base. Then we moved up to ounces, began dealing to people we barely knew. Always breaking the units down, skimming off the top, putting out those lines from dusk, when we got out of bed, till dawn. The parties didn't start until after we closed the bars."

"I wish I could say that I hated the life, but I didn't. For the first few years, I don't think I even minded Byron's slapping me from time to time. We weren't dealing on the street. Our customers were mostly freaks of one kind or another. Performance artists, mad poets, painters with beards that dropped to their belts, uptown rich kids with enough bank to feed the monkey. Those kids didn't give a damn about anything. Not as long as they were stoned and had daddies to bail them out.

"Then I got popped the first time. I was walking along Broome Street, on my way home, and this undercover forced me into the lobby of an abandoned building, found a couple of grams in my bra. Later, when he testified before the Grand Jury, he swore he'd eye-balled me tossing a package into the gutter.

"Maybe the jurors didn't believe him, because they indicted me for a misdemeanor instead of a felony and I pled it out in return for probation. Then, six months later, I caught another case. Same deal, probation, but the judge started making noises like he was tired of seeing my face. Like if it happened again, he might have to get serious."

"As time went on, Byron's hands got heavier and heavier. I think it was the juice, not the coke; he was buying vodka by the case. And then I got pregnant, which just made it worse, because I cleaned myself up, didn't even smoke cigarettes, and he hated me for it.

"It wouldn't be the first time a woman kicked a habit in the interests of her child. I kept telling myself I wasn't going back to drugs, but I didn't leave Byron, so I guess there has to be a lie somewhere in the mix. It all became meaningless anyway, because the baby only lived a few days and I was stuffing powder up my nose before the funeral was over. Thinking it was my fate, what I deserved, *all* I deserved."

"For a long time after that, more than a year, I couldn't bring myself to care about anything but cocaine. Humiliation became a way of life. Petty arguments were ended with a casual slap; the serious beatings came closer and closer together. I thought he was going to kill me and I thought it would be okay. I wanted him to just do it. Do it and get it over with.

"Then, one day, about a year later, I came close to getting my wish, this time in public. I was in a bar, having a drink with a dealing buddy, when Byron showed up, ripped me off the stool, beat me so bad I was sure I was going to die. The bartender—his name was Lance—pulled Byron off and called the cops. They took one look at me and placed Byron under arrest.

"I stayed in the hospital for two days. Long enough for the social worker, a woman named Miriam Farber, to convince me to press charges. I didn't have any faith in the system, but the way it turned out, Byron's eight months in Rikers scared the piss out of him. Remember, Byron's folks were middle-class and for all his tough-guy attitude, Byron had been a good boy for most of his life, just like I'd been a good girl.

"I still ran into him from time to time, at parties or in the bars. He was always so, so sorry. It was very convincing, very real, and I might have taken him back even then, but fate intervened when the cops busted Johnny Fabriello, an old friend. Fabriello traded his time for mine by introducing me to a narc and I got taken down a few weeks later."

"Once I understood the politics, prison was actually good for me. In order to survive, I paired up with a dyke, a lifer named Latisha Freemason. The sex was pretty ugly, but Latisha convinced me to pull my life together. Or at least to make the attempt.

"She told me, first of all, that I *had* a life and that it was mine. I was entitled to it, responsible for it. She told me that my life was my baby, that I had to treat it the way I would have treated my child.

" 'You got *family*, girl. Family that's willing to help when the board cuts you loose. So don't be makin' no excuses 'bout how you gotta go right back to the life. This is all about you doin' it to *you*.' "

"You've been to see my boss, Sid, and you know that I made my parole visits on time, that I was clean. You've got the letters, too, so

I won't get into why I let Byron move back after he was released from Sing Sing except to say that if I could redeem my life, why couldn't he?

"I've read those letters again and again, looking for a clue. Because Byron didn't revert after he came out of prison. No, prison was a great leveler for Byron; it reduced him, eliminated any trace of the good Dr. Jekyll. He took those group sessions, all right, the ones on coping with violence, but he did it to impress the parole board and it must have worked, because they cut him loose as soon as he was eligible. I was the second prize, like the peanut inside the M&M.

"Byron made his trip to Panama a week after his release. The fact that he could be remanded for leaving the state without permission didn't bother him for a second. He was a master at manipulating his PO, skipping sessions, showing up late, always going to the edge without slipping over. He kept a bag of clean urine strapped to his belly, a bag with a tube on the end that he held against the side of his penis when he had to pee in the bottle.

" 'Funny thing,' he once told me, 'is a white man doesn't really wanna look too close at a black man's dick. Not unless he's planning to suck it.'

"There was no pretense at sophistication, no more bohemian parties. For the first time, there were guns in the apartment. The people we dealt with, buying and selling, had razor-blade eyes. Byron could still be sweet when he was in the mood, but he made the deal plain to me early on.

" 'I own your ass. There's nothing more to it. You try to leave before I'm finished with you, I'm gonna hurt you before I kill you. And I don't give a shit about what happens afterward. You do thirty months, you can do thirty years.'

"I tried anyway, that time with my parents. The neighbor, Mr. Cassadina, saw it, too. Byron didn't give a damn. He was going to be a player in the drug world; he was going to have the yachts, the offshore accounts, a villa in the British Virgin Islands. If he had to leave a trail of bodies in his wake . . . well, that's what comets are all about.

"It was such a joke. Byron was just a flunky. Yeah, he dealt in weight, but he was getting the cocaine fronted to him at an outrageous price and he was cooking base at the rate of an ounce a day.

When his connection demanded payment, he was always short. Then he'd grin and shuffle, beg for a little more time, accept a slap in the face like it was a kiss. After they left, of course, he'd take it out on me.

"Byron used me in another way, too. Most of the time, when there was a pickup to be made or he needed to move coke around the city, I was the mule, the one who carried it. This happens all the time in prison. The weaker convicts ferry weapons and contraband through the institution; if they get caught, they take the beating and do the time in the box. Believe me, especially in prisons for men, the alternative is far worse."

"There were times when I actually decided to hand the coke over to the first cop I saw. I thought, Fuck it, I'll just do the time, whatever it is. At least, I'll survive.

"But I didn't have the courage. Or maybe I thought Byron would straighten out. Sometimes, when he was really behind with the money, he'd talk about taking treatment, about how he fucked up his life, about how he was gonna change, get himself together. Then he'd cry those crocodile tears, turn to me for comfort.

"I'll tell you this, whenever Byron left the apartment carrying drugs, I prayed for him to get busted. I'm talking about on-my-knees, hands-folded prayer. And the funny part is that I should have done it myself, should have turned rat, set Byron up for a long bit. But I couldn't make the phone call and God wasn't listening, either, so, in the end . . ."

"The final beating came on a Sunday, when the television went out in the middle of a football game. Byron ordered me to fix it and when I couldn't, he slapped me a few times, kicked me in the ass when I turned away. I fell down and started crying.

"He said, 'You think you've got something to cry about? That what you think?'

"It went on for a long time. In fits and starts. I tried to get away to the bedroom, but he dragged me back. Finally, I lost consciousness.

"I spent the next two days in bed; I couldn't move and didn't want to. When I finally came out, Byron was sitting in the chair like a cat at a mouse hole. He was smoking a cigarette and he held it up, blew on the coal.

"He said, "Got about a bellyful of your bitchin'. Think I'll make a fire.'

"I knew where he kept the gun in the bookcase and I picked it up without thinking much about what I was gonna do with it. Then I pushed the little lever on the side, figuring it was some kind of safety, and the cylinder popped out. Byron started laughing, but I shoved it back and pointed the barrel at his chest.

"He said, 'When a *man* pulls a weapon, he knows he's got to use it. Too bad you're a bitch. Too bad you gotta pay the price.'

"What he was doing was giving me a choice. I could either shoot him or let him kill me. Maybe he didn't care which way it went, maybe he was that stoned. I know I stood there, holding the gun for what seemed like an hour. Then he started to get up out of the chair and I pulled the trigger.

"Byron fell back into the chair, put his hands over the hole in his shirt as if he could hold the blood inside. Then he came forward, dropped onto his knees, and started to crawl away from me. I remember expecting him to say something, I don't know exactly what, but he finally collapsed onto the carpet.

"I didn't think about calling for help, because I knew Byron was dead. And don't ask me *how* I knew. The way he went down, there wasn't any doubt. I remember putting the gun on the table and waiting for the cops to show. I didn't have any doubt about that, either."

It would play. That was my first thought. I didn't judge her story, didn't subject the narrative to any test of truth. Priscilla had touched all the bases, delivering her story in soft, almost wistful tones. She'd seemed smaller, her hands folded on crossed knees, her downcast eyes dropping the occasional tear, the nape of her neck exposed and vulnerable. If the jurors believed her, they would have to acquit. And I wouldn't need to spell it out (though I would, again and again). After closing arguments, when the judge instructed the jurors on the statutory requirements for the defense of self-defense, Priscilla's tale would conform to every demand of the law.

She looked up at me, her brimming gray eyes as lustrous as pearls. For a moment we were absolutely silent, as if the courtroom had been removed to a museum and we were an exhibit. Then she reached up, stroked the side of my face and kissed me on the mouth. It was a short kiss, over almost before it began.

"All right, let's wrap this up." The court officer's gravelly voice didn't exactly inspire debate. Nevertheless, I put up a token defense for the sake of my client.

"Seems a bit arbitrary, sergeant."

"A half hour, counselor. That's what I was told." He turned to Priscilla, snapped the word, "Up!"

Priscilla's mouth curled into a sardonic smile even as she obeyed. I watched her walk toward the holding pens alongside the courtroom, head erect, stride loose and natural. Even after the door snapped shut, I stood there for a moment. As if she'd simply gone into another room to retrieve her purse. Then I picked up my briefcase and walked out.

Twelve

When I strode into Judge Winokur's packed courtroom a little before two o'clock every head swiveled in my direction. I stopped in the doorway, swept the room with imperious eyes, carefully repressed the smirk pulling at the corners of my lips. Thelma Barrow was there, sitting on the left side of the room next to Julie and Caleb. She was wearing a navy dress, its long sleeves and throat-high collar trimmed with lace. Over her left breast, an enormous scarlet pin shouted: FREE PRISCILLA SWEET.

Yes, fine, I remember thinking, but not for a while.

I was on the comeback trail, an aging actor handed a juicy role, and I didn't want my part left on the cutting room floor. After all, the quality of my performance would not only serve to restore my celebrity status, it would also be my revenge on those who'd written me off when I was on the downside.

A few minutes later, Priscilla was standing next to me, shoulders squared, chin up. "Not guilty, your honor," she declared in the firm voice I'd suggested.

Winokur accepted the plea, then asked for bail applications. Buscetta, with a sly glance at the spectators, fairly shouted, "Ms. Sweet failed to make an appearance on April 15, 1990 in the misdemeanor part. A bench warrant was issued and served on April 17.

For this reason, and in light of the seriousness of the charges, the state requests that Ms. Sweet be remanded without bail."

I managed to accept the news without flinching, reminding myself that clients like Priscilla Sweet, who'd sworn to me that she'd made her appearances, always lie, often for no discernible reason.

"Bail denied."

Winokur was about to bang the gavel, when, in my best oratorical tones, I moved for an immediate dismissal on the grounds that my client's right to a fair trial had been irreparably damaged by the state's willful failure to allow her to be examined by a physician of her choice. As I wound it up, I pointed to the fading bruises on Priscilla's face and throat. "Perhaps the prosecution, in its wisdom, hoped any evidence of my client's state prior to the events of January 16th would simply vanish. And if her arraignment had been postponed over the weekend, they would have gotten their wish."

Buscetta started to speak, but Winokur silenced him with a wave. "I now order that the accused be examined by physicians at the Rikers Island clinic and that the results, including laboratory and X-ray results, be turned over to the defense and to the court. Today, Mr. Buscetta."

Buscetta nodded glumly. I suspect he was already formulating a defense of his actions for the media. "I'll contact the Department of Corrections as soon as I leave the courtroom."

"Good. Now, gentlemen, let's go to the wheel, see if we can find a trial judge." He nodded to the court clerk. "Mr. Fariello?"

The clerk produced an object that looked like a bird cage mounted on a cross bar. He placed it on his desk, handling it with the reverence due a Vatican relic, then gave it a spin. When it settled down, he unfastened a little door, reached inside, withdrew a card. "Trial Part 71," he announced. "Judge Thomas Delaney."

Carlo and I glanced at each other, exchanged the barest of smiles. Tommy Delaney was a holdover from the days when the Irish ran New York, a lawyer out of the Democratic clubhouses who'd been rewarded with a judgeship in the last days of Mayor Wagner's reign. He was pro-prosecution on motions to exclude evidence (routine in New York where judges have to ask a technicality-hating citizenry to reelect them), but once the trial began, he usually gave both sides as much leeway as possible.

"I do love a battle, boyo," he'd once told me over a shooter of Wild Turkey. "It's in me blood."

I marched out of the courthouse, into blinding winter sunlight, to face the guardians of the public's right to know. I stood before a forest of microphones attached to a metal stand. The microphones were tipped in my direction like sky rockets about to launch.

Thirty minutes later, it was all over, the cameras and microphones packed away, the reporters already composing their stories. I watched them for a moment, feeling a mix of regret and relief, then strolled over to where Caleb and Julie stood on the sidewalk beside a middle-aged woman in a belted, red coat. The woman, shorter than Julie, and a good deal heavier, had a thick head of nearly white hair that fell in a smooth line to the wide collar of her coat.

"Sid," Julie said, "this is Rebecca Barthelme. From the New York Women's Council."

The woman turned, extended a gloved hand. She had an oval face, well-lined, with large brown eyes over a thin nose. Her smiling mouth was generous to a fault, dominating a button of a chin.

We cut a deal over lunch, Ms. Barthelme and I: In addition to a spousal abuse expert, Dr. Elizabeth Howe, the Women's Council would supply an experienced attorney to sit in the second chair. That attorney was Rebecca Barthelme. In return, the Council would get to associate their organization with Priscilla Sweet, *cause celebre*, and the right to use that association in their various fund drives.

"Most of my experience is in civil law," Rebecca explained, "but I've been a litigator throughout my career. I know how to examine, and how to *cross*-examine, a witness."

Buoyed no doubt by my earlier triumphs, I was very nice to Rebecca, and very charming, until we were well into dessert and coffee. Until I got to the bottom line.

"Priscilla and I share a single agenda," I explained. "She wants out and I want her out. I see no reason to confuse the issue with the Council's politics. We don't need an overview."

"Which means?"

"Which means that you sit in the second chair. Which means that you're my assistant and I'm your boss. Which means that you don't approach Priscilla Sweet without my permission."

To my surprise, Rebecca began to laugh. "Don't bullshit me, Sid. You're afraid I'll steal your client."

"Well," I admitted, after my rat partners, Julie and Caleb, joined in the merriment, "there's that, too."

I woke up the next day riding the manic end of my bipolar personality like a bobcat on the back of a raging timber wolf. I felt on-target, as if life had a purpose (which I didn't believe, not even at the time) and I'd hooked myself into its central energy. Losing seemed less than a possibility, as remote as one of those galaxies that can only be seen with an orbiting telescope. Looking back, I realize that what I needed was grounding, but for then, and for the six weeks that followed, I was having much too much fun. I was winning.

By ten o'clock, Byron's phony passport had passed into the greedy hands of Phoebe Morris. Within three days of receiving it, she'd secured the original application, wheedled a handwriting sample in the form of a prison letter from Byron to his brother, William, and verified Byron's handwriting on the application and passport with a recognized handwriting expert. Then she managed to convince her editors at *Newsday* to run Byron's passport photo on the first page.

A day later, when Carlo Buscetta demanded that the passport, as evidence, be turned over to the state, Phoebe met him on the courthouse steps with a *Newsday* photographer and a camera crew from CBS.

"How," she asked him as she handed over the document in question, "does this passport bear on the case against Priscilla Sweet? Does it mean the drug charges against her will be dropped?"

Phoebe's efforts that week were neatly balanced by a salvo from the other side. Jay Harrison ran a column in which an unnamed drug dealer from the Lower East Side declared that he'd done business with Priscilla Sweet and didn't even know that she was married. "She was in charge, all right. She was definitely running the show. Her and that .38 she carried."

Though Caleb, Julie, and I enjoyed the media attention, not least because we knew it would be good for business, we were far too busy to give the various stories much attention. Earlier that week I'd sent Carlo a letter outlining the material I wanted on discovery, including all police reports, autopsy reports, lab analyses, and ballistic test results related to the death of Byron Sweet. He'd responded, as he was bound to do before Friday's scheduling conference in Judge Delaney's chambers, agreeing to provide the data as it became available to him. In fact, he would put my request to one side, figuring to stall until the start of Priscilla's trial or until Delaney got in his face, whichever came first.

In the course of our pre-trial conferences, I would demand to receive the material as soon as possible. Maybe I'd get it, maybe not, but those conferences were still in the future and there was a second group of documents to be secured in the here and now, documents crucial to Priscilla's claim of self-defense, documents that could be secured with a simple subpoena. There were twenty different items in this group, everything from my client's probation reports to her hospital records to the results of her drug tests.

The downside was that each subpoena would have to be individually prepared (with every *i* dotted, every *t* crossed), then served on the proper agency. It would take weeks to accomplish, even if there weren't other tasks, like finding and interviewing witnesses, requiring immediate attention. Still, there was one piece of paper I wanted right away, mostly because I wasn't sure it existed. I drew up that subpoena first, then dragged Caleb with me to the 107th Precinct where we confronted the officer who'd taken Thelma Barrow's complaint after the attack on Priscilla at the Barrow house a year before. We had a date, but no complaint number, and I was afraid that the original report (assuming Thelma had actually made it) had either vanished into a central warehouse for unverified civilian complaints or never been filed at all.

I needn't have worried. Encouraged by a little cop-to-cop charm on Caleb's part, and a double sawbuck, Sergeant Patrick Shannahan tracked the report to a filing cabinet in the basement. "I don't remember taking this complaint," he announced as he handed over a single sheet of paper, "but if I wrote it down, it must have happened."

As that was a position I, myself, intended to maintain, I accepted the report and made a graceful exit. Before he changed his mind.

"Thelma was telling the truth, at least about making the report," Caleb told me as I drove off toward the Long Island Expressway. "Check this out. *The complainant alleged that when her husband tried to call police, the alleged perpetrator threatened to kill the alleged victim.*" Caleb folded the paper, put it back in his pocket, and sighed. "I may not know anything about literature," he said. "But I know what I like."

I knew what I liked as well. The complaint would be offered as proof that Priscilla, in fleeing to her parents' home, had exercised her duty to retreat. Later, when the police failed to act on her mother's complaint, she was out of options. She had to defend herself and she did.

Thirteen

We were still preparing subpoenas by night, serving them by day, when Caleb, accompanied by a very tiny, very old lady, walked into the office. Though unable to suppress a grin, Caleb said nothing as he helped the woman off with her coat, shrugged out of his own, then led her across the room. It was nearly midnight.

"Miss Higginbotham, that's Julie Gill sitting by the computer. And these two are Rebecca Barthelme and Sid Kaplan. They're both lawyers, so you might wanna watch your step. Folks, this is Miss Maybelle Higginbotham."

Julie rose, extended a hand. "*Little* Maybelle Higginbotham?"

The old lady's face, a smooth, mahogany mask, came to life as if at the command of a stage magician. Her brown eyes glittered with pleasure, her full mouth rose into a joyous, professional smile. "Ah, darlin', I thank you for rememberin'." She touched Julie's hand with the tips of her fingers, the gesture both regal and intimate.

"Little Maybelle is a blues singer," Julie said to me and Rebecca. "Must have started out . . ."

"Sixty years ago," Maybelle said. She was wearing a jade green, velvet dress, the collar and sleeves trimmed with lace, and a matching, wide-brimmed hat. "I was livin' in Chillicut, Mississippi, and Depression times was goin' full blast. Figured my possibles in

Chillicut was mostly *im*possibles, if you take my meaning. So I got on the road." She sat down, folded her hands on her lap, allowed her back to bend ever so slightly. "Course, I'm retired now."

Caleb nodded happily. "Maybelle lives on Broome Street, right down the hall from Priscilla and Byron. She made the 911 call that brought the cops that day."

"Miss Higginbotham . . ." I began.

"Maybelle, please."

"Great, and I'm Sid to my friends." I crossed my legs, glanced from Julie to Rebecca. The exact wording of Maybelle's call for help was crucial to our motions to exclude evidence found in Priscilla's apartment. The more specific the wording, the greater the justification for the entry by the first cops on the scene.

"Who's the reporter?" Maybelle asked, looking from one of us to the other.

"Not here yet." Caleb glanced at me. "Maybelle's written an autobiography. She's hoping a little publicity will help her find an agent."

"One thing I learned in life," Maybelle said. "You got to take advantage of the advantages that come along. Specially if you're an old black woman livin' on Social Security and food stamps. Jus' don't be askin' me to tell no lies. I stopped fibbin' right after my last divorce. At my age, you got to get yourself right with the man upstairs."

Phoebe Morris chose that moment to make her entrance. She pushed her way through the door, put her briefcase on my desk, tossed Julie a brief smile, then pulled a tape recorder from her briefcase. "You mind?" she asked.

Maybelle Higginbotham shook her head. "Uh-uh. But I *was* hopin' you'd bring a photographer. This hat ain't been out the closet in fifteen years."

I went into the drawer of my desk, pulled out my Olympus, and passed it to Phoebe Morris. Then I motioned to Maybelle. "You're up."

Maybelle smiled, then got right to the point, "What I told the woman was, 'I want to report a gunshot in my building.' Then I give her Priscilla's apartment number and the building's address. You know what she had the nerve to ask me? As if I was some kinda senile fool? 'Could what you heard have been a firecracker? Or a backfiring truck?'

" 'Best get your butt over here,' is what I said. 'I think the boy done killed her this time.' "

The last sentence brought the five of us, Rebecca, Phoebe, Caleb, Julie, and myself, to full alert. Like circus poodles gazing at a piece of steak dangling from a trainer's fingertips.

"That's exactly what you told them?" Julie asked. "About Byron killing Priscilla?"

"Course, I knew the both of 'em from when they first come to the Lower East Side." Maybelle raised her chin, announced, "I'm something of a celebrity in the neighborhood." Then she laughed. "Among the hipper folk."

Julie slid her chair up to Maybelle's. "So, you must have known what Byron was doing to her."

"Don't recall him tryin' to hide it." She paused to accept a cup of tea from Caleb, to add cream and sugar. "They was good people when they first come downtown. Then the drugs got 'em like they got so many. I used to know Billie Holliday. Charlie Parker, too." She looked from Julie to me, her eyes wide, questioning. "Byron got mean and Priscilla . . . well, Priscilla wasn't no angel. She went along with it until one day he come close to killin' her. Then they separated for a couple of years when they were the both of 'em in jail. After Priscilla got paroled, I thought she was gonna make it, but she took him back in the end. That happens."

"Yes, it does," Julie said. "But there's one more thing you can help us with. We need to know if the cops spoke to you before they went to Priscilla's apartment."

Maybelle shook her head. "By the time they knocked on my door, Priscilla was already standing in the hallway. Had the handcuffs on, too."

Later, when Caleb, Julie, and I were alone, I remember hugging Caleb, then demanding to know why he hadn't found her sooner.

"Wrong question, partner," he responded without hesitation. "Miss Higginbotham spent the last two weeks in South Carolina. Visiting a niece. The question you oughta be askin' is what you've done in your miserable life to deserve an investigator who kept going back until someone answered the door."

I wasn't surprised to find a knot of reporters gathered before the

Criminal Courts building when I arrived on February 1 for a scheduling conference in Judge Delaney's chambers. After all, I'd phoned
many of them to announce that Priscilla would take the occasion to
demand a speedy trial which meant that she'd be making an appearance. What surprised me were the demonstrators, predominantly
female, who sported FREE PRISCILLA SWEET buttons, and the demonstrators, mostly male, who carried NO JUSTICE/NO PEACE placards.
One and all, they were so busy trying to keep warm, they failed to
notice my entrance until I was right on top of them. Then a tall, fat
woman in a down overcoat shouted, "There he is," and both fac-
tions began to chant. Looking between them, I saw a video crew near
the entrance to the building.

I remember thinking that I should find all this depressing. That I'd
been through far too much to overestimate my own value. Or to
underestimate those things in my life that were actually valuable.
Nevertheless, I straightened my back, squared my shoulders, lifted
my chin, marched between the demonstrators as if walking a gaunt-
let. I continued past the camera crew and the poor *schmucks* waiting
to go through the metal detectors, entering the building through a
door bearing a painted sign: COURT PERSONNEL ONLY/ALL OTHERS SUB-
JECT TO SEARCH.

Delaney was sitting at his desk, bent over a foot-high stack of
paperwork, when I walked into his chambers. He was a mild looking man with a long oval face. His features, small and pale, were
overhung by a shock of thinning, silver-white hair, the net effect
that of an old (if not actually wise) soldier slowly fading away. He
nodded good morning, told me to help myself to coffee. Buscetta
hadn't arrived and Delaney wasn't about to waste his time on
social conversation.

Buscetta made his appearance a few minutes later, and I put forth
Priscilla's determination to exercise her right to a speedy trial.
Delaney was clearly unhappy, but when I told him that I'd tried my
best to talk her out her foolishness, he sighed and moved on to the
matter of discovery.

"By time of trial," Carlo said as he passed a copy of my request
to Delaney. "At the latest."

"That's not good enough," I interrupted.

"Your Honor, according to the statute . . ."

"Forget the statute." I turned to Delaney. "Judge, we're looking at a warrantless search of my client's home based on a 911 call. The responding cops didn't even bother to stop at the door of the woman who made the call. They went directly to Priscilla Sweet's apartment and forced their way inside. The detectives who arrived later conducted another warrantless search when they could have gotten a warrant by phone. Without the evidence discovered as a result of those searches, the prosecution has no case against my client. I need the notes, logs, and reports filed by the cops, as well as the text of the 911 call in order to prepare motions. I need that material and you have the right to compel the prosecution to deliver it. These are records made immediately after my client's arrest; they exist, intact, right at this moment. If Mr. Buscetta doesn't have them in his possession, let him pick up his lazy butt and walk over to the 7th Precinct and use their copier."

Buscetta was furious, but Delaney simply waved him off. "Was there a warrant?" he asked.

"No," Buscetta admitted.

"I want you to make an effort, Mr. Buscetta. We'll come back in two weeks and discuss the matter again. Let's move on."

This was a crucial moment for Priscilla Sweet. Delaney (though I didn't think he had the balls, not when so many voting citizens were looking over his shoulder) could rule that any reference to Priscilla's and Byron's past was irrelevant. Certainly, Buscetta would fight, point by point, for that position. What I needed from Delaney was the widest possible latitude. In the great tradition, I wanted to put the victim on trial.

"Your Honor," I began, "if given the opportunity, I'm prepared to put forward a claim of self-defense that conforms to every element of the statute."

Buscetta jumped in before Delaney could respond. "What he wants to do is attack the victim. The prosecution will file motions to exclude any such testimony."

It was all very predictable, the opening salvo in the pre-trial wars. A judge's ruling on what may or may not be presented to a jury is often more crucial than the actual trial, but that ruling wouldn't come until just before the trial itself. In the meantime, I gave Delaney something to consider.

"My client was systematically abused over a period of years. I can document this abuse with medical records, police reports, eye witnesses, and an order of protection." I leaned forward, tapped Delaney's desk with my forefinger. "The evidence is overwhelming. Priscilla Sweet was in fear of her life. She was trapped. The media has already dug up a good piece of that history, your Honor. It cannot be excluded."

"Enough." Delaney pulled on his chin, a sure sign he was annoyed. "I'm not going to try the case in chambers." He glanced at his watch, shook his head. "Let's go out and talk to Ms. Sweet about her speedy trial. It's Friday and I have a mid-town appointment with a glass of Dewars."

The room was full when Priscilla emerged from the holding pen. I remember her scanning the room, that half smile painted on her face, as she took the chair next to mine. "My mother's left town," she told me. "The phone calls, the reporters showing up at her door—she couldn't take it. She's in Oklahoma now, visiting her sister."

"That's fine, Priscilla. As long as she's back in time for your trial. Her testimony, along with that complaint, establishes the fact that you exercised your duty to retreat. Without your mother, we lose everything."

Priscilla laughed and tapped the back of my hand with the nail of an index finger. "Don't worry, she'll be back. Even if I have to go get her myself."

Fourteen

New business. It still has a sweet sound, even all these years later. And not just because vindication, according to my own definitions, could be measured only by the size and quality of my caseload. Thelma Barrow's five grand had, by then, dwindled to a small pile of c-notes; the successful defense of her daughter was utterly dependent on an inflow of fresh capital.

The first entreaties came through just after Priscilla's arraignment, a series of calls from low-level mutts with the wherewithal for a minimal defense. I accepted their pitiful retainers with every intention of postponing their cases until after Priscilla's trial. Then, on February 7, a much larger fish swam into view.

It was just after four o'clock when my personal shylock, Benny Levine, took a chair opposite mine, rubbed his watery allergic eyes with the blue handkerchief in his breast pocket, said, "Jesus, Sid, I'm fucked."

Music to my ears. "How, Benny? How are you fucked?"

"It's the feds." For a minute, it looked as if he was going to cry, but then he pulled himself together. "It's the goddamned RICO."

Benny, as he subsequently explained, was in danger of being indicted under federal racketeering statutes for participating in a continuing criminal enterprise. His source for this information was a co-conspirator's attorney. "It ain't fair, Sid," he protested. "Do I look like some kinda mob guy?"

He did, actually, what with his charcoal suit and his pinky ring and his pointy Italian shoes. But I'd known Benny for years, long enough to be sure he was small potatoes. I suspect the feds knew it, too, but that wouldn't prevent their portraying him as a key member of some Mafia superfamily. And while I'd have to actually see the indictment to calculate the number of years Benny was facing, not only were the penalties for RICO violations very severe, at the time there was no parole in the federal system. What you got, you did.

"It's unbelievable, Sid. What they're sayin'." Benny pulled his chair up a little closer, examined the palm of his hand as if it held an explanation for his predicament. "Every so often I run short of capital, like any other businessman. But can I go to the fuckin' bank, take out a loan? Will the bank manager sit me down in a chair, light up my cigar? Or do I gotta run to somebody else in the biz, somebody a little bigger than me?"

What Benny did was borrow from another, better-connected shylock at a mere ten percent per week, then put the money on the street at twenty percent. He didn't do it often for fear that one of his clients would welsh on a big loan, and he was always careful to repay the principal as soon as he had the money. It was a matter of professional pride.

"Now, the joke," he explained, "is that the feds say because I went to this guy for money, and this guy went to that guy for money, and that guy went to another guy for money, we're all part of some kinda gang." He dug a fleck of grit out of his right eye with his thumb, then looked up at me. "You call this a fuckin' life? Huh? You call *this* a fuckin' life?"

What I called it was, "Fifteen grand up front. As a retainer, Benny. So I can poke around without worrying you're gonna panic and run to some other lawyer."

A week later, an even larger fish rose to the bait, a fish named Manuel Bergman. Supremely confident, he strolled into my office, dropped his narrow butt onto a chair, tossed off his cashmere overcoat to reveal a cascade of gold chains that spilled over a white silk shirt.

Manuel was my favorite kind of client. Already bailed out, he'd been indicted (solely on the testimony of co-conspirators) for conspiring to distribute several tons of Colombian cocaine. He showed no fear, had already fired his attorney of record, and knew, having accumulated more than fourteen years in various institutions, his law. Manuel knew his law and what he wanted was delay.

"Snitches," he told me toward the end of the conversation, "they can change their minds. If they have enough time to think about it."

I told him I could give his snitches the better part of two years to reconsider, and I told him how I'd go about it, motion by motion.

Manuel must have liked my strategy, because he parted with twenty-five thousand dollars in banded fifties before he walked out the door some three hours later, leaving me to a crushing workload and a bank balance that for the first time in years I wasn't ashamed to contemplate.

The media war between Phoebe Morris and Jay Harrison continued unabated, as it would continue right through Priscilla's trial. Julie was in charge of feeding tidbits to our side of the battle, and she never failed to read the various columns over breakfast. I paid little heed, for the most part, especially after I had Bergman's retainer in hand. With enough money to see the trial through, I was focusing more and more of my attention on Priscilla. I was confident that I could get her off on the murder charge, but the cocaine was still a huge problem.

There was, however, one item that caught my attention, this courtesy of Jay Harrison. Jay's nugget emanated from an unnamed source in the Office of the Medical Examiner, said source declaring, "Mr. Sweet's liver was cirrhotic throughout. Personally, I find it amazing that he lived long enough to be murdered."

Though the implications were pretty obvious—Buscetta would now claim that Byron was too sick, as well as too drunk to mount an attack—Harrison spun them out for the length of his column. It was only at the very end that he conceded the obvious. Whatever the condition of Byron's liver, he was alive when Priscilla Sweet pulled the trigger.

We were still at breakfast, still discussing the Harrison column, when I got a call from Carlo Buscetta. "The plea board has decided to make you the following offer." His tone made it clear that he did not agree with that decision. "If your client pleads to man-one and third degree possession, she will receive concurrent seven-year sentences."

"I'll put the offer to my client this morning," I said after a moment, "but if she asks me if we can win outright, I'm gonna tell her that not only can we win the legal argument, we can win the moral argument as well."

The last part inspired Carlo to a burst of laughter. "Is that supposed to mean you actually believe your client is innocent? Get back to the real world, *Sid*ney. Priscilla Sweet isn't a sixteen-year-old kid who made a mistake. She's a thirty-five-year-old woman who's been a criminal for all of her adult life. No matter what else might have happened to her." He stopped abruptly, took a deep breath. "Ya know something, *Sid*ney, I liked you better when you were just another sleazy defense lawyer out for the money."

Two hours later, I walked into the Rose Singer Jail on Rikers Island, Carlo's latest deal in hand. The officer manning the reception desk, a stranger, began our relationship by ignoring the twenty tucked inside my briefcase. After a thorough shuffling of my papers, she called up to the PC unit, listened for a moment, then hung up the phone. "There's been a disturbance," she informed me. "Your client will be delayed."

When I asked for something more specific, she glared at me over the top of her reading glasses. "If your client was dead, counselor, I wouldn't be asking you to wait."

By the time I actually got to my client, I'd pretty much calmed down. Still, I remember that Priscilla smiled as I came into the little room and that I, even as I returned her smile, checked her teeth to make sure they were all there.

I outlined Buscetta's deal first, advising Priscilla to think about it for a couple of days. In light of the charges against her, I explained, it was the best offer she was going to get.

After a moment, she nodded and I changed the subject. "They told me you had some trouble," I said. "I've been waiting for over an hour."

She was sitting behind the table, her legs crossed, a finger curled in her dark hair. "Me? Uh-uh. One of the bugs went off on a CO, but it didn't have anything to do with me."

I put a pack of cigarettes on the table and watched her shake one out. "You're telling me it took the staff all this time to gain control?"

Priscilla stared at me for a minute, her gaze frankly speculative, then shrugged her shoulders. "The bug got her ass kicked in a hurry. She was on her way to the exercise yard when she went off. Then the rest of us were locked down. As an object lesson, I guess." She lit the cigarette, blew out a long stream of smoke. "Afterwards, the CO's put us through the usual bullshit."

"Which was?"

For once, her eyes flashed a little fire. "What they did first, counselor, was toss our cells. Then they had us strip down and bend over so they could look up our vaginas and rectums for contraband. The usual, like I said."

When I flinched, Priscilla reached across the table to lay her fingertips on the back of my hand. "It's all right, Sid. Doesn't hurt a bit. And you can tell Buscetta to shove his deal. Tell him he can do it privately. He doesn't have to have a CO watching to make sure he does it right."

Before I could respond, a grossly overweight corrections officer rushed up to the viewing window and knocked on the Plexiglas. "Hey, hey, hey. No touching."

Instinctively, I pulled away, the little boy caught with his hand in the cookie jar. Priscilla leaned back, shifted her weight in the chair.

"Look, Priscilla, what happened the other day, I'm not saying I blame either one of us, but it's not gonna happen again. Understand? Because I'm telling you, as plainly as I can, that there's no emotional justification on my part. What I want to do here is win. That's good for me and good for you. It doesn't require complication."

Instead of answering directly, Priscilla sat back in the chair. She drew up her shoulders and shook her head. "Sometimes," she told me, "I can't believe I'm still trying." Her eyes were bright, almost feverish, as if she was making an effort beyond her capacity. "You know, even in your darkest moments, your heart beats, you breathe, your body does everything necessary to maintain itself. It won't stop just because you want it to." She let her fingers run beneath my shirt cuff, the gesture seeming to me curious rather than seductive, a search for information that could only be received through the fingertips. "I remember lying in bed, wishing that Byron had finished the job, that he'd actually killed me, while my body went about the business of healing. Like it didn't belong to me, like I was a demented tenant who had to be protected from herself."

Fifteen

To this day, I think of the six weeks following Priscilla's arraignment as a period of grace, a little gift to console me for the storm that followed. Without doubt, it was a time of small victories, a truth Buscetta acknowledged with his seven-year deal. It was also a time of high spirits and high energy. We worked until we were ready to drop. We laughed at each other's jokes. We were drunk on the mere possibility of success.

The high point of that period, the white froth at the apex of the wave just before it began to curl down over my family, occurred on February 15, in the chambers of Judge Thomas Delaney. The session was to be purely off the record, with no court reporter present, a chance to air complaints, review progress. Under other circumstances, Delaney would have pushed for a plea bargain, but I think by this time he was looking forward to a trial.

After a few minutes of verbal sparring in which Buscetta accused me of withholding the state's generous deal from my client, I renewed my demand for all paperwork pertaining to the search of Priscilla's apartment and her arrest. "You ordered the state to produce this material, judge, but I can't even get Mr. Buscetta to return my calls."

Delaney gently pushed a wisp of silvery hair away from his fore-head. "Mr. Buscetta?"

Carlo folded his arms across his chest. His dark eyebrows formed twin arches above his black eyes. When he spoke, his voice was cold. "This is a two-forty matter, your honor." He was referring to Article 240 of the Criminal Procedure Law. "The prosecution is not oblig-ated to produce this material until after direct examination of those witnesses the prosecution chooses to call."

Delaney stared down at his desk for a moment. I could see his scalp redden beneath his feathery hair, a sure sign that I should keep my big mouth shut and let nature take its course.

"I read Mr. Kaplan's motion, Mr. Buscetta, and the first question that occurs to me is how the responding officers knew the 911 call wasn't a hoax?" Delaney's voice was thin and strained. "I've never been much for warrantless searches. Perhaps that's because I was appointed in an era when the legislature respected the Constitution of the State of New York." He drummed his fingers on the desk, finally looked up to stare directly into Buscetta's eyes. "Did I tell you that I'm considering retirement? That's partly because I can't make the adjustment to being shit upon by pissant prosecutors."

I intoned a silent prayer to my ancestors, wishing with all my heart that Carlo's resistance would stiffen into outright defiance. If Delaney ruled the original entry into Priscilla's apartment unjusti-fied, the cocaine and the gun would go out, along with Carlo Buscetta's case against my client.

"Your honor, the statute is clear," Buscetta began.

"Today is Friday, Mr. Buscetta." Delaney's voice hardened as he went on; his small nostrils pinched together until they virtually closed. "Let's say by Monday morning, ten o'clock, in Mr. Kaplan's office. Copies of the 911 tape, all written material requested in the motion, anything else relating to the search which might, by any stretch of the imagination, be considered relevant."

Buscetta actually shuddered, producing a doglike wiggle that ran from the base of his spine up into his neck. "Your honor . . ."

"I'm not asking for any assurances," Delaney said, waving Carlo into silence. "After all, the statute *is* clear."

We celebrated, Julie, Caleb, and I, with a lunch at the Union

Square Cafe, one of New York's better and more expensive restaurants. I remember the general mood as amused. Carlo, as he'd exited Judge Delaney's chambers, had almost bounced off Caleb who was standing in the hall. He'd stared at Caleb for a moment, his face reddening, then whipped around to stare at me.

"I can't get the material to you by Monday morning," he finally said.

"Sorry to hear that, Carlo." I threw Caleb a wink. "Because if you don't, I'm gonna snitch you out. See if I can have your sorry ass thrown into solitary."

I told the story over lunch, went on at length without overestimating the extent of our victory, finally predicting that Carlo would provide the data on time.

"Delaney won't back off," I concluded. "He once told me that his great-grandfather learned the art of New York politics from Boss Tweed and that it boiled down to a pair of mandates: reward your friends, punish your enemies. Carlo's been around for a long time. He'll figure it out once he cools off."

Rebecca Barthelme joined us for coffee, accompanied by Elizabeth Howe. It was my first meeting with the good doctor and I don't know exactly what I was expecting (perhaps the anorexic, chain-smoking, shifty-eyed shrink who'd supervised my own therapy) but Elizabeth Howe, a fortyish black woman, radiated the kind of inner warmth usually associated with coffee and pie around the kitchen table. Her voice was honey-warm.

Julie did her best to maintain a neutral expression as she made the introductions, but, though she did manage to erase an incipient smile with the tip of her tongue, she failed to control the amusement in her, for once, sparkling green eyes.

"And this," she said, extending her open palm in my direction, "is Sidney Kaplan, Defender of the Downtrodden, Champion of the Underdog."

I celebrated the morning's triumph by taking an afternoon snooze in my office, a matter of pure self-indulgence and a good measure of my personal contentment. I would get Priscilla off, then Benny Levine, then Manuel Bergman, then all the rest of them. I was Sidney Kaplan, Esq. I could not be beaten. I would count my clients, or the dollars they poured into my coffers, instead of sheep.

I was still half-asleep when Elizado Guzman and Adelberto Garcia rang the office bell. I heard Julie mumble something, then press the security buzzer to release the lock on the outer door. A moment later, her voice sounded on the intercom.

"Two gentlemen to see you, Mr. Kaplan."

I shrugged into my jacket, took a second to straighten my tie and run my fingers through my hair, finally walked across the room and opened the door. Elizado Guzman, maybe thirty years old, caught my eye first. He was standing in front of Julie's desk, a pearl gray overcoat draped over his right arm, wearing an off-white, double-breasted suit and a sun-yellow shirt buttoned to the throat. His features were darkly handsome and very full; inky brows framed a pair of round, widely-spaced eyes that locked me in a frankly evaluating glare.

"My name," he lied, "is Manny Gomez." His broad mouth opened into a bright smile. "And this is my associate."

The unnamed, much younger companion, standing some fifteen feet behind his master, neither smiled nor looked in my direction. Tall and thickly built, he wore black jogging pants over white, unlaced basketball shoes, and a matching, hooded sweatshirt devoid of any fashionable logo. His broad face, half hidden beneath the folds of the hood, was dark and ruddy, his features noticeably *Indio*, his unblinking reptile eyes expressionless. A wide shiny scar ran from the inside corner of his left eye to the outer edge of his jaw.

"What can I do for you, Mr. Gomez?" I glanced at Caleb, was immediately glad for his presence. Volatile clients are an occupational hazard for defense attorneys and although it seemed a little early in the game, I'd been threatened many times in the past.

Gomez looked disappointed, as if he'd been expecting a hero's welcome. "I got some business," he finally said. "You open for business, right?"

I nodded, stepped out of the way, motioned him into my office. He entered without hesitation, followed by what I took, at the time, to be his bodyguard. Once they were inside, I gestured to Caleb and he preceded me into the room.

"This is my investigator, Caleb Talbot. Anything you tell him is privileged, just as if you were speaking to me alone."

Gomez took one of the chairs in front of my desk, waited for his buddy to sit next to him. "Naw, thass no good. What I got to say, I got to say to you an' nobody else. *Por favor.*"

"I'm sorry to hear that." I walked around the desk, sat in my leather chair, swiveled slightly to the right as Caleb crossed the room and dropped into an armchair against the wall. "Because Mr. Talbot has my complete confidence."

For the first time, Gomez actually glanced at his companion. I don't know what he was looking for, but his partner's eyes didn't move. They remained fixed on something a foot or so behind my head.

"Okay, if thass the way you wanna do it." Gomez laid his overcoat across his lap, unbuttoned his jacket. "Now I'm gonna tell you the story and please to no interrup' me 'til I'm done." He waited for an encouraging nod, then continued matter-of-factly. "You got a client named Priscilla Sweet. Me an' her old man, Byron, we're business associates before she decides to shoot him. I don' blame her for this, because he was no too nice to her. But a' this time when she's killin' him, he owes *muy dinero* to me an' my people. I send a message to Priscilla in the jail: Where is my money? You know wha' she say? The pigs steal all the *coca* before we can sell it. So sorry."

Gomez shook his head. Again, he glanced at his partner, again received no response. "Too bad for her that Byron tole me tha' shit was all sold. He tole me the day before she's shootin' him. Well, you know, like I send word back, stop with the bullshit or somethin' bad is gonna happen to you. Like in jail you got enough problems. You know wha' she done, *Señor* Kaplan? She goes into the protective custody where I can no get to her.

"I tell myself, Thass a pretty smart girl. She knows what she's doin', but I also know what I'm doin' and tha' is visitin' her mother in Flushing. I tell her, Mrs. Barrow, your *chingada* daughter's owin' me a lot of money and if she don' pay up I'm gonna take your fingers and grind them for *chorizo.*

"Tha' Mrs. Barrow, you know wha' she tell me?" He took off his jacket, laid it on top of his overcoat. "She tell me she give all the money to the Jew lawyer for Priscilla's defense. Then she disappears.

"At first, I ain' believin' tha' bullshit. But then I'm seein' your face in the newspapers and on the television. Even *El Diario* carries this big story about the big lawyer. So maybe Thelma ain' lyin'. Maybe she runs away because she's scared I won' believe her. Maybe the lawyer got all my fucking money."

"How much?" I asked. "How much money are we talking about here?"

"One-five-zero. Very large, my man. Very, very large."

My first reaction, at least it wasn't a million, quickly gave way to the truth: repayment was not a possibility. I was going to have to deal with the situation through Priscilla.

"I got an idea." Caleb stood up. "What do you say to a little refreshment? Maybe take the edge off the conversation, see if we can work this out." He crossed the room to the small refrigerator we kept near the bookcase, removed four cans of Coke, and put them on a tray. I was served first, then Gomez, then his silent companion who ignored Caleb, his stare fixed, until it became clear that Caleb wasn't going to move. Finally, at a nod from Gomez, he wrapped his fingers around the can as if holding a hand grenade.

"That Berto," Gomez said, identifying his partner for the first time, "he got a fixed mind. You know, like he can only think abou' one thing at a time."

"Yeah?" Caleb said, his tone suddenly and shockingly hard, hard enough to make me flinch though neither Gomez nor Berto reacted. "Well that's half a thing more than I gave the asshole credit for." Still standing, he waved his soda can in Berto's direction. "In fact, when I first saw him, I thought he was an insect on steroids. Now I think I overestimated his talents."

Berto's only reaction was a blush that left the rubbery scar on his cheek as white as a maggot. Gomez, on the other hand, looked over to Caleb as if seeing him for the first time. "You shouldn' talk to Berto like tha'. He got like a Latino *macho* attitude concernin' insults."

"No shit?" Caleb's hand snaked beneath his jacket, reappeared clutching an automatic which he pressed against the side of Berto's head. Berto didn't flinch, didn't take his eyes off mine. "Think if I pull the trigger, it'll get him over his hangup?"

"Go ahead if thass wha' you gotta do." Gomez lifted his chin, extended it toward Caleb. "Me, too, if you wanna. But we ain' car-ryin' no weapons, so you gonna have a hard time esplainin' to the cops."

For the briefest moment, I thought Caleb was going to pull the trigger. Then I saw his body droop ever so slightly as his weight settled back on his heels.

"Why don't we all calm down." My chest was so tight, my voice failed to rise above a whisper. "Try to work this out."

Gomez put his untouched Coke on my desk, waited for his partner to follow suit. "Is real simple, *hombre*. Priscilla give you money tha' di' no belong to her and now you gotta give it back. *Pronto*." He leaned forward. "You know how it is in the business, right? The people I owe don' take no escuses. They gotta get paid and I gotta collect. Is so simple I'm hopin' I don' have to say tha' shit again."

"There's no money," Caleb said before I could find a place to begin. He was seated again; the pistol was back in its holster. "If Priscilla stole your money, she didn't give it to us."

"Don' insult me, *señor*, 'cause I also got a *macho* attitude." Gomez frowned, then continued without looking at Caleb. "Hey, you know in my life I been arrested, right? Thass jus' the way it is." He waited for me to nod. "Plus all kinds of my people been arrested, so like I know the price for a lawyer, okay? Don' insul' me with bullshit. You ain' no public defender."

"There's no money," I insisted. "We're doing it for the publicity."

Gomez crossed his leg, took a pack of Benson & Hedges from his shirt pocket. "Thass your final position?" He lit the cigarette, let his head drop back, then blew the smoke out through his nose.

"Yeah," Caleb said. "That's the whole thing. So why don't you and Fido take a hike before I call the cops."

"The cops?" Gomez, as he stood up and put on his jacket, began to laugh. "Wha' you gonna tell 'em, my man? Tha' your client is a fuckin' drug dealer who don' pay her bills?" He carefully buttoned his jacket, then shrugged into his overcoat. "*Mira*, you say she din' give you no money? I could believe tha' shit. But like, you know, it don' help nobody. Cause if she din' give the money to you, she gotta still have it. And if she have it, then you gotta get it."

Gomez stood, tapped Berto's shoulder, and the two of them walked to the door. There, with his hand on the knob, he executed a perfect half turn. "*Mira*, I mus' to have tha' money. Okay? I mus' to have it and I'm gonna be callin' you Monday for a delivery."

Neither Caleb nor I moved until we heard the outer door close.

Then, as Julie's worried face appeared in the still open door to my office, Caleb picked up the soda cans Gomez and Berto had held, grasping them by the top and bottom edges. Moving quickly, he carried the cans into the bathroom, emptied them into the toilet, finally came back into the room, and laid them on the bookcase.

"Hard times a'comin', Julie. Better sit down."

She did as he said, settling into the chair vacated by Gomez. When she spoke, her normally soft voice carried a much harder edge. "What's with the cans?"

"I'm gonna let the condensation evaporate, then dust 'em for prints." Caleb's tone was matter-of-fact, as if he was working through a task he'd performed many times before. "The job has prints on computer, now. And these bad boys definitely have records."

He went on to recount the message delivered by Gomez and Berto. It didn't take him very long, and I remember thinking how simple it really was. No obfuscation, no equivocation, no intent to deceive. No opening statement, either, and no closing argument, no rules of evidence. Give me my money or I'll kill you, Sidney Kaplan. Whether you've got it or not.

Part II

Sixteen

At some point in middle boyhood I stopped going directly home after school. (This in the great golden age of the 1950s, a time when children roamed the streets without fear of crack-dealing street gangs or trolling pedophiles.) I was, I think, all of nine years old, a fiercely independent third grader, the first time I walked to the house of my grampa, Itzy, and my *bubbe*, Ethyl. It's easy, now, for me to say that I was fleeing the ghosts that haunted my mother's life (the same ghosts later enshrined on my living room wall) but I doubt that I saw it that way. No, more than likely, since my grandparents' house was directly between school and home, it'd merely seemed a good idea, a harmless whim designed to please my doting grandmother whose daughters now lived with their husbands and children in far-off New Jersey.

If that was my motivation, the affair was an unmitigated success. Grampa Itzy was semiretired by that time and I have a clear memory of the smile that brightened his habitually sour expression, that raised drooping eyes and mouth, that deepened the long, vertical lines that ran from the inner corners of his sharp black eyes to the edge of his jaw.

"Please to come in, Mister Kaplan."

My *bubbe*, so round and warm and full of energy she was almost a caricature of a Jewish grandmother, filled me with honey cake and cold milk (which she sent Grampa Itzy to fetch). It was only then, after I'd been fed, that she called to let Magda know I was safe.

I believe I've already said that I wasn't a popular kid. Looking back, I'm more or less convinced (depending on the day of the month and the phases of the moon) that I really didn't care whether or not my peers liked me, that I was one of those odd children who thrive on loneliness. Whatever the case, I clearly had three possibilities from which to choose at the end of every school day. I could have gone home to Magda, or home to my grandparents, or I could have run with the other boys in the neighborhood. Sheepshead Bay was filled with Jewish and Italian refugees, men and women who'd found success after WWII and wanted nothing more than to flee the slums that had confined their immigrant parents. They came from Little Italy and the Lower East Side, East Harlem and Hell's Kitchen, South Brooklyn, Williamsburg, Greenpoint, Bushwick. Almost universally, they believed in large families and their children swarmed the residential streets.

My choice was no choice at all. It was as if I'd turned a corner into Oz, made that jump from the dull grays of Kansas to the rainbow world of Munchkin land. My grandparents' household was intensely verbal; my grandparents, the both of them, seemed to live by words, debating everything from the quality of the kosher dairy on Nostrand Avenue to the execution of the Rosenbergs. After the eerie silence that surrounded Magda's intense longing, an emptiness observed by my father who loved her more than he loved himself (and certainly more than he loved me), I absorbed the chaos like a leaf absorbs sunlight. For the next four years, until my *bubbe* died suddenly and Grampa Itzy moved into his son's home, I virtually lived with my grandparents. And I don't recall any objection being made, don't recall discussion of any kind.

It was only a matter of weeks until a routine was established. Grampa Itzy was home from the store by noon, bored to death (not to mention getting on his wife's nerves) by 3:15 when I'd show up. He'd wait impatiently while I was fed and did my homework, then, after my work was checked and I'd packed up my schoolbooks, he'd shrug into his coat.

"*Nu*, you're ready for a trip?"

Grampa Itzy's 1952 Pontiac was his pride and joy. Not only was it his first *new* car, it was his first car of any kind and he worried about it as if it was an exotic pet whose biology he barely understood. Still, he was a terrible driver, wandering from lane to lane, missing traffic lights and stop signs even when he tried to pay close attention, which he rarely did. Maybe that's why we seldom went further than the mile or so between his home and the boardwalk at Brighton Beach.

"The family," he told me early on, "you have to know from the family, the way it was." By family, of course, he meant the Kaplans, the family of his father and his son. I don't remember my grandfather ever mentioning his daughter-in-law's name. Not in this connection.

I'll say this for Itzhak Kaplan. He didn't romanticize the past. "The rats had it better than us. They got to live in our building for nuttin'; we had to pay for the privilege. Take it to the bank, Sidney, in them days a life wasn't worth a bag of coal. Which is what for lack of, people froze in their beds. And there wasn't no welfare, neither. For help, you went to the family."

There were calamities everywhere, living behind the walls like cockroaches. First and foremost, Hyman Baruch's death in the wilds of New Jersey and the vagaries of economic survival afterward, a survival complicated by cholera, smallpox, typhus, polio. All aggravated by a pervasive malnutrition.

"Sidney, we wasn't eatin'. We had no resistance. In 1905, I was seven years old when cholera came to the neighborhood. From everywhere, there was families burying babies. We were afraid to go outside, we were afraid even to breathe. Then I got it and my sister, Molly, also. I lived and she didn't and that was it. My mother sat *shiva* and the rest of us went to work. We worked right around her, in the apartment, and when the rabbi came to pay a call, he didn't complain."

Grampa Itzy's father, Hyman Baruch, had come to the New World accompanied by two married brothers, a married sister and a dozen children. They were also family and if my grandfather Itzy attended to their needs less dutifully than to those of his mother and siblings, I couldn't tell from the sound of his voice. All his stories were told in a rush, spoken from whatever corner of his mouth happened to be closer to my ear.

"I'm not saying from this you should conclude we loved each

other like in the movies." He took hold of my arms, stopped me for a moment. I remember it being midwinter, January or February, with the sun seeming to jump from behind the small, intensely white clouds, to blind us with its glare. A bitter wind carried a salt spray that tore at the exposed skin of my face like a sandstorm. "We had plenty bums in the family, criminals even. My cousin Leo and his wife, you couldn't rely on them for spit. But . . ." He raised a gloved finger as if testing the wind, grabbed his lapel with his free hand. ". . . if they should have a problem, they wouldn't hesitate to place a call. *Schnorrers* the two of them."

We walked on for a moment, the boardwalk creaking beneath our feet. Off in the distance, a man wearing a knit cap plodded toward us. He was bent far over, trying to keep the wind off his face. Grampa Itzy glared for a moment, as if he'd been deliberately interrupted, and waited until the man turned off onto one of the streets. "When Leo was starting out in manufacturing, the factors had him by the balls. Later on, he made it big. Then he would come to weddings in a limousine. In 1934, the landlord was gonna throw me and your father out from the store and I went to Leo for a loan. Like a beggar I went to him. He told me, 'Itzy, I haven't got dollar *one*.' Meanwhile, he was going around with a showgirl from the Tropicana. A *shiksa*."

Inevitably, my grandfather's narrative wandered from relative to relative, as if he, himself, was moving along the strands of a spider's web, pausing at each junction, examining, explaining, then sliding past. Leo had a mother he neglected. Her name was Rachel and she was too sick to care for herself. Itzy's Aunt Celia took Rachel in, though Celia was already burdened with a daughter-in-law and two grandchildren.

"Celia was mourning her son, Alan, who died from cancer, but she didn't say, 'No, it's too much for me.' She took the old lady into her apartment, nursed her for three years. Then, after Rachel died, Leo came around asking, 'So where's my mother's money?' "

I believe my grandfather had a dual purpose for these boardwalk stories. Without doubt, he felt a strong need to pass along the essential truths that had brought him through every disaster, from the death of his father to the ultimate nightmare of the great holocaust, a need brought to urgency as the Kaplans began to drift apart. His own two daughters, Iris and Miriam, had moved out to New Jersey; he saw them on family occasions, at *seders*, weddings, *bar mitzvahs*, funerals. Every summer, he and Ethyl spent a month traveling from one daughter to the other, visits that left him depressed for weeks.

"Sidney," he once complained, his tone bewildered, almost wistful, "the children, they are like strangers to us. Like the *kinder* of strangers."

Grampa Itzy's daughters weren't the only Kaplan children to move away. The family had money, now; its sons and daughters pursued careers far removed from those of their parents and grandparents. They attended colleges in distant cities, moved up to the mainstream model, the nuclear family, a split-level in the suburbs, a station wagon in the garage. I suppose, in the late 1950s, when most of these conversations took place (and while my *bubbe* was still alive), the losses couldn't have amounted to much. But Grampa Itzy was always shrewd; he had an ability to sniff the air, taste disaster on the wind.

Years later, I came to realize that my grandfather had a second reason, this one more personal, for our trips to Brighton Beach. He wanted to tell *his* story, the story of the Kaplans, and whenever he tried it in the house, he butted heads with his wife. Not only did they disagree on the details, they disagreed on whose family history was to be preserved.

"I was a Fidelman before I was a Kaplan," she insisted. "From 1875 my family was here."

"*Nu*, you shouldn't remind me." With the exception of a cousin or two, Grampa Itzy disliked the Fidelmans. Descendants of a famous rabbi, the most important goal in their miserable lives (or so he loudly proclaimed) was to out-orthodox friends and relatives. "They wouldn't eat in our house," he once told me, "because we are not enough kosher. My dishes might send them to hell on the express train. Meanwhile, they don't got two pennies to rub together."

When my grandparents really got excited, they broke into Yiddish and I eventually learned the language well enough to follow their arguments. My darling *bubbe*, it turned out, had been a union organizer and a socialist in her youth, a rabble rouser who made impassioned speeches in Union Square. Grampa Itzy found her efforts to extend the obligations imposed by family to the society at large pitifully naive. She, on the other hand, declared his capitalist *macher* aspirations nothing more than *chutzpah*.

"You owned a store on the Lower East Side, Itzy," she told him in Yiddish. "And you think it makes you a John D. Rockefeller. *Feh*."

All of their arguments eventually came down to this essential difference in their worldviews. And when I heard the term *rachmones*, I knew the discussion had reached its zenith. It might be my grandfather accusing Ethyl of being excessively compassionate, using the word like conservative politicians use the phrase *bleeding heart*. Or Ethyl accusing her husband of possessing a heart of stone. A *shtarker* is what she called him, a tough guy, though I doubt very much if she understood how perfectly the word suited his self-image.

After my grandmother died, Grampa Itzy went from sitting *shiva* directly to his son's spare bedroom. I don't remember him ever returning alone to his own house. It was my job to accompany him as he arranged to close and sell his home. Magda, though she didn't work, was never a possibility.

Grampa Itzy still spoke of his family as we waited for this or that relative to cart away this or that piece of his life, but the basic theme of his narrative took a definite turn.

"We was tough kids," he told me. "We had to be tough. When Papa died the family helped out, also Jewish relief and the Bialystokers, but there was never enough."

I remember him getting up, pacing with his hands behind his back as if we were still on the boardwalk. His house was slowly emptying and the faded carpet in the living room showed a brilliant blue in the space once covered by his sofa.

"The rich *goyim* called us street Arabs. To this day I don't know what it means. We was always running wild through the streets. Fist fights was an everyday thing. When the Italian kids from Mulberry Street came to the neighborhood there was regular wars."

My aunt Sylvie arrived a few minutes later, she and two men who worked in her husband's appliance store. The men covered the walnut breakfront, a massive piece, with furniture pads, then hauled it to a van parked in the driveway. Aunt Sylvie watched them like a hawk. "They'll break it for spite," she told us after the van drove away. Then she hugged my grandfather. "Thank you Uncle Itzy. I know *Tante* Ethyl would have wanted it this way."

Later, as we approached my parents' home, Grampa Itzy slapped his hands together, shook his head as if clearing it after a blow. "The furniture, it has to go to the family, this I know. But I'm telling you, Sidney, if the house burns down tonight, I wouldn't lose a minute's sleep." He led me into the backyard, sat on the edge of a small patio. It was early summer and the grass was ankle high.

"I better cut this before the weekend," I said, "or Dad's gonna be pissed."

Grampa Itzy ignored my comment. "Starting tomorrow," he announced, "we don't see each other so much. Sitting around in somebody else's living room don't agree with my constitution, so I'm going to the store with your father." He grinned, showing tiny, faded teeth. "I'm gonna make a comeback."

I was well into my teens by then, a prisoner of my hormones. The time for a boy and his grandfather was past and both of us knew it.

"When things was tough," he said after a moment, "we was all *gonifs*. We stole from the peddlers on the street, food and sometimes clothes, a pair of pants or a dress. My brother, Nathan, would start a commotion, a fight, maybe, and I would snatch and run. We got vegetables this way, also butter and eggs. Sidney, the first few times I was so scared I nearly *plotzed*, but when the belly hurts, you do what you gotta do." He leaned down to me, his eyebrows rising into narrow black semicircles. "After a while, I got used to the stealing, then I got to like it. A few times the Irisher bulls chased after me, but I knew the alleys and the basements and the rooftops. Itzhak Kaplan they couldn't catch. Never."

A static image, as complete as a photograph, jumped into my consciousness at that moment, an image I can pull up to this day. A small, thin, bandy-legged boy wearing an oversized coat and a cap that falls below his ears charges down an alleyway. The featureless walls on either side of the child narrow to a thin rectangle and the light from that rectangle frames the child. At the mouth of the alleyway, a helmeted policeman, a giant, waves his billy over his head. The cop's breath steams in the air and he appears to be shouting. From behind the boy, a white dress streams like the plumage of an exotic bird.

Seventeen

For the next several hours after Guzman's call I sat in my chair (sat there in a state of suspension, like a pickled frog in a jar of formaldehyde) while Caleb and Julie tried to solve our mutual problem. I remember their measured conversation in bits and snatches, remember that I was preoccupied not with survival, but the sudden, internal flip from big-time, New York lawyer to hapless, hopeless jerk. Self-pity was the emotion of the hour. Self-pity as a tightrope suspended over a pit of clinical depression.

"I wasn't about to shoot anyone," Caleb insisted. "The point with the gun was to find out if they were punks. It was a test and they passed."

"That doesn't make them kingpins in the Cali cartel." Julie's voice was firm, without the slightest quaver of indecision. "In fact, I'd bet my left hand that Gomez is a low-level jerk who got in over his head. The key is what he said at the very end. He *has* to get the money, because he has to pay off his own suppliers. If he doesn't . . ."

I don't remember Caleb arguing that or any other point until Julie got to the bottom line of her argument, until she said, "What we should do, Caleb, is stall until we track them down, then. . . . Then we should protect the family." Julie was sitting next to Caleb, bent slightly forward at the waist, her crossed forearms resting on crossed knees.

"Just like that, huh? Just take a life and forget about it?"

"Actually," I finally interrupted, "I like the stalling part." I tried, and failed, to smile reassuringly. "Look, today's Friday and Guzman isn't calling back until Monday. Let's take the time to check him out and see what develops. It's too early to make any hard decisions."

"I know what it's like," Julie insisted, "to be a dog locked up in a back room waiting for massa to come in and kick me. I'm not going back to that." She shifted in her seat, frowned, jabbed a bony finger in Caleb's general direction. "Just find them."

"Well, I don't plan to sit on my ass and wait for Gomez to come looking for me." He sat back, chuckled manfully. "Course he wouldn't actually be looking for *me*. Uh-uh. Most likely, ole Gomez'd come looking for Sid." When his joke fell flat, he shrugged, continued: "Way I see it, Julie, it might be that Gomez and his boyfriend are just a couple of messenger boys. That the real muscle stayed home."

I was up early the following morning, before 6 A.M., staring into the bathroom mirror. Tracing the lines of my face with the ring finger of my right hand. The rims of my eyes were swollen and nearly purple with fatigue. My nose was heavier than I remembered, the bridge shot through with curling red veins; my lips drooped at the corners except when I smiled and I couldn't bring myself to smile.

And what I understood, as I turned on the shower and waited for the hot water to rise, was that I didn't have the energy for a second comeback. If Priscilla Sweet told me to get lost (or, just as bad, if I simply walked away from the case and hoped Gomez and Berto got the message), I'd spend the rest of my life chasing the rent.

Three hours later, Caleb and I were sitting with Priscilla in a Rikers interview room, trying to gauge her reaction to the story I told at great length. I noted confusion when I identified Gomez, a slight nod of recognition at Berto's name, a minor tightening of her lips when I described her sainted mother's role in the proceedings. Beyond that, there was, as usual, nothing; Priscilla's face retained its ordinary composure. The only thing I saw in her eyes was my own tired reflection.

"And that's it," I concluded. "That's where we stand right now. Gomez is gonna give me a call on Monday to arrange delivery. If there's no money, he plans to hurt the only folks he can reach."

Priscilla looked down at the table, ran her fingers through her hair. "Sid, if you think . . ."

"Forget about what I think. Let's see if we can establish the facts. Do you know who these people are?"

She nodded, raised her eyes to meet mine. "The smooth one, his name is Elizado Guzman. The other one is Adelberto Garcia. Berto's as crazy—and as stupid—as he looks. They're both Dominicans."

"Not Panamanians?" I made an attempt to keep the sarcasm out of my voice, though I don't believe I succeeded.

"They're middlemen. They receive small shipments, maybe twenty kilos, split them up, and pass them on to people like Byron. There's no trick to it. Everything's done on credit. That's why the shipments are relatively small."

I looked over at Caleb. He was sitting quietly, his hands resting on his belly, looking at Priscilla. "What about the passport?" I finally said. "If Byron was just another mid-level dealer, what was he doing in Panama?"

That brought a quick, hard smile. "If you want the coke fronted, which Byron did, you have to go to Panama City for an interview. But the trip's really not about you, because you've already been recommended. It's so you can see for yourself how bad they are, how many killers and guns they have. They tell you stories about feeding you and your family to their pet crocodiles."

"You told me that Byron was always behind in his payments. What was he planning to do, Priscilla, play Daniel in the crocodiles' den?"

"You serious?" Priscilla's brows arched in surprise. "Look, when Byron went to Panama, he was fresh out of jail and still basically clean. That's why they set him up. Then he became an addict. It doesn't call for a lot of explanation."

"That's true, Priscilla. And, of course, he was just a little behind. It's not like he was planning to rip them off, right?"

The question caught her by surprise, as it was meant to do. Priscilla's chin came up and she waggled a finger at me. "I have to stop forgetting that you're a professional," she said without revealing any of the things I needed to know.

"How about answering the question?"

She looked at Caleb who smiled brightly, said, "You know, Priscilla, they *are* threatening to grind our fingers up for *chorizo*."

"I don't know why my mother told them I gave you the money. If I wasn't sure Elizado was too stupid to make it up, I wouldn't believe it."

"They don't care whether or not your mother told the truth." I shook my head, managed a brief smile. "With Thelma gone, the only way they can get to you is through us. Me and Caleb and Julie, we're the only game in town."

Priscilla didn't respond immediately and I saw the pause as my chance to hit her with the one essential lie I could prove. "Any chance," I asked, "that your mother will agree to come back to New York, tell the boys she made a slight mistake?"

"I'll call her and . . ."

"Why don't you give me the number, let me call her?"

The question was loaded. If Priscilla refused to give me the number, it would be a tacit admission that she knew exactly why her mother had taken off, that she'd known all along. On the other hand, if she did give me the number, who's to say I wouldn't pass it on to Elizado Guzman?

"Look," Priscilla said after a slight hesitation, "the reason I took PC is because Guzman threatened me through another inmate. I lied to you and I'm admitting it. I also lied to you about my mother. She left to get away from them and she's not coming back. Berto scared the crap out of her." She leaned across the table, touched the back of my hand with a by now familiar forefinger. "But I did not know my mother told Guzman that she'd given his money to you. And I never expected, not for a fucking minute, that anybody would threaten you. Maybe I should have seen the move coming, but I swear that it never crossed my mind. Never."

I took out a cigarette, offered her the pack. "They gonna follow through, Priscilla? Do they have heart?" I got up, sucked on the cigarette, began to pace. "Am I supposed to go about in fear of my life while I prepare your defense? Or am I supposed to resign, lose my access, hope Guzman doesn't believe Thelma? Or that he won't spank me for my impudence?" I stopped talking abruptly, but continued to pace. Waiting for a response that was a long time coming.

"I don't have the money, Sid. What I said about muling the coke around the city was the truth. And when I told Guzman that the cops took the coke, I believed what I was saying. Maybe there's a lockbox stuffed with cash in some bank, but I don't know where it is." Her face was composed again, her voice matter-of-fact, as if she was reminding herself that, after all, her basic position was still defensible.

Three hours later, I was sitting across from Benny Levine, pouring my heart out. We were in the Slipper, on opposite sides of a narrow booth set against the rear wall. The stench of booze was overwhelming, despite the cigarettes I lit, one after another. Each time I drank from my glass of ginger ale, I tasted a highball.

"What I'm looking for," I concluded, "is somebody to run these guys a strong message. I don't have their fucking money and I don't know anything about their money. And neither does my client."

Benny dug a finger into his ear, rooted for a moment, then withdrew the tip for inspection. "A big trial like this," he finally declared, "you're telling me it's on the house?"

"You want to inspect my bank statements, I'm more than willing. But don't think I'm in it to save my soul. Every time my face appears on the little screen, I get phone calls from new clients." I took a deep breath. "If I'm not mistaken, it's what brought *you* to my door."

That produced a grunt of understanding. Benny liked to think of himself as a businessman, had told me on several occasions that the bottom line was as close as he got to God. Maybe that's why he hastened to define it.

"Me, also," he declared with a little shake of his head. "I also want a freebie."

"In return for exactly what?"

He toyed with a wet swizzle stick for a moment, turning it in a little circle on the tabletop, finally said, "Gimme their names again, tell me where they hang out. I'll see if they could be spoken to."

"Well, that's not quite good enough, Benny. But if it turns out they *can* be spoken to, if you take them off my back, then you can have your freebie. Just remember, it's gonna be real hard to collect if I'm dead."

The most obvious option, simply vanishing, was not a possibility for us. We had seven clients by then, each of whom needed attention.

There were motions to prepare, a bail hearing to attend on Wednesday, four different A.D.A.'s to corner before the end of the week. That was why we decided, after a long discussion over a long dinner in the apartment on Sunday evening, not to dump Priscilla Sweet. At least not right away.

The only advantage to withdrawal was that Guzman couldn't realistically hope to reach Priscilla through me. But I'd still have to convince Guzman that I didn't have his money and if I could convince him of that, maybe I could convince him that either Priscilla didn't have it or wouldn't give it up, that there was no way her poor, abused lawyer could alter the facts.

Surprisingly, in retrospect, we gave almost no time to Priscilla that night, neither exonerating nor condemning her. Yeah, she'd lied to us, but unless she'd instructed Thelma to point Guzman in our direction, her lies were lies of omission. Seen from her point of view, until Guzman began to threaten us, the fate of his money was none of our business.

What I remember is wrangling with the practicalities, finally coming to a half-assed plan that was geared to response, not initiative. I would take Guzman's call on Monday and record it just in case we finally decided to bring in the police. Beyond that, I'd try first to persuade him that I did not have and could not get his money. When that failed to appease him—as we were certain it would—I'd offer to put more heat on Priscilla, beg him to give me until Thursday or Friday.

While I stalled, Caleb would visit Guzman's Washington Heights territory, see how close he could get. Benny Levine, presumably, would be working his own end of the equation, trying to play the mediator, the voice of reason. Meanwhile, Julie would explore the economics of hiring professional bodyguards in case we decided to hunker down, wait it out.

Eighteen

It was Julie who took Elizado Guzman's first call on Monday morning. As per agreement, Julie informed Mr. Guzman that I was on my way out to Rikers and a visit with Priscilla Sweet. No, she wasn't sure when I'd be back, but if he wanted to leave his number, she'd beep me.

Needless to say, Guzman, who'd identified himself as Mr. Gomez, did not want to leave his number. (Just as well, because I didn't have a beeper.) But he didn't make any threats, either, just said he'd call back later, which he did, at two, four, and six o'clock when he finally caught up with me.

Meanwhile, ever the diligent shyster, I spent the afternoon in pursuit of my clients' various prosecutors, running down four A.D.A.'s, including Manuel Bergman's. Her name was Lois Santana and she was a tall, broad-shouldered woman in her mid-forties who nodded thoughtfully as I explained the need for delay.

"I'll be tied up with Priscilla Sweet for the next six months. There's no way I can start on Bergman's case before then." I shrugged my shoulders, willing myself to appear cooperative. "That's assuming we go to trial, of course."

Santana outlined her case, which verified Bergman's account. Five hundred pounds of cocaine had arrived on a Liberian freighter, then, with the cops in hot pursuit, been delivered to a private home in Bay Ridge, Brooklyn. Though Bergman owned the house, he was out of town when the cocaine arrived. His indictment was based solely on statements given by the five individuals arrested with the product.

I ran directly from Lois Santana's office to a payphone in the hallway, dialed Bergman's phone number. He picked up on the fourth ring, his husky voice making it clear that he'd been asleep.

"Wake up, Manny," I said, "because I got some good news for you." I went on to tell him that his basic goal, long-term delay, had been achieved. Lois Santana, perhaps not in love with her case, was in no rush to go to trial. "Plus," I concluded, "you've got a decent shot at an outright acquittal. The state's case, from what I can see of it, is very thin."

I remember my client being pleased, but not what he actually said. That's because I had something else on my mind. "Manny, you ever know a dealer named Elizado Guzman, works uptown near the bridge?"

"You're saying that Guzman, the Weasel, is snitching on me? That right?"

For a moment, I was tempted to confirm his hasty conclusion, send him after an unsuspecting Elizado Guzman, unleash the kind of drug feud that shredded babies in their strollers.

"No," I finally said, "Guzman has nothing to do with your case. What I'd like to get is a character report. For instance, would you recommend him to a prospective employer? Or to a bank that wanted to extend credit?"

Bergman took his time framing an answer. I heard him sip at something liquid, the clink of a cup dropping onto a saucer. Finally, he said, "The Weasel is a climber, looking to get up and out. What I heard, Sid, was that he was having trouble with his bank, that he climbed too fast, got himself spread out thin and now he can't collect." Another pause, then, "You can't collect, you can't pay, right? In the Weasel's line of work, that's a definite no-no."

On my way out to Rikers early that afternoon, I stopped long enough to meet Caleb for a quick lunch at Georgie Petrarkis's diner on 21st Street in Long Island City. Caleb was there when I arrived, hovering over a bowl of split pea soup in a rear booth. He waited until I was seated, then returned to his lunch while I detailed my conversation with Manny Bergman.

"I won't say I wasn't tempted, because I was," I concluded. "But a drug war? See, the thing about it, Caleb, is that I trust someone like Benny Levine to handle Guzman quietly. Manny Bergman on the other hand . . ." I leaned back in the booth as Georgie dropped a cup of coffee and a bowl of soup in front me. When he was gone, I pushed the soup to one side and leaned across the table. "But the impression I got is that if we stall for a while, Guzman's Panamanian handlers are gonna take care of our problem."

Caleb nodded, continued to spoon soup into his mouth. When the bowl was empty, he carefully wiped his fingers before looking up to me. "I can take him out," he said. "I'm talkin' about Guzman. He hangs at a social club on the south side of 180th Street near St. Nicholas Avenue. There's three abandoned buildings down the block on the north side. Be an easy shot with a rifle."

"I thought Julie was the hawk and you were the dove?"

"What you said about Guzman being desperate?" Caleb ignored my remark. "That if he can't pay his debts, somebody's gonna kill him real soon? That's bound to make him eager to collect, partner. More I think about it, the more pissed off I get." He hesitated, looked down at his hands. "Seems like I worked real hard to get my life in shape. Be a shame to die just when I was startin' to enjoy it."

I carried that message to Priscilla, watched her eyes carefully, hoping for some proof that she'd actually received it. No such luck. After the shortest of pauses, she issued the expected denials: there was no money to return, the matter was beyond her control. So sorry.

For the first time, as I listened to her, I thought about how I might feel if she was lying to me. If she had the ability to take Elizado Guzman off our backs and was deliberately sacrificing us. If she had supplied her mother with the big lie.

"Sid?" She reached across the table, laid her fingertips on the back of my hand. The gesture was shockingly intimate. "Look, it's okay if you can't do it. The trial can be delayed. I can find somebody else."

I responded by putting her to work. Priscilla's success or failure at trial would depend on personal testimony that persuaded as much with posture and tone of voice as with the literal meaning of the words she spoke. Detached amusement was not going to cut it.

"It's my job," I told her just before we began, "to put a little sparkle in those flat, gray eyes. That way you won't spend the rest of your life in scenic Bedford Hills."

On the way back to the office, I met briefly with Benny Levine at the Slipper. Benny was pretty sure his people would be able to arrange a meeting with Guzman by the end of the week. Meetings were no problem at all.

"But it's not like the old days," he was quick to add. "We had real men back in those days, men of honor. Now we're like the fuckin' liberals. Nobody's scared of us."

It wasn't, he went on to explain, that today's mob didn't have balls. No, they were as quick to protect their honor as their forebears. But they wouldn't kill a man's entire family to make a point. They wouldn't slash open a kid while the parents watched.

"We're not fuckin' animals." Benny paused long enough to shake his head mournfully. "Them spics, Sid, they got no respect for anything."

Still, even that judgment didn't mean—motivated as they were by profit—that the new breed was beyond reason. In the case of Elizado Guzman, for instance, it was simply a matter of convincing him that slaughtering Priscilla Sweet's impoverished attorney would gain him nothing, while at the same time offering a little hope. A little hope in the form of a large loan at the usual rates.

"What I'm thinkin' here, Sid," Benny concluded, "is that we could maybe work ourselves up to a piece of Guzman's action. Not with threats, like in the old days, but by offerin' our management skills along with enough capital to keep the operation afloat."

It was cold when I left the bar, and near dark; I remember pausing a half block from the Slipper to button my coat, tuck in my scarf. What was clear to me was that everybody was working an angle, from Guzman to Priscilla to myself, while Benny Levine was working two or three at the same time.

Julie was on the phone when I came through the door. She mouthed a single word, *Guzman*, without taking the phone away from her ear. I nodded once, heard her say, "Mr. Kaplan just came in, Mr. Guzman. He'll take your call in a moment." Then she put him on hold and smiled up at me.

"Our boy a little anxious?" I hung my overcoat on a hanger, dumped my hat on the rack.

"Not so you could tell. He's been propositioning me for the last fifteen minutes."

I walked into my office, set the answering machine to record the conversation, picked up the phone. "Elizado," I said, "how's it going?"

"I don' know till you tell me." He didn't flinch at the sound of his real name, leaving me to wonder if he'd noticed my using it. "How am I doin'?"

"Well, not as good as you might be," I admitted. "See it's kind of hard for Priscilla to admit that she has your money when she got me for nothing by telling me she was broke." I paused, hoping he'd make an incriminating statement, but he was smart enough to keep his mouth shut. "I don't know if you know this, Elizado, but Priscilla's mother owns a house in Queens. Priscilla thinks her mother can be persuaded to take out a small mortgage. Not enough to pay you what you claim Byron owed you, but maybe enough to get you out of a jam."

"Tha's no good. I don't got no time for no mortgage."

"Don't be so pessimistic. A home equity loan can be approved in a couple of days. Priscilla said that she'd call her mother tonight, start the ball rolling." The door to my office cracked open, revealing Julie's anxious face. I winked by way of demonstrating that Elizado hadn't dispatched me via telephone, then returned to the conversation while she watched. "Figure, if everything goes right, Priscilla will have something for you by the end of the week."

"Tha's too slow." His smooth voice cracked on the last word, hinting at an inner desperation that scared the piss out of me.

"C'mon, man. What did you think? That she had the fucking money in her cell? That she was gonna pass it over to me on Rikers Island? Look, Elizado, my client is telling me that she doesn't have your money and I believe her. Despite that, she's willing to pay if that means you'll get off her back. But if you can't hang on until the end of the week, we're both wasting our time here. I don't do miracles."

I held the phone away from my mouth, said, "Julie, bring me in the files on Benny Levine and Manny Bergman, lemme update them while I have a chance."

"Who you talking to?" Guzman asked.

"I'm talking to my paralegal, Elizado. An incredibly talented woman, just in case you need representation sometime in the future."

"What I'm needin' is my fuckin' money."

"Elizado, lemme ask you this: Do you really think Priscilla, if she did steal your money, gave that money to me?" Even as I asked the question, I knew the rational answer was, no, of course not, nobody in their right mind would rip off the keeper of the crocodile pit in order to pay a lawyer.

Another long pause, thankfully the last of the series. "Friday, I'm gonna call you up at nine o'clock right where you sittin' now. Wha' you gonna say to me is yes or fuckin' no. Tha's it. You got it or you don't. No more Jew lawyer bullshit."

It was snowing the next morning as Caleb, Julie, and I made our way to the office, a sharp, painful snow pushed to near-horizontal by an unrelenting wind. Almost instinctively, we followed each other in single file, heads bent, shuffling our feet along the sidewalks like timid figure skaters. My cheeks were half frozen by the time we got to Union Square, despite the wool scarf wrapped around my face, excuse enough I felt to justify a quiet day in the office. We'd catch up on our collective paperwork, indulge in caffeine-driven strategy sessions, feast on meals delivered by undocumented aliens, maybe even drag out the polishing rags and a vacuum cleaner.

A lazy day filled with necessary tasks. It was the kind of vacation that can only be fully appreciated by another junkie. After a year of intensive rehabilitation, Caleb, Julie, and I had simply switched addictions. Instead of alcohol, coke, or dope, we were addicted to work and to each other—addictions that not only didn't harm us, but which, arguably, had lifted us out of degradation and poverty.

The snow, which had been tapering off all morning, stopped just before eleven. Still, we managed to stick to the game plan until after we'd put away two small pizzas and a cold antipasto between noon and one. The phone rang then, while I was tearing the pizza boxes into pieces small enough to be stuffed into the wastebasket, bringing with it an offer guaranteed to drag me out of the office.

The caller, Susan Veraci, identified herself as the producer of the

CNN panel show, "Real Opinion Live," which was doing a segment on spousal abuse at three o'clock and had lost one of its panelists, an attorney from Connecticut who claimed to be snow bound. Ms. Veraci understood that she was calling at the last minute, but if I had the time and wanted to substitute, they'd interview me, along with a copanelist, remote from a studio in Rockefeller Center. The show, of course, would be aired nationally.

To my credit, I showed no untoward eagerness besides asking her which cheek of her ass she wanted me to kiss first. And I wasted no time getting out of the office, shrugging into my coat while I explained the mission to my comrades.

"What I'm gonna do, I think, is go with the question of who deserves protection. Do you have to be white, middle-class, and heterosexual before society grants you the right to self-defense? Maybe we should limit self-defense to virgin princesses, let the carnal commoners take the beating and like it." I jammed my hat on my head. "I should be out of the studio by four. You guys gonna watch the show?"

"Well, I don't know, Sid," Julie returned without missing a beat. "There's a "Honeymooners" rerun on Comedy Central that I've only seen a couple of hundred times."

I was much too egotistical to ask the obvious question: Why had CNN chosen Sidney Kaplan from among the ten or twenty thousand feminists in New York City? But the answer became obvious when I met my copanelist at the studio. Phoebe Morris was grinning broadly as she extended a hand. "Mr. Kaplan," she said, "we meet at last."

The show went well, considering the logistics. The host, a woman named Eleanor Kelly, shuffled back and forth between the two panelists by her side in an Atlanta studio, and Phoebe and me in Manhattan. The first part of the discussion centered on a trial in Miami about which I knew nothing, but then a merciful caller brought up the O.J. Simpson case, allowing me to make a well-prepared point.

"Let's suppose," I told an audience of millions, "that Nicole Brown decided to take matters into her own hands, say when that fourteen minute 911 tape was made. Suppose she killed O.J. Simpson and the Los Angeles District Attorney decided to put her on trial." I remember, at that point, turning slightly to look into the camera. "What the prosecution would have done is put Nicole Brown's whole life on trial. The Hollywood parties, the sleeping around, the dabbling in drugs and homosexuality, sex on the couch while the kids were sleeping upstairs. That last would have been enough, all by itself, for a conviction."

Phoebe, who'd been introduced as a Pulitzer Prize winner for a series on battered women (a series evidently written during my blotto years, because I had no memory of it), nodded thoughtfully before jumping into the debate.

"My research demonstrated that the lower a woman's socioeconomic status, the more likely a jury to reject a claim of self-defense. Prostitutes who killed their pimps were in the worst position of all. These were women, Eleanor, who'd been reduced to virtual slavery; one and all they'd been scarred by their masters. But in each case, the prosecutor jumped on their backgrounds. They were whores and petty thieves who took drugs and neglected their children and were therefore guilty of murder. It may seem ridiculous, but, trust me, Eleanor, I went through the transcripts carefully and that's exactly what happened."

After the show wrapped up, Phoebe invited me and my crew to join her for an early dinner. I tried to call Julie and Caleb at the office, got the machine, hung up without leaving a message.

"The work ethic personified," I explained to Phoebe as we tried to flag down a cab on 6th Avenue. The snow had stopped, but the wind, if anything, had picked up. It was bitterly cold, and my feet half froze in the few minutes it took us to abandon surface transportation in favor of the subway.

We rode uptown, to an Indian restaurant on Amsterdam Avenue, and talked about Priscilla Sweet while we feasted on *samosas*, mulligatawny soup, fiery lamb *vindaloo*, and mango ice cream. Toward the end of the meal, I called Elizabeth Howe, our spousal abuse expert, and arranged an interview for Phoebe, then trudged off in search of a taxi.

A full moon hung over Lexington Avenue as I made my way downtown, bright enough against the inky sky to be my personal spotlight. I watched it through the windshield, looking over the driver's shoulder. The radio, tuned to a Latin station, was playing softly through the rear speakers. And I remember thinking, as the cab worked its way around a Con Edison dig at 34th Street, that one day, and sooner rather than later, Elizado Guzman would become the subject of one of those fascinating anecdotes I used to relate at important cocktail parties. The kind of parties to which, five years before, I'd been routinely invited.

Nineteen

I was home from school on the day my *bubbe* died. It was February 12, 1956, Abraham Lincoln's actual birthday and not merely the closest convenient Monday. My father was at work, as he would be on George Washington's birthday later in the month. That left Magda or myself to answer the phone when Grampa Itzy called.

It was raining outside, a cold steady downpour, the kind of weather I favored at fourteen. Now I had a good excuse to stay in my room all day, putter with a science project due in a couple of weeks, maybe finish Harold Gray's novel, *The Hoods*, which I'd begun reading the night before.

My only friend at the time, Vinnie Barrone (who went to Bishop Loughlin and didn't have the day off) had given me *The Hoods*, just as he'd given me *A Stone For Danny Fisher* and *Knock On Any Door*. Defiant heroes who lived short, violent lives fit my self-image perfectly.

But I wasn't in my room when Grampa Itzy called. I was in the kitchen, fussing with an onion omelet. Magda was sitting at the other end of the table, sipping at a cup of coffee while she composed one of her letters. She wrote, as she always did, with a fountain pen on pale blue stationary, her handwriting small and precise.

The phone startled the both of us and I remember Magda looking across the table, almost imploring me to answer it, to leave her wrapped in the cocoon of her obsession. A few years earlier, I would have picked up without thinking twice, but at fourteen, with the sexual fires raging, I'd begun to cultivate a sullen quality. Perhaps by way of complementing the acne blossoming on my cheeks.

In the six times the phone rang before Magda finally got up, I crisscrossed my omelet with an unbroken line of ketchup, added salt and pepper which it didn't need, and buttered a slice of toasted rye bread. I wore my hair in a well-greased pompadour back then, with the forelock pulled down to cover my brow. The hair was my barrier whenever I needed to disappear while in the company of my parents or my teachers or my schoolmates. I used it then, at lunch, while the phone in the small foyer continued to ring, letting it hang like a spider's web between myself and my mother's entreaty.

"Hello?"

After a long silence, I finally raised my head to find Magda with her right hand pressed against her chest, her fingers raised to the hollow of her throat. Her breath popped from her lungs in a series of sharp, hollow coughs.

When Detective Sergeant Harold Knapp, his shield extended, jumped out of an unmarked Ford and strode across the street to intercept me as I approached the door of my apartment building, I flashed straight back to my mother as she'd stood in the doorway between the foyer and the kitchen of our Brooklyn home. I remembered her exactly as she'd been, one hand against her throat, the other extended, offering me the phone receiver as if it explained everything.

And I experienced that same catch in my lungs, was unable to draw a breath, felt my chest squeezed down as if by a heart attack. Knapp's pale face swam into view. He was a middle-aged man, hatless despite the cold night and his nearly bald scalp. I remember that his brows and eyelashes were thin and blond, that his watery blue eyes were two circular ice cubes floating beneath a pair of soft, fleshy lids.

"Sidney Kaplan?" He watched me for a moment, his stare as frankly evaluating as that of a two-year-old. "You all right?"

I nodded once, caught the glint of a reflection in the Ford across the street, became aware of a man in the car, another detective, though I couldn't see his features clearly.

"I'm here about a man named Caleb Talbot. You know who he is?"

My breath began to come back to me, as it had come back to my mother, in little sips at first, then in a deep, sucking rush. Again, I nodded.

"Talbot's dead." Knapp raised his chin, looked down at me along the length of his nose. "Murdered, up in the Heights."

When I still didn't reply, he said, "You don't seem surprised."

I shrugged, turned, rang my apartment buzzer. If Julie was home, I wanted to know it. Then I realized that Knapp must have already tried the bell, that our home was empty. "You know who I am?" I asked, turning to face him again.

"Yeah," he admitted. "Your name is on Talbot's business card. That's how I found you."

"Then stop with the games and tell me what it is you want."

"We need someone to identify the body." He shifted his weight from one foot to the other, rubbed his hands together. "Christ, it's cold."

I expected to be taken to the morgue. Instead, Detective Brown, the man I'd seen inside the car, turned left on Third Avenue and headed straight uptown.

"The M.E.'s gonna be delayed," Knapp said. He was half turned in the front seat, watching me over his shoulder. "I figured, what the fuck, let's see if we can find a relative, get the I.D. over and done with. By the way, you guys live together?" His fleshy mouth expanded into a smirk. "You guys roommates or somethin'?"

He continued to throw questions at me as we rode, and with no real choice, I answered. The radio squawked from time to time, its terse messages blending into the traffic noise, the hum of the tires, the occasional blaring horn. I remember closing my eyes at some point, and a powerful sensation of being sucked forward into a narrowing tunnel. As if even the pretense of volition was to be denied me.

Knapp asked me where I'd been that night and I answered. He asked if anyone else lived in the apartment and I told him about Julie. He asked where she was and I told him that I didn't know. He asked me if I knew what Caleb had been doing in Washington Heights, if Caleb had enemies, if I knew anyone who might have a motive for murder.

I lied on each of the last three questions, answering with a simple, "No." There wasn't a chance in hell that he believed me, but there wasn't a hell of a lot he could do about it. Still, he continued to chatter away, asking how long Caleb had been working for me, what it was he did, what he'd been working on recently. And I continued to answer, even as I tried to conjure up some real, actual place Julie could be except in the hands of Elizado Guzman.

The crime scene was deserted except for a single cruiser sitting with its engine running at the head of the alleyway. For some reason, I saw this as an affront, an insult to the body lying back in the darkness. Caleb needed protection, if not actual attendance. There had to be rats back in that alley, rustling through the garbage, hungry, searching for any bit of flesh.

"For Christ's sake," I told Knapp, "he was one of yours. He was a cop. He shouldn't be alone."

For the first time, Brown turned to look at me. He was a black man, tall enough to brush the car's liner with the top of his head. His round, nondescript features were dominated by a pair of round eyeglasses, their lenses tinted pink. "He ain't gonna mind, counselor. It's cold in the morgue, too."

Knapp spoke briefly to the uniformed cops inside the cruiser, firing off a series of questions to which he received short respectful answers. Yes, the crime scene unit had finished and was gone. No, the ME hadn't shown. Yes, they'd remained in place for the whole time. No, nobody had approached the alley. In fact, the locals had been driven indoors by the cold, just as he and his partner had been driven into their unit.

Finally, at a signal from Knapp, Brown pulled forward and to the curb. "Leave it running," Knapp said, "and leave the goddamn heater on."

I don't know what I expected, but I didn't move, just sat their dumbly, my hands jammed in my pockets, until Knapp finally opened the door from the outside, snapped on a flashlight, shone it briefly in my face. "You ready, Mr. Kaplan?"

The wind hit me like a slap and I ducked my head instinctively, pulling my exposed neck down into the collar of my coat. Knapp nodded, smiled, turned the flashlight to the mouth of the alley.

"Way I figure it," he said, "Talbot was shot somewhere else and ran into the alley to get away. You see this here?" His light flashed to a black pool. "That's blood." The light swung forward. "There's more of it, here and here." He was walking now, swinging the flashlight from side to side as he went. "That garbage can was knocked down when I got here. Most likely, he stumbled against it. There's a palm print on the wall where he must've leaned. See the blood?"

As we moved forward, as Knapp rattled on and Brown watched me from behind, I felt myself tightening down. There'd been times in my life when I'd lived on defiance alone, on the pure refusal to submit. In that space, anger was sustenance, misery a badge of honor. Caleb would have understood, of course. Julie as well. Knapp, on the other hand, was after something entirely different. He wanted a murderer.

"Well, this is as far as he got."

My head jerked up, following the beam of the flashlight as it swung quickly forward. I picked out the skeleton of a rusted shopping cart, a tilted, doorless refrigerator, a stack of paint cans against the wall. But I didn't see Caleb, even when I looked at the dark circle in the center of the light.

"You wanna get a little closer, Mr. Kaplan? We gotta be sure it's really your roommate here."

What I wanted to do was turn and run, hit the nearest bar, drain a bottle of scotch. And I might have done it, too, if Knapp and his partner weren't there to witness my shame. I flashed back to my grandfather, seeing his tiny round eyes in the darkness, his shy, sincere smile. "In dem days, Sidney, we was all tough guys. We had'a be."

I stepped forward, sliding my feet as if on skis. Caleb was wearing a black coat, lying in a puddle of black blood; his round body seemed to flow into the larger shadow and for a moment I couldn't locate a top and bottom. I could find neither his head nor his feet.

"Way I see it," Knapp said, crossing the blood with the flashlight beam, "your buddy musta bled out. Exsanguinated. That's what the ME will say in court. Exsanguinated."

I slid up next to him, looked straight down his arm at Caleb's unmarked features. Caleb was lying on his side, with his open left eye locked on his hand which lay, palm up, in front of his face. I wanted to touch him, felt it was somehow expected, but Detective Brown, as if he'd been lying in wait, yanked me back to reality.

"The guy's frozen. Gotta be. Like a rock. The ME's gonna have to nuke him in a microwave before they do the autopsy."

They took me downtown, from the crime scene on 185th Street and Audubon Avenue, to the headquarters of the Manhattan North homicide squad on West 52nd Street. It was still early, barely ten o'clock, and the Upper West Side was just gearing up for its nightly run at oblivion. As we drove (and while Sgt. Knapp groused to his partner about a woman named Iris, a cop groupie who hung at his favorite bar, but wouldn't give him the time of day) I stared into the windows of the bars and the nightclubs, drawn to the shadows, the glow of neon, the imagined hum of sexually charged conversation.

For most of my life, I'd walked into bars like an animal in search of a den. The best ones enveloped you, smothered you in quiet and safety, in the mixed odors of alcohol and tobacco, in the protective cloak of your personal fantasy. I could be whatever I wanted, even a big shot lawyer who won cases by day, partied until the break of dawn, never looked back to see who or what was gaining on him. Now, I'm not sure there was ever a time when I could sustain that life, that I wouldn't have been a better (though less amusing) attorney if I'd stayed at home with a cup of cocoa.

They gave me a mug of coffee after we settled into chairs around Knapp's desk, and offered me an oozing jelly doughnut which I refused. As before, Knapp asked most of the questions while his partner fixed me with what was surely meant to be an intimidating glare. Unfortunately, the tinted glasses only drew attention to the watery, allergic eyes behind them, so that Brown's gaze had a tentative, almost pleading quality to it.

"Awright." Knapp took a microcassette recorder from a desk drawer, held it up for my inspection. "Just for the record, this interview is being recorded." Speaking very clearly, very slowly, he stated the day, the date, and the time, then my name, his own, his partner's. After the first hour, Brown left the room to check my alibi and I stopped paying attention. I'd already established the most important point, that my time was accounted for, and I wasn't going to mention Guzman or his threats, not until I knew more about Julie's situation. In truth, I was still holding out hope. Thinking maybe she'd gone out to interview a witness, or to visit an old lover. Maybe there was a note back at the apartment, stuck into the hall mirror, the proper place for notes in our household. Or maybe Julie was there now, afraid for her family, wondering where I was.

Brown was in a much better mood when he returned. "Hey, good news, counselor. I checked out your alibi and you come up clean as a whistle." He bit into a doughnut, swallowed. "Yeah, I called that reporter, Morris. She says you were with her every minute. Course, bein' as the public has the right to know, I had'a tell her what happened to ya buddy. She's headin' uptown with a photographer even as we speak."

I sat down, shrugged my shoulders. "Is there something else we have to do here?"

He took me back over the same ground: what were Caleb's duties, what was he working on when I left the office, did he keep a log of his activities, did I have any clients or witnesses who lived in Washington Heights, why didn't I want to help the police find my roommate's killer?

"Maybe what I should do," he said after thirty minutes of verbal sparring, "is hold you as a material witness while I get a warrant, search your office."

It was so stupid, I didn't bother to reply directly. "The problem with cops is that they only have room in their heads for one idea at a time. You have no reason to believe that . . ." I hesitated, unable, for a moment, to say his name. ". . . that Caleb Talbot's presence on 185th Street was work related. Maybe he was up there visiting a friend, maybe he was the victim of a street mugger, maybe your line of inquiry is pure bullshit." I took out a pack of cigarettes, lit one up. "Better get out the Visine, Brown," I told Knapp's partner when he protested. "You want me to stay, I gotta access my nicotine delivery system."

In the end, I promised to go through Caleb's desk (this after refusing Knapp the same privilege on the grounds of client confidentiality), and pass along any piece of information specifically

related to the day's activities. I also gave them Caleb's lover, Ettamae
Harris, who they were going to find sooner or later. Ettamae lived in
Harlem, the neighborhood directly south of Washington Heights.

"What I'm gonna do," I told him as I stood up, "is call Ettamae,
tell her what happened. And what I'm hoping is you'll let me notify
her before you knock on her door."

"Hey, no problem," Knapp said. "Everybody knows me, knows
I'm a sensitive guy."

I walked into a dark empty apartment and went directly to the phone
in my office. I was determined to put it simply, get it over with:
"Ettamae, Caleb's dead." But when she picked up, when I heard her
sleepy, Southern voice mutter a querulous, "Helloooo," I couldn't
get past the first word.

"Ettamae . . ." Again, something in my chest, some previously
undiscovered organ, squeezed into a tight ball. My eyes filled, over-
flowed, my nose as well. I heard my own grunts—"Uh, uh,
uh"—from so great a distance I couldn't be sure I was making the
sound. Nor, for a moment, when Ettamae's wail exploded in my ear,
was I sure the cry hadn't come from my own throat.

Eventually, I managed to convey the two essential facts: dead and
murdered. Eventually, Ettamae decided that she would inform the
family. Eventually, I agreed to deal with the ME's office, to retrieve
the body after the autopsy, to have Caleb's butchered remains trans-
ported to an unnamed funeral home.

Then I was alone, sitting in my swivel chair, the smoke from a cigarette spiraling upward, from control into chaos. I heard a siren
outside my window, soft at first, then louder, more intrusive, as it
came up Third Avenue. Though it might easily be coming from a fire
engine or a police cruiser, I imagined it an ambulance, imagined
Caleb's body inside, still dressed, still bloody, in the final stage of its
journey from an uptown alley to the morgue a few blocks away.

I'm not sure how long I sat there, lighting one cigarette after
another, before the phone rang. I know I didn't retrieve the messages
on the answering machine, though I'm not sure why. Maybe I just
wanted a little space, a few minutes of zombie calm before I began
tilting at the windmill of New York violence.

The first call was from Phoebe Morris. Always the journalist, the consummate professional, she wanted my reaction to Caleb's death. I refused, told her I wasn't ready to make a statement, hung up when she persisted. The second, third, and fourth calls, which followed in quick succession, were from various television and print journalists whose names and affiliations were forgotten before they were off the line.

The fifth call, from Elizado Guzman, the only one I'd been expecting, was the only one that shocked me. I remember coming up out of the chair, pulling the phone off the table, being seized by a hatred so pure as to be actually cleansing.

Twenty

"**H**ey, *Señor* Kaplan, where you been? I'm tryin' ta contac' you all fuckin' night." His voice was actually gleeful, as if he'd pulled off a great practical joke. "You shouldn' be keepin' so late hours when you gotta work tomorrow. It's gonna fuck you up."

I watched the red light on the answering machine blink for a minute, watched the spools as they pulled tape across the heads, finally asked, "Why did you do it, Elizado? I thought we had a deal."

"You know, *Señor* Kaplan," he responded without hesitation, "I was also thinkin' tha' same shit. Tha's why I'm takin' it so hard when your peoples come up here messin' in my business. Hey, *maricon*, tha' was no part'a no deal."

I pulled the phone away from my ear, took a deep breath. It was the basic lie, the one I'd been hearing on the lips of my criminal clients for most of my career. Though it had any number of variants, the lie always supported the same conclusions: don't blame me; it wasn't my fault. And I'm not sorry, either.

"Where are you, man? I don' hear you."

I put the phone to my ear, said, "Tell me what you want."

"You secretary, *Señor* Kaplan, she agree to hang with us 'til you pay up your debt." He hesitated briefly. "Course, I'm no sayin' eza-ckly where she is. But she is definitely havin' a good time."

"Can I speak to her?" I was consciously avoiding the use of Julie's name, was afraid of another breakdown.

"Oh, man, why you always makin' troubles?"

"If I don't speak to her, how do I know she's alive?"

"I think wha' you gotta worry about, man, is keepin' you*self* alive. I'm gonna call you up in your office at six o'clock tomorrow night, see how you doin'. Meantimes, have a nice day."

"Elizado, if I don't speak to her, you can take your threats and stick them up your ass. *Comprende*?"

I hung up, waited for him to call back. When he didn't, I lit a cig-arette, dug the Slipper's number out of my Rolodex. Benny Levine was there, of course, still conducting business despite his pending indictment. He listened to my story, muttering, "No shit, no shit," as I went along. When I finished, he said, "See what I told ya? About these guys bein' animals? I had a meet set up for the day after tomor-row, but this fuckin' spic, he couldn't wait forty-eight hours."

I cut him off before he could work up a head of steam, dragged him back to the problem at hand. If I could somehow satisfy Guzman, Julie might still be saved. "What I need now is money. A loan, at the usual rates."

"How much?"

"A hundred thousand, Benny. Between that and what I have in the bank, I can swing it." I didn't add, If Julie's still alive. I kept that one to myself.

"I'll make a few calls, see what's what, get back to you in the morning," he finally said. "But don't be expectin' no miracles."

I remember falling asleep that night, though I don't recall when. Only that I woke up in a chair in Julie's room, the window was open slightly and a pair of light green curtains were fluttering in a very cold breeze. Outside, the pre-dawn sky was pale gray and flat, as if somebody had pressed a sheet of tin across the window frame. The net effect was cinematic ghostly, and the insistent ring of my door-bell, in those first moments of consciousness, seemed like the wail of a lost spirit.

I opened the door to find Phoebe Morris standing in the hallway.

She was carrying New York's three tabloids beneath her arm and she offered them to me without saying a word. I accepted her gift, thanked her, then closed the door in her face. To her credit, she didn't ring the bell again.

At ten o'clock, Priscilla called from the bowels of the Rose Singer Jail on Rikers Island to offer condolences. We were, the both of us, constrained, knowing the DOC might well be monitoring the call. I think she wanted to tell me that it wasn't her fault, but I refused to respond to her hints. Instead, I told her I'd be up to see her in a couple of days, that her defense would go forward, was going forward even as we spoke.

After I hung up, I went into the kitchen, made a pot of coffee, sat down at the table with a pad and pencil. An hour later, I'd compiled a list that raised as many questions as it answered:

1. Priscilla chooses a lawyer she has to pay instead of the free lawyer offered by the Women's Council.
2. Priscilla has no money to pay this lawyer, and her mother, who has resources, refuses to finance a serious defense.
3. Priscilla's apartment is burglarized.
4. Priscilla takes protective custody.
5. Thelma disappears.
6. Sid is threatened.
7. Caleb dies.

Beneath this list (and a mass of cross-outs) I'd written a series of questions. Why was there cocaine in the apartment when the cops arrived? How advanced was Byron's liver disease at the time he was killed? Why is Priscilla so confident? What does it mean to be crushed? What does it mean to be a prisoner? How does helplessness actually feel? Can you be helpless and powerful at the same time?

As I said, my work created as many questions as it answered, questions that could only resolve themselves over time and with a great effort. Still, I knew, even as I listened to Benny Levine's voice on the phone, that I was now obligated to seek a justice that went far beyond Elizado Guzman. And that in order to seek that justice, I would first have to define it.

"We gotta do a face-to-face, Sid," Benny explained. "The phone don't cut it for what you want."

I agreed to meet him at a Second Avenue coffee shop, hung up, and shrugged into my coat. The phone rang as I unlocked the door, but I ignored it. I wanted to run, to burn off the tension, calm my body the way I'd calmed my emotions. And I might actually have done it, just lumbered off down the street, if I hadn't met Phoebe Morris in the lobby.

"Please, Sid," she said, falling into step alongside me, "hear me out. It won't take a moment." She grabbed my arm, perhaps by way of precluding a negative response. "I'm not talking about now, okay? You say you can't talk and I accept that, but later on, after the trial, I want the whole story. Remember, I can help you here."

We were standing on the sidewalk just outside my building. It was bitterly cold, as it had been for the better part of a week. A relentless wind stung my cheeks, filled my eyes so that Phoebe's small features seemed about to melt.

"Start with this, Phoebe. Caleb Talbot's death was in no way related to his professional life. You have this from Sidney Kaplan and . . ." I hesitated, wiped my eyes with a coat sleeve, cocked a malicious grin. ". . . and from the cops. From a highly placed source within the NYPD."

Phoebe stepped away from me, her intensity dropping off in a series of tiny jerks. "And for me?" she asked.

"For you, Phoebe," I said, putting a hand on her shoulder, "the truth. When it's all over, you get the truth." I waited for another nod, then let my hand drop to my side. "And write that I was Caleb Talbot's partner, not his employer. That he was my friend, that I loved him, that I'll never stop missing him."

It was crowded inside the Athenian Coffee Shop on Second Avenue, crowded, overheated, and very noisy. For a moment, coming in from the cold, I was disoriented; I literally couldn't remember why I'd come. The restaurant was very bright, the Formica walls, counter, and tabletops reflecting the glare from a dozen hanging fixtures. I remember staring at the hostess, a heavy, middle-aged woman in a black dress that was too tight and too short for her years and her body, raising my hands to cup my half-frozen ears.

"One?" the woman repeated. She was holding a stack of menus, pressing them against her chest.

Before I could respond, I spotted Benny Levine half standing in a booth against the back wall. He was waving to me. "Hey, Sid, over here."

I nodded to the hostess, crossed the room, shook Benny's hand, dropped onto the bench seat like a sack of potatoes.

"You okay, Sid?" Benny's smile faded. "You think you're up for this?"

I took a deep breath, opened the menu lying on the table. "Lemme put it this way, Benny. After yesterday, I don't think you could surprise me."

Benny nodded, then sipped at his coffee. "The most I could get for you is twenty-five large, Sid. I asked around, but after what happened, nobody wants to take a chance on you. The twenty-five comes from me alone and it's all I could spare."

"You're sure?"

"Yeah, I'm sure. And even that's a strain."

I shrugged my acceptance. "I expect to hear from Guzman around six. You'll have it then?" With my forty-plus, I could now offer Guzman sixty-five thousand dollars. Maybe it would be enough.

"I'll be ready, Sid. Whenever you need me."

The tone of the incoming calls changed during that endless, empty afternoon. People who'd known Caleb began to phone with their condolences. I was caught off guard the first time, as if the solicitous voice on the other end of the line was driving a nail into Caleb's coffin. As if the muttered sentence, "I'm sorry," made Caleb somehow more dead.

Everybody wanted to know when and where the funeral would be held. The when, of course, depended on the medical examiner who could, according to law (and if he had the space), hold the body until the end of time. The second question was answered by Ettamae who called just before three. The family, she explained without preamble, was determined to bring Caleb back to Brantley, Alabama, to bury him alongside his parents. I was welcome to come down, join the mourners, even share in the post-burial feast, but the peculiar relationship Caleb and I had developed over the years did not confer rights of any kind.

"I spoke to Miss Vera Benton," Ettamae explained, "Caleb's first cousin. I told her about you, Caleb, and Julie. I don't think she got past the part about roommates."

"It's all right, Ettamae." I could see Caleb's family spread out on the wall as I spoke, see each and every smiling face, and the small white church in the background of so many of the photographs. "You going?"

"If I can scare up the money."

"That's no problem, Ettamae. Caleb had a little cash in a savings account. Not much, about five thousand dollars. He told me if anything happened to him, he wanted you to have it."

It was a lie, a small act of generosity. Caleb had no money, had, instead, a closet filled with designer clothing.

"Shouldn't that money go to his kin?"

"It was a joint account, Ettamae, with my name on it, so if you don't take the money, I don't think I'm gonna be able to resist temptation."

The calls tapered off as the afternoon progressed, finally stopped altogether about four. Six o'clock came and went, with no call from Guzman, then seven, then eight. I'd like to report that time slowed down, that the minutes and seconds attained the individuality of descending knives, but I believe what happened is that in some important way, my mind (not to mention my heart) went numb. I know, for sure, that I should at least have called Benny, asked him to stay in place, and I never considered doing so.

If I'd remembered to lock the outer door I might have sat that way forever, a dusty figure in a secondhand chair behind a secondhand desk. As it was, at ten, when Harold Knapp finally strolled into my office, I didn't jump, didn't move at all for a moment or two. I recall Knapp slowly unbuttoning his coat to reveal a neatly pressed gray suit, a fresh white shirt and a red tie. His eyes were bright now, the dark shadows beneath them faded to a smoky beige.

"I just come from the scene of a multiple," he told me. "Up in the Heights." He took the chair in front of my desk, fixed me with a familiar childish stare. "About a block from where your buddy got hit. Way I read it, the main target was a mutt by the name of Elizado Guzman, but they slaughtered everybody in the apartment. The kids, everybody."

He stopped abruptly, began to rummage through his pockets, finally produced a business card, one of mine, and tossed it on the desk. "I'm really not supposed to do this, being as the card's evidence and all, but I thought you might wanna take a look. I mean, it came out of Guzman's pocket, so it's gotta be important, right?"

I remember pulling myself up at that point, a long process that began somewhere in my bowels. "What do you want, Knapp?"

He responded, in typical cop fashion, with a question of his own. "How come you're in the office so late? You got an appointment?"

"The clock's ticking." I met and held his stare.

"Nine dead, Kaplan. Four males, three females, two children. I got a fucking right to ask what your card was doin' in Guzman's pocket."

"I don't know. And I don't want to know."

"You don't wanna know?" His voice jumped a full octave. "And I suppose you don't wanna know if Julia Gill was one of the victims?"

I think the question was supposed to shake me. After all, I hadn't told Knapp about Julie being missing. But there were a dozen ways he could've learned about Julie, a dozen friends and enemies who'd have been more than happy to tell him. "If she was, I'm sure you'll let me know."

Knapp stared at me for a moment, mouth slightly open, eyes empty of all expression. He loathed me, I was sure of it, but he wouldn't show his feelings. He wouldn't give me the satisfaction. "Counselor," he said as he picked up my business card and headed for the door, "I'll be in touch. Count on it."

I went for a walk before lunch on the following day, up to Macy's, where I killed a half hour fingering ties and sport coats, then walked directly back, as if afraid I was going to miss something. The phone was ringing when I unlocked the door of our Third Avenue apartment, but I don't remember hoping it was Julie, despite understanding that if she wasn't part of the slaughter, she might well be alive. It wasn't Julie, of course; it would never be Julie. The voice on the other end of the line belonged to Jay Harrison from the *Post*.

"On the record, Kaplan," he said. "What was your business card doing in the pocket of a murdered drug dealer? And what did Elizado Guzman have to do with Caleb Talbot's death?"

Too depleted to trade quips, even with an asshole like Jay Harrison, I hung up without answering. Not that I actually escaped. The red light on the answering machine in my office was flashing rapidly. I made an effort to count the calls, stopped after the eighth blink and simply pressed the replay button. Harrison was there, along with six or seven other reporters, including Phoebe Morris.

I remember sitting at my desk for a long time after the machine reset itself, staring at the now steady red light. And I remember thinking that if Julie was alive, she would have called, that I ought to take the phone off the hook, avoid the media until I prepared a useful comment. But I couldn't do it, not that night or any other night for weeks to come. Each time the phone rang—and it rang every fifteen minutes for the first few days after the massacre—I felt that pressure in my chest, like a fist pushing against my diaphragm, as I raised the phone to my ear.

The contradiction, looking back, is obvious. On the one hand, I declare myself to have been without hope. Yet whenever I heard the phone ring, I also heard Julie's voice. In defense, let me say that the head can decide whatever it wants, that the heart makes its own decisions. In its own good time.

I spent that night floating back and forth between Julie's and Caleb's bedrooms and my own room, packing my clothes in fits and starts. We had a convertible sofa in the office and that's where I was going to sleep until I was done with Priscilla Sweet. I would never again willingly enter our home.

As at my mother's house in Sheepshead Bay years before, I became a ghost in search of ghosts. I wandered from room to room, opening drawers, handling the most mundane items as if I'd discovered them in the tomb of an Egyptian pharaoh. As if Julie's brush and comb, her lipstick and powder, had a significance beyond all but the most intuitive understanding.

The phone rang again and again and again. Phoebe Morris called at one point and I told her, for the record, that Elizado Guzman had come into my office a few days before, that we'd discussed the possibility of future representation, that he must have taken my card at the time.

"Is Julie around?" Phoebe asked when I'd finished my statement.

"No."

Her voice softened. "Off the record, Sid. Are you expecting her?"

"Every minute."

Phoebe didn't press it, but I think she recognized the fact that I'd used *every* instead of *any*. "When it's over," she said before hanging up. "I want it all."

"When it's over," I answered, just as if I could imagine an ending, a conclusion, a line that could be drawn, much less crossed.

Twenty-one

A psychiatrist (a drinking buddy, not my therapist) named Milton Morton once told me that I ran on momentum. "You get up a head of steam, Sidney, get it all in motion. Then you have trouble stopping." This after an hour of my ramblings on how the corrupt inner nature of the criminal justice system mirrors the corrupt inner nature of humanity in general.

I thought of Milton as I set up housekeeping in my office the next morning. Milton had been a thoughtful man, calm and deliberate, traits that hadn't prevented his taking that midnight leap from his bedroom window one fine spring night. I remember going to his funeral, tossing a handful of earth onto his coffin, wondering if this was the fate of a man who'd lost his momentum, who'd rooted himself in reality, who'd given himself time to think.

The first thing I did after closing the door behind me was hang the photos of Caleb's and Magda's respective families on opposing walls of my inner office. Then I took the crumpled paper on which I'd written the list of Priscilla's actions and the questions those actions had raised, and taped it to my desk. Finally, I unpacked my clothes, hanging what could be hung in our smallish closet, leaving the rest in a suitcase which I slung on top of the filing cabinets.

Satisfied, and purposeful for the first time since Detective Knapp

entered my life, I went back to my desk and made a series of
reporter-punctuated phone calls. The first went to a customer rep at
NYNEX who instructed his computer to have calls made to my
apartment automatically forwarded to the office. The second went to
an employment agency called NowStar where I arranged to have a
legal secretary, a woman named Wendy Houseman, and a paralegal
named Janet Boroda, sent over on the following morning for an
interview. Then I called Rebecca Barthelme at her office, got put on
hold, and finally cut off when I took an incoming call from a
"Hardcopy" producer named Jason Weinstein. ("I'm talkin' bucks
here, Kaplan. Big bucks.") Ten minutes later, when I finally reached
Rebecca, she wasted no time getting to the heart of the matter.

"You need to talk to Priscilla, Sid. Before we discuss the case."

"Does that mean you've already been to see her?"

"Under the circumstances . . ."

I let her go without reacting, punched in the number of a PI
named Patrick Hogan. A retired cop, Hogan had been Caleb's partner for the six years preceding Caleb's abrupt resignation from the
NYPD. We'd had him to dinner maybe a year before, had watched
him pump down a pint of Dewars in the course of the evening. He
was a short man with a broad face dominated by a fleshy, drinker's
nose. His brown eyes were set extremely close together, giving him
the look of a startled bird even when he was so drunk he could
barely stand.

Hogan recognized my voice before I announced my name. I
arranged to meet him at seven in my office. To his credit, he didn't
push me, didn't beg for details, simply asked, "This about Caleb?"

I said it was, hung up, went to Caleb's desk, and spent the next
couple of hours rummaging through Julie's files. I was half expecting
Priscilla to call, wanted to make sure she'd receive me at Rikers.
When she didn't, I got up to leave and nearly tripped over a large
unmarked box. Curious, I opened it and found the police reports
Judge Delaney had ordered Carlo to deliver.

I had to think a minute to place the date of Delaney's ultimatum:
Friday, February 15, less than a week before.

Two hours later, after fighting my way through an enormous traffic jam caused by a misplaced tractor-trailer wedged beneath an
overpass on the Grand Central Parkway, I walked into an attorney-

client room to find Priscilla already seated. Without greeting her, I took out a pack of cigarettes and tossed them on the table, waited patiently while she shook one out, lit it up.

"Sid . . ."

I turned my back, walked to the window behind my client, stared at the corrections officer on his stool. He was a skinny man with a large red boil near the corner of his left eye. As I watched, he gently rotated the boil with a fingertip.

"Sid, I don't know how to tell you . . ." Again, Priscilla's voice trailed off.

"It wasn't your fault."

"I wish I felt like it wasn't my fault, that I didn't have blood on my hands."

The CO turned to look at me. His gaze, confused at first, became rapidly more challenging and I finally turned away. "We have a lot of work to do, Priscilla. There's no percentage in playing the blame game." I sat down, lit a cigarette, tossed the match on the floor.

"Look, Sid, under the circumstances . . ." She stopped, sent her dark hair flying with a shake of her head. "Shit, I don't know how to say this."

"Say what? That you don't want me to represent you? That you've decided to go with the Women's Council and Rebecca Barthelme, tap those deep, deep pockets? Or maybe that you're afraid I'll fuck it up deliberately, pay you back for Caleb and Julie?" I crossed my legs, straightened the crease on my trousers. "Because Julie's not coming back either. Julie's gone the way of Caleb."

Priscilla's face hardened as she sucked in a deep breath. "What I think, Sid, is that you're too upset, that you need time to recover, deal with your grief."

I smacked the tabletop with the palm of my hand. "Caleb and Julie, they're gone. Now and forever. Me, I've got a life to live, the quality of which depends almost entirely on the outcome of this case. You dump me, I'm right back in the sewer. On the other hand, if I defend you successfully . . ."

"I've already made my decision." She dropped the cigarette to the floor, stomped it out. "There's no going back."

"You sure about that?" When she didn't answer, I delivered the essential message: "You dump me, I'm gonna hold a press conference, let the world—and the cops—know exactly what happened to Caleb and Julie. I'll be punished for doing so, maybe even disbarred, but the way I see it, there'll be enough money in the book I'll write to make up for the loss of a dead-and-buried career. Meanwhile, Priscilla, what *you'll* do is spend the next twenty years in Bedford Hills."

She stared at me for a moment, then let her mouth expand into that familiar ironic smile. "You're a hardass mother-fucker, Sid. It's not what I expected."

"Tell me something," I persisted. "Did you steal Elizado Guzman's drug money?"

"No," she quickly replied, "I didn't."

"Then you're not to blame for what he did. As for Thelma and the lie she told? Well, what I did, last night, was put myself in her place. I pretended I was an elderly, middle-class woman living alone, that Berto Gomez showed up one day and threatened to grind my fingers into sausage. Would I have tried to push the problem onto somebody else? Without doubt. I would have done *anything* to get those men out of my house." I paused for a moment, rolled the cigarette between my thumb and forefinger, stared at the rising smoke, finally said, "I want you to call Rebecca, tell her I'm your lawyer, that either she accepts her role or I find somebody else. And what we, you and I, are going to do between now and your trial, is prepare your testimony. We're going to do it every afternoon for as long as they'll let us hold onto the room. Remember, words alone won't save you. The jury will read your body language, listen to the tone of your voice. If you want to walk away from all this, you're gonna have to be perfect."

She looked at me for a moment, her smile firmly in place, then nodded once. "My mother's coming home tomorrow. You might wanna go over there at some point, calm her down. Right now, she's afraid of you."

"Lemme see if I got this right, boyo. What you want me to do, the entire thing of it, is find Priscilla Sweet's pot of gold, assuming it exists?"

Pat Hogan raised his glass, held it between us for a moment. He was drinking Chivas (in deference, undoubtedly, to the fact that I was paying the bill), chugging doubles, one after the other. Beyond highlighting his already florid complexion, the booze seemed to have no effect on him, though it was definitely giving me the shakes. I kept hearing a little voice whisper, *So what's your excuse for staying sober now, asshole?*

"There's more to the story, of course." I squeezed a wedge of lemon into my Perrier. "But I don't want to tell you what it is. I don't want to give you that much power over my client."

"You don't trust me?" He sliced off a chunk of rare steak, worked it into a puddle of fat and blood at the bottom of his plate.

"There's no need to know here, Pat. Nothing in it for either one of us."

"There's still Caleb."

I put down my glass, let my shoulders settle against the back of the booth. Hogan seemed even more dissolute than when I'd last seen him. He was wearing a well-stained tweed jacket over a well-stained yellow shirt. His brown tie looked stiff enough to shatter.

"I trust you enough," I finally said, "to ask you to do whatever it takes. And to back up the request with cash. That gives you power over *me*." I paused long enough to get a nod of recognition. "Look, if that money exists, all I want is to know it. You, on the other hand, should feel free to put the cash in your pocket."

Hogan's mouth, virtually lipless, expanded into a shadowy grin. His close-set eyes drew together as if he'd suddenly gone cross-eyed. "And that's all ya want? To know?"

"Asked and answered." I sipped at my Perrier, set the glass on the table. "As for Caleb, in my opinion the newspapers have the facts pretty close to right. Which means those directly responsible are beyond punishment."

To his credit, Hogan didn't press me further. He took the envelope I passed across the table, jammed it into a pocket without looking inside. "To the wars," he said as he rose, ignoring the check. "You'll be hearing from me within a few days."

When I returned to the office, I found, along with the usual jumble of media come-ons, a message from Rebecca Barthelme on the answering machine requesting that I call her at home. I can honestly say that I didn't expect to hear Julie's voice on the tape, but that doesn't mean I wasn't listening for it. Or that I didn't take out my disappointment on my cocounsel.

"So what's it gonna be," I said after learning that Rebecca had spoken to Priscilla, "you in or out?"

"That's not fair," she responded. "I've acted in good faith."

"You went behind my back after my partner was killed."

"Not so. Priscilla called me in my office, asked me to come to Rikers." Her voice was angry, now. "Look, there's something you need to know. Priscilla never really dismissed the Council. She asked us to stay in touch, just in case things didn't work out with you. I remember Priscilla's words exactly: 'He used to be a great lawyer, but he used to be a drunk, too. I don't want to be left out in the cold.' "

I responded before the words sunk in. "You still haven't answered the basic question. You coming or going?"

After a few choice epithets, Rebecca admitted that neither she nor her organization was going anywhere. To do so would prejudice our client. "Besides," she concluded, "everything's falling into place. Byron Sweet was a brutal son-of-a-bitch and we're going to prove it."

I didn't argue the point, told her, instead, that I expected to ask for the earliest possible trial date and that our work schedule was going to change. From now on, we'd spend our mornings preparing friendly witnesses for cross-examination. "Time to get the folks ready for Carlo Buscetta. Let's bring them into the office, put them through a little basic training."

We went on for a few minutes, but I didn't pay close attention. Instead, as I hung up, I added a line to the list of numbered statements I'd taped to the surface of my desk: *8. Priscilla pays $5,000 to retain bankrupt ex-drunk while keeping well-heeled, pro bono counsel in reserve.*

I managed to work until midnight before my concentration gave out. With no hope of sleep, I put on my coat and hat, jammed my .32 into my pocket, and went for a walk. I don't remember having any specific destination, no goal more complex than exhaustion. It was very cold outside, and Union Square was deserted. Above the soft puddles of orange light thrown by the streetlamps, the bare branches of a dozen oaks and maples cut the skyline into small, sharp fragments. Sheets of cardboard, the abandoned homes of the homeless, skidded over the grass, piled up against the empty benches. A small rat, jaws working furiously, stuck its narrow head over the rim of a trash basket as I walked by. It regarded me through round black eyes for a moment, then dove back into the garbage.

As I left the park and walked east along 17th Street, I felt the emotional mix that had driven me into the cold, the pain, the anger, the fear, begin to settle. I slid my right hand down into my coat pocket, circled the pistol's stock with my fingers, caressed the trigger as if stroking the throat of a kitten. The wind pushed between my shoulders, urged me forward, told me not to be afraid, that nothing more could be done to me. That I was free at last.

Twenty-two

Somewhere around eleven the next morning, while Janet Boroda, my new paralegal, read motions, and Wendy Houseman, my equally new secretary, explored the computer systems created by Julie, I opened the box of police reports sent over by Carlo Buscetta. The package included reports filed by the forensic unit, by Alfonso Rodriguez and Oliver Kapell, the two patrolmen who'd responded to Maybelle Higginbotham's 911 call, and by Detective Shawn McLearry who'd discovered the cocaine. The reports were in no particular order, the various pages mixed together as if they'd been shuffled as they came off the copier. The strategy on Buscetta's part may have been one of harassment; if so it backfired, because I was forced to examine each page carefully in order to reconstruct the entire sequence. In the course of that reconstruction, my attention was drawn to several pages, each bearing the signature and badge number of Patrolman Alfonso Rodriguez, that had obviously been copied from a small, spiral notebook.

One of the jobs assigned to the first officers responding to a homicide, after making sure the deceased is actually deceased and securing the scene, is the maintenance of a log. Theoretically, the names and ranks of individuals entering or leaving the scene are recorded in the log, along with the time of day. In actual practice, on the rare occasions when the log was included in discovery material supplied by the prosecution, I'd found it to be sloppily kept with personnel logged in, but not out, names badly misspelled or completely illegible, time of day left off altogether.

Patrolman Rodriguez's log, on the other hand, might have come out of an academy training manual. Not content with mere names, Rodriguez had recorded ranks and functions, badge or civilian identification numbers, time entering and leaving to the minute. All in a small, precise handwriting that could only have been taught by a ruler-wielding nun.

That precision was very good news for Priscilla Sweet because Rodriguez had logged Detectives Shawn McLearry and Boris Karansky onto the crime scene at 6:31 P.M., then back out at 6:53. According to McLearry's report, on the other hand, he and his partner, on their initial entry, had checked Byron for a pulse, walked through the apartment in search of other victims or perpetrators (discovering the cocaine in the process), then exited immediately. Even by the most generous estimate, the detectives' initial, warrantless search should not have taken more than five minutes. McLearry and Karansky had been inside for twenty-two.

I took that information to Rikers Island and Priscilla Sweet, offered it as a prelude to our regular work session. Priscilla had come out of protective custody the day before, and seemed in decent, if subdued, spirits. I recall her gaze as frank, but not challenging, her customary smile as absent.

"The questions I'm gonna put to Judge Delaney go something like this," I concluded. "If the cocaine was in plain view, why didn't Rodriguez find it when he went through the apartment? If all McLearry and Karansky did was look for other victims, why did they spend twenty-two minutes inside?" I stopped to light a cigarette. "What I might do, if Delaney allows it, is put on a little demonstration, maybe time a cursory search of the courtroom and the judge's chambers, see how long it actually takes." I tossed the match on the floor, dropped the pack on the table. "If I convincingly demonstrate that McLearry's a liar, Delaney might exclude the cocaine."

"Might?" Priscilla ran her tongue across her front teeth. "If you prove the bastards are lying, how can he do anything else?"

I allowed myself a quick smile, but kept my voice even. "It's a law and order age. All those reporters in the gallery, everybody who reads or watches those reporters? Let's just say the body politic doesn't care for technicalities. The public may accept your defense, but they want to hear it, so judges mostly rule for the prosecution and let the Appellate Court reverse." I got up suddenly and turned away. Caleb had first posed the question: why hadn't Priscilla gotten rid of the cocaine before the cops arrived? The obvious answer was that she'd wanted the drug to be found, that it made the initial lie she'd told Elizado Guzman, the one about the cops booking just enough cocaine to make it look good while stealing the rest, believable. And that was true whether she'd left it locked in the trunk, or out where the cops were sure to find it.

"We do have one thing going for us," I said, my face to the wall. "Delaney needn't fear the wrath of the voting public, because he's about to retire. It all depends on how he wants to be remembered, and what I'm hoping is that he's contrary enough to exit with a raised finger."

In the days that followed, I settled into a routine that if not actually comforting, was at least endurable. I spent the mornings with Rebecca Barthelme, preparing witnesses, the afternoons at Rikers Island with Priscilla, my nights roaming the island of Manhattan in a fruitless search for an unambiguous fact. On Tuesday afternoon, I met Carlo Buscetta in Delaney's chambers, received a manila envelope stuffed with various technical reports. I didn't read them immediately, because Carlo, a malicious grin bisecting his hatchet-thin face, then introduced me to his newly appointed cocounsel, a black ADA named Isaiah Hazleton. I'd been up against Hazleton before, knew him to be quiet and competent, knew also that he had not been chosen for his attitude or his ability. Carlo had decided to play the race card, a fact his triumphant smirk made abundantly clear.

Judge Delaney had a surprise of his own. In response to my request for the earliest possible trial date, he announced, "April Fools Day seems appropriate. I'll hear motions, then we'll proceed directly to trial."

"April 1 is fine by me," I told Delaney before informing him that

I expected to present a dozen witnesses to a pattern of physical abuse stretching back ten years. Carlo protested on the grounds of relevance, announced that he would file motions to exclude such testimony. I promised to respond in a timely fashion.

All very predictable. Carlo knew he would lose on this issue, but he had to go forward. If he got lucky, Judge Delaney might limit the scope of the testimony, but since I didn't intend to document Byron's violence in mind-numbing detail, I wasn't particularly worried about it.

Outside, in the hallway, as Carlo sped off to make an appearance in another courtroom, I again shook Isaiah Hazleton's hand. "You don't look real happy, Isaiah. That because it's been ten years since you had to sit in the second chair?"

Hazleton was a handsome man, tall and powerfully built, with a pair of liquid brown eyes that would have been more appropriate on a social worker. He raised those eyes to the ceiling, laid his hand over his heart. "Sacrifices must be made," he intoned. "Sacrifices for which there will be an eventual reward."

"Only if you win," I said as I turned away. "If you lose, you join Carlo in the toilet."

"Thank you for sharing that, Sid," he called to my retreating back. "And please try not to weep as you read 'em."

I puzzled over his last remark until I got to the waiting area at Rikers Island and examined the forensic material handed to me by Carlo. I remember glancing at the autopsy results, discovering no surprises, then jumping to a serology report from Mount Livmore Technical Laboratories. An examination of Byron's blood established both that he was extremely drunk (blood alcohol level: .42, as predicted) and that he'd been using cocaine at the time of his death, also no surprise.

I made a mental note to fax the autopsy results to Kim Park that evening, then finally got to the document that inspired Isaiah's parting comment. According to the NYPD's forensic lab, a print of my client's right thumb had been found in two places: on the gun, just below the cylinder, and on the side of an unspent cartridge within the cylinder.

Priscilla was brought down a few minutes later, but I didn't confront her until I was ready to leave. Then, as I packed my bags, I said (just as if I hadn't demanded that she craft her story to meet the legal definition of self-defense), "You should have told me, Priscilla, you should have told me about loading the gun."

"It was Byron's gun," she said, her voice dropping away toward the end, wary now.

"It was an unregistered revolver found in an apartment leased in your name. That's presumptive evidence that you possessed it. And the fact that your fingerprint appears on a bullet found *inside* the chamber . . ." I was tempted to produce a smirk worthy of Carlo Buscetta, but settled for a distasteful sniff. "The question that arises, Priscilla, is how, if you were in immediate fear of your life, you found time to load the gun?" I smiled. "Just something else to think about. I'm sure we'll get past it."

Two days later, I was on my way to Caleb's burial, flying tourist class to a tiny airport outside Brantley, Alabama. The trip was actually torturous, with a stopover in Raleigh-Durham, and a change in Mobile to a plane so small it might have been launched with a rubber band. It was close to eleven at night when I finally reached the Paradise Motel, the only motel in the area rated by the AAA. At the time, I feared that I'd walk into a hot sheet hotel, be plagued with screeching bedsprings and groans of illicit ecstasy. Instead, quotations from the Christian bible adorned virtually every surface, from the office door to the pillow on my bed.

Sometime after dawn—I remember the drapes across the window edged in pale orange light—I woke up to find myself crying. I'd been dreaming of Julie, that she was in terrible trouble and that it was my fault. I couldn't recall the details of the dream and I couldn't stop crying, either. A sorrow as pure and grim as the pale shoots rising from the black Alabama soil enveloped me. My chest tightened again, until I was sipping at the air like an asthmatic at a cat show. For a very long time, I couldn't formulate a coherent thought. Instead, ideas and images whirled through my consciousness like swarming bees.

I don't know how long I remained in that state. When I slowly came back to myself, the light behind the drapes was sharp and clear. I was sitting on the floor with my back pressed up against the foot of the bed, my arms wrapped across my chest. On one level, I knew it was time to move, to get into the shower, pull myself together; and if it was simply a matter of attending Caleb's funeral, I might have done so.

Priscilla's image wandered into my consciousness; she was smiling that tight, ironic smile, the one that claimed a special knowledge, a knowledge which you could not share, which you could barely comprehend. I remember holding that image, clinging to it, my face covered with a mix of tears and snot. Long ago, my mother had written DEATH MAKES FREE at the end of her journal. But Caleb, lying in his coffin, and Julie, for whom I held out no hope, put the lie to that declaration. Magda had been looking for an excuse; she'd hoped to justify her life, as if she'd actually chosen it. And what I understood, sitting on the floor in Room 208 of the Paradise Motel, was that despite my self-created, day-to-day frenzy, I was trapped in a state close to paralysis. And no jury verdict could free me.

Twenty-three

I arrived at the home of Miss Minerva Talbot, Caleb's great-aunt and the family matriarch, at ten o'clock. Caleb's body was laid out in the parlor, but I didn't go in right away. Instead, I agreed to a second breakfast, sat in the kitchen while Minerva mixed pancake batter, poured out coffee and orange juice, dropped spoonfuls of batter into a cast iron skillet. We were alone when she started, but relatives began to drift in as we spoke. They entered without knocking, men, women, and children, pushing through the back door, calling out familiar greetings. The adults shook my hand politely, the younger children simply stared.

Most of them, I assume, knew little or nothing of my relationship with Caleb; they seemed surprised, perhaps even impressed, that I'd made the journey. Minerva, on the other hand, had assumed the role of family confidant after Caleb's parents died. A very small, very old lady, she cocked a wooden spoon in my direction as she spoke of the decade she'd spent in New York.

It wasn't until Ettamae Harris arrived, just before eleven, that I found the courage to approach the open coffin. Jews don't look at their dead. The most orthodox wrap the body in a shroud, secure the coffin lid with wooden pegs, drop the box into the ground within twenty-four hours. But even those Jews like myself, whose Jewish identity is wholly tribal, keep the coffin closed. Perhaps that's because we came late to the idea of an afterlife, that prior to the beginning of the common era, death promised little more to the Hebrew people than rot and corruption.

The upshot was that, despite having been to Christian funerals before, I couldn't bring myself to look down on Caleb's face. And not because I feared collapse. The truth of it, which I understood at the time, was that I was temporarily cried out, that the emotion which kept my eyes glued to a spray of flowers mounted on a wire stand just behind the coffin was much closer to dread than sorrow.

I remember Ettamae dropping to her knees, folding gloved hands, starting to pray. I remember that clearly, but the rest of the day returns to me only in small fragments. At noon, four men heaved the coffin from the rolling platform on which it rested to a waiting hearse. A long train of cars followed the hearse as it made its way to the First Church of Christ, Pentecostal. Fourth in line, I rode next to a pair of restless children in the back seat of a green Buick. The service was long and very emotional, the choir well rehearsed, yet it was obvious that Reverend Powell had never met Caleb Talbot.

By six o'clock, I was strapped into a tiny seat in a tiny airplane. We were off the ground, banking away from Brantley and toward Mobile. Ettamae was sitting beside me, her cheeks wet.

"Why'd Caleb go up there, Sid?" she asked without preamble.

"Then you know about it?" I returned. "He told you about Priscilla and Guzman?"

"Yes, he did. And I was gonna tell the police, but I was afraid about Julie. Then Guzman got himself killed, so I just figured it didn't matter."

The skin of the plane was vibrating beneath my feet, the wing outside my window flapping wildly. Lightning flashed on the horizon. Ordinarily, I would have been terrified.

"To answer your question, Ettamae, I don't know why Caleb and Julie went up to Washington Heights. Without doubt, I told them not to go. And when I left the office that afternoon, I was certain they'd stay put."

She nodded once, then rummaged in her bag for a tissue. "Caleb," she finally said, "he didn't ever listen. That was his biggest problem. He always thought he knew exactly what to do."

It took us six grueling hours to make New York, hours passed mostly in silence. I think, by the time we touched down at La Guardia, Ettamae was as numb as I was. She'd stopped crying somewhere outside of Raleigh-Durham, had taken a compact from her purse, repaired her makeup, accepted a drink from a concerned flight attendant. As we collected our luggage from the overhead rack, we promised to stay in touch, a promise neither of us expected to keep. I was looking forward to a quick ride back to my office, a shower in the tiny bathroom stall. Maybe I would even sleep.

Those plans evaporated a few minutes later when I caught sight of Sergeant Harold Knapp and his partner, Detective Brown, standing a few yards from the exit ramp. Knapp straightened, waved me over.

"Not you, Mrs. Harris," he said after explaining that he'd gotten my schedule from Rebecca Barthelme. "I need to speak with the counselor."

Ettamae looked at me for a moment, then, after a parting nod, drifted off.

"I guess this must be important, Knapp," I said, "because you brought your dog along."

Neither Brown nor his partner responded to the taunt, though Knapp took a moment before saying, "I think we found your girlfriend in the river. You wanna ride over to the morgue, take a peek?"

I should have seen it coming, of course, should have read the message in his flat smile, his empty stare. As it was, I stood there, speechless.

"Sure," Brown said, "take a ride with us, save the cab fare. You like to save money, don't ya?"

Knapp jumped in as if reading from a script. "We're not sayin' you gotta do it, counselor. Only thing, if we can't make an identification, the city's most likely gonna dump her in an unmarked grave."

Instead of leading me down into the basement when we arrived at the morgue on First Avenue, Knapp and Brown took me to a small office on the second floor where I found two cops waiting. Knapp introduced them as Detectives Fisher and Brinkmann. "They're workin' the Guzman case," he explained, "and they were hopin' to

ask you a few questions. Meanwhile, Brown and me'll go downstairs, see if the body's ready to view."

Fisher did most of the talking. Like his partner, he was middle-
aged, overweight, and rapidly balding.

"Looks like you're famous," he began, offering me a copy of
Newsday.

I grunted, remembering a time when I'd welcomed fame, then
quickly scanned the article. The reporter had it, from a trusted
source within the NYPD as well as several drug dealers who wished
to remain anonymous, that Elizado Guzman had been the primary
cocaine supplier to Byron and Priscilla Sweet.

"Whatta ya think, Mr. Kaplan?" Fisher asked when I returned the
paper. "Think they got it right?" He had a gray mustache that bris-
tled above a mouth that turned down at the corners, making him
look, to me at that moment, like a depressed walrus.

"Ask me a question that isn't actually stupid," I said. "I've been
traveling for the last six hours and I don't have the energy for
stupid."

Fisher and Brinkmann exchanged a significant cop look, then
Fisher said, "You told Knapp you didn't know how Guzman got
your business card. Then you told a reporter that Guzman was a
client. Which is it?"

"The latter."

"Then why'd you tell Knapp . . ."

"I'm not gonna stand for an interrogation, Fisher. I'm much too
tired."

He nodded, scratched the back of his head. "Did Guzman tell you
that he was in trouble?"

"What Guzman told me falls under the heading of attorney-client
privilege."

"Not if he's dead. If he's dead, he has no right to privacy."

I took off my coat, folded it over my arm, finally sat down. "Do
you really think he named his murderers, maybe left me a sealed
envelope to be handed over in the event of his death?"

That brought an actual smile. "You mean he didn't?"

"Afraid not. But I will say this: What you and your partner oughta be looking for is who Guzman bought drugs *from*, not who he

sold them *to*. Priscilla Sweet, incidentally, has an alibi for the time of the murders."

"That doesn't mean she didn't order it done."

"Now we're back to stupid."

Knapp returned a few minutes later. "All ready," he announced. When I didn't move, he looked disappointed. "You wanna come downstairs or not?" he asked.

"What happened to the Polaroids?"

He shrugged, waited for me to get up, then led me to a small room in the basement. "Thing is," he said as he pulled down the sheet, "there was a whole lotta ice on the river and Julia got a little beat up. You might have to look close to make an identification."

The figure beneath the sheet, except for a few shreds of skin, had no face. Bits of the scalp remained, as did the lobe of one ear and both eyes, but the bones and cartilage of the nose were completely torn away.

"See, that part of the river has a hell of a current to it, so the ice formed in blocks instead of a solid sheet. Gill was trapped a few inches below the water and what I figure is that her head was a perfect target. For the ice, I mean."

Something hardened inside me at that moment. I heard a door slam, understood it as the end of my fear, the end of any life I might actually want to live. The game would simply play itself out; the game would carry me along like a block of ice on a polluted river. There was no way out.

"I don't know who this is," I said without turning away. "It could be anybody."

"That's what I thought the first time I saw her. But then I found this locket." He waited until I was facing him. "Right here, on the back, it says, *FROM SID WITH LOVE.*"

Twenty-four

I'm not sure what Knapp was trying to accomplish. Maybe it was simple payback. I had information that might be useful, but wouldn't give it up. He couldn't force me to come clean, but he could deliver enough pain to make sure I didn't forget him. If that was the case, then he got his wish because, though I never saw Knapp again, neither he nor his pink-eyed partner, images of Julie lying in the morgue, sometimes distorted by dreams, continue to haunt me. I do know that a month later, Fisher and Brinkmann charged three Jamaicans, all members of a Brooklyn posse, with the Guzman homicides. The case drew a lot of attention because the Jamaicans, whose names I can no longer recall, were prosecuted under New York's death penalty statute. They were convicted of murder for hire after a typically contentious Bruce Cutler defense, but missed being part of history when the jury voted for life without parole instead of lethal injection.

In the days that followed my return to New York, I continued to plod along. The fingerprint evidence went by fax to Marilyn Tannhauser, an expert based in New Orleans, who responded within a few hours. The latent prints lifted from the murder weapon, she wrote, belonged to Priscilla Sweet and she, Marilyn, was not prepared to testify otherwise. Kim Park, to whom I faxed the autopsy and serology reports, was much more positive. If the prosecution, he told me by phone, wished to contend that Byron's .42 blood alcohol level precluded his offering a threat, Dr. Kim Park would be delighted to present a thorough, jury-convincing refutation. Especially in light of the fact that I was now prepared to cover his fee.

"One other thing," I said when he was through promoting himself. "The cirrhosis. Just how sick was Byron?"

"Without a liver transplant, I don't believe he would have lived until summer."

"Would his wife have known?"

"Without a doubt," Kim replied. "There would necessarily have been acute episodes. Why don't you check with his doctors?"

Rebecca Barthelme showed up on Sunday, stealing time from her family to present me with a new witness, a woman named Margaret D'Cassio. D'Cassio was important to us for a number of reasons, not the least of which that after a crisis of conscience, she'd sought us out. A college friend of Priscilla's, Margaret had not only been witness to Byron's abuse in the early years of their marriage, Byron had threatened to "kick her white ass up and down the block" when she attempted to interfere. That was enough for D'Cassio. A straight-arrow type who'd never taken drugs, she'd quickly declared her friend a lost cause and gotten on with her life.

"I've been carrying the guilt," she told me, "for all these years."

D'Cassio was a professor of Ancient Languages at New York University. She presented herself as a trim, immaculately groomed blond in a maroon skirt and matching bolero jacket over a starched white blouse. Her voice was deep and well modulated, her enunciation precise, as befitted a woman of her station. The jury would love her, especially because the violence she described was graphic and she'd taken the time to detail it in the journal she'd been keeping since childhood.

I carried that little victory to a dinner with Pat Hogan later that evening. Hogan had pulled Thelma's and Priscilla's credit records. Predictably, Priscilla's demonstrated a pattern of credit abuse, while Thelma's revealed only the information Julie had gotten on the day she strolled into our office.

"This was not unexpected," Hogan explained, "so I took it a step further. I got Thelma's bank and credit records." He waved a hand, shook his head. "Don't ask me how. I got 'em and what matters is that they show *bupkis*. You wanna go further, I got a friend who's got a friend at IRS. For a price, Sidney, I can get a check of safe deposit boxes. At least find out if Thelma's got one. Ditto for the daughter."

"A lot of people have lock boxes, Pat," I said. "What would it prove?"

"I thought about that," he admitted. "But a hundred and fifty large takes up a lot of space. You'd have to have a very big box, much bigger than the kind families use for the jewelry and the deed on the house. Which means if the mother's got the money, she probably took out the box recently. That would go for your client, too."

Hogan stopped at the approach of the waiter, drained his glass while our chile was served, finally signaled for a refill before sprinkling grated monterey jack over the red beans. "That kind of money," he said before plunging his soup spoon into the chile, "you gotta figure it's well hidden. If it was mine, I wouldn't put it anywhere the government might look. Not if I was figurin' to spend six months in Rikers waiting for trial."

Though I continued, over the next few weeks, to spend the mornings with my cocounsel, preparing witnesses, and the nights roaming the Lower East Side, the messages I gathered from those sources were decidedly mixed, the pea stubbornly elusive. Priscilla, on the other hand, if not exactly forthcoming, at least had the answers. And I'm certain she knew that I was looking for answers. Although our distinctly grounded sessions were anchored in the practical, in my charitable moments, I truly believed that Caleb and Julie had penetrated that blank facade, had gotten beneath it, reached into her heart. More likely, though, Priscilla's need for reassurance sprang from the fact that her own life was on the line. There was simply no way she could be sure I wouldn't betray her in the course of the trial.

Toward the end of the week following Caleb's funeral, Priscilla directly approached the question of absolution. I remember striding into the cubicle, tossing the customary pack of smokes on the table, then launching into a monologue.

"I've come up with a way to deal with the fingerprint and how it got on the bullet." I turned away from her, began to pace. The scenario I'd invented as I drove from Manhattan was slick enough to

excite my lawyerly instincts. The fact that it actually created the per-
jury it suborned, that I'd crossed a line, interested me not at all.

"Now, if I remember correctly, you told me the gun belonged to
Byron, that it was in the living room when you picked it up. I think
we both realize that's not gonna wash if you want the jury to believe
that you were in immediate fear of your life when you pulled the trigger. Remember, Byron's physical condition is in play here. He was
very, very drunk. If you claim, for instance, that the bullet fell out
when the cylinder popped open, that you picked it up and put it back
in the chamber, the prosecution will contend that Byron didn't attack
you before you reloaded because he was physically unable to do so."

I stopped with my back to Priscilla, traced a crack in the particle
board with a fingernail in need of cutting. In the past, I'd always
been fastidious and I couldn't help but wonder, as I listened to the
mope in the next cubicle lie to his attorney, what other small attach-
ments to ordinary life I'd surrendered. "For the last week, Priscilla,
we've been drifting away from a claim of pure self-defense." I turned
to face her. "We've been preparing a psychological defense. You did-
n't flee because you believed that Byron would come after you, that
he'd find you and kill you no matter where you went. And why not?
When you tried to run away, he came to your parents' home and
took you out by force. With Dr. Howe to back you up, it's a legitimate defense, even for a predicate felon. Or, it would be except for
one indisputable fact: your husband was terminally ill. His liver was
rotten and he was sick almost all the time. Even your own witnesses, Priscilla, the ones prepared to testify in your defense, tell me there
were times, even days, when Byron couldn't get out of bed.

"What prevented you from leaving, hiding for the six months it
would take your husband to die of natural causes? The jury's gonna
want to know and Carlo's gonna raise the question with every witness we call. You haven't told me whether Byron spent any time in
the emergency room or if he had a personal doctor, but Carlo will
have already pursued that angle. In any event, the autopsy results are
definitive. They've convinced my own expert."

Priscilla's gray eyes bore into mine. They remained fixed, even
when she tilted her chin up to exhale a stream of gray smoke.

"I think what we can do here is make a virtue of necessity," I continued. "Byron knew he was dying and he was determined to take

you with him. After he beat you that last time, as you lay in your own excrement, he told you that you would never again leave the apartment, that he was going to kill you, then kill himself.

"You spent two days in bed, trying to devise a means of escape. You thought, for instance, of climbing down the fire escape, but the window was covered with a locked grate and Byron had the key. You thought about waiting for Byron to go into the bathroom, then dashing out into the street, but the bedroom door was kept closed and the one time you opened it, Byron, after repeating his threat, again attacked you.

"Finally, Byron came into the bedroom, told you that your time was short. He'd been up for two days, drinking heavily, snorting cocaine every fifteen minutes to stay awake. His eyes were yellow and he was bent forward in pain. He seemed on the verge of collapse, but he was coherent enough to display that lit cigarette you told me about, to threaten you with a very slow, very painful death.

"He left then, for a final snort of coke, a last celebration before the final act. In desperation, without any real plan, you took the gun from a shelf in the bedroom closet and examined it carefully. Of course, you didn't know that revolvers don't have safeties, so the cylinder popped out when you pushed the lever and one of the bullets fell to the floor. You picked it up, reloaded, put on your clothes, went to confront Byron.

"When Byron saw you with the gun, he just laughed. That's when you knew there was no way out. You were trapped and your choices had narrowed to life or death. Then Byron started to come out of the chair and . . ." I pointed my finger at her, whispered, "Bang."

We stared at each other for a moment, then I sat down, lit a cigarette, sucked the smoke down into my lungs.

"That's nasty," Priscilla finally said. "That's very, very nasty." Her tone, as I read it, was admiring.

A few minutes later, we got down to our regular work. I wanted the jury to know something about the early phase of Byron's and Priscilla's relationship, the pre-drug, pre-violence days at Columbia. Priscilla, though she could understand why she needed to convince black jurors that she'd once been in love with her husband, was having a hard time. Her presentation was lifeless and unconvincing, her tone that of a bored child forced to recite.

We went at it for an hour, until Priscilla finally stopped me with a shake of her head. "I can't get it back," she insisted. "I can't get any of it back." Her eyes dropped to her folded hands. "There were no limits to my life, to what I could become. At least that's what I believed when I left my parents' home for Columbia. When I think about it now, I feel like a jerk. I feel like one of those cheap roses you buy at the fruit stands, the kind that fall over when you put them in water." She raised her head, fixed me with a pair of glistening gray eyes that reminded me of rain-streaked pavement. "What it's come down to is mere survival. I can't get beyond that, to actually want my future. Survival isn't something you want. It's like sleep; it has no promise."

She took another cigarette from the pack on the table, lit it quickly. "I've ruined too many lives. I'm responsible for Byron, for Caleb and Julie. When I look back, I can't think of a single individual whose life I made better. Not one."

As before (and as expected), I was completely unable to gauge Priscilla's sincerity. But I was sure the apparent emotion she displayed would impress the jury and I was about to tell her so when somebody at the other end of the corridor began to scream. The corrections officer outside our room hopped off his stool and ran off.

It was as if we'd been sucked into a vacuum, as if we'd stolen the privacy and now had to make use of it. I was standing at the time, leaning forward with my thighs against the edge of the table. As I continued to stare into Priscilla's gray eyes, I was seized by an urge to yank her up out of the seat, to press my mouth against hers, unzip her jumpsuit, run my hands across her body. She wouldn't resist, I was sure of it, but that wasn't the point. I knew it would be a descent into madness. And not the delusional world of the paranoid schizophrenic. There would be no voices to whisper in my ear; I would not conjure demons or angels from the empty air. Instead, I would achieve the perfect clarity of the psychopath, would seek no higher good than personal satisfaction: Priscilla's small breasts beneath my fingers, the slap of her teeth against my tongue, the nearly unbearable pleasure as I pressed between her legs.

I turned before I could act, took a step away from the table, then spun to face her. "Show me the scars again," I said. "The burns. Show me the burns and tell me again how you got them."

She smiled, then, her fingers rising to the zipper of her jumpsuit, sliding it down to her waist. "Byron thought I was skimming profits," she told me as she unhooked her bra. "He couldn't face the fact that we were doing so much coke there weren't any profits to skim." The raised weals between her breasts were white and smooth. They looked, to me at the moment, like the paired eyes of an insect. "What Byron would do, in the early days, is buy an ounce, throw in four or five grams of cut, calculate the profit if we sold it all. Then he'd pull out a gram, snort it, then pull out another. Most of the time he was so stoned he couldn't keep track and when the ounce was gone and we didn't have the money to buy another, he'd blame me."

"And you were completely innocent?"

"Not exactly, Sid. Remember, the profits were going up my nose, too."

Twenty-five

Later that afternoon, after a long soggy walk from the garage to my office, I sat down before a desk piled with notes and began to search for the name of the man who referred me to Priscilla Sweet. Though I'd been trying to remember his name since leaving Rikers, I could only recall that I'd neither recognized the individual when Priscilla first named him, nor been surprised by my failure. A good deal of my life had been lost in the fog of cocaine and alcohol that preceded my collapse, a fact I'd learned, of necessity, to accept. I did, however, recall being a lot more interested in Thelma Barrow's five thousand dollars, and Priscilla's publicity value, than in the identity of some nothing client I'd most likely fobbed off on a subordinate.

It was only as I sat in my car, watching the guard stationed on the Rikers Island side of the Hazen Street Bridge search my trunk, that I'd reviewed the question in the light of something Rebecca Barthelme had told me a week before. Rebecca had insisted that Priscilla, while refusing an offer of pro bono representation, had asked Rebecca (and the Women's Council) to stay close in case I didn't work out. At the time, I'd asked myself why Priscilla would choose me instead of the Women's Council with its deep pockets. The more pertinent question was why Priscilla had chosen me at all.

I was interrupted in my search twice. The first time by Pat Hogan who informed me that an IRS inquiry had produced no record of a safe deposit box in either Byron's, Priscilla's, or Thelma Barrow's name.

"Look, Sid," he concluded. "I paid a fortune to get the search done in a hurry. If you still wanna go forward, I'm gonna need a lot more cash."

I told him to come by later that night for a discussion of how much and what for, then hung up. A few minutes later, the phone rang and I picked it up to hear Thelma Barrow's thin voice offer a tentative, "Sid?"

For the next several minutes I listened to her alternately tell me how sorry she was for everything, and that she was still afraid of me. I told her not to worry. "It's done and we have to go on." The good news was that she wouldn't have to face me, at least not right away. "My co-counsel, Rebecca Barthelme, is preparing defense witnesses. You come in the day after tomorrow, in the morning. I'll make sure I'm somewhere else."

"Thank you, Sid. And I'm sorry. I'm so, so sorry."

Fifteen minutes later, I was kneeling before a filing cabinet stuffed with folders, looking for the records of a man named Peter Howard. The name, when I'd finally dug it out of my notes, had evoked no memories. I couldn't remember Howard at all and was on the verge of concluding that Priscilla had invented him, when I came upon his file half buried between Grabosky and Green.

Whatever relief I might have felt at verifying Howard's existence vanished when I read the paperwork. Five years before, Peter Howard, having been charged with the criminal sale of a controlled substance in the third degree, had retained the famous mob lawyer, Sidney Kaplan, to defend him. The prosecution, according to notes in my own handwriting, had offered an excellent deal: criminal sale in the fifth degree, a D felony. I'd advised my client to stand pat and we'd proceeded to a one-day trial after which a jury had taken all of fifteen minutes to find him guilty as charged.

Although I still couldn't remember Howard's face, I could, by then, clearly picture his back as a pair of court officers led him away. His back and the upraised finger he'd thrust in my direction.

Two days later, while Thelma prepared her testimony in my office, I drove out to the home of her next-door neighbor, Gennaro Cassadina, the only living witness to Priscilla's kidnapping besides Thelma. The last time I'd seen Cassadina, he'd approached me in a yellow slicker, an umbrella thrust above his nearly shaved skull, and bragged of his sexual prowess. I'd listened to his drunken rant for a moment, then decided that even sober he couldn't be trusted before a jury. Maybe, if I hadn't been able to verify the report Thelma gave to the cops at the 107th Precinct, I would have come back to Gennaro, tried to work with him. As it played out, I'd simply dismissed his testimony as irrelevant. Dismissed it without actually hearing it.

Now, motivated by the need to fill several hours before my afternoon session with Priscilla, I drove down 164th Street, parked my car in front of Cassadina's house, shouldered the door open. My expectations were decidedly low, but I do recall harboring some vague hope of being entertained.

"Yeah?" The woman who opened the door was close to fifty. Blond, heavy-boned, and devoid of makeup, she wore a man's white shirt, tails out, over faded jeans.

"My name is Sid Kaplan." I retrieved a card, handed it to her. "I'm an attorney and I'm looking for Gennaro Cassadina."

She held the card at arm's length while she read it. "You the lawyer for next door?" she finally asked.

"I'm Priscilla Sweet's attorney, yes."

"Well, better come on in." She held the door open for me, waited until I stepped inside and shucked my overcoat. "I'm Jenny Cassadina. My father somehow involved in this?"

"Maybe. According to Thelma Barrow, your father witnessed an incident about a year ago . . ."

"Lemme stop you there." She rolled her eyes toward the ceiling. "Right now, as we speak, I've got my father's act pretty cleaned up. But I'm tellin' you flat out, Mr. Kaplan, he doesn't remember a whole lot about the last couple of years."

She walked away from me, then, into the living room where her father sat in front of a gigantic television set. On the set, a very cute, very sexy young woman was urging viewers to leave AT&T for MCI. Before she could finish her appeal, Jenny Cassadina snapped the set off.

"Pop," she said, "this is Priscilla Sweet's lawyer. You know who Priscilla Sweet is? Your neighbor, Thelma Barrow's daughter?"

Gennaro had gained weight since I last saw him, his face swelling from skeletal to merely gaunt. His hair had been cut, too, and his face smoothly shaved. Beyond that, he looked absolutely miserable, an ex-drunk without the consolation of Alcoholics Anonymous.

"I'ma no dead yet," he declared.

His daughter looked at me, again rolled her eyes, then stalked into the kitchen.

"Fuckina bitch," he whispered to me once the kitchen door was safely closed. "You got a drink?"

"I don't drink, Mr. Cassadina. That's because I'm a drunk."

"Me, too," he admitted. "And I'ma no wanna die sober." His stick-thin legs were crossed at the knee; his hands, resting in his lap, washed each other relentlessly. "So, whatta ya doin' here?"

I told it as a story, setting time and place, beginning with Priscilla's unexpected arrival, ending with Byron dragging his wife across the lawn. "Now, according to Thelma Barrow, Mr. Cassadina, you were standing there when Byron came out of the house with Priscilla. You saw him force her into a car."

He continued to stare at me, as if he'd fallen asleep and forgotten to close his eyes.

"Yes? No?"

"I don' know. Maybe it could'a be. I can't say." His head waggled on its stalk of a neck, describing something between a nod and a shake.

"Do you remember any of it? Even vaguely?"

Now his head was definitely shaking. "But that don't mean it dinna happen. These'a days, my memory, she's soft as my dick."

The response, as far as I was concerned, was definitive. I got up, reached out to shake his hand. "Well, I had to try."

"This Byron, he's a fuckina spook, right?"

I ignored the slur, answered with a nod.

"Because it'sa kinda funny. See, Joseph, he no fuck around. One time, he take me into the house, show me thisa big gun. Then he say, 'That nigger mess with me, I'ma kill him.' "

Late that night, I rewrote the small list I'd taped to my desk, adding and revising as I went along, until I was satisfied with the result. The list now read as follows:

1. Thelma Barrow files a false report with the local cops.
2. Joe Barrow dies.
3. Priscilla kills Byron.
4. Priscilla leaves just enough cocaine in the apartment to support her claim (to Guzman) that the cops stole the bulk of the drugs.
5. Priscilla has her mother pay $5,000 to retain Sidney Kaplan, a lawyer she believes to be an incompetent drunk, while keeping a well-heeled, pro bono attorney in reserve.
6. Priscilla's apartment is burglarized.
7. Priscilla takes protective custody.
8. Thelma tells Guzman that she gave his money to Sid Kaplan.
9. Thelma disappears.
10. Sid is threatened.
11. Caleb dies.
12. Julie dies.

As I taped the new list to my desk, a single question began to pound like a woodpecker against the side of a rotting oak. If I, as prosecutor, judge, and sole juror, should find that Priscilla Sweet caused the deaths of Caleb Talbot and Julie Gill, what, if anything, was I prepared to do about it?

Twenty-six

Carlo and I went head to head over the following two weeks in a series of bitter pre-trial conferences, Carlo proving himself as tenacious as ever. Arguing that any evidence of Byron's abuse would be inflammatory, he fought to limit testimony to the incident that immediately preceded the killing, presenting written motions in support of his verbal arguments. Delaney shot Carlo down, point by point, as he was bound to do, but Carlo, unfazed, merely shifted his line of attack.

"If there's to be no limit to the defendant's 'abuse excuse,' " he told Delaney, "then there should be no limit to the state's right to present evidence of the defendant's real motive. What we have here, Judge, is a falling out between drug dealers."

As he went on, it became clear that Carlo not only wanted to present the jury with Priscilla's felonious past, he wanted to present witnesses to whom Byron had complained about Priscilla's skimming of the profits. I argued that these conversations were both hearsay and irrelevant. Priscilla Sweet, after all, hadn't been charged with stealing her husband's money. She'd been charged with killing him.

I don't know if Carlo thought he could prevail on any of these points, but what struck me, as we argued, was that despite everything I still wanted to win. I wanted to crush Carlo Buscetta and the

State of New York, and nothing could change that, not even the loss of the two people I loved most in the world. The fact, even stated baldly, didn't mean that I'd forgotten Caleb and Julie in the intervening month. Or even that I was trying to forget. I still hadn't returned to the apartment we'd shared and I didn't intend to return. I still missed them terribly, still heard Julie's voice from time to time, still glimpsed Caleb in the subway, on the streets, in crowded restaurants. Nevertheless, without doubt, I wanted to win.

Carlo waited until the last day to make his final move, his goal, undoubtedly, to give me as little time to prepare as possible. "While incarcerated," he told Judge Delaney, "at the Rose Singer Jail on Rikers Island, the defendant made certain damaging admissions relating to her motive for committing this crime. We intend to present this witness in our case in chief."

"Great," I responded, "the defense employs medical and police reports to show motive, the prosecution employs felons and snitches."

Delaney nodded once, then shrugged. He could not prevent the jailhouse rat from testifying. If he tried to exclude her, the credibility of witnesses being a problem for the jury, Buscetta would simply take the ruling to the Appellate Court and obtain a reversal.

"Any more business?" he asked, glaring at each of us in turn. "Are we ready at last?"

It was Friday, March 29. The trial was scheduled to begin on Monday, April 1, with a Mapp Hearing on my own motion to exclude evidence seized at Priscilla's apartment.

"The state is ready," Carlo replied.

I nodded agreement. "Yes, your Honor, the defense is ready."

"You won on every point," Priscilla told me that afternoon in Delaney's chambers. "You were simply amazing."

I'd asked for and gotten permission to confer with my client for ten minutes before she was taken back to Rikers Island. Ten minutes of freedom that had apparently gone to her head.

"The only victory here is the glimpse Carlo gave us of his case." I didn't bother to explain. We both knew I was talking about the snitch testimony. "By the way, do you know a woman named Margo Robertson?"

Beyond lighting a cigarette, Priscilla showed no reaction to the sudden change of subject. "Sure, I know her."

"She's a friend of yours, right? Not Byron's. And she was also a customer?"

Priscilla stared at the match in her hand for a moment, then tossed it next to a well-chewed cigar butt in Judge Delaney's ashtray. "Why don't you just cut to the bottom line, Sid."

"Margo's gonna testify against you. That's what I hear on the Lower East Side. She took a bad bust a couple of weeks ago and she wants somebody else to do her time."

"Do you know what she's going to say?"

"What I think she'll say is that you were stealing from Byron and he knew it and you killed him so you wouldn't have to give the money back."

"Mutt versus mutt? Is that the way of it, Sid?"

"That's right. A swearing contest between villains. Except that we have all the physical evidence on our side."

I had dinner in the office that night, a working dinner with Rebecca and my paralegal, Janet Boroda, during which we studied elaborate questionnaires filled out by a pool of two hundred prospective jurors. Janet Boroda was very young, very intelligent, and eager to a fault. She and Rebecca debated the minutiae while I, apart from answering direct questions, observed in silence. Aside from eliminating obviously prejudiced jurors (which Delaney would do in any event), my only goal was to put genuine New Yorkers on the panel. I wanted individuals who'd grown up in the city and I didn't give a damn for their religion, race, or gender. I'd treated hundreds of jurors to post-trial dinners, questioning them closely, and what I'd discovered (and later used to my advantage) was a general anger at the disruption to their lives caused by a long trial. They resented any delay, from overlong opening and closing statements to nitpicking technical objections and frequent bench conferences. Many of them had attempted to avoid jury duty altogether and wanted only to put it behind them; others had walked naively into the pit. In either case, they were looking for someone to blame, the judge, the prosecution, the defense, anybody.

Carlo Buscetta was a perfect candidate for that blame. Though I knew he'd be compulsively thorough in his tight-ass way, and absolutely ruthless, I didn't believe he could disguise his ugly personality for the length of a major trial. Especially if I, while appearing to move the case forward, provoked him by asking questions to which he could make technical objections.

I slept well that night, dropping off almost as soon as my head found the pillow, and by six the following morning, as the sun rose over the projects along the East River, I was up and working. Now that the public end of the battle was about to begin, I experienced a familiar mix of rising tension and narrowed concentration. The courtroom was the arena, the boxing ring; the outside world existed only to witness the combat.

The phone calls started before seven, continued one every ten minutes until my secretary, Wendy Houseman, showed up at eight and I stopped keeping track. By then, I'd managed to take a shower and don my armor, a conservatively cut blue suit over a white shirt and a muted red tie. I'd even found time, between phone calls, to clip the hair in my nose and ears, tuck a white handkerchief into my breast pocket.

"You look beautiful, Sid," Wendy decided after a careful inspection. "A lawyer looks that good, he can't lose."

"Yeah, well we always have that edge on the prosecutors. They don't get paid enough to afford a decent wardrobe."

I left her with instructions to call every defense witness on a list compiled by Rebecca, let them know it was time to get ready, that they'd be called upon to testify in a week or so. "Anybody you can't locate," I said as I shrugged into my coat, "I wanna know about it. Ditto for anybody who seems reluctant."

It was still a few minutes short of nine o'clock when I arrived at the Criminal Court Building, but long lines had already formed outside both Centre Street entrances. Searches were mandatory for all visitors, including the press. Pockets had to be emptied, bags and briefcases examined; every individual walked through a metal detector. The process was slow and demeaning, as it was undoubtedly meant to be.

As an officer of the court, I, on the other hand, was entitled to stroll through a side door and go my way unmolested. Or, I would have been if a bank of reporters hadn't had the doorway blocked. They shouted questions, thrust microphones and video cameras in my face. In another time, with another client, I would have made a carefully prepared speech. As it was, I limited myself to a terse declaration of my client's innocence as I forced my way through.

Inside, I was met by two burly court officers. Though court officers, like most other cops, have little use for defense attorneys, this pair greeted me respectfully.

"We're your escort," the older of the two, Sergeant Mason according to his name tag, explained. "In case you want to avoid the reporters." When I looked over my shoulder at the mob outside the building, he continued. "There's more upstairs, but we've established a press area on the south side of the building, so if you take the north elevators you could get to the courtroom without speaking to them."

I nodded my thanks, followed the pair up to Trial Part 31 on the eleventh floor. The case had been moved there from Part 71, Delaney's turf, ostensibly because Part 31 was the largest courtroom in the building. By happy coincidence, it had also been renovated within living memory and wouldn't disgrace the city in the eyes of out-of-town reporters.

The move was extremely unusual, but it wasn't the only accommodation made in the name of public scrutiny. Ordinarily, I would have had to confer with my client in the holding pens. For the duration of this trial, however, the small hearing room adjoining Part 31 would serve as my private office. A court officer would be stationed outside the locked hallway entrance, not only to make sure Priscilla didn't try to escape, but to guarantee our privacy.

My client was already present when Sergeant Mason unlocked the door to let me in, along with Janet Boroda and Rebecca Barthelme. Priscilla was wearing a white dress with a flowing skirt; the collar was so high it might have been a choker. A small pin, constructed with bits of colored glass in the shape of a butterfly, gleamed above her right breast.

"Very nice," I said. "But I'm not sure white is what we want to emphasize here."

"Tomorrow I'll wear *kente* cloth," Priscilla answered. "Over a Malcolm X t-shirt."

Her response was amusing enough to have drawn a smile in happier times. As it was, I simply nodded, then said, "We're going with a warts-and-all defense, Priscilla. Fairy princess just won't cut it."

Before she could reply, Isaiah Hazelton came through the side door leading to Delaney's courtroom. He nodded to Rebecca, then handed me the prosecution's witness list.

"Right off the press, Sid. Get 'em while they're hot."

I led him to the door, shook his hand, fired a parting shot. "I got a pair of Ben Franklins says Carlo doesn't let you cross-examine my client."

Carlo's witness list, as I'd predicted, was short; Carlo was going with a bare-bones prosecution. On the murder charge, he would prove that Byron was seated, that he was extremely drunk, that Priscilla pulled the trigger; he would infer that she'd loaded the gun in advance, that Byron couldn't defend himself, much less attack her. For the drug charge, he would need only to demonstrate that the cocaine was actually cocaine and not powdered milk.

Of course, that wouldn't be the end of it. After Rebecca presented our defense, Carlo would have an opportunity to call rebuttal witnesses, witnesses already chosen, already coached. What he didn't have to do is reveal the names of those rebuttal witnesses to the defense. He could hold them back, arrange any number of painful surprises.

"You recognize this name?" Rebecca asked Priscilla. "Kaisha Norton?"

"No. I've never heard of her, but she must be the snitch Buscetta mentioned on Friday." Priscilla leaned back against the bench. We were sitting in the gallery of a very small courtroom, just a few rows of benches in front of a tiny well. The room was used exclusively for motion hearings.

"And you never met her?" Rebecca asked. "Never spoke to her?" The implication, apparent in Rebecca's skeptical tone, was that Carlo wouldn't be putting Ms. Norton on the stand unless at some point she and Priscilla had shared the same cell.

Priscilla lit a cigarette, brushed a few strands of dark hair away from her face. "Before I went into protective custody," she explained, "I was held in an open housing area. Imagine a room with fifty bunks, two rows of twenty-five set three feet apart and lined up head-to-head." She paused for a moment, then smiled. "Now imagine fifty felons sleeping in those beds at night, walking around the housing area during the day. What do you think the chances are that I'd tell one of those assholes I had money hidden on the outside? Or, if I did, somebody wouldn't put a shank to my throat, convince me to give it up?" She held the cigarette aloft, blew at the tip, then turned to look at me. "I couldn't have told Kaisha Norton or anybody else that I killed Byron over money because there wasn't any money. Not then, not before, not now, not ever."

Twenty-seven

Everything stopped when the four of us, Priscilla, Janet, Rebecca, and myself, entered Judge Delaney's packed courtroom a few minutes later. We walked through the hush as through a still photograph, forming a solemn procession, our heads slightly bowed. I remember glancing at Priscilla as I held out a chair. She was smiling her familiar smile, one corner of her mouth pulled slightly upward, the tip of her tongue just visible between her lips. Whatever else might be at stake, this was her moment, a fact everybody present, even her enemies, even her lawyer, was forced to acknowledge. Priscilla Sweet was the only necessary player in this drama.

Ten minutes later, Carlo called Alfonso Rodriguez to the stand and Priscilla Sweet's day in court began with a preliminary hearing on our motions to suppress the gun and the cocaine, a hearing at which Delaney would serve as judge and jury. Formal jury selection would follow immediately afterward.

Guided firmly by Carlo, Rodriguez testified that while on routine patrol he'd been instructed by his dispatcher to investigate a 911 report of shots fired inside the Sweet apartment. Eight minutes later, Priscilla had opened the door in response to his knock and uttered a single word after he explained his reason for being there and requested permission to enter the premises: "Okay." Upon discovering

Byron, Rodriguez had left Priscilla with his partner, then checked Byron for any sign of life. Finding none, he'd noted a revolver lying on a table near the body, but hadn't touched it. Instead, he'd gone quickly through the apartment in a fruitless search for another victim or a perpetrator, then withdrawn into the hallway, called for help, and established a perimeter for the crime scene outside the only entrance to the premises.

Carlo turned the witness over to me at that point. His examination had taken less than fifteen minutes.

The first twenty questions I asked were meant purely as a smoke screen. They revolved around Priscilla's consent to the officers' original entry and were edged with sarcasm. Finally, after repeated objections by Carlo, Delaney asked me to move along. I shook my head, returned to the defense table, and pretended to study my notes for a moment.

"All right, officer, let's go through the rest of this quickly. The first thing you did inside the apartment was examine the deceased. Is that right?"

"I checked for a carotid pulse, yes."

"And you found none?"

"I found no sign of life."

"Then you went through the apartment in search of . . ." I picked up my notes, stared at them for a moment. "In search of a perpetrator or another victim."

"Correct."

"You were standing in the living room when this search began?"

"Yes."

"And where did you go from there?"

"I drew my weapon and went into the kitchen."

"What did you do in the kitchen?"

"I searched it."

"Exactly where did you look, Officer Rodriguez?"

"I looked in the pantry and underneath the sink."

"And where did you go next?"

From the kitchen, he'd gone to the bathroom where he'd pulled the shower curtain aside. Then he'd gone into the bedroom, checked the closet, and glanced under the bed. Finally, almost as an afterthought, he'd opened the door to the hallway closet by the front door.

"I guess I should have done that first." He was very young, barely finished with his rookie year. When he grinned sheepishly and lowered his head I could sense the gallery's sympathetic response. That was fine with me, as was anything else that made Officer Rodriguez feel safe.

"Now, officer," I said after a moment, "when you searched the bedroom, did you have to cross it to get to the closet?"

"Yes, I did."

"And then you walked to the side of the bed, knelt down, and looked underneath. Is that right?"

"That's right."

"Finally, you rose and left the room?"

"Yes."

"Did you, at any time while you were in the bedroom, happen to notice a clear plastic bag the size of a small book on the nightstand right next to the bed?" I held up the papers in my hand by way of reminding him that he'd already answered that question in the negative while testifying before the Grand Jury.

"No," he said. "I didn't." He should have stopped at that point, but, as I'd hoped, he felt it necessary to justify the oversight. "Only I wasn't in there very long."

"Really?"

"Remember, I wasn't actually searching the apartment. I was looking for a perpetrator or another victim."

I could see Carlo out of the corner of my eye. He was glaring at his witness. I wondered, briefly, as I launched into the next question, how many times he'd instructed Rodriguez not to volunteer information.

"Tell us, Officer Rodriguez, just how long would you estimate this search took?"

"Maybe five minutes. There weren't that many places a human being could hide."

"Five minutes to search the whole apartment?"

"If that."

I turned him back to Carlo for redirect, an opportunity Carlo quickly declined. Then, as Delaney began to dismiss Rodriguez, I requested that he remain available as I expected to recall him. That brought a sharp look from Carlo, but there was nothing he could do except proceed with his case. He called Detective Shawn McLearry.

Detective McLearry's testimony, up until the moment when he described his discovery of the cocaine, was strikingly similar to that of Rodriguez. After conferring with the responding officers in the hallway, he'd rechecked Byron, then rechecked the apartment in search of a second victim or a perpetrator, proceeding from the kitchen to the bathroom to the bedroom, finally discovering the cocaine in a large Ziploc bag on the nightstand. His direct testimony, like that of Rodriguez, took less than fifteen minutes.

When my turn came, I walked McLearry through the apartment, room by room, just as I'd done with Rodriguez. Only this time I produced a large graphic created by Janet Boroda that clearly demonstrated just how small the Sweet apartment actually was. McLearry had walked eighteen feet from Byron's body to the kitchen, twenty feet to the bathroom, ten feet to the only bedroom, thirty feet to the front door.

"While you were in the kitchen, Detective, did you look in the cabinets over the sink?"

"No."

"Why not?"

"Because the cabinets were too small to conceal a human being."

I'm giving the impression that McLearry's answers were delivered rapidly, which is the way they look in the Q&A format on the trial transcript. In fact, McLearry was hesitating for a few seconds before responding, as he'd undoubtedly been trained to do, and Carlo was objecting at every turn, despite being routinely overruled.

"And when you went into the bathroom, did you look in the medicine chest?"

"No."

"For the same reason?"

"That's right."

"And, in the bedroom, did you look in the dresser drawers?"

"No, I didn't."

"For the same reason?"

"Correct."

"So, you only searched six areas: in the pantry, under the sink, in the bathtub, in the bedroom closet, beneath the bed, and in the hall closet. Is that right?"

"Yes."

"And how long did that take you?"

"I don't know. I wasn't keeping track of the time." He crossed his legs and leaned back in the chair, confident that he'd anticipated the thrust of my attack.

"Give us your best estimate, Detective. An approximation will do."

Before he could answer, Carlo objected. "Asked and answered," he declared. "And defense counsel is badgering the witness."

I raised my hands in amazement. "I haven't raised my voice, your Honor."

"Overruled." Delaney was leaning forward, one elbow on the desk, cradling his chin in his palm. "Mr. Buscetta, is it absolutely necessary to object to every question?"

Buscetta sat without responding.

"You may answer, Detective," Delaney said.

"I don't recall how long I was inside the apartment."

"So, you're saying it might have taken you as long as, for instance, thirty minutes to look in six places? Five minutes for each place? Five minutes to look under the sink? Five minutes to look under the bed?"

Carlo was on his feet again, but McLearry answered before he could object. "Not that long," he admitted.

"Then how long, Detective, how long do you think it took you to search that apartment?"

"I didn't keep track," he insisted. "I didn't see any reason to keep track." He hesitated, his mouth tightening down, then said, "Maybe eight or ten minutes."

"No more questions," I said to Delaney, "but I'd like this witness to remain in the building and I ask that he be instructed not to discuss his testimony, or any further testimony from Officer Rodriguez, with anybody."

Twenty-eight

Carlo rested at that point and I quickly recalled Alfonso Rodriguez. He seemed reluctant as he approached the witness box, and I suspected that someone from the prosecutor's office had dressed him down while McLearry was on the stand. In any event, I left him to stew for a moment while I instructed my paralegal.

"I want you to go out in the hallway, Janet, see if McLearry's standing there. If he is, keep an eye on him, make sure he doesn't get wind of what's happening with Rodriguez."

She nodded, then left me and Rebecca to handle the single exhibit we'd be using, Officer Rodriguez's log.

"How long have you been a member of the force, Officer Rodriguez?" I began.

"Fourteen months," he answered.

"So, you were a rookie when you responded to the Sweet apartment?"

Carlo shot to his feet. "Objection, your Honor. Relevance."

"I'm laying a foundation, your Honor. If I may be permitted."

Delaney scratched his ear. "I'll allow it for the moment. Just try to make it brief."

"Yes, I was a rookie," Rodriguez said after exchanging a glance with Carlo.

"Then you must remember your Police Academy training pretty well. It's not a distant memory?"

"I don't remember every minute." Rodriguez laid a little foundation of his own.

I walked to the defense table, picked up a thick book, turned back to face the witness. "Did you take a written examination at the end of your Academy training based in part on an instruction manual called *The New York Police Department Patrol Guide?*" I held the book up.

"That's right."

"And did you apply the instructions in the Patrol Guide for handling crime scenes on the night you responded to the Sweet apartment?"

"You do the best you can."

I dropped the book on the table. "Well, let's see exactly *how* well you did. Would you describe for us the instructions detailed in the Patrol Guide for officers responding to the scene of a homicide. As you remember them."

He took a second to think it over, then began to tick off the items on his fingers. "First, to give aid to any living victims. Second, to secure the scene. Third, to preserve the evidence."

"And that's it?"

"You're also required to keep a log," he finally admitted.

"A log of what, Officer?"

"Of anybody entering the crime scene."

"That's it? Just the names of individuals entering the scene?"

"No, you have to include their ranks, badge numbers, time of entry, and time of exit."

I took a deep breath. It was out there now. "And on the night in question, did you maintain a log as you'd been instructed to do as a student at the Police Academy?"

"Yes."

"And you logged the names, ranks, badge numbers, time of entry, and time of exit for each individual entering or leaving the Sweet apartment?"

"That's right."

"And you performed these tasks carefully?"

He raised his head to look at me. "Yes, I did."

"Were you wearing a watch on that night?"

"Yes."

"And, to the best of your knowledge, was it working accurately?"

"Yes."

"Officer Rodriguez, is that log with you today?"

Carlo shot to his feet, fairly shouted, "Your Honor, may we approach?" He was off before I could respond, speeding across the well of the court in answer to Delaney's weary, "All right. Approach."

"If your Honor recalls," Carlo began, "you gave the prosecution three days to compile, copy, and deliver all paperwork relating to the police investigation. Somehow, in that process, the log maintained by Officer Rodriguez was misplaced. I have effected due diligence in a search of the prosecution's files and am prepared to say that it cannot be located."

"That's funny," I said, "because I've got a copy in my hot little hand."

Carlo, his mouth locked into a tight line, his jaw barely moving, again blamed Delaney for the loss of the log, then demanded a copy of my copy and the rest of the day to study it and prepare his witnesses. Later, after the trial was over, I learned that Carlo's wife had left him a week before the trial began, taking their six children with her. The story, at least the way it came to me, had her running off to northern Montana with another prosecutor.

"Look, Judge," I said, "the witness ought to be able to identify his own handwriting. Why not let him take a look? If he says it's his, then we can run off a copy for the prosecution and proceed immediately. Otherwise, I feel we're looking at an indefinite delay while the prosecution searches for the original. You might also consider that the witness, when asked about his activities at the crime scene, told the court that he, in fact, kept a log."

Carlo argued for a few minutes, until Delaney ordered him back to the prosecution table. Then Delaney personally handed Rodriguez my copy of the log and asked him if he recognized the handwriting.

"Yes," Rodriguez said, "it's mine. It's the log I kept on the night of the murder." He was smiling now, pleased, perhaps, that everybody could see he'd been a good boy and done his job.

Delaney had a copy run off for Carlo, then motioned me to proceed.

"Officer Rodriguez, is the document you hold in your hand an accurate copy of the log you kept on January 16 of last year?"

"Yes, sir."

"Now, I want to draw your attention to the first entry. Would you read it to yourself, please?" I looked toward the gallery as I waited, noted the rapt attention, and, despite everything that had gone before, I felt a visceral pleasure that bordered on joy. "Now, would you read that entry to the court?"

"McLearry. Detective. 4573. 18:31."

"Would *4573* refer to Detective McLearry's badge number?"

"Yes."

"And *18:31* refers to time of entry?"

"Correct."

"And *18:31* is military time for 6:31 in the evening?"

"Yes."

"All right. Now, please read the fifth entry."

"To myself?"

"Yes, to make sure it's accurate." I paused again, then asked him to read the entry aloud.

"McLearry. Detective. 4573. 18:53."

"Does *18:53* refer to the time of exit?"

"That's right."

"Could it refer to anything else? Anything at all?"

"No. That's the time Detective McLearry left the scene."

I took a second before asking the next question, brought my tone from crisp and peremptory to gentle and encouraging. "Officer Rodriguez, do you take pride in the performance of your duties as a police officer?"

Rodriguez let his eyes swing over to Carlo before answering. The smile on his face grew slightly, making it apparent that whatever passed between them before the hearing had been less than pleasant.

"Yes," he said, "I certainly do."

"And do you have an independent memory of creating this log?"

"I do."

"And do you remember taking care to keep it as accurate as possible?"

"Yes."

"And when you personally went through that apartment, before the detectives arrived, you didn't see any cocaine, did you?"

"That's correct."

"No more questions."

Carlo made a half-hearted attempt to get Rodriguez to concede that he might have made an error, an attempt Rodriguez resisted by answering, "That's the way I remember it," thus reinforcing the fact that he had a memory of events independent of his notes.

Delaney cut him off after a few minutes, reminding Carlo that there was no jury present, then declared a fifteen minute recess. I remember following Priscilla into the courtroom next door, noting the swing of her hips, her determined stride. As if she hadn't a care in the world.

Priscilla wasn't the only one happy with the turn of events. Rebecca termed my cross-examination "marvelous" and "outstanding." Even though it hadn't produced any tangible results and no jury would ever hear it. But I didn't spoil the celebration. Instead, as I listened to Rebecca go on, I found myself wishing with all my heart that it was Julie speaking, that it was Caleb hoisting a glass of Sprite to my legal prowess.

When McLearry retook the stand, I had him repeat his estimate, that he'd only been inside for eight or ten minutes, before confronting him with the log. To his credit, he took some time to think it over, but there was no place for him to go, a fact I proved to him by reconstructing the search. I walked eighteen steps, as McLearry would have, pantomimed opening a pantry door, looking under a sink. Then I took twenty steps into the bathroom, then ten to the bedroom, finally thirty to the front door. At each point I went through the motions McLearry had described earlier. The whole thing, even done slowly, took six minutes.

"Rodriguez must have made a mistake," McLearry, his legs crossed, his face a mask, kept insisting. "I couldn't have been inside that long."

"And that's because it could not have taken twenty-two minutes to perform the search you described?"

"That's correct."

"And you're saying that if you were inside the apartment for twenty-two minutes it's because you were doing something other than what you've described?"

"That's argumentative," Carlo interrupted. "The witness had already stated that the log is inaccurate."

"I withdraw the question. Detective McLearry, did you keep a record of the time you entered and left the crime scene? Did you write anything down?"

"I already told you I didn't."

"Did you look at your watch before and after you searched the apartment?"

"No."

"But you want us to believe that the only *written* record is inaccurate?"

"It has to be."

"And that's because if the log is, in fact, accurate, you did something other than perform the search you described?"

Carlo objected again, as well he might since I'd asked exactly the same question I'd withdrawn a moment before. Delaney sustained him, then asked me to move on.

I signed off then, figuring I'd done all the damage I could. If Delaney decided to believe McLearry, or if he concluded that the time discrepancy was irrelevant, there was nothing I could do about it.

To my surprise, Carlo didn't try to rehabilitate McLearry, perhaps because he couldn't accomplish the task without tainting Rodriguez. In any event, I clearly surprised him when I recalled Rodriguez to the stand.

"Mr. Kaplan," Delaney asked, "is this absolutely necessary?"

It was like asking a trapeze artist not to finish his act with a triple somersault. "I only have a few questions, your Honor. On a matter not yet examined. It won't take more than ten minutes."

Rodriguez, when he came back, seemed considerably subdued. Apparently, his testimony hadn't drawn rave reviews.

"While you were in the Police Academy, Officer Rodriguez," I began, "did there ever come a time when your instructors discussed a concept called 'in plain view'?"

"Yes."

"And was the concept of 'in plain view' mentioned in connection with general search and seizure law as it pertains to police officers?"

"That's right."

"And would you explain 'in plain view' as you understand it?"

Carlo rose from his chair to object on the grounds of relevance.

"It's foundational, your Honor. And goes directly to the credibility of the witness."

The irony of my attempt to establish the credibility of a prosecution witness wasn't lost on Delaney who smiled before instructing Rodriguez to answer the question.

"To me it means that I never have to ignore evidence that's lying out in the open."

"When you say 'evidence,' would that include, for instance, a weapon?"

"Yes."

"Would it also include a clear plastic bag filled with cocaine?"

"That's right."

I took a few steps forward, my hand extended as if about to offer a blessing. "And were you aware of the 'in plain view' concept when you searched the Sweet apartment on the evening of January 16?"

"It occurred to me."

"And did you look for incriminating evidence lying 'in plain view' as you walked through the apartment?"

"I didn't go through the rooms with a magnifying glass, but I did look around."

"And did you notice a plastic bag filled with cocaine lying on a nightstand in the bedroom?"

"No, I did not."

Twenty-nine

When Delaney, after listening to fifteen minutes of closing argument from each side, tossed out the cocaine (and with it, of course, the charge of possession), the crowd behind me let out a collective gasp. A babble of conversation surged upward, blended smoothly with a shuffle of feet as several reporters fled the courtroom. Carlo, standing to my right, slapped a palm to his forehead; his lower lip rose almost to his nose and actually quivered. I turned slightly, tried to suppress a grin, then distinctly heard Caleb's voice in my left ear.

"The boy is *back*," he whispered. "Ohhhhh, yesssssss."

Before I could react, Delaney slammed his gavel down, plunging the courtroom into a sudden, complete silence.

"We'll take our noon recess, now," he said, "start the *voir dire* this afternoon. Be prepared, gentlemen. I want jury selection completed before we go home."

Carlo, apparently recovered, demanded a continuance while he appealed Delaney's ruling to the Appellate Court. It was a mistake; he couldn't win, but he could (and did) make an enemy of Judge Thomas Delaney.

"If you want to appeal, Mr. Buscetta," Delaney replied evenly, "that is, of course, your privilege. But there will be no delay in the start of this trial. Your request for a continuance is denied."

A few minutes later, with Janet out fetching sandwiches and Rebecca searching the hallways for a working telephone, I explained it to my client.

"The only issue here is credibility. Rodriguez claims that you consented to his entry. McLearry says the cocaine was out in the open. Delaney believed the one, but not the other. It's that simple. The Appellate judges who hear Carlo's appeal weren't sitting in the courtroom this morning. They can't extract McLearry's body language, his posture, and the tone of his voice, from the trial transcript."

It was a speech, the kind of pompous lecture Julie might have grinned at in times past, and I was acutely aware of my own voice as I made it. I was aware of an underlying fear, as well, a fear no amount of self-congratulatory bullshit could erase. And what I again feared was a descent into pure madness, a descent that some distinct obscure and thoroughly debased aspect of my being was prepared to welcome.

Priscilla was sitting next to me on the front bench of the little courtroom. The knee-length skirt of her dress lay in bunches across her legs. At that moment, I wanted to flip the skirt up into her lap, run the fingers of my right hand over the inside of her thigh, get my descent off to a good start. Some piece of me was absolutely certain that I could make it all the way back, that I could enjoy a life of wealth and celebrity with an appreciative Priscilla Sweet on my arm, that she would know me in a way (and to a depth) that no other woman ever had. If I could just bring myself to forget.

Priscilla touched my arm. "You know, Sid, after . . . everything that happened, I was afraid . . . I was afraid that you'd sell me out."

I recognized the hesitant tone immediately. It was one I'd been coaching her to produce when she spoke of her love for her dead husband.

"But after listening to you out there today. . . . Well, I know it's not true."

Rebecca Barthelme returned at that moment, passed through the outer door by the attentive Sergeant Mason.

"I managed to reach Pat Hogan," she said. "He's going to check out Kaisha Norton, see if she's testified in other cases. He told me to tell you that he's making progress on the other job you gave him and you should look for results as early as tomorrow."

I remember Priscilla's eyes jumping over to mine, her head cocking slightly to the right. "You working on another case?" she asked.

"Several." I returned her gaze evenly. "Pro bono doesn't pay the rent. Meanwhile, what do you say we get to work on winning this one?" I held up the jury questionnaires. "By the end of the day, twelve of these citizens will be charged with deciding your fate. It'd probably be good if they were the *right* twelve."

Delaney brought the potential jurors down in panels of fourteen, the number of chairs in the jury box. Carlo and I were each allowed fifteen minutes of questioning per panel, slightly more than one minute per individual. Ordinarily, we'd be working completely in the dark, picking jurors by pure instinct. In this case, we had the questionnaires, filled out to screen jurors influenced by the pre-trial publicity, but while they were certainly helpful, the most obviously prejudiced jurors had already been removed. As advocates, Carlo and I shared two distinct problems. Not only were we tasked with finding the liars, we had to uncover the direction of their prejudice. There was nothing I would have liked more than to place a single individual already committed to my end of the argument on that jury.

I handled my end of the problem by asking the same general questions over and over again. Jumping them from juror to juror as if addressing the entire panel at once.

"Do you believe, Mr. Abernathy, that people have a right to defend themselves against physical attack?"

"Mrs. Kenzick, how about you, do you believe in the right to self-defense?"

"And you, Ms. Battle, do you think *everybody* has the right to defend themselves? Is there anybody who doesn't have that right?"

"What about a murderer in a prison, Mr. Goldstein? Would a murderer in a prison have the right to self-defense if he was attacked by another prisoner?"

"And a drug dealer, Mr. Guidanzo, would a drug dealer have the right to defend herself? Or would a drug dealer have to let herself be killed?"

I stood close to the jury as I worked, kept my voice as friendly and intimate as possible. My posture was relaxed, my hands spread out before me or folded just above my waist, my expression quizzical, as if I didn't know the answer and needed the jurors' help. Most of them responded positively, with a nod or a word. Occasionally, one of the more assertive declared, "Only if they try to get away first." I used their declarations to my advantage, asking other jurors, often the same individuals who'd replied with a simple affirmative to my original questions, if they felt that way, too.

"How about you? Do you believe that people have to try to get away before they're allowed to defend themselves with deadly force?"

"Well, yes," I remember one woman, Latisha Garret, saying as she raised a lace handkerchief to her lips, "I think you must at least *try*. Otherwise it's revenge, isn't it?"

Isaiah had a different problem. Though his manner was far more deferential than Carlo's, he was forced to ask pointed questions. A number of female jurors had indicated that they or someone they knew had been a victim of domestic abuse. Isaiah had asked that they be excused *en masse*, a request Delaney had quickly turned down. Instead, he'd put a single question to each.

"Do you believe that despite your experience you can reach a fair and impartial verdict?"

I watched this part of it from the defense table, knowing that jurors hated questions that challenged their honesty. Isaiah must have known this, too, because he smiled as he worked, managing to convey an implied apology while he dug for the information he needed. His goal was to evoke a revelation grave enough to produce a dismissal for cause, thus conserving his peremptory challenges for the hard cases.

Unfortunately, Isaiah was almost exclusively targeting women and they clearly didn't like it. Of course, with a bare fifteen minutes in which to question fourteen individuals (Delaney, predictably, was keeping us to a tight schedule), there was no way Isaiah could reach everyone. But I felt that he could have been more subtle, and when a hand dropped lightly to my shoulder halfway through Isaiah's examination of the fourth panel, I turned to share my insight with Julie.

For a moment, a very long moment, I was completely disoriented. The face of the woman opposite me was vaguely familiar, the face of a friend of a friend to whom I'd been introduced in the distant past. I watched her lips move without understanding a word she said, found myself wondering why she wasn't smiling. Had I done something to offend her?

I was just about to ask, "Where's Julie?" when I came back to myself. Rebecca was staring at me. Her white hair, curled into a shoulder-length pageboy, seemed to float away from her skull, a pure halo.

"You okay, Sid?" she asked.

The concern in her voice seeming to me, at that moment, perfectly sincere, I felt it best to reassure her. "Never better," I said with a smile. "Never fucking better."

By five o'clock we had a panel of nine women and five men. There were five whites, four blacks, two Latinos, and one Asian on the standing jury, plus two black alternates. Isaiah had spent thirteen of fifteen peremptory challenges dumping women, but had still failed to produce a male majority because Delaney, may God bless his chauvinist heart, readily dismissed men who claimed hardship while retaining women, thus virtually guaranteeing a gender-biased panel. If it had gone the other way, Delaney's rulings might have formed part of an appeal after conviction. The prosecution, on the other hand, could do no more than bemoan an acquittal.

I went directly back to the office after dinner, paused only to make a pot of coffee before I sat down to work on my opening statement. A number of recent studies, published in various law journals, had concluded that many jurors decide guilt or innocence solely on the basis of the opening statements. And why not? If consumers are dumb enough to be motivated by television advertising, and voters dumb enough to be influenced by twenty-second TV spots, why shouldn't jurors convict or acquit before actually hearing the evidence? It's the American way.

For the next few hours, I buried myself in work. Except for the most complex trials, it was my practice to deliver my opening statement without reference to notes of any kind, not even index cards. My primary job, as I understood it, was to sell myself to the jury. Or at least, to sell my boy-from-Brooklyn *persona*. I couldn't appear to be reading from a script.

Beyond that bit of self-aggrandizement, I had several substrategies. In theory, the purpose of an opening statement is to outline the evidence you intend to introduce at trial. Lawyers are not supposed to argue their cases. In practice, you get away with whatever you can. Some judges will put you back on track without an objection from opposing counsel. Others, like Delaney, prefer to let the attorneys fight it out. As I've already stated, juries don't like frequent objections, especially in the course of opening and closing statements which provide the only real drama present in most trials. Carlo would know this, of course. But provoked by declarations like, "The prosecution would have you believe that the only time a woman has the right to defend herself is after she's dead," I was sure he wouldn't be able to contain himself.

On still another level, my opening, taken as a whole, would form the first skirmish in what would soon become an all-out attack on the victim. Maybe the claim of self-defense would rise and fall on Priscilla's credibility, but there was hard evidence that her husband was a brutal manipulator. It was not only possible, but actually likely, that some of the jurors, once they got a good look at the photographs and medical reports, would vote for an acquittal even if they believed that she'd killed him over money.

Around eleven, just as I was about to assault a pint of macadamia brittle ice cream, the phone rang. I'd been screening my calls through the answering machine, avoiding reporters, but when I heard Ettamae Harris's voice, I ran into the office and picked up.

"Ettamae? It's Sid. Wait a minute while I shut off the machine." I sat down in my chair, pressed the button. "There. How you doin'?"

"Not so good." Though her tone was free of inflection, it somehow carried a measure of desperation. "I keep thinking that he's here. I keep seein' him." She went on, changing the subject as if Caleb's presence was an unavoidable reality she'd simply come to accept. "Tell me why Caleb and Julie went up there, Sid. I know I asked you this before, but it keeps comin' back to me. What were they tryin' to do?"

"It's real simple, Ettamae. They went there to protect Sid Kaplan." I let the words hang for a moment, as hard as if they'd been ground into glass. "It wasn't what I wanted or what I expected. In fact, I told them *not* to go. Be that as it may, I was the only one at risk. They, themselves, were in no personal danger."

After a brief silence, Ettamae took an audible breath. I could hear her lips brushing the mouthpiece as she spoke. "Caleb really loved you, Sid. He talked about you all the time, the crazy things you did in court, the way you acted with your clients. Caleb said you tried to come off real cynical, but underneath you were soft as butter."

"Softer, Ettamae, much, much softer. Just ask my girlfriends."

The humor, weak as it was, served its purpose, deflecting the conversation away from my relationship with Caleb and Julie. But it couldn't obscure the central truth: Sid Kaplan, miserable mutt that he was and is, had for a brief period in his adult life been actually loved. And it was obvious to Sidney Kaplan, as he listened to Ettamae Harris, that he would never be loved in that way again.

"You gonna win, Sid? You gonna get her off?"

"Most likely, Ettamae. Most likely she'll walk."

"And then you'll be famous again. Is that the way of it?"

"I'm already famous." When she didn't respond, I continued. "The only real question here is whether it was Priscilla's fault. Guzman's beyond punishment."

"And that's supposed to make some kind of a damn difference?" Her voice turned hard, reflecting the anger she needed so desperately to feel. "Seems to me like it don't matter what Priscilla did. Don't matter if she pulled the trigger on Caleb her own self. Don't matter if she pushed Julie into the river. Priscilla's still gonna go free and y'all are still gonna be famous."

Thirty

I saw Caleb twice on the way to court the next morning, once getting out of a subway car at the other end of the platform as I boarded, then again buying a newspaper at an outdoor newsstand on Chambers Street. Each time, some logical corner of my brain jumped through the usual hoops. It wasn't Caleb; it couldn't be; Caleb was dead and buried. Furthermore, confusing him with every overweight black man I came across actually insulted his memory. But on another deeper level, I was absolutely serene. Caleb was free to come and go as he wished. Julie, too. Their appearances, whether visitations from the other side or mere wishful thinking, meant less than nothing.

Both of these denials came unbidden, proceeding from a corner of my brain I no longer used or needed.

It was very early, barely eight o'clock, when I approached the courthouse, but not early enough to avoid a knot of demonstrators and camera crews from CBS and NBC. Two blond women, so close in appearance they might have been sisters, came rushing forward. They thrust foam-covered microphones in my face, jabbing them at me as if fending off an attacker.

"The prosecution claims she killed him over money," the one on the left shouted. "How do you respond to that?" Her name was Sissy

Crowley and she wore a fetching lime-green dress that neatly complemented her frosted hair.

I was at the door by then, the door marked AUTHORIZED PERSONNEL ONLY. Behind the glass, a skinny, middle-aged court officer stared glumly at my chest. "Wake up, Sissy. Prosecutors don't trot out their jailhouse rats unless they, meaning the prosecutors, are desperate." A little shot for Carlo, one he was sure to take personally. "I intend to present medical and police reports, have doctors and cops testify. The prosecutor intends to present a repeat felon who wants to get off the hook." I pushed the door open with my left hand, took a half-step forward. "Ya know, the sad truth is that if it wasn't for the publicity surrounding this case, it would never have come to trial."

Priscilla was already present when Sergeant Mason let me into the courtroom that served as our impromptu office. She was leaning forward, huddled over a cigarette, her hands crossed on her knees.

"Good morning, Priscilla."

She turned at the sound of my voice, unfolding like a wild flower in a nature movie. "Good morning."

"You look great." I gestured to the navy suit she wore, the white rayon blouse beneath it. "Much better than yesterday."

"My mother bought it last night. The skirt's too big. I had to pin it."

She raised the hem of the jacket, showed me the safety pin binding the waist of her skirt. I reached out, touched the head of the pin as if about to unsnap it. Priscilla held herself steady, her gray eyes seeming curious as they stared into mine.

"After you're acquitted," I asked, "where will you go?" My right hand hovered by her waist.

"I guess I'll have to go back to my mother's." Her smile vanished. "Being as I have no money."

"Then you'll be looking for a job?"

Janet Boroda, dragging her evidence bag on a wheeled luggage carrier, came into the room before I got an answer. She set down a paper bag, began to pull out coffee and bagels. Janet was a Sephardic Jew, both parents having come to this country as young children from Morocco. She had the exotic good looks, the olive complexion, and large round eyes, common to Mediterranean Jews. "A mini-feast," she declared, adding a tub of cream cheese and a package of sliced lox. "To celebrate victories past and future."

Delaney spent the first hour of the court day outlining the basic structure of trials to the jury. Then he cautioned them, first, to not make up their minds without hearing all the evidence and, second, to not discuss the case, either with each other or with outsiders.

"And you are not to read about this case in the newspapers or watch news reports dealing with the case on television," he piously intoned. "Media reports are not evidence and you are not to be influenced by them."

The whole business was routine and I'm sure Delaney knew, as did we all, that the jurors would go home every evening, discuss the case over dinner, watch every bit of the coverage. And why not? It was their fifteen minutes, too.

I studied the jurors closely as Delaney droned on. They were fidgeting in their chairs, casting sharp, quick glances at Priscilla, longer looks at Byron and myself. Under other circumstances, I would have been extremely nervous, but on that day I felt entirely at ease. Even Carlo's powerful opening statement failed to penetrate my confidence. He would prove, he told the jury when his turn finally came, that Priscilla had loaded the gun herself, that Byron, desperately ill and utterly intoxicated, had been sitting in a chair when his wife pulled the trigger.

"Byron Sweet didn't die immediately. No, no. Byron Sweet, though he was shot through the heart, fell to his knees and crawled through a pool of his own blood in an attempt to get away. And his killer, the woman who pulled the trigger, his wife and business partner, did nothing to help him. She didn't call an ambulance or a doctor or the police. Oh, no, ladies and gentlemen. What Priscilla Sweet did was watch her husband bleed to death."

The performance was vintage Carlo Buscetta, his hatred for the defendant apparent in every stiff gesture. Priscilla Sweet was the embodiment of evil, a clear-eyed, cold-blooded killer. If the trial had ended after his opening remarks, the jury would have sent out for a rope.

I could have objected at any number of points, but I didn't. My restraint stemmed in part from a determination to play the good guy, the one who kept the trial moving. Beyond that, I realized that Carlo was making a fundamental mistake by promising more than he could deliver. Though he might be able to present a case for Priscilla's technical guilt, he would never prove that she was a monster.

Maybe he'd been overly influenced by years of prosecuting defendants without the resources to mount a serious defense. Or maybe he was so filled with anger that he just couldn't stop himself. Either way, when my turn came, I attempted to elevate the emotional tone of Carlo's delivery into the central issue of the trial.

"Listening to the prosecutor," I began as I slowly approached the jury box, "I got the distinct impression that it was Priscilla Sweet who used to beat the hell out of her husband. Instead of the other way around."

Carlo was on his feet before I finished the sentence. "I object, your Honor. Mr. Kaplan is arguing his case."

Delaney sustained the objection, tossing in an additional caution against the use of profanity.

I apologized to the court, then continued in the same vein. Carlo objected again and again. At first, I barely reacted to the interruptions, then, as the jurors' annoyance became apparent, I began to show my own feelings. By turns, I sighed, let my shoulders slump, shook my head, tightened my lips, shrugged apologetically.

"Your Honor, I allowed Mr. Buscetta to complete his opening remarks without interruption."

I made the statement a half dozen times, my inflection as sharp as that of an unfairly punished child. Delaney, of course, wasn't moved. Though he smiled from time to time, he sustained most, but not all, of Carlo's objections.

Eventually (and inevitably), a few of the brighter jurors pulled back in their seats, holding themselves away from me. Their annoyance had begun to swing from Carlo to myself as they realized, perhaps, that I was doing it on purpose. By that time, I was keying off a juror named Rafael Fuentes, an electrical engineer with a master's degree from Columbia. Fuentes, in contrast to the other jurors, had been taking notes, his eyes moving from the pad resting on his knee to my own. When he finally closed the pad and shoved the pen into his shirt pocket, I walked back to the defense table and pretended to consult my files.

A few minutes later, instead of returning to my former position in front of the jury box, I stepped up to a lectern near the witness stand and began to outline the case I intended to present. I named my witnesses, specified the medical and police reports I would introduce, promised the jury that they would hear from the accused. Carlo, though I hadn't expected him to take the bait, again jumped in with both feet, launching one objection after another. Only this time, Judge Delaney systematically overruled him.

Finally, Delaney, his pink complexion now florid, called us both to the bench. As we approached, he waved off the court reporter.

"For Christ's sake, Mr. Buscetta," he hissed between clenched teeth, "we haven't called our first witness." Before Carlo could reply, he turned to me. "And I've had about enough of your games, too, Mr. Kaplan. Even if Mr. Buscetta wants to play, I don't."

I apologized immediately, though I didn't intend to stop, not even if he cited me for contempt. Carlo, on the other hand, continued to insist that I was arguing my case. Delaney listened to him for a minute, then shut him down.

"Mr. Buscetta and Mr. Kaplan," he said, "I have a trial on my calendar scheduled to begin two weeks from today and I intend to start on time. Now you people go back out there and get *this* trial going."

I moved purposely across the courtroom to the jury box and rested my palms on the rail.

"Ladies and gentlemen, the defense will not tell you that Priscilla Sweet did not kill her husband." I spoke slowly, and evenly, separating out the various pieces of information I wanted to convey. "Instead, even though we are required to prove nothing, we will clearly demonstrate the *fact* . . . the fact that Priscilla Sweet exercised a right *fundamental* to every human being, the right to preserve her own life. Thank you."

Thirty-one

With Delaney pushing hard, we managed to work our way through the clerk who'd taken Maybelle Higginbotham's 911 call and the dispatcher who'd sent Rodriguez and his partner to the Sweet apartment before the one o'clock recess. Because I didn't intend to dispute the basic facts, I asked very few questions. I wanted the prosecution's case done with as quickly as possible, so the jury could focus on the victim as a beast, instead of the victim as a victim.

I did take the first witness, Ms. Irene Gordon, back over a tape of Maybelle's call, emphasizing the last sentence: "I think he done killed her this time."

"Did you understand the words, '*he* killed *her*,' to mean the caller believed the victim to be a woman?" I asked.

"I've already said that I don't remember the call."

"Well, did you communicate the fact that the caller believed the victim to be a woman to the dispatcher?"

"We don't speak directly to the dispatchers. We write down the complaint and send it along a conveyer belt."

"And do you have that written complaint, Ms. Gordon?"

"No, we don't keep every scrap of paper."

Gordon's voice was edgy and suspicious. She held herself stiffly with her head pulled back and her arms folded just below her breasts. There was no reason for her attitude, because I wasn't trying to discredit her testimony. Still, if she wanted to appear evasive and the jury concluded that she was holding something back, it was, as Grampa Itzy would say, fine by me.

"When you made up the complaint for the dispatcher, do you remember writing that *he* killed *her*?"

"I don't remember the incident, sir."

"Is it your practice, Ms. Gordon, to note the gender of a victim in your complaints?"

"Would you repeat that? I didn't get the question."

We went at it for another few minutes, with Gordon refusing to give a direct answer. I didn't really care about the answer one way or another, but I did, according to the transcript, take the opportunity to repeat my basic '*he* killed *her*' message an additional six times.

After Delaney sent the jury off to lunch, I asked to approach the bench, and Carlo followed me over. When I requested permission to have Thelma Barrow visit her daughter during the lunch recess, he tossed me a suspicious look, then said, "I assume she'd be willing to submit to a search?'

"She was searched on the way into the building," I responded, "but if you wanna do body cavities, maybe we could use an NBC camera crew for the video." The implication, of course, was that if Thelma was subjected to a thorough search (or, worse, refused permission to visit her daughter), the media would be informed and, through the media, the jurors.

After a few minutes of wrangling, I agreed to have Thelma's purse reexamined before she went inside. That done, I reunited mother and daughter, then took off for a lunch meeting with Pat Hogan in a McDonald's on Chambers Street. Hogan's message, delivered a day earlier by Rebecca Barthelme, had been positive enough to get my senses tingling, but when I saw his face, I knew it wasn't to be. Hogan was sitting by himself at a table near the counter, huddled over a Big Mac and looking distracted. When he saw me, he shrugged apologetically and motioned me to get some food.

Five minutes later, the proud bearer of an incredibly greasy fish sandwich and a container of scalding hot coffee, I laid my tray on the table and took a seat.

"All right, Pat, let's hear the bad news."

"The bad news is that there's no news." He shoved a french fry into his mouth, washed it down with a drink of Sprite, then he leaned across the table and tapped my wrist. "Thing was, buddy, I thought I found the money. There's this friend of Priscilla's, woman named Pauline Yager, got a dumpy one-roomer over a *bodega* on Grand Street. Looks like it couldn't go for more than a few hundred a month, meanwhile the windows are alarmed." He loosened his tie, opened the top button of his shirt. "The first thing I figured, naturally, was that she was in the drug business, but when I asked around, I was told she was clean. So, what I did, after duly considering the penalties, was arrange a visit one afternoon when she wasn't home. The alarm system was a phony, just a bunch of magnetic strips stuck to the glass. She must have put 'em there to scare off the junkies."

"And there was no money, either," I said.

"Yeah," he responded, "you might say it was a false alarm." When I didn't smile, he continued. "What could I do? It was a mistake, that's all. I'm gonna keep tryin', but I don't have a good feeling. It looks like you're gonna have to live with your doubts."

If I was forced to live with my doubts, Priscilla, when I rejoined her, appeared to have no doubts at all. She and her mother were in extremely good spirits. They were talking about a trip she and her parents had taken to California many years before. I ignored the both of them, spending the last few minutes before returning to the courtroom with Janet Boroda. The afternoon's testimony would, I was certain, wipe the smile off her face. I found myself looking forward to it.

Fifteen minutes later, Carlo put Officer Alfonso Rodriguez on the stand. An hour after that, the jury got its first look at Byron Sweet's body. He was on his stomach, his head turned to the right, lying in a pool of dark red blood. A wide irregular swatch of blood trailed off behind him, reaching to the lip of the chair in which he'd been sitting.

I was seated behind the defense table when the photo went up. Priscilla was beside me and I watched her out of the corner of my eye. Naturally, we'd discussed this moment and her reaction to it at length, finally deciding that she should glance at the photo for a fraction of a second, then turn away.

"You've got to show the jury that some part of you still loves him," I'd told her. "Despite everything that happened."

Priscilla followed my instructions exactly, even managing to flinch as she turned her eyes downward. Then she took it one step further and began to cry. There were no sound effects, no sobbing, no sniffles. Just tears running along the side of her nose to drop onto the table. As I took out my handkerchief and passed it over, I thought of Caleb lying in that alley, wondered if Priscilla had reserved even a single tear for his passing.

"Mr. Kaplan," Delaney asked, "does your client need a recess?"

As I turned back to face the jury, I realized that Priscilla's tears had done their job, that every juror, including the alternates, were looking at her and not at Byron's corpse.

"No, your Honor," Priscilla answered before I could speak. "I'm all right." She raised her chin, looked straight at the jury. Her normally flat gray eyes, at that moment, were so filled with sorrow as to appear actually wise.

When Carlo ended the pantomime by slapping his pointer against Byron's photo, Priscilla's gaze turned down to her folded hands. In recognition, perhaps, of the fact that her scene had been completed. A few minutes after that, photos of Byron's corpse, taken from several angles, were circulating through the jury box. The eyes of the jurors moved from the photos in their hands to Priscilla, a typical progression. As victim photos go, this group was fairly benign. Still, I was certain that most of the jurors were staring at that pool of blood and thinking that somebody would have to pay.

There was nothing I could do about it beyond feigning indifference while Carlo pinned the photos up on a board, then turned to Rodriguez who told the same basic story he'd told to the Grand Jury, then repeated at the preliminary hearing. As cop witnesses go, he was strong and believable, his youth a definite asset. But, again, since I wasn't disputing his testimony, I was able to use his credibility to Priscilla's advantage.

"How many times did you knock on the door," I asked, "before someone responded?"

"Once."

"And was Priscilla Sweet the individual who responded?"

"Yes."

Rodriguez, having heard these questions before, was answering quickly, though I don't believe he knew where I was going.

"And did she call to you through the door?"

"No, she opened the door."

"And did you then explain why you were there and request permission to enter?"

"Yes."

"And did Priscilla Sweet ask to see a search warrant?"

"No."

"And did she refuse permission to allow you to enter?"

"No."

"If she had refused permission, Officer Rodriguez, tell the court what you would have done?"

Carlo, the first on the prosecutorial team to awaken, objected. "Calls for a conclusion, your Honor."

"Overruled. You may answer."

"Would you repeat the question?" Rodriguez's voice had dropped a full octave. He was now suspicious.

"If she'd told you to take a hike, Officer, what would you have done?"

"I don't know."

"You don't know whether you would have retreated or forced your way inside?"

"I don't know."

"Officer Rodriguez, you've already testified that you have an independent recollection of that evening. Is that correct?"

"Yes."

"And now you're telling this court that you never gave a thought to what you were going to do if you were refused entry to that apartment?"

"I might have thought about it. I just don't remember."

Rodriguez's features tightened down to match his voice, turning his boyish good looks childishly sullen. Carlo tried to protect him by claiming I was badgering the witness and Delaney, though he overruled the objection, told me I was walking very close to the edge. I apologized, then went back to work.

"Officer Rodriguez, the 911 call was logged in at 5:52 P.M. Would you tell us what time it was when you knocked on the door of the Sweet apartment?"

"Approximately 6:20."

"And then you went inside and observed a body on the floor and a gun on the table?"

"That's right."

"And the gun was lying in plain view? No attempt had been made to conceal it?"

"Not that I could see."

"And had any attempt been made to move or conceal the body in the twenty-eight minutes between the time the 911 call was made and the time you arrived on the scene?"

Carlo objected again, stating that Rodriguez hadn't acted as an investigator and was not competent to render a judgment. Delaney, as expected, sustained the objection.

"Officer Rodriguez," I said after a moment, "when you entered the Sweet apartment twenty-eight minutes after the 911 call was received, did you find Byron Sweet lying in the center of the living room and not behind the couch?"

Carlo was on his feet before I finished the question, but this time Delaney overruled. "Make your point and move on, Mr. Kaplan," he said.

"He was lying very close to the center of the living room."

"And had any attempt been made to conceal his body?"

"No, he was lying where he crawled after she shot him."

Score one for the cops. I finished my cross-examination by having Rodriguez describe Priscilla's physical condition. To my surprise, instead of resisting he turned poetic, comparing a bruise on Priscilla's face to the skin of a green plum.

Thirty-two

On the following morning, I woke chasing a dream in which Julie's voice rolled through my consciousness like oil beneath the fingers of a masseur. I was certain Julie's message was of great importance, something I very much needed to know, but I just couldn't catch up and her voice was gradually replaced by the soft drumming of raindrops against the window. I left the bed and crossed the room. According to the clock, the sun was already up, but the northern view from the window was of an angry, dark sky. Below me, a dense fog shimmered beneath the amber streetlights in Union Square Park. It hung just above the floodlit tower on the Metropolitan Life building ten blocks to the north, completely obscured the Empire State Building on 34th Street.

I walked away from the window and over to the coffee machine on the filing cabinet. Without thinking, I began to spoon fresh coffee into a clean filter. I was in the process of adding tap water, when a single fact, one I already knew, but had failed to act on, jumped into my consciousness. It was Thelma Barrow, not Priscilla, who'd led Guzman to my door. In order to convict Priscilla, I would have to build a case for a pre-planned conspiracy between Priscilla and her mother, a conspiracy that began when Thelma falsely reported her daughter's kidnapping, then continued up through the actual murder to the day Thelma told Guzman that I was holding his money.

According to that line of thought, Priscilla had left the cocaine in order to make the first lie she'd told Guzman, that the cops had stolen most of the coke, more believable. I was pure backup, a second line of defense in the event Guzman rejected the first.

I marched into my office and dialed Pat Hogan's home number. He picked up on the seventh ring, his raspy whisper revealing his compromised condition. "Ohhhhhh, shit," he moaned. "Who the fuck is this?"

"Nobody important, Pat. Just your client."

"Sid?" His voice oozed disbelief. "You oughta know better. It's goddamned 6:22 in the morning."

I started to say that, being as I was already into him for ten grand with more to come, I'd call him whenever I felt like it, then stopped myself.

"Okay, I hear ya, Pat, but I've made a decision and we don't have a lot of time. I wanted to be sure I got to speak to you before I left for court."

He moaned softly, drew a deep breath. "I think my brain is leaking into the telephone."

"Actually, I'm sucking it out from this end." I smacked my lips.

"Awright, awright, I'm movin'." The bedsprings groaned in the background. I heard footsteps cross a room, the sound of water running, the squeak of a closing faucet. A moment later Hogan was back on the phone. "Let's do it, Sid," he said. "Before my eyeballs fall out."

"What I wanna do is concentrate on Thelma Barrow. If Priscilla was running a scam, Thelma was part of it from the beginning." I went on to describe the fracas in the Barrow kitchen when Byron allegedly kidnapped Priscilla, and the fact that Gennaro Cassadina didn't remember it, though he could describe the gun Joe Barrow kept. "I thought you might start by checking on Joe Barrow, maybe with the shopkeepers near his hardware store. See if he's the gentle soul his wife makes him out to be."

"How 'bout I skip to the chase," he responded. "Go into Thelma's house, give it a toss? That be okay?"

"It'd be better if you hadn't told me."

That brought a phlegmy, choked laugh. "Hey, Sid, you know the story. If I get taken down, the first thing I'm gonna do is cut a deal." He laughed again, then moaned. "I gotta go. I think I'm gonna throw up."

The jury was barely seated when Detective Shawn McLearry began his testimony. Carlo, as he'd done with Alfonso Rodriguez, used McLearry as an excuse to wave a series of bloody photographs at the jury. This time we had Byron from the front, staring up at the camera through blank eyes that seemed only a bit more empty than those of his living wife. There were several photos of the blood trail as well, and a stark closeup of the murder weapon lying on the table. Finally, like a schoolboy at the climax of a show-and-tell project, Carlo had Byron's chair brought out by two of the biggest court officers I'd ever seen.

After putting the chair into evidence, he pushed it up to the jury box, had the jury leave their seats to examine the small hole in the tightly woven green fabric, the circular bloodstain surrounding it. Then he let McLearry speculate that Byron was fully seated when he was shot. I might have objected, but I let it go, more than satisfied that McLearry had opened a door through which Dr. Kim Park would eventually drive.

On the other hand, I objected vigorously, demanding a sidebar, when Carlo asked McLearry if Priscilla had shown remorse.

"The fact, your Honor," I said, "that my client exercised her Fifth Amendment rights cannot be used as evidence of guilt."

Delaney agreed, then made it worse by allowing Carlo to pose specific questions relating to Priscilla's demeanor.

"Was," Carlo asked, "the defendant crying when you arrived at the Broome Street apartment?"

Again, I objected, only to be again overruled.

"No," McLearry replied.

"Did she appear agitated?"

"No."

"Was she hyperventilating?"

"No."

That was enough for Delaney. "Move on, Mr. Buscetta," he demanded. "You've made your point."

Carlo took a deep breath, nodded once, then asked McLearry to estimate the length of time it had taken Byron to crawl from his chair to the place where he collapsed. The question was clearly without foundation and my objection was immediately sustained, but it was a victory for Carlo nonetheless. Not only had he introduced Priscilla's failure to call for help, he had me objecting to nearly every question.

"No further," Carlo said after tossing a final glare at Priscilla.

I pushed myself up, strolled over to Byron's green chair, then casually plopped myself down. The assembled multitudes let out a collective gasp which I studiously ignored. I also ignored Carlo's angry objection, leaning forward slightly to slide my right index finger between my suit jacket and the bullet hole. As I rose and approached McLearry, I kept the finger pressed to my back.

"Detective McLearry," I said, pointing at a photo of Byron tacked to a display board, "you were kind enough to circle the wound on the deceased's back for Mr. Buscetta." I turned to let the jury see the exact position of my finger. "Would you point out that spot again?"

Carlo rose to his feet. "Your Honor, can we dispense with the theatrics? The defense is asking the jury to make a comparison that assumes facts not in evidence."

Delaney sustained the objection, a ruling that offered no surprises. That was why I'd covered the tip of my index finger with white chalk, why I'd worn a charcoal gray suit. Standing as I was, with my back to the jury, the white dot on my jacket was invisible to both the prosecution team and the judge.

I let my hand drop to my side, then repeated the question. "Would you please indicate the wound on the deceased's back. In fact, would you approach the photo and actually touch the spot?"

"It's right here," McLearry said.

"Now, the place you're touching, it's in the exact center of the wound, right?"

"Yes."

The exit wound on the left side of the victim's back was several inches above the rise of his buttocks. And well below the dot on my suit jacket. I gave the jury a moment to comprehend the obvious, then continued.

"You're quite sure?"

"That's it, counselor." The best cops are able to feign cooperation when they're fighting you tooth and nail. The worst make no effort to conceal their bias. McLearry was definitely (and defiantly) among the latter.

"And it's your opinion, Detective, that the deceased was fully seated when he was shot?"

Carlo objected. "Lacks foundation," he declared, even though he'd established these same responses on direct. Delaney overruled before I could argue.

"Yeah, he was sitting down."

"Tell us, Detective, are you absolutely certain that the deceased could not have been rising?"

"I'm ninety-nine percent convinced," McLearry said, as if the surrender of a single percent rendered his testimony less absurd.

I walked quickly back to the defense table, leaned over my notes while Janet Boroda casually wiped the dot off my back, then took McLearry through the same set of hoops Rodriguez had negotiated the day before. I gradually forced him to admit that Priscilla had made no attempt to remove the body, to conceal the gun, or to flee, and I made him describe the bruises on Priscilla's face. Finally, I gave him back to Carlo who soon had him repeating much of his original testimony. Delaney took it until Carlo began rapping his fingernails against the crime scene photos.

"Mr. Buscetta, despite my advancing years, I haven't lost my memory. It seems to me we've heard this before." Delaney allowed himself a quick smile, in recognition, perhaps, of his own wit. "If you have nothing to add, then wrap it up. I believe it's time for lunch."

Thirty-three

After spending forty minutes trying to make small talk with Thelma Barrow while I worked my way through a stringy corned beef sandwich and a soggy knish, I was more than glad to get back into the courtroom. Thelma was sure the jury hated Buscetta and took every opportunity to repeat her insight. Priscilla kept silent, for the most part, though she favored her mother with an occasional fond glance. They even went so far as to exchange a quick kiss before Thelma went to her place in the gallery.

Inside, after a five-minute delay while Delaney attended to the needs of a lawyer involved in another case, Isaiah Hazleton called Dr. Gideon Fitzgerald, the assistant medical examiner who'd performed Byron's autopsy. I waited until Fitzgerald was sworn, then requested a sidebar. Once out of the jury's hearing, I formally objected to any testimony relating to Byron's inebriation or his liver disease, declaring both irrelevant at this point in the proceedings.

"If," I conceded, after a few minutes of back and forth argument with Isaiah, "we open the door when we present our case, Byron's condition might become relevant as rebuttal. But for now, your Honor, its only purpose is to rouse sympathy for the deceased in the minds of the jurors. Byron Sweet's death resulted from a bullet wound, not alcohol poisoning or cirrhosis of the liver."

"The state," Carlo declared, leaning over his cocounsel's back, "is prepared . . ."

Delaney waved him to silence. "This isn't a tag team match, counselor. Whoever examines the witness argues the objections. No exceptions."

"Your Honor," Isaiah said before Carlo could further piss Delaney off, "the prosecution believes the defense introduced a claim of self-defense, first in their opening statement, then by having both Officer Rodriguez and Detective McLearry describe the bruises on the defendant's face at the time she was arrested. Surely, a claim of self-defense makes the victim's ability to mount an attack relevant."

Delaney still wasn't convinced. "The cirrhosis, Mr. Hazleton, the liver disease. Do you intend to maintain that the victim was unable to rise from his chair as a direct result of his disease? More to the point, are you prepared to make this court an offer of proof?"

Isaiah danced around the questions for a moment before Delaney cut him off, ruling the liver disease out, the intoxication in. I took this back to Priscilla as a victory. She rewarded me with a smile, laying her hand on my shoulder for a moment before turning to face the jury. As per my instructions, she'd been making brief eye contact with individual jurors, absorbing their suspicions (and sometimes their outright hostility), projecting her own vulnerability.

Gideon Fitzgerald's testimony was direct and to the point. Byron Sweet had died from a bullet that entered the upper part of his chest, proceeded on a downward path through his heart, finally exiting his back. At the time of his death, his blood alcohol level had been .42. This in addition to the presence of cocaine in his system.

"A blood alcohol level of .10," Fitzgerald explained in response to Isaiah's gentle questioning, "is considered sufficient to render an individual legally impaired. A level of .40 will be marked lethal by hospital laboratories."

"And would," Isaiah asked, "a level of .42 be incapacitating?"

The question called for a conclusion well beyond the expertise of a forensic pathologist, but I didn't object because I believed the whole line of testimony to be easily rebutted. The only person who could accurately testify to Byron's condition immediately before the shooting was sitting next to me. In that light, the prosecution's attempt to render Byron harmless smacked of desperation, a point I intended to make to the jury in the course of my closing argument.

"Almost certainly," Fitzgerald equivocated.

"Dr. Fitzgerald," I asked when my turn came, "did Byron Sweet die of alcohol poisoning?"

"No." Fitzgerald looked at Carlo for a moment, then back to me. When he spoke again, his voice was a good deal stronger. "No, he didn't."

"You'll excuse me, Doctor, but I seem to remember you telling the jury that his dose was fatal?"

Isaiah was on his feet, explaining, accurately enough, that I'd completely mischaracterized Fitzgerald's testimony. Delaney sustained the objection, but it gave the jury a starting point from which I could, step by step, force a retreat.

Actually, Fitzgerald admitted when I rephrased the question, the word fatal, written on a lab report, only indicated a potentiality and the need for immediate treatment. It did not mean that the person testing .40 was actually dead. It didn't even mean that he or she was necessarily unconscious. Yes, the presence of a central nervous system stimulant, such as cocaine, would mitigate the effects of a depressant, like alcohol. No, he could not be certain that Byron Sweet was incapacitated when the bullet that actually ended his life actually entered his body.

"Dr. Fitzgerald, have you ever done an autopsy on an individual with a blood alcohol level of .50?"

"Yes, I have."

"Ever do a six?"

"I once," he told the jury, "did an autopsy on a woman who registered a level of .62."

"And was alcohol poisoning the cause of the woman's death?"

"No, Mr. Kaplan, it wasn't."

"If she didn't die of alcohol poisoning, Doctor, how did she die?"

"She walked off the edge of a roof."

It was almost 3:00 when I let Fitzgerald go. Isaiah (wisely, I thought) didn't attempt to rehabilitate the doctor's testimony. Instead, he called Sergeant Benjamin Fish, who'd supervised the crime scene unit. I had no questions for Benjamin Fish and he was off the stand by 3:30. Delaney looked at the clock, then asked, "Mr. Buscetta, is your next witness ready?"

"Yes, your Honor," Carlo said. "She's waiting outside." He glanced back over his shoulder as if he could see through the wall. "Lieutenant Grushko has obligations in Part 33 tomorrow afternoon. If we can get her direct testimony in today . . ."

The reason for Carlo's eagerness soon became apparent. Lieutenant Lena Grushko had been working in the NYPD's Fingerprint Division for nearly ten years, and had testified hundreds of times. She would (and did) tell the jury that on January 18, two days after Byron Sweet was murdered, she'd gone to the lab armed with a set of Priscilla Sweet's fingerprints. Once there, in the presence of Detective Shawn McLearry, she'd first dusted the pistol seized at the Sweet crime scene, lifting an identifiable partial print from the barrel of the gun. Then she'd removed the cartridges, dusted them one at a time, discovering still another print. The fingerprint on the barrel matched Priscilla's left ring finger (nine points of comparison); the print on the cartridge her right index finger (eleven points of comparison).

When Lena Grushko told the jury that Priscilla Sweet's fingerprint had been found on one of the bullets in the gun, her tone was so matter-of-fact that it took them a moment to realize the implications. Then, one by one, they shifted in their seats as each turned to look directly at Priscilla.

Juries are hard to read, but I took those looks to be reevaluations. Up to this point, we'd been winning the little skirmishes; now, all of a sudden, they were imagining Priscilla dropping those cartridges into the chambers, pushing the cylinder up into the frame. And maybe they were also imagining Byron Sweet in that chair, drunk and helpless, unable to offer the least resistance. Albert Wong, follower of the gentle Christ, seemed almost disappointed. He held his mouth in a little circle, cleaned his glasses with a handkerchief before fixing his gaze on Priscilla.

By the time Carlo finished, it was after five o'clock and Delaney quickly recessed the jury, allowing each member to carry home Grushko's uncontested testimony. That was why Carlo had been so anxious to get Grushko on the stand, why he'd strung out her testimony until he was certain Delaney would call it quits for the day. Tomorrow, on cross-examination, I would open up a line of doubt that Priscilla would define when she finally testified. But for this one night, the prosecution's theory would stand by itself, a reality to be discussed at dinner, perhaps over a good stiff drink.

For once, Priscilla seemed a bit off center. Maybe she realized that I'd made a mistake, that I should have cross-examined Benjamin Fish, kept him on the stand until Delaney was ready to call it a day. In any event, she resisted briefly when a court officer took her arm, then rose to her feet. Her eyes remained on mine for a moment and I believe I saw, just below their flat gray surface, a hint of fear.

"I had a bad night," Priscilla admitted on the following morning. "The looks the jury gave me . . . I felt like I was being convicted on the spot."

"Well, I had a bad night, too. I screwed up, Priscilla. I should have kept Sergeant Fish on the stand until Delaney was ready to adjourn, but I didn't. I let the jury sit with Lena Grushko's testimony and now we have to live with it." I sipped at a container of steaming coffee, chased it with a sharp pull on the cigarette in my hand. In fact, I'd slept very well the night before, slept a dreamless sleep after an apparition-free evening. Perhaps it had to do with Priscilla's fear, a fear I somehow found comforting. "Today," I announced, "Carlo hands the jury a motive."

"You're talking about Buscetta's snitch?"

"That's right. But don't worry, by the time I finish with Ms. Norton the jury will think she's a witness for the defense."

As if to prove my point, Janet Boroda showed up a few minutes later, bearing a diagram she'd been trying to get from the Department of Corrections for the last two weeks. It depicted an open housing area in the Rose Singer Jail, two rows of twenty-five bunks arranged head-to-head, a twenty-by-twenty foot area containing sinks, showers, and toilets, a few tables and benches. There were no partitions anywhere, and thus no privacy.

I intended to use the diagram (along with her criminal record and the deal she'd cut) to impeach Kaisha Norton's testimony. Juries love physical evidence, objects they can see or touch. Janet was carrying fifty-one stick pins in her evidence bag, forty-eight blue representing the other prisoners, two red for Priscilla and Ms. Norton, one yellow for the corrections officer who patrolled day and night. I would ask Kaisha to place the blue pins first, knowing full well that she wouldn't remember the position of every other prisoner. But the jury would get a good look at those pins in my hand, and they'd get the message as well. Especially if I dropped a few as I put them away.

I was in the process of congratulating Janet when Sergeant Mason pushed open the door and stuck his head inside. "Delaney wants you in chambers," he said. "Pronto."

Carlo and Isaiah were already present when I arrived, as was a court reporter. Delaney waved the reporter off when her fingers drifted up to the keyboard. "Let's keep this off the record for now." He indicated a chair, tossed me a copy of the *Post* opened to page three. The article, under the headline: GAMES LAWYERS PLAY, featured a courtroom drawing of my back as I questioned Shawn McLearry. The chalk dot on my jacket was now the size of a ping pong ball.

"Any response, Mr. Kaplan?" Delaney asked.

"To the *New York Post*? No, I don't think so."

"How about," Delaney continued without missing a beat, "a response to *Newsday,* the *Times,* the *Daily News*, ABC, NBC, CBS, or the Fox Network?"

"Whatever they're referring to, assuming it wasn't fabricated from whole cloth, must have occurred accidentally."

"Like your abuse excuse?" Carlo snarled.

"You'll have to forgive Mr. Buscetta," Delaney said. "The Appellate Court turned down his appeal of my ruling on the cocaine evidence and he's a bit peevish this morning."

"I want him put under oath." Carlo ignored Delaney's little dig, though by this time he must have been regretting his decision to appeal. "It should be on the record."

"And why is that, Mr. Buscetta? Are you planning a *second* appeal?"

Under other circumstances, I might have been severely chastised, perhaps even held in contempt. But no judge likes to have his rulings appealed, especially while the trial is proceeding. After the cocaine charge was dismissed, Jay Harrison had written a column profiling judges who "never met a technicality they didn't like."

"I'm going to take you at your word, Mr. Kaplan," Delaney continued. "As long as it doesn't happen again. You might want to think about changing dry cleaners. Just to make sure."

A few minutes later, he reminded the jury that they were only to consider actual testimony. "Under no circumstances are you to allow yourselves to be influenced by rumors or unchallenged demonstrations." Then he called Lena Grushko back to the stand.

I watched the jury while Delaney reminded Grushko that she was still under oath. They'd spent the night imagining Priscilla loading her own gun and they weren't happy about it. Latisha Garret, who'd told me that women have an obligation to escape their abusers, sat with her arms folded across her chest, her mouth drawn into a frown of disapproval. Rafael Fuentes, his notebook already out and on his lap, stared straight ahead when I tried to make eye contact.

"Good morning, Lieutenant." I didn't try to approach the jury, thought it better to let them sit with their judgments.

"Good morning, Mr. Kaplan."

"Lieutenant Grushko, did you find any other fingerprints, either on the gun or on the cartridges, besides the two you described yesterday?" I picked up the revolver, let it dangle from a finger.

"There were no other identifiable prints."

I responded, my voice loud enough to make Delaney jerk in his chair, before she finished the sentence. "That's not what I asked you, Lieutenant. Try to answer the questions I ask you. Instead of the ones you want to hear."

"Objection, argumentative."

"Sustained. If the witness needs instruction, Mr. Kaplan, I'll instruct her."

Instead of repeating my first question, I abruptly changed direction. "Lieutenant Grushko, you found two fingerprints belonging to Priscilla Sweet, one on this revolver and one on an unspent cartridge. Is that correct?"

"Yes."

"When were they put there?"

She straightened in her chair, the question obviously expected. "I don't know."

"Forty-eight minutes before the gun was fired?"

"There's no way . . ."

"How about forty-eight hours or forty-eight days?"

Carlo was on his feet again, requesting that the witness be allowed to answer. Delaney arched his right eyebrow, a warning gesture, before instructing me to slow down.

"You can finish your answer," he finally told Grushko.

"It is not possible," she told the jury, "to ascertain with any degree of certainty when a given fingerprint was placed on an object."

"So, for all you know, those fingerprints were placed there months before you saw them. Is that right?"

"It's possible."

I put the gun down, returned to the defense table, picked up a copy of Grushko's report. "Now, Lieutenant, would you tell us if there were any other fingerprints, besides the two you identified yesterday, found on the gun."

"No other identifiable prints were found."

If she wanted to fight, that was perfectly okay with me. I had Delaney instruct her to answer the question, then forced her, inch by inch, to admit that she'd found smudged prints in eight different places on the gun and the bullets, that some were overlapping, that the weapon might have been handled by a dozen individuals.

"Now, you've told us that you recovered partial fingerprints that were too small to identify. Is that correct?"

"That's correct."

"Did you compare these partial fingerprints to those of the defendant?"

"Yes, I did."

I finally turned to the jury, noting their interest with satisfaction. "In the course of those comparisons, Lieutenant, did you conclude that *any* of those partial fingerprints could *not* have belonged to Priscilla Sweet?"

"Yes," she finally admitted, "I did."

"So, even though these partial fingerprints were too small to identify as *belonging* to a specific individual, they could still be used to *exclude* a specific individual?"

"That's right."

"And how many partial fingerprints did you find which could *not* have belonged to the defendant?"

"Four."

"You found *four* partial fingerprints that could *not* have been put there by Priscilla Sweet?"

"Yes."

I turned then, directed my full attention to the witness. "Would you explain to this jury, Lieutenant Grushko, exactly why you didn't say this yesterday and save us all a lot of time?"

Thirty-four

It took Carlo all of sixty seconds to demolish my thoughtful cross-examination. As I dropped into my chair, he strode across the courtroom, picked up Byron's .38, and released the cylinder. Still without speaking, he dropped six blank cartridges, one at a time, into the chambers before snapping the cylinder shut with a quick twist of his wrist. "Lieutenant Grushko," he asked as he slowly turned to face the jury, "is there any way, any way at all, that the defendant's fingerprint could have gotten on that cartridge case . . . *after* the weapon was loaded?"

I remember Priscilla's fingers tightening on my forearm when the cylinder slammed home, but I didn't turn to look at her. Instead, I kept my eyes on Carlo, expecting him to flash some measure of his little triumph, but he didn't even make eye contact as he addressed the court.

"Call Kaisha Norton."

Even dressed in an obviously new, smoke-gray pants suit and a pair of sensible, low-heeled pumps, even sporting a jet-black, shoulder length wig, Kaisha Norton's bony frame and battered face read like a memoir of life on the street. A long, near-miss scar ran directly across her throat, two of her teeth were badly chipped, and she was missing her right canine. I thought of Julie when I saw her, of how this might easily have been Julie's fate, and I felt a momentary twitch of sympathy for Kaisha Norton, and for Carlo, as well. He would never have purchased her testimony if he hadn't been desperate.

Kaisha's history of drug possession, larceny, prostitution, and burglary ran to four pages in her rap sheet and included two felonies. Her last bust, the one she was trying to get out from under, occurred six months before Byron's death. Charged with criminal sale of a controlled substance in the second degree, a B felony, she'd been unable to make the twenty-five-thousand-dollar bail and had been incarcerated on Rikers Island when opportunity in the form of Priscilla Sweet knocked on her bunk.

As a persistent felon, Kaisha had been looking at a twelve-year minimum sentence if convicted. The deal she'd made with Carlo (and which he put on the table at the start of his direct examination) was simple. In return for her testimony, her charge would be reduced to criminal possession of a controlled substance in the seventh degree, a D Felony, and her sentence reduced from twenty-five years to fourteen months. As she'd already been incarcerated for nearly ten months, Kaisha would be on the street before the end of Priscilla's trial.

Her testimony, delivered in a hoarse, raspy whisper, was equally simple. On January 18, the day before Thelma Barrow entered my office, Kaisha had offered Priscilla a cigarette, then struck up a conversation. In the course of that conversation, Priscilla had admitted shooting her husband.

"He thought I was stealing," she'd told her new friend.

"And was you?" her new friend had asked.

"I got what I needed from that asshole," she'd answered. "I got everything he had to give."

Priscilla had done hard time in Bedford Hills; she knew the rules and she knew about prison snitches. I remember her leaning forward to catch the details, then settling back with a shake of her head. For a moment, I thought she was going to flash that sardonic smile. Instead, she picked up a pencil and began to doodle on a yellow pad.

"Do you recognize her?" I asked when Carlo turned the witness over.

"Kaisha was in the dormitory." Priscilla shrugged, raised an eyebrow. "It's not the kind of face you can forget."

"And not the kind of face that inspires confidence?"

Instead of a smile, I got a lecture. "Mother Theresa," Priscilla told me, her voice tight, breathless, "wouldn't inspire confidence on Rikers Island."

I spent the first thirty minutes of my cross-examination taking Kaisha back over her criminal history. Until I felt the jury's collective attention begin to wander. Then I switched to show-and-tell. I had Janet Boroda set a blow-up of the diagram supplied by the Department of Corrections on an easel while I picked up my colored push-pins. "Miss Norton," I asked as I crossed the courtroom to stand next to the easel, "do you recognize this diagram as an accurate representation of the D233 housing area where you were incarcerated on the eighteenth of January?

She stared at it for a long moment before replying. "Yes, I do."

"And were all fifty bunks occupied that night?"

"Yes, sir."

Those were the only affirmative answers I got from Kaisha Norton. She thought her conversation with Priscilla had taken place on Priscilla's bunk, but she wasn't sure where Priscilla's bunk was. She couldn't place the corrections officer who walked the housing unit, couldn't recall her (or his) name. When I asked if any of the closest bunks had been occupied, she replied, "Might have been. I don't remember."

"Miss Norton, besides you and Priscilla Sweet, there were forty-nine women in that housing area, is that correct?"

"I guess."

"But you don't remember the position of a single individual, is that also correct?" I shook the heap of pins in my hand, held them up for the jury to inspect.

"I must'a been not payin' attention."

"And why is that, Miss Norton? Why, with forty-nine other people in the room, were you so preoccupied with Priscilla Sweet, a woman you'd never met before that night?"

"I don't know. We just got to talkin'."

"And in the course of that 'just talking,' Priscilla Sweet admitted to committing a premeditated murder? Is that what you want this jury to believe? That she admitted this to *you*?"

Rafael Fuentes was scribbling furiously. Latisha Garret was leaning away from Kaisha Norton as if trying to avoid a foul odor. Several other jurors were looking at their hands. One, Maureen Baker, kept glancing at her watch. Wondering, undoubtedly, what she was going to have for lunch.

If Kaisha was aware of the fact that her performance was bombing, she didn't let it show. Her deal was cut, this appearance her end of the bargain. If her testimony failed to convict Priscilla, it was no skin off her nose.

"What I'm tellin' you," she rasped, "is that's how it went down." I caught Alfred Wong's eye, held it while I asked my next question. "Miss Norton, will you please describe Priscilla Sweet's appearance on the night you had this conversation?"

"She was beat up," Kaisha responded without hesitation. "She was beat up bad."

Margo Robertson told a story very similar to Kaisha Norton's, a story made all the more effective because it came from the mouth of a very pretty, very white young lady. On Margo, the dark blue dress, the black pumps, the gold circle pin over the breast looked natural. When she spoke, her Connecticut origins were readily apparent in her clipped tone and precise diction. "Yes," she told Isaiah, "Priscilla and I were good friends. Best friends, I think."

The word on the street, according to Caleb, was that Margo Robertson was a dabbler, a slice of whitebread come to the Lower East Side for a taste of the wild before settling into a safe, middle-class life. An accounting major with a degree from N.Y.U., she'd taken her first bust three days after Priscilla shot Byron. Ordinarily, middle-class white women are forgiven their first offense, but Margo's boyfriend, Carlos Azzirre, who owned the four kilos of cocaine in the trunk of Margo's Honda, had chosen to shoot it out with his Dominican connection. When the smoke cleared, Margo was the only one left to take the weight and she'd been charged with criminal possession in the first degree, an A1 felony punishable by fifteen years in prison. Fifteen years to life.

A quarter of a century ago, the deal offered to Margo Robertson would have gone unheard by the jury. Margo, if asked directly, would have replied that she had received no promises from the District Attorney, that she'd been driven by conscience to come forward. Today, these deals are negotiated by counsel and etched in stone: this for this, that for that. The state's this was Margo's testimony; Margo's that was a sentence of probation to a C felony. Isaiah, like Carlo before him, revealed the terms of Margo's deal at the opening of his direct examination. His tone was mild, his questions to the point and directed to the jurors. He stood exposed, his jacket unbuttoned, shoulders spread. Telling the jury that the prosecution had nothing to hide. Telling them, beyond that, to transfer the state's apparent honesty to the witness before them.

Margo Robertson told the expected story. She and Priscilla were confidants, they shared every facet of their lives, including Priscilla's troubled relationship with Byron. In fact, on two occasions, Margo, who ordinarily avoided Byron, had been present when Byron went off on Priscilla. Both times, he'd charged her with stealing his money. After the second incident, while Priscilla nursed a cut lip in Margo's apartment, Margo had asked her, point blank, if Byron's accusation was true.

"I'm not gonna come out of this broke," Priscilla, according to Margo Robertson, had replied.

"And did you return to this subject in the future?" Isaiah asked.

"Yes, from time to time."

"And did the defendant ever tell you that she was in fear of her life?"

"Yes. In November of last year—I don't recall the exact date—Priscilla told me that Byron had threatened to kill her if she didn't return the money."

Isaiah let his voice drop a notch, forcing the jurors to lean forward. "Did Priscilla Sweet take this threat seriously, Ms. Robertson?"

"Yes." Margo stole a glance at Priscilla before replying, a glance that seemed, to me, full of regret. "What she told me was that if it came down to him or her, it was going to be him."

Delaney called the noon recess before Isaiah got to his chair. Ninety minutes later, after a stringy roast beef sandwich in a packed deli, I rose from my chair, pitched my first question across the well of the court. "How many days, Miss Robertson? How many days have you spent in jail since you were arrested for possessing more than nine pounds of cocaine?"

Margo recoiled slightly, then curled her cupid's bow mouth into a pouty frown. Her nostrils flared into perfectly rounded circles. Her right hand fluttered to the silver cross at her throat.

"Miss Robertson, did you hear my question?" I was in motion by then, striding up to the lectern, buttoning my jacket, slapping down a stack of notes. My aim was to clean the jury's memory, to turn Margo Robertson into a witness for the defense.

"Yes, Mr. Kaplan."

"Then please answer it."

"I was in jail for one day."

"A full day? Twenty-four hours?"

Margo stole a glance at the prosecution table. Judge Delaney's eyes followed. Her message: Please help me. His message: If you try to coach the witness, I'll make you pay for it. Delaney being the man wearing the black robes, Isaiah and Carlo maintained deadpan expressions.

"Let's make it a little easier," I said. "According to your police file, you were taken into custody at 10:45 P.M. on Monday, February eighteenth, then released at 3:30 P.M. on the following day. Would you disagree with that?"

"No."

"So you were incarcerated for exactly sixteen hours and forty-five minutes. Is that right?"

"I guess so."

"Miss Robertson, you were charged with an A1 felony. Is that correct? Criminal possession of a controlled substance in the first degree."

"Yes."

"And you are guilty of that crime, are you not?"

It was a trick question. Margo Robertson might very well not have been guilty. The cocaine might have belonged to her boyfriend. She might not even have known it was in the trunk of her car. But she was going to take a plea; she was going to admit that the drugs belonged to her. That was also part of the deal.

"I am," she said after a long moment.

"Miss Robertson, did your attorney, Alice Blankman, ever tell you that if convicted of an A1 felony, the minimum sentence you could expect to receive was fifteen years in prison?"

"She told me that," Margo said.

"And did Mrs. Blankman negotiate a deal with the prosecution in return for your testimony? Or did you speak to the prosecution directly?"

"Mrs. Blankman negotiated."

"And the deal she negotiated for your testimony against a woman you characterize as your 'best friend,' calls for a reduction of your sentence from fifteen years to the sixteen hours and forty-five minutes you've already served. Is that right?"

Isaiah objected and Delaney sustained him. There was no way Margo could predict her actual sentence if she'd gone to trial. But the point was made and I was certain the jurors would carry my version of the deal into their deliberations.

"Miss Robertson, have you ever been incarcerated in a state prison?"

"No. Never." Margo straightened in the chair, squared her shoulders, slid her hands from the arms of the chair to her lap.

"And before your recent arrest, had you ever been confined to a county jail?"

"No."

I turned slightly, pitched the next series of questions to Latisha Garret. From time to time, our eyes met and locked. I understood that she was weighing me, that I was offering myself to her. Throughout, I kept my voice soft, my manner relaxed.

"Are you afraid of prison, Miss Robertson?"

Isaiah, who saw what was coming, tried his best to protect her with a series of objections, but I refused to react. The truth was that Margo Robertson, like any other son or daughter of the middle-class, was terrified by prison and would do anything short of suicide to avoid it.

"Bad things," Margo finally whispered some ten minutes later, "can happen to you in prison."

I stepped back, turned to face Margo. "You ever see Priscilla Sweet with a split lip?" I barked. "A black eye? Bruises on her face?

On her neck? On her arms, her legs, her back, her breasts . . . ? Would you say that bad things can happen to you *outside* of prison?"

Delaney stopped me with a bang of his gavel. "No more of this," he warned.

"I apologize, your Honor," I responded before putting the questions to Margo one at a time. After a series of affirmative responses, I asked her if she'd ever urged Priscilla to have her injuries treated at a hospital.

"Yes. About a year ago. I thought she might have broken one of her ribs."

"She? You thought Priscilla Sweet broke her own rib?"

"I thought Byron might have broken her rib."

I rotated my shoulder toward the defense table, then spun back to again face Margo. "How much, Miss Robertson, did Priscilla steal from her husband? A thousand dollars? Ten thousand? Fifty? A hundred thousand?"

"I don't know."

"But whatever the amount, it was enough to justify her remaining with her husband. Would you agree with that?"

"I don't understand the question."

"Miss Robertson, if Priscilla was stealing all this money from her husband, why didn't she just buy an airline ticket and leave him?"

"She was afraid he'd kill her," Margo answered before Isaiah could object. Delaney, after instructing Margo not to respond if either counsel voiced an objection, told the jury to disregard her answer as a matter of pure speculation.

I tucked my notes under my arm, stole a glance at Latisha Garret. "Are you saying, Miss Robertson, that Priscilla Sweet was afraid to *leave* her husband, but she was not afraid to *steal* from him?"

Somewhere in the course of my summation, I would urge the jurors to use their common sense. Nobody would endure the abuse endured by Priscilla Sweet for money. I would point out that we, the defense, had proven that Byron's abuse extended back for more than a decade. Had she been stealing all that time? Dr. Elizabeth Howe would tell the jury that abusers virtually always justify their abuse, that Byron's accusation was no more rational than that of a husband who attacks his wife because he can't find his favorite pair of socks.

"I know it doesn't make sense," Margo responded after a long hesitation. "I'm just saying that's what happened."

It was time to get out. "No further," I told Delaney.

Carlo was up before I got back to my chair. He moved to the lectern quickly, head erect. "Your Honor," he announced, "the prosecution rests."

Thirty-five

I walked all the way back to Fourteenth Street, a little over two miles, straight up the Bowery. Even through the commercial district above Canal Street, there were knots of strolling pedestrians, mostly young, on every block. The temperature was still up in the mid-fifties and I could smell the odor of spring as surely as I had in Brantley, Alabama, the night before Caleb's funeral. It rose above the exhaust of the taxicabs, the trucks, and the buses, pierced the acrid stink of urine in the doorways, so insistent I found myself wondering if the light breeze had carried the fragrance from some little valley in New Jersey, had conserved it explicitly for winter-weary Manhattan. Within a week, thousands of daffodils in Central Park would extend yellow trumpets from stiff, determined stalks. On the following Saturday, half of Manhattan would come out to pay their respects. I could remember a time when I'd watched this pilgrimage from the balcony of my Central Park West apartment, cradling a morning cup of Hennessy-laced coffee, wearing my green silk robe over my green silk pajamas.

Somewhere near Houston Street, I passed a derelict wearing enough layers of clothing to obscure every curve and angle of her body. She was sitting on a square of torn cardboard, her back against the stone wall of an office building, staring up at the sky as if about to ask a question. As I passed, she grabbed a Styrofoam cup with a few pennies at the bottom and shook it in my direction. I fished a quarter out of my pocket, dropped it in.

"Survived another winter?" I asked. "Congratulations."

She put the cup next to her right hip, kept her eyes on the firmament above. My quarter didn't entitle me to a conversation, not even a thank-you.

As I turned away, I suddenly realized that I was jealous. Not of this old woman, but of the good citizens who moved around us. A year before, Julie, Caleb, and I had joined the pilgrimage to Central Park, had carefully observed hyacinth, daffodil, and crocus, had played audience to street singers, jugglers, even a robed magician. Now that it was time to renew the compact, I could not imagine returning alone.

A few minutes later, as I reached Fourteenth Street, still wallowing in a sludgy mix of self-pity and righteous anger, I had a sudden vision of myself strolling past the Central Park Zoo, arm in arm with Priscilla Sweet. And why not? If things went well, and I intended to make sure they would, she'd be out of jail before the end of the following week. Central Park in springtime would be the perfect place for a born-and-bred New Yorker to begin a new life. Maybe we'd take a carriage ride up to the Metropolitan, stroll through the exhibits, accept congratulations from the assembled (and appreciative) multitudes. All I had to do was put Caleb and Julie to rest. Then, like Priscilla, I could get on with my life.

I came out of the elevator expecting to pass a long night alone with my thoughts, took several steps toward my office at the end of the hall, then pulled up short. Pat Hogan was sitting on the floor, legs splayed, his flabby torso as shapeless as that of the homeless woman I'd run into on Houston Street.

"Hey, Pat, you alive down there?" I resisted an urge to drop a quarter in the upturned hat next to his right hand.

He opened his eyes, stared up at me until the light of recognition dawned, then opened his hand to reveal a set of lockpicks in a small metal box. "I told ya I couldn't use 'em," he said. "I ain't got the fingers for it." It took him a long minute to gather his hat, rise to his feet, and shake off the cobwebs. Finally he said, "The chickens have come home, Sid. Now let's see if you really wanna play rooster."

Once inside, he flopped into a chair, pulled a nearly empty pint of Absolut from his jacket pocket, drank without apology. I took the chair behind my desk, put its weight between us, suddenly afraid of the message I'd paid thousands of dollars to hear.

"I did what you asked, Sid. I went back to the neighborhood where Joey Barrow had his hardware store and asked around. No problem. When I told 'em I was workin' for the great Sidney Kaplan, they got in line to talk to me. In fact, one or two went so far as to actually tell me the truth." Hogan scratched his jowls, settled his bulk against the back of the chair, and lit a cigarette. "You were right about Joey Barrow. He kept a gun in his store, showed it off to the neighbors, liked to play the macho man. Guy who owns the barber shop down the block, Eddie Bogolio, told me him and Joey dabbled in stolen goods. Small appliances mostly, toasters, clock radios, electric shavers, like that. Joey referred to his son-in-law as the nigger, never called him anything else. 'You know what the nigger did this time?' That's the way he began his haircuts. He ended his haircuts as follows: 'One day I'm gonna shoot that nigger.' "

Hogan brought the bottle to his mouth, took a judicious sip. "Wanna hear somethin' else?" he asked. "Joey used to take his darlin' daughter to a gun range in Middle Village. Story I got from the manager, Werner Bergman, the kid wasn't a bad shot with a .38."

I maintained my silence for a moment, remembering Priscilla's insistence that she knew nothing about guns, had accidentally opened the cylinder on the revolver she used to kill Byron, thinking the cylinder release was a safety. Hogan unbuttoned his jacket, exposing the grip of an automatic beneath his right armpit, then rubbed his gut. "I'm fuckin' torn up inside," he complained. "I'm livin' on Pepcid."

I dropped my elbows to the top of the deck, looked at the bottle in his lap. "Price of the ticket, Pat. Take it from a reformed drunk."

"Now you're preaching?" He looked disappointed as he raised the bottle to his open mouth.

"Beg pardon. You were saying?"

Hogan stared straight ahead for a minute, stared unblinking at the window behind my back. "What it was was luck," he finally announced. "The Long Island Expressway was terminal this afternoon. The worst I've ever seen the fucker when it was actually open.

Or maybe it wasn't open. Maybe they were taking the traffic off a couple of exits ahead. What matters is that I gave up on it, jumped ship at Main Street with the intention of working my way toward Northern Boulevard."

"But Northern Boulevard was also jammed with traffic," I said, my dinner turning in my stomach. "And you went to Thelma Barrow's house which just happened to be in the neighborhood."

"Wrong. What I did was go to the neighbor's house. Gennaro Cassadina's house. Figured I'd ask him if Joey kept a gun at home and not just in the store. Sometimes these gun freaks, their wives won't let 'em bring a gun into the house. Maybe that was why Joey didn't try to prevent his daughter's kidnapping." Hogan lit a cigarette with an old Zippo lighter, blew smoke in my general direction. "They were very nice to me, Sid. The daughter and the old man. Served me coffee and cake while Gennaro told me his life story. I was there maybe a half hour when the alarm went off in Thelma Barrow's house.

"It took me a minute to realize what was happening, that it wasn't an ambulance or fire engine. That's because the Cassadinas didn't react. They didn't go to the window, check it out, didn't even complain. When I asked them why they weren't concerned, Jenny told me the alarm would shut off in a few minutes, that it had happened so many times in the past the cops didn't show up anymore. The noise was a pain in the ass, but what could you do? An old lady without a husband in New York? You couldn't blame her for taking precautions.

"I left the Cassadinas a few minutes later, walked right across the lawn and pretended to knock on Thelma's door while I checked the house. There were no sensors on the windows, no alarm company sticker on the door and from what I could see through the living room window, no motion detectors in the corners. Sid, there's only one other possibility for a home system and that's pressure pads under the carpeting."

Hogan stopped speaking long enough to drop back into the chair and cross his legs. He flicked his ash on my floor, looking thoroughly pleased with himself. "Installing pressure pads means ripping the carpet up, then putting it back down. It's expensive which is why you never see it in middle-class homes. Plus, it lets an intruder into the house before it triggers. Most people wanna scare off the bad guys before they gets inside. The advantage is that the system's invisible and burglars set it off before they even know it's there. It's also invisible to lawyers who come to interview their clients' mothers. Lawyers who might put two and two together."

He stopped abruptly, wriggled even deeper into his chair while I absorbed the information. "You'd think," I finally said, "if Thelma could afford an expensive system, she could afford one that worked."

"Rule of thumb in the precincts, Sid, more than two false alarms in a month, the cops don't respond. That's how bad most of these home systems are. Of course, you don't know that until after you buy the system. Pressure pads, for instance, start out fine, but when you walk on them day after day, you throw off the calibration. Then you gotta rip the rug up to fix 'em, which is a major pain in the ass." He took a drag on the cigarette. This time he blew the smoke over my head. "Cut to the chase, Sid. You want me to dig under that rainbow? You want me to go in, toss the house? It's your call."

I made the call without hesitation, though my mind was running in a thousand directions, my thoughts scurrying off like cockroaches beneath a descending fist. "Do it, Pat. Do it and get it done."

"First, I gotta find a time."

"For Christ's sake, Thelma's in court all day."

"That's the problem. All *day*. I'm not goin' in while it's still light outside. Too easy to be spotted."

I thought it over, then said, "Thelma's scheduled to testify on Monday. I'll ask her to come into the office on Saturday afternoon to review her testimony. Thelma takes the subway back and forth—two subways, actually, and a bus from Flushing. Figure she won't get home until eight-thirty. That give you enough time?"

Hogan nodded, ground the stub of his cigarette into an ashtray. "About the money, Sid. If I find it, what happens next?"

I'd flipped on the overhead fluorescent lights as we'd come through the door and now the fixture above our heads was buzzing softly. I looked up at it for a moment, made a mental note to replace the tubes. "What you do is you count the money," I told him without looking down. "You count the money, then you tell me how much, then you disappear from my life."

Hogan didn't move a muscle. "I don't think so," he finally said.

"You don't think what?" For a moment, I thought he was going to balk, to assert his cop scruples.

"You gotta take a piece, Sid. Understand?" He drained the inch of vodka in the bottom of the bottle, deposited the bottle on my desk, then rose. "If there's money in that house, you gotta take a piece. I don't wanna be in this by myself."

I crossed the room, opened the door. As Hogan came abreast of me, he fired a parting shot. "An alarm system like that, you gotta figure it cost the better part of five grand. I mean I been all over Thelma Barrow's finances and I know she didn't take the money from either one of her bank accounts. Ditto for putting the bill on her only credit card." He grinned happily. "Let's be positive. Let's presume innocence. Maybe she's got a penny bank the size of a steamer trunk."

Thirty-six

I got my body up the next morning, got it showered, shaved, and dressed, got it out of the office, onto a subway, and into the court-house without mishap. It behaved very well, my body, didn't once flinch away from its obligations, demanded a bare minimum of attention. Which was just as well because the rest of my attention, the larger part by far, was committed to a stream of words that flapped thorough my consciousness with the determined anarchy of bats leaving a cave at sundown. I told myself that an alarm system in the house of a Queens widow, even an exotic system, didn't prove that the crown jewels were buried under the foundation, that it made perfect sense for an elderly widow to protect herself in bad old New York where personal jeopardy was an article of faith. It wasn't her fault that a salesman had sold her a bill of goods.

I told myself the scenario that had Priscilla setting up Byron's murder shortly after the death of her father was absurd on its face. It insisted that she accepted Byron's punishment, endured attacks that clearly threatened her very life for nearly eight months before pulling the trigger. Why would she do that if she'd already stolen enough to warrant her mother's purchase of an expensive alarm system? Why?

Even beyond the pain, if Thelma had purchased an alarm solely to protect her daughter's loot, then mousy little Thelma was a co-conspirator. She'd not only known that her daughter was a thief, she'd known, at the very least, that her daughter was going to put a permanent end to her marriage. Had Thelma encouraged Priscilla to stay the course, persist until the sky, in the form of Elizado Guzman, finally began to fall? Did she put an arm around her daughter's shoulder, say, "C'mon, Priss, it isn't that bad. Nothing a dab of liniment won't fix. Remember, personal fortunes are made through sacrifice. No pain, no gain"?

As the day passed, I kept rearranging these ideas. Or, better still, they rearranged themselves, adding a bit of dialogue here, subtracting a hypothetical there, the unspoken (and actually stupid) assumption being that precise wording and perfect order would somehow reveal a tangible truth. At no time do I remember fearing that Pat Hogan would be caught in the act, a distinct possibility. Nor can I now recall, with any degree of accuracy, the course of the trial on that Friday. My general impression, at the time, was that Rebecca did very well. I can visualize her white hair flowing down over the collar of a light blue jacket and I can hear her voice working in the low registers as she examined this or that witness. But when I look at the transcript, read the Q&A line by line, it's as if my knowledge of the day's events came to me in two minute chunks on the six o'clock news.

Rebecca began our case by leading Dr. Kim Park, our forensics expert, through a concise recitation of his formidable credentials. Then she had Byron Sweet's bullet-scarred chair and a mannequin pierced with a quarter-inch wooden dowel brought into the courtroom. Park used these exhibits to prove that Byron had not been sitting when the fatal shot was fired. "The dowel," he explained as he plopped the model into the chair, "follows the bullet's path through Byron's torso exactly. It will not line up with the bullet hole in the back of the chair if the model is placed in a sitting position. If, however, the mannequin is raised several inches, like so, then tilted forward, dowel and hole line up perfectly."

Carlo's cross-examination, centered on Park's botched analysis of a crime scene more than eight years before, lasted until the noon recess. The tactic, obvious to any courtroom veteran, was a common one. The defense wanted to pile witness on witness, to overwhelm the jury with a fusillade of cumulative evidence. The prosecution, unable to effectively discredit that evidence, could at least nullify the basic strategy by putting the jury to sleep. If, in the process of delay, Carlo and Isaiah aroused the ire of Judge Delaney, as they knew they would, each could drop his shoulders, turn to the jury with a pained expression and a tight, narrow smile, play the prosecutor victimized by technicalities. All the while hoping the jury wouldn't blame them.

After lunch, it became clear that Isaiah was going to follow the pattern of delay established by his boss. He began by challenging the qualifications of Dr. Arthur Goldbaum. Goldbaum, with more than two decades of emergency room experience, was in court to convince the jury that very high levels of inebriation do not preclude the possibility of aggression, the highly visible scar on his own forehead being tangible proof. Isaiah, with some justification, pointed out that Goldbaum had never participated in any scientific study, had never published in any scientific journal, and had written no books. His testimony was therefore anecdotal in nature and should not be presented to a jury as expert. Delaney, with no real choice, sent the jurors off to cool their heels while he conducted a full hearing.

About a half hour into the hearing, with Goldbaum testifying and arguments still to come, I realized that Thelma Barrow would not take the stand before Tuesday morning. At the earliest.

Five minutes later, I was hunched over a pay phone in the hallway, listening to Pat Hogan's answering machine request the favor of a message. At the beep, I dutifully introduced myself, getting as far as "Pat, it's me," before Hogan picked up.

"Hey, Sid, whatta you doin' out of the courtroom at two o'clock in the afternoon? They find your client guilty?"

I quickly explained the situation, finishing with, "I can't find a good reason to drag Thelma into Manhattan on a Saturday if she's not gonna testify until Tuesday. So what I'll have to do is bring her in after court on Monday."

Another lie, a lie buried in truth. Beyond all considerations of Thelma Barrow's comfort, beyond any fear of rousing her suspicions, I was afraid of what Pat Hogan would find in that house, afraid that I'd have to do something when I wanted to do nothing.

"You know, Sid," Hogan said, "you might wanna think about lettin' it go. I mean what're you gonna do if I find what you're lookin' for? I was Caleb's friend, too, and the way I see it, neither one of us has a lot of options. Plus, you might wanna consider that if Priscilla capped her old man for money, she might be willing to do the same to her lawyer."

I shook my head at the phone, muttered what I believed to be an irreducible truth. "I gotta know, Pat. Whether I do anything about it or not, I gotta know."

"What could I say? I've been there a time or two in my life." He sighed into the phone. "Might as well look at the bright side, pretend the goddamned glass is half-full. Maybe ripping your client off will be enough. One thing for sure, this is a woman who really cares about money."

I might have chosen that moment to put my thoughts to the test, might have laid my exculpatory scenarios before Hogan, absorbed his inevitable refutations, but I don't recall even considering the possibility. Instead, I hung up and returned to the legal fray.

Beyond a sharp glance as I took my seat, Priscilla maintained the demure courtroom demeanor we'd worked so hard to perfect. She was wearing a green, long-sleeved dress with a bit of lace at the cuffs, a bit of ruffle at the throat. Sitting with her legs crossed under the table, her hands folded in her lap.

Arthur Goldbaum was lounging in the witness box, trying not to yawn while he listened to Rebecca Barthelme tell Judge Delaney that twenty years of emergency room experience, twenty years during which her witness had dealt directly with tens of thousands of inebriated patients, counted for more than the odd article published in the odd scientific journal. Goldbaum wasn't there, she declared according to the official transcript, to make an assessment of Byron's condition on the day he was killed. No, Dr. Goldbaum's purpose was to counter testimony introduced by the prosecution through the medical examiner. In fact, she casually informed Delaney, if the prosecution was willing to stipulate that Byron was perfectly able to mount an attack on the day in question, the defense would dispense with the witness altogether.

Carlo, needless to say, demurred, and a few minutes later, Delaney having pronounced Goldbaum's clinical experience expert enough for the jury to consider, the trial was again under way. As for myself, I went back to my ruminations, gradually becoming more and more self-absorbed until a burst of laughter snatched me back to the present.

Humorous moments are rare in the courtroom, especially when a jury is present, a fact which makes them, when they do occur, all the more memorable. Goldbaum, when asked if he'd ever encountered a belligerent drunk with a blood-alcohol level above .4, responded by pointing to a scar on his head, then explaining that he'd received it from a bedpan-wielding drunk with a level of .48.

Barely able to repress a smirk, Delaney popped his gavel once, then again, as several jurors, including Latisha Garret, continued to chuckle. A moment later, Rebecca turned Goldbaum over to Carlo who worked the other side of the question for the better part of an hour, forcing Goldbaum to admit that extremely high levels of inebriation often produce a loss of consciousness and sometimes a loss of life. Goldbaum, though he'd never before testified in a trial, came up with the proper response. "Sometimes," he told Buscetta, "isn't always. If you want to know the condition of a specific individual, you have to ask someone who was there to observe that individual."

Delaney recessed for the weekend before Goldbaum was out of the courtroom. I expect he could already smell the Chivas, already feel his butt against the seat of his favorite bar stool. I watched him leave, watched two court officers lead Priscilla back to the pens, then went out to corner Thelma Barrow in the hallway.

"I want you to come into the office after court on Monday afternoon," I told her. "To go over your testimony one more time." I put my hand on her shoulder, looked into her eyes. "You're the keystone, Thelma, and you've got to get it right."

"I thought I was going to testify on Monday?" Her palms were pressed together and she was working them in a slow circle.

"Buscetta's decided to slow the pace down. We'll be lucky to get through the trial by Memorial Day."

As if summoned, Rebecca chose that moment to approach. She had her coat slung over the shoulder and appeared supremely confident. "Looks like Carlo doesn't have any pressing engagements," she announced. "We'll be lucky to get a verdict by the Fourth of July."

"I was telling Thelma I want her to come into the office on Monday evening," I said. "To go over her testimony one more time."

Rebecca cocked her head, looked hard into my eyes. Thelma's testimony was her responsibility, not mine, and she didn't like being reminded of her second-chair status. "Yeah," she said after a long moment, "that might not be a bad idea."

"We could order in some dinner. Make it a party." I finally took my hand off Thelma's shoulder. "And by the way, Rebecca," I announced, "you were great today."

Thirty-seven

Over the weekend, I became my great-grandfather, Hyman Baruch. I wandered the galleries of the Metropolitan, the Whitney, the Jewish Museum, the Museum of the City of New York, and the National Museum of the American Indian. I sat through two utterly boring (and utterly obscure) black-and-white films at a Peter Lorre retrospective in a packed Greenwich Village theater.

I remember almost nothing of what I saw, not surprising because my trek had little to do with nature or culture or even entertainment. No, my goal was only to outrun a fear that continued to build despite my efforts, a fear that had, if not a name, at least a message that winked on and off like a prompt on a computer screen: What, my fear asked me, are you going to do about it?

I carried that fear into Judge Delaney's courtroom on Monday morning, sat with it as Rebecca Barthelme put Amelia Green and Lance McCormack, the waitress and bartender at Pentangles the night Priscilla was attacked, and Margaret D'Cassio, Priscilla's college chum, through their paces.

For the first time, the jury was presented with irrefutable evidence of Byron's violence and they reacted appropriately. When Lance McCormack declared, "I was really scared, but I knew he was going to kill her if I didn't pull him off," Latisha Garret's fists clenched in her lap and Rafael Fuentes, who'd been scribbling furiously, capped his pen, then wiped the corner of his eye with a wrinkled handkerchief. When the photos taken at Bellevue Hospital were passed around, the jurors' eyes went from Priscilla's image to the living Priscilla as if seeing her for the first time.

Carlo objected at every turn, asked nitpicking questions, challenged the admissibility of nearly every piece of evidence. His strategy not only reeked of desperation, it was poorly chosen. He should have let this testimony rush by, should have gotten Priscilla on the stand as soon as possible. After all, she was his only hope. If she failed to hold up on cross-examination, if she broke, he could still win. By delaying, he not only made it harder for himself, he made it harder for me, as well. It was becoming more and more obvious that the state would not exact punishment, not for Byron or Caleb or Julie.

Despite everything, I was very good that evening. With Rebecca, Thelma, and Janet Boroda for an audience, I delivered anecdotes about clients and judges, defense attorneys and prosecutors, ordered in prime rib dinners from the Chelsea Steak House, analyzed the course—future, past, and present—of Priscilla Sweet's trial.

Over dinner, I told a long story about the first time I'd practiced before an abusive judge; over coffee, a shorter story about a client who shot off his mouth to every reporter in New York. Thelma endured it all. She said little, sat with her back and shoulders hunched, as if fending off a cold rain. When I finally let her go, at seven-thirty, she rose, slipped into her coat, pulled a knit beret down to her ears, and was out the door without changing expression. Janet and Rebecca followed almost immediately.

I crossed the room to a window, watched my paralegal and my co-counsel exit the building, then hail a northbound cab on Broadway. Suddenly, I realized that I didn't know where either lived, if they were heading for an uptown co-op, or to Grand Central for a train ride to Connecticut. Maybe they'd told me at some point, but their lives had so little interested me that I'd simply forgotten. Or maybe I'd never asked.

As if determined to rescue me from my thoughts, another of those I'd used, Pat Hogan, stepped from the doorway of a small coffee shop and crossed Broadway. Despite his bulk and the large brown suitcase he held in his gloved hand, Hogan moved very quickly, very lightly, with a freaky grace that instantly reminded me of Caleb's.

A minute later, as I stood by the open door, I heard the decrepit motor that drove our elevator start up with an angry screech, then quickly settle into an uneven rumble as the elevator began to move. The elevator took its time, crashing, as usual, into the steel frame that caged it between the second and third floors, then again between the fourth and fifth. Finally it stopped to disgorge a wildly grinning Pat Hogan. "Buck, buck, buck," he said as he walked past me into the office.

"Buck what?" I closed the door and followed him inside.

"I was imitating a chicken." He dropped the suitcase on my desk, flicked both clasps at the same time, jerked up the lid to reveal stacks of neatly banded greenbacks. "You know, as in the chickens are coming home to roost."

For a moment, I said nothing, my eyes riveted to the money. Then I recalled an obscure bit of testimony from some long forgotten trial. The witness, a Treasury agent, had announced, with a proud flourish, that 450 bills of any denomination weigh exactly one pound.

"They're all hundreds?" I asked, knowing full well that wholesale drug dealers (the problems of counting, storage, and transportation obvious enough) commonly refuse to accept any bill lower than a fifty.

Hogan snorted, said, "No. There's stacks of fifties on the bottom."

"But nothing smaller?"

This time he didn't bother to respond. "I found the case in the basement, Sid, in an old cabinet stuck behind a bureau stored behind the furnace." His face was flushed; his scalp glistened with sweat. "Wanna hear a good joke? When I came through the basement window an alarm went off." He chuckled manfully. "Thelma had motion detectors all over the basement. Might as well have put up a sign: End Of Rainbow/Dig Here."

"What'd you do?"

He grabbed a handful of cash, held it in front of my nose as if offering a bouquet of flowers. "What does it look like I did?"

"I mean when the alarm went off?"

"That's a joke, right?" He shook his head. "Hey, Sid, I already knew the cops wouldn't respond, remember? So I just turned the motion detectors to face the wall and went about my business. The system recycled a few minutes later and the alarm shut down."

I circled the desk, sat in my swivel chair, feeling like I deserved a rest I wasn't going to get. "How much, Pat?" I asked. "How much?"

"You think I counted it?"

"Yeah, I do."

He grinned happily and I suddenly realized that he wasn't drunk, that for the time being the money was enough. "Well," he said, "you're right. Being as I was out of there in fifteen minutes, I had a little time to kill."

"So, how much?"

"A mere pittance, Sid. Three hundred and twenty-five thousand. Give or take a few bundles."

"She could have saved Caleb and Julie. She could have saved Caleb and Julie and still had a hundred and seventy-five thousand left over."

Hogan began to slap bundles of hundred dollar bills down on my desk. "You're lookin' at it the wrong way, counselor. Caleb and Julie weren't the ones who got threatened. Uh-uh. Way I remember it, the bad guys were after Sid Kaplan. It was you she didn't wanna save."

"I don't want that money," I told him, though I made no move to put it back in the suitcase.

"Throw it away, burn it, donate it to AIDS research. I don't give a shit." He stopped abruptly, closed and locked the case. "Fifteen percent, my little co-conspirator. Sixty thousand for the man who hired me to get the answers." He jerked the suitcase off the desk, held it against his chest with both hands for a moment, finally let it drop to his side. "Well, I'm off, Sid. I'm off to Las Vegas, see if I can drink myself to death like Nicholas Cage in that movie. You need me, I'll be the fat guy with the drop-dead call girl at the hundred-dollar blackjack table."

I wanted to maintain a silence, let him walk off into the sunset, but I lacked the courage. "Wait a minute, Pat. Before you go, I have a question. How do we know the money belongs to Priscilla? How do we know it doesn't belong to Thelma?" Again, I tried to stop myself, again I failed. "Guzman told me that Priscilla owed him a hundred and fifty thousand. That's a lot less than you've got in that suitcase."

Hogan crossed the room before turning to face me again. His knuckles, wrapped around the handle of the suitcase, were bone white. "You wanna answer those questions, put 'em to your client. You want a real question, ask yourself what you're gonna do about it when she tells you she paid for that money in blood."

Thirty-eight

When I saw the huddled silhouettes of Priscilla Sweet and Thelma Barrow on the following morning, I was instantly reminded of a client I'd represented many years before on the afternoon Judge David Guttman sentenced him to three consecutive twenty-five year terms in prison. His name was Abel Code and somehow, despite an extensive history of violent crime, he'd expected the judge to show him mercy, had told me, in the few minutes we had together before his sentencing, "I'm a white man, Sid. Even a Jew wouldn't treat a white man like a nigger."

As Guttman passed out years like Christmas candy, the blood had drained from Abel Code's face, leaving his skin the uniform dingy gray of prison underwear. Priscilla's skin, despite the face powder, the hint of blush on her cheeks, was the same dingy gray when I entered the little courtroom at a quarter to nine. Thelma's skin, by contrast, was the color of alabaster; her blue eyes looked as if they'd been painted over china.

"You seem nervous today, Thelma," I said as I tossed my coat onto a bench. "I hope you're not worried about your testimony. Like I already told you, not even Carlo Buscetta would be stupid enough to browbeat the loving mom."

"It's not that, Sid," Priscilla answered for her mother as I took a seat directly behind them. "My mother was burglarized last night." Her green eyes pushed into mine, as if opening the door of a closet.

In the hours following Hogan's departure, I'd attempted to devise a plan of action, but I still wasn't sure, at that point, if there was anything I could do to effect the outcome of the trial short of screaming, "She did it," to the jurors. (Which would result, not in a guilty verdict, but in a mistrial and probable disbarment.) Even if I blew my final argument, even if I asked Priscilla, on direct examination, the sort of questions Carlo would eventually ask anyway, as long as Priscilla kept her cool, we would probably win.

"I hope you didn't lose anything valuable," I said to Thelma. Then, before she could respond, I again turned to my client, "I think I'll come out to Rikers this evening. To go over your testimony. You'll be on the stand first thing tomorrow morning."

"Like you went over my mother's testimony yesterday?"

"Exactly, Priscilla." I stood up, stretched, said, "If I don't get a cup of coffee, I'm gonna fall asleep in the courtroom. I'll see you guys in a few."

Rebecca put on four witnesses that day, beginning with Dr. Theodore Grace, the physician who'd treated Priscilla at Bellevue after the Pentangles incident. Though Grace claimed to have no independent memory of Priscilla Sweet (and, indeed, had only come to testify upon receiving a subpoena), he identified his signature on the hospital records, then compared those records to the photographs taken by Miriam Farber, finally pronouncing the injuries visible on the photos consistent with his own painstaking documentation.

An extremely agitated Thelma Barrow followed. Thelma sat with her legs pressed together, her palms turning slow circles on the tops of her thighs, her back rigid. She delivered her testimony in a monotone that must have driven Rebecca Barthelme to distraction. Whenever Rebecca tried to lead her witness, Carlo objected and was sustained, turning what should have been a naturally told horror story into a series of terse responses to a single, repeated question: "And what happened next, Mrs. Barrow?"

"Your mother," I told Priscilla at one point, "is blowing it."

Priscilla thought about that for moment, then turned to me and whispered, "Well, she was ripped off last night."

"C'mon, Priscilla." I struggled to keep my own expression neutral, to keep from laughing at my own punch line. "What could your mother have lost that's more valuable than the next twenty-five years of your life?"

Sgt. Patrick Shannahan, head of the Domestic Violence Unit at the 107th Precinct in Fresh Meadows, followed Thelma to the stand. After establishing the basics, that Shannahan had received a complaint that included allegations of kidnapping and assault, then jammed his written report into a filing cabinet and left nature to take its course, Rebecca tore into him. Why, she wanted to know, was there no investigation? Did he, Patrick Shannahan, consider kidnapping a minor crime? Or was that the official policy of the New York Police Department? If Priscilla Sweet had been kidnapped by a stranger instead of by her husband, would the police then have acted? Or did the police need a ransom note first? Or a dead body?

Rebecca continued to pound away until Judge Delaney stopped her with a polite tap of the gavel. "Your point is made," he told her. As indeed it was. Priscilla had tried to escape, but the police had let her down. I would ask the jurors to imagine themselves trapped in a downtown tenement, subject to attack at any time, hoping for rescue. Just as if the entire incident hadn't been manufactured.

Maybelle Higginbotham, in a lavender gown with puffy shoulders and black velvet trim (as far as I knew, she was still trying to sell her life story), followed Shannahan to the witness box. Invited by Rebecca to explain her statement to the 911 operator, *I think the boy done killed her this time*, Maybelle told the jury, over a series of thundering objections, that she'd heard Byron shouting and Priscilla screaming on many occasions, felt ominous thuds and bangs against her bedroom wall, had seen Priscilla bruised and cut, had been told by Priscilla that her husband had inflicted the injuries. In theory, these responses went to Maybelle's state of mind at the time she'd made the call and were not offered for the truth of the matter. In fact, they served to establish a consistent pattern of abuse from the time Priscilla was kidnapped until the night she pulled the plug on her husband.

I kept up an almost constant patter as the day's witnesses presented their testimony, leaning over to whisper into my client's left ear. I commented on individual jurors, our various witnesses, Judge

Delaney, and especially Carlo Buscetta. "Look at him," I told Priscilla as Carlo made a desperate attempt to rehabilitate Sergeant Shannahan. "That's the face of a loser, a guy who cries himself to sleep at night. See Delaney? That bored look? He knows it's over, too. Only the jury's still interested."

And, indeed, individual jurors continued to study Priscilla as if she was a puzzle piece left in the box. Their scrutiny forced her to maintain a rigid control over her expression, her posture. I remember that she sat with her legs pressed together under the table, back and head bent slightly forward, that her lower lip trembled when Maybelle described the bruises on her face, that her jaw came up and her mouth tightened when Shannahan (who, like Dr. Grace, had no independent memory of his role in the events preceding Byron Sweet's death) tried to defend his inaction.

Despite the tension, Priscilla did very well, undoubtedly because she'd been thoroughly trained by a professional at the top of his game. Still, for the first time her gray eyes acquired sufficient depth to afford me a glimpse of the rage that lay there, motionless, like a snapping turtle on the bottom of a pond.

Delaney adjourned early that day, at four o'clock, and I left for Rikers Island at five, figuring to arrive just after Priscilla's bus. But the rush hour traffic on the Drive was so bad I diverted to the 59th Street Bridge which was even worse. It was nearly seven when I parked the car, and after seven-thirty by the time Priscilla, wearing an orange jumpsuit, was brought down from her cell. She smiled when she saw me, a smile that didn't come within light years of her eyes, and said, "Hey, Sid, you got a smoke?"

I tossed a pack on the table, watched her shake out a cigarette. Her movements were slow and sensual, as if she hadn't a care in the world. I recalled the elaborate rationales I'd constructed over the weekend, the forced march I'd made through the streets of Manhattan, my plan to shake the confidence of Priscilla Sweet. The letters CFA came to mind, New York cop shorthand for Complete Fucking Asshole.

"Where did you lose it?" I asked her. "Did he beat the humanity as well as the shit out of you?"

She thought about it for a moment, her blank eyes fixed on my throat, finally shrugged and said, "I love my mother. That's enough for me."

I thought of my own mother as she floated through our kitchen, remembering, for some reason, that Magda had kept her fingernails long enough to slice neatly through the tops of envelopes. It was her only affectation.

"Your mother? I don't think so. I think what you loved, Priscilla, was the money. The money and the cocaine."

"I paid for that money," she told me, her voice cold enough to raise goose bumps on the backs of my arms. "I paid in blood."

"As did Byron and Caleb and Julie and those kids who were slaughtered when person or persons unknown took down Elizado Guzman. If there's a point here, why don't you explain it to me?"

"You're the one who called this meeting, Sid. Remember?" She leaned back in her chair, raised her chin, blew a stream of gray smoke at the ceiling. "I'm the one in prison."

"What I want," I told her, though I didn't know why, "is the truth. First, I want the truth."

"And then? What do you want after you get the truth? My blood? Because I'll tell you up front that I'm bled out. Byron got every drop."

I let that go, let my eyes drift around the little cubicle though there was nothing at all to see. The space was as gray and blank as my client's eyes. "Did you ever love him?" I asked. "Byron? Did you ever love him?"

The question brought forth a contemptuous smile. "Who knows, Sid? When I think about that time at Columbia, I feel like an archeologist studying a dead civilization." The smile disappeared. "Next question."

"Why did you take him back?"

This time her smile was genuine. "I hated that nine-to-five bullshit. You can't imagine how much I hated it. Paulie Gullo would hand me that paycheck like it was a gift, like he was Columbus passing trinkets to the Indians. Just enough to pay the rent, of course, just enough to buy groceries, to put clothes on my back, to get me to work on Monday morning." She crossed her legs, looked directly into my eyes. "The check was like dope, Sid. Like a fix. By the time payday came around, there was always some bill overdue. Friday nights, I'd be running to the bank instead of the clubs, trying to cover checks I'd already written. What kind of life is that?"

It was the kind of life I'd lived with Julie and Caleb, the kind of life I'd never live again. "You haven't answered the question, Priscilla. Why did you take your husband back?"

She fiddled with the zipper on her jumpsuit, slid it down a few inches, then back up. "When I came out on parole, I was assigned to a parole officer named Adrienne Whetmore who should have been running a concentration camp. I never once visited her, not even after a year of producing pay stubs and testing clean, when the bitch didn't threaten to violate me at the drop of a hat. I didn't see any point in going back to prison, so I followed the party line.

"As for Byron, I started hearing from him just about the time I was coming off parole. I wanted to get back in the life, but I didn't have any money. What Byron told me when I went up to see him was that he'd made a connection in prison, that he wanted me to help set it up before he came out on parole."

I stopped her with a wave of my hand. "Why you, Priscilla? Why did Byron choose you?"

"Byron didn't have any money, Sid. He'd arranged to have coke fronted, but he had to move it in a hurry. My job was to contact our old customers, get everything in place before the parole board cut him loose. Besides, like he told me again and again, 'Baby, there's no one else I can trust.' " She burst out giggling, brought her palm up to cover her mouth. "Ironic, isn't it? Because I came into the deal intending to rip him off. Because I'd spent two years in Bedford Hills eating the pussy of a man-hating bull dyke who taught me everything I know about survival. Because I thought of Byron Sweet every time I pissed in Frau Whetmore's plastic bottle, every time Paulie Gullo jammed his hand into my crotch."

"Didn't you know what Byron would do to you? Weren't you afraid?"

"Are you asking me if I believed those letters?"

"Yeah."

"The letters were for the parole board, Sid. What Byron told me, face to face, was that he was looking for a business relationship. He would purchase and I would sell."

"And he would beat you up whenever the fancy took him?"

Though she continued to study me closely, Priscilla didn't respond immediately. I met her gaze, told myself not to show fear, that animals and ex-convicts can smell fear, that fear provokes aggression.

"I was raised on pain, Sid," she finally told me. "Good old Joe Barrow, he was smarter than Byron. He knew where to hit, how to conceal the bruises. By the time I got married, a slap didn't mean all that much to me. I thought I deserved it." She shifted in her seat as I continued to stare at her. Again, she seemed to be weighing her thoughts carefully, though whether in search of the right words to convey the truth, or to deceive, I couldn't tell.

"I don't think," she finally said, "that I can make you understand, so let me put it simply. I was in the cocaine business where your life is always at risk. Byron was just another factor in a violent equation. True, there were times, though not as many as I've led you to believe, when I couldn't handle him, but I wasn't going anywhere, not while there was money to be made. That's the deal I cut with myself going in. That's the way it finally went down." She smiled. "Of course, knowing I was gonna kill him made it a lot easier."

She looked at me for a moment, still smiling. "You want to hear the ironic part? I needed to keep Byron stoned, so he'd lose track of the product and the money. But when he was stoned, of course, is when he was most dangerous. You wanna hear another one? I had to engineer the last attack, the one we're using to justify Byron's death. It wasn't easy, Sid, because the poor fuck was halfway to dead at the time."

In the cubicle alongside ours, an attorney, a woman, was trying to convince a reluctant client to accept a harsh plea bargain. As I listened, she told the hapless mutt, over and over again, "But you have no defense, Carrie. You have no defense."

"You knew that Guzman would eventually turn to you for repayment," I finally said. "That's why you left the cocaine where the cops would find it. But when Guzman didn't buy your story about the cops stealing the bulk of the shipment, you took protective custody and turned to your second line of defense. Isn't that right?" When she didn't respond, I continued, anxious now to get it out in the open. "Thelma deliberately pointed Guzman in my direction. That was why you hired me in the first place. I was the sacrificial shyster." Again I hesitated, again she refused to respond. "It was a good story,

Priscilla. Much better than your bullshit about the cops, which Guzman never believed. In fact, it was good enough to get Thelma off the hook, at least temporarily. And, of course, good enough to get Caleb and Julie murdered."

I searched Priscilla's gray eyes, looking for rage, fear, sorrow, for any hint of what she was feeling at that moment. But Priscilla was clearly beyond revealing any fragment of her inner life. "I paid," she calmly repeated, "for that money. I paid in blood."

"You could have saved them. You could have taken care of Guzman and still had enough to start a new life." My own voice was trembling. I wanted to kill her and I wanted to run away and hide; I wanted to come over the table, take her throat in my hands, and I wanted to be at home, lying on my bed in the dark. All my life I'd been a control freak, convinced, even in my darkest moments, that I could pull myself together with an act of will. Now I knew, fully and for the first time, that I'd never been the one giving the orders, that my life had simply happened.

"When my mother took off, I ran out of options. Even if I wanted to, I had no way to get him the money." Priscilla's tone was matter-of-fact, her expression, if anything, even more relaxed. "That wasn't part of the plan," she declared, "leaving the money unprotected. But after she panicked, there was nothing more I could do."

"Don't bullshit me, Priscilla. You could have contacted Guzman. You could have called him on the phone, told him that I didn't have his money, that I never had his money. You could have told him where the money was, given him the code to shut down the alarm, and invited him to pick it up. If you'd done that, Caleb and Julie would be alive. You didn't and now they're dead."

I lit a cigarette, offered the pack to my client, let the silence build. A corrections officer walked by the cubicle, a young *latina* with a butt the size of a watermelon. She glanced at us as she passed, tossed me a hard look devoid of curiosity, then passed on by.

"Are we done with the confession?" Priscilla finally asked. "Can we get down to business?" She laid her cigarette on the edge of the table, ran her fingers through her hair, announced, "I'm getting sleepy."

I ignored the comment. "How did you fix it?" I asked. "So that it looked like Byron was getting out of the chair? Did you provoke him? Did you put the gun in his face, tell him to get up?"

"None of the above," she told me. Then she repeated, "None of the above."

"Do you mean he was really in the process of attacking you?"

"No, I mean that his liver was hurting him and he was sitting on a cushion. I mean the cushion didn't get any blood on it, so I moved it over to the couch. I mean I didn't just sit around and wait for the cops to arrive." She leaned forward, stared into my eyes, her sardonic smile firmly in place. "When I get out of here, Sid, I want to take you to bed, fuck your brains out." She went on before I could interrupt. "Face it, you're a bastard. You've always been a bastard. I didn't set out to get anybody killed, anybody except Byron, but it happened and now it's done with and I'm a bastard, too. What a couple we'd make."

I still saw nothing in her eyes, no glimmer of emotion, no hint of guile, nothing at all. "Does that mean you want your money back?" I laughed loud enough to attract the attention of the corrections officer in the hallway. "Hey, I'm a bastard; you're a bastard. You stole from Byron; I stole from you. You paid in blood; I paid in blood. I've got the money; you *don't*." I stopped abruptly, waited until I was sure she had no answer. "Look at the bright side, Priscilla. If I'd been charging by the hour, as I would have been if you hadn't feigned indigence, you'd have spent most of the money by now anyway. Spent it well, I might add, on a perfect defense."

She let me in, then, just for a moment, flashed me a look of such hatred that I flinched involuntarily. My fear, momentary though it was, seemed to calm her. She leaned back in her chair, looked around as if remembering where she was. Finally, she turned back to me, said, "I'm willing to cut you in, Sid. As long as you make it reasonable. Otherwise, you and Byron can say hello to each other in hell."

"Really? You might keep in mind that you'll be charged with first degree murder this time. In case a sentence of life without the possibility of parole means something to you. Or do you expect to get away with this one, too?" I glanced at my watch. "Well, it's growing late and I don't want to keep you from a good night's sleep. You testify tomorrow and jurors like their mutts alert and healthy." I stood up, pushed my chair against the table. "As for the money . . . well, Priscilla, there's always Tucker Trucking. They really love you down there."

Thirty-nine

Priscilla was perfect. Priscilla was perfect. Priscilla was perfect. I can no longer think of Priscilla Sweet's performance on the day she testified without that sentence preceding all further considerations. And not only in front of the jury, but earlier, at eight-thirty when I arrived, shook the rain off my trench coat, and sat down next to her. Looking back, I believe I can understand her strategy. An incarcerated woman with few resources and fewer friends, she was simply playing the cards in her hand, all the while assuming there'd eventually be a reshuffle, another deal.

"Where's your mother?" I asked.

"My mother's very upset." She stared at the backs of her hands, at her freshly manicured fingernails. "One of the C.O.'s did them for me," she announced. "What do you think? Butch enough for the jury?" She went on before I could answer. "I didn't want to come to court looking like an uptown princess, but I didn't want to look ratty either."

Her nails had been cut just beyond the tips of her fingers, coated with clear polish, the cuticles trimmed back. "Perfect," I told her. "They're perfect."

She dropped her hands to her lap, drew in her shoulders. "My mother's not coming to court today. She's too upset."

"Maybe," I suggested, "your mother doesn't love you anymore. Now that you're broke."

She turned to look into my eyes. "Aren't we past the words? The taunts? I thought we were past that."

It had been raining hard when I made my way into the building a few moments earlier, the clatter of the rain overpowering even the relentless push of the buses and trucks along Centre Street. But in that small, windowless courtroom the only sound besides our hushed voices was the scrape of Priscilla's shoe on the tile floor. She was running the ball of her foot in a slow, steady circle. "I've been thinking about what you told me last night," she continued after a long hesitation. "About the quality of the defense you're providing. And what I think is that a hundred thousand ought to cover it." She smiled, tapped me on the knee. "As long as I get off."

I turned away from her, looked over at the door leading to the pens. With no hearings scheduled for the little courtroom we occupied and Delaney's courtroom on the far side, the pens would be empty. I imagined Priscilla as she'd come up on the elevator, as she approached the bars, working over her deal. Should she offer me seventy-five? A hundred? Or should she go all the way, make that offer I couldn't refuse? Come with it right out of the box.

"Try two-fifty," I said. "Start at two-fifty and let's see what happens."

Priscilla responded without skipping a beat. "It's been a great defense so far," she said, "but not an expensive defense. No Dream Team. No army of experts. There was just you, Sid, which I guess makes it all the more amazing, but still . . ."

"What about the blood money?" I leaned toward her, pressed my shoulder against hers. "Caleb and Julie, they ought to be worth something, no?"

She looked down at her folded hands as if contemplating the problem, drawing her dark hair forward in the process to veil the side of her face. Priscilla was wearing her courtroom best, a pleated navy skirt, a white blouse that looked to be woven of silk, but was probably synthetic, a green cardigan sweater, long sleeved and demure. A small gold earring, a sea shell, glistened in her ear, echoing the glitter of a matching pin on her sweater.

"It's not like they can be compensated," she finally said.

"That, as you already know, Priscilla, is not the point."

"A hundred and fifty, Sid. You have to be reasonable here."

"Why? Why do I have to be reasonable?" The word itself—reasonable—seemed to me so absurd that I came close to laughing in Priscilla's face. "What does reason have to do with it? Don't forget, I'm the one with the cash." When she didn't respond immediately, I said, "Hey, look at the bright side. I could always throw you to the wolves, let you rot in prison while I spend your money."

She shook her head, dismissed the possibility, said, "I feel better. Now that I don't have to lie to you anymore."

The door opened at that moment, opened with a painful creak, and Thelma Barrow, followed by Janet Boroda, stepped through. Priscilla was on her feet before I could react, stretching one arm toward her mother.

"I had to come," Thelma said. "It wouldn't look right if I didn't come."

As Thelma unbuttoned a clear plastic raincoat, slid it over her shoulders, a drop of water fell from the brim of her hat to the corner of her mouth. In an instant, her tongue, a pink blur, snaked out to capture the drop and pull it inside. I looked at Priscilla, looked directly into her eyes. The emotion I saw there was powerful enough to shock me. She really did love her mother, a factor which changed the basic equation not a whit. "Don't worry, Sid," she told me. "I know we'll be able to work this out. We don't have to be enemies."

When Priscilla spoke of college as an adventure, the excitement of her first freedom, finally her head-over-heels love for Byron Sweet, her gray eyes, wistful at first, became deeply regretful. The single tear she erased with an impatient swipe of her hand was far more powerful (and far more effective) than a flood. I remember stealing a glance at Albert Wong, follower of the gentle Jesus, watching his head bob, his eyes fill, and realizing that the poor jerk had already passed through reasonable doubt, that he was standing with both feet firmly planted on exoneration.

Latisha Garret's eyes clouded with rage as Priscilla (careful to make the important point that she'd only begun to use cocaine in response to Byron's fists) narrated the Sweet family's slide into drugs and violence. As Priscilla spoke, her breathing tightened down. She narrowed her shoulders, drew her breasts together, rubbed her left shoulder with her right hand. The look in her eyes shifted from regret to anger to unfathomable sorrow as she finally described the Pentangles assault. "I thought he was going to kill me," she declared. "I thought I was going to die."

Just in case the jury didn't believe her, I resurrected the photos taken immediately after the Pentangles incident and again passed them around. I remember Rafael Fuentes sliding a fountain pen into his shirt pocket, carefully folding his notebook, staring down at each photo. He seemed disbelieving, the implied chaos an affront.

"When I was finally arrested for possession of cocaine," Priscilla declared two hours into her testimony, "I think I was relieved." Up until then, she'd only stolen occasional glances at the jury. Now, she looked directly at the jurors for the first time. "I was a drug addict," she said. "I was addicted to cocaine. I could see that it had to end this way, that I couldn't get clean on my own."

And prison had done its job, at least in regard to drugs, because she hadn't, she told them, gone back to cocaine, had resisted temptation despite all that followed, despite the kilos of white powder moving through her apartment.

"Priscilla," I asked just before Delaney called a fifteen minute recess, "were you asked to take a blood test to determine if there were drugs present in your body after your arrest early this year?"

"Yes, I was."

"And did you take that test voluntarily?"

"I did."

"And do you know the results of that test?"

"Yes."

"And what were the results?"

"I was clean."

"No cocaine? No heroin or marijuana?"

"No."

"No barbiturates? No amphetamines?"

"Nothing."

During the break, I watched Priscilla wolf down a custard-filled doughnut, sip at her coffee while she accepted encouragement from Janet and Rebecca. Her wool sweater was a pure green and very dark; if she dripped custard onto the wool, no amount of Kleenex and water would take it off. But, of course, being perfect, she didn't. Her movements were precise and delicate as she set her coffee on the railing, held a napkin beneath her chin, snipped off chunks of dough-nut with her front teeth. All the while engaged in vivacious conversation.

Priscilla added another facet to her performance after Delaney called us back to work. As she described her release from prison, her job at Tucker Trucking, the pure joy of living a free life, her manner became animated, almost perky. Her head tilted to the left and her smile broadened; her hands came together several times in an abbre-viated, silent clap. "I felt like I was going to family instead of work," she explained.

"And how often did you report to your parole officer?"

"Every two weeks at first. Then once a month."

"For how long?"

"For more than a year."

"And you were employed at Tucker Trucking for this entire period?"

"Yes."

I watched Latisha Garret, she of the stony face, nod her head in time to Priscilla's responses, as if listening to music.

"Now, Priscilla, were you tested for drugs when you reported to your parole officer?"

"Yes."

"Every time?"

"Yes."

"And did your parole office make unannounced visits to your home and place of work from time to time?"

"Yes."

"And were you routinely tested for drugs in the course of these unannounced visits?"

"Yes."

"Did you ever come up dirty, Priscilla? Were you ever found to have drugs in your system?"

"Never."

I turned to face the jury, changed the subject, while Priscilla, seemingly without effort, shifted personas. "Did there come a time, Priscilla, during this period, when your husband attempted to contact you?"

We flew, Priscilla and I, through this phase of her life, left it deliberately hazy. Yes, she'd come to believe that Byron had changed, that he, too, was ready to begin a new life. But, no, driven by cocaine and alcohol, he'd lied to her, trapped her, tortured her, promised to eventually kill her. Then, after she tried to escape, he'd placed the lid on the kettle.

"He told me if I left him, he'd kill my mother."

From behind, I heard Thelma begin to sob. In front of me, a frowning Delaney snatched up his gavel, then slowly returned it to the desk as Thelma, muttering, "I'm sorry. I'm sorry," fled the hushed courtroom.

"I think," Delaney said after informing the jury that courtroom outbursts were not to affect their deliberations, "this would be a good time to break for lunch." Once the jury had been safely removed, he turned to me, barely able to repress a smile, and said, "Mr. Kaplan, I trust you'll see to it that Mrs. Barrow remains under control. Assuming she wishes to sit through her daughter's remaining testimony."

The air in the adjoining courtroom, once the team had gathered, was celebratory. Thelma Barrow, I remember, despite her pain, was especially exuberant. She took her daughter's hands, stared, dry-eyed, into her daughter's face, said, "You were perfect, darling. Just perfect." A smiling Rebecca Barthelme stood behind them, her white hair floating out in seeming benediction.

With no place at this particular feast, I decided to go for a walk, maybe clear my head. I think if I'd made it, things might have turned out differently, but as I came into the corridor, I saw Rose Sweet talking to a reporter. She was very tiny, Rose Sweet, and a good deal older than Thelma, a hunched black woman standing in the shadow of a hulking reporter.

"How," I heard him ask, "did it feel to hear your son's character attacked by the woman who killed him?"

Behind them, a knot of reporters, including Phoebe Morris and Jay Harrison, waited by the elevator. They watched me, their eyes positively feral, for several seconds before they began to move. I wanted to flee, but I remained still as they swarmed around me. Somehow, despite having brushed off several of the same reporters as I'd entered the courthouse earlier that morning, I'd forgotten that the trial had meaning for the rest of the world, that there was a world beyond Sidney Kaplan and Priscilla Sweet.

"You can see for yourself," I told them as I stepped back through the door and closed it in their faces, "exactly what's happening."

Later, I parked myself on a bench several rows behind Priscilla, pretended to busy myself with my notes while I ate a ham sandwich, tossed down a bottle of Coke. Priscilla was again animated, vivacious, but when I caught her eyes from time to time, I felt as if I'd cannonballed into an empty pool. Finally, in a quiet moment, she slipped away from her mother to join me.

"How'm I doing?"

I looked at her, tried and failed to produce a smile. "Your lipstick's smudged," I told her. "You need to fix it."

Her smile remained in place; her eyes remained cold. "C'mon, Sid," she urged. "Don't be a party pooper. Life can be wonderful, if you choose to live it. If you refuse to let the past destroy the future." She fiddled in her purse, produced a small compact, flipped the lid open, finally said, without a trace of detectable irony, "Life is all we have."

I brought Priscilla to those final hours with Byron right after lunch. Ordinarily, I would have stretched her testimony through the afternoon, left the jury to sleep on our version of the evidence. But I'd laid a trap for Carlo, a small packet of prison letters now resting in one of Janet Boroda's files, and I knew he'd step into it before the afternoon wore down. Priscilla had admitted to dealing drugs, both before and after her separation; she'd spoken of her love for Byron in the same light. Carlo would try to convince the jury that drugs, and not love, had brought the Sweets back together, because it was the most obvious point of vulnerability in Priscilla's testimony. At that point, the letters would become relevant.

Priscilla, by design, kept her responses short and to the point as she described the final beating, two nights and a day unable to leave her bed, Byron's waving a cigarette in her direction. I'd urged her to show a small measure of reluctance to speak about those last hours, a proper respect for the horrific nature of the final act.

"When Byron threatened to burn you, Priscilla, did you believe that he would actually do it?"

"Yes."

"And would you tell us why you believed him?"

"Because he'd done it before."

Over Carlo's thunderous and quickly overruled objection, Priscilla, her breath coming in little chuffs, slowly unbuttoned her blouse to reveal a pair of shiny scars. The entire courtroom, the prosecution, the defense, the jurors, the spectators, came to an abrupt halt, as if posing for a photograph. If I'd had my way, I would have passed my client around, let the jury run its collective fingers over her wounds. Instead, I waited only long enough to let Priscilla button up, then asked, "And what happened next?"

I let her go through the rest of it without interruption, how she'd gone back into the bedroom, picked up Byron's gun, the gun he'd already told her she didn't have the courage to use, and pressed the cylinder release.

"Two of the bullets fell out," she said, "fell on the floor. I picked them up and put them back into the gun, then went into the living room. My hands were shaking and it took me a long time." She was rocking slowly in the chair, eyes down, back curved, and her voice was slightly hoarse, as if she lacked the breath to fully form her words. "When Byron saw me, he just laughed. He asked me what I was going to do with the gun, and I didn't have an answer. I wanted to get out of there, but I knew he wouldn't let me. I knew I didn't have any place to go." Her hand rose to briefly cover her mouth. Then she drew a deep breath, raised her chin, said in the saddest voice I've ever heard, "He started to get up, to get up out of the chair and the gun. . . . No, he started to get up and I pulled the trigger. I did it. I killed him."

I fought an urge to say, "Poor baby," stepping back instead to give the jury an unobstructed view. Priscilla was sobbing silently, her chest heaving. She clutched the edges of her sweater, drew them together, shook her head in disbelief. The jurors stared at her for a moment, then, one by one, turned away in embarrassment.

I milked the tableau for all it was worth, waited until Delaney ordered me to proceed before asking, "Will you tell us what happened next, Priscilla?"

"Byron fell to his knees. He crawled a few feet. . . ." Again, the hesitation, the sharply drawn breath. "And then he collapsed. I think I expected him to get up because I just stood there for . . . I don't remember exactly how long. Forever, it seemed like, until I knew he was dead. Until I knew I couldn't take it back."

"And what did you do then?"

"Do?" She looked at me, head cocked, eyes round and questioning. "I did nothing. I sat in the chair and I waited for something to happen."

"Did you think about escaping before the police arrived twenty minutes later?"

"No."

"Did you consider what might happen to you when the police arrived?"

"No."

"Even though you'd been in prison? Even though you knew what prison was like, you didn't think about running away?"

"I felt," she told the jury, "like I was paralyzed. Like I couldn't move. I felt like I wanted to go to sleep and never wake up."

I walked back to the defense table, shuffled a handful of papers, finally said, "No further, your Honor," before sitting down. Rebecca Barthelme, her courtroom face appropriately solemn, gave my sleeve a little tug before whispering, "Priscilla was perfect, Sid. Absolutely perfect."

According to the trial transcript, Carlo leaped eagerly into the trap I'd set for him. I can't draw the tone of his voice from the printed words, but I know his first task was to obliterate the emotion of the moment, to demonize Priscilla before the jury voted for canonization. His initial question—"Mrs. Sweet, did you ever sell drugs to children?"—set the stage for a barrage of similar questions. Priscilla, for her part, admitted to dealing drugs only before her separation from Byron. After they came back together, she'd been, she declared, nothing more than a mule, a prisoner forced to transport quantities of cocaine, to take the risks, from the police and from Byron's clientele, with no hope of eventual reward.

"I thought Byron was going to kill me," she told Carlo and the jury at one point. "What good would money do me if I was dead?"

They went back and forth for perhaps thirty minutes before Delaney, without an objection from me, ordered Carlo to move on. Carlo, as if on cue, asked, "Mrs. Sweet, is it your contention that after your and the victim's separation, he forced you to reconcile?"

At this point I was supposed to object. And not only because Carlo had completely mischaracterized Priscilla's testimony. It was my job, as it would be the job of any trial lawyer, to give my witness a little breathing room. Still, according to the transcript, I remained silent, partly, I'd like to believe, because Carlo, by attacking Priscilla's credibility, opened the door, not only for the admission of Byron's prison letters, but also for Byron's phony passport. The further Carlo went, the more latitude Delaney would grant when my time came on redirect.

There was something else, however, something obviously more important to me and which I still remember clearly. As I sat next to Rebecca and Janet, my legs crossed beneath the defense table, wishing for a cigarette, I began for no apparent reason to recall a long-forgotten period of my mother's life.

I believe I was six or seven years old, still young enough to spend virtually all of my time in the house of my parents, when Gregor Glitzky, via telephone, introduced himself as a trade minister attached to the Soviet U.N. mission. By then, of course, Magda had been sending out her letters of inquiry for several years and so the call may have seemed to her the logical culmination of an overwhelming effort. Or perhaps she was merely seduced by Gregor's enthusiasm. Without doubt, he expressed unbounded confidence, a belief in a world where things got done, where he, Gregor Glitzky, got them done.

In either event, what Gregor told my parents on the following Saturday, as he sat sipping tea in our kitchen, was simple enough and true on its face. Tens of thousands of European Jews (the exact number could not be known), faced with almost certain death at the hands of the Nazis and with no hope of escape to the west, had fled into the broad bosom of Mother Russia. Unfortunately, given the post-war political atmosphere, these refugees could not be allowed to leave and were now scattered throughout the vast Soviet empire.

"How to find them, eh? This is big problem for families in West." Gregor, as I resurrected him in Judge Thomas Delaney's courtroom, was a tall muscular man with enormous shoulders and a belly to match. His narrow Slavic eyes, pale blue and veiled by epicanthic folds at the corners, flicked from my father to my mother as he made his points. "But for Gregor Glitzky is simple matter. Cut through tape, this I say." He leaned as far forward as his gut would allow, flapped pale bushy eyebrows. "Somewhere in KGB, I tell myself, there is records of refugee foreigners. This must be so because in KGB there is records of every Soviet citizen."

I doubt very much that my father was impressed with Gregor's confident manner, any more than he was impressed with Gregor's cheap, double-breasted, Soviet blue suit. I remember him sitting there, my father, arms folded over his chest, staring along the length of his nose at Gregor Glitzky, smoking one cigarette after another. For Magda, it was an entirely different matter. As she listened to Gregor describe encounters with one or another Jewish exile, the efforts he made to establish contact with whatever remained of their families, she at first displayed a nervousness that masked an emotion she'd already come to fear. I don't know if Gregor sensed her hesitation or if he was simply in love with the sound of his own voice, but he continued on, hands flying as if the conversation was being conducted in sign language, until finally hope emerged, until Magda's sallow cheeks began to glow, until the bait was thoroughly taken. Only then did he set the hook.

"Corruption is sad fact of Soviet life," he declared. "For price, if you are knowing the right people, anything can be did."

The price, a mere one thousand dollars, would guarantee access to all KGB records in perpetuity, he told my parents. There would be no further payments. "I take nothing for self," he explained as he fumbled in a battered briefcase, drew forth a stack of worn testimonials. "For me is love labor."

Gregor Glitzky's love labor stretched out for nearly three years and eventually cost the Kaplan household more than five thousand dollars. I remember, early on, a flood of letters posted not only from Moscow and Leningrad, but from a host of smaller industrial cities. I remember Magda's face, as she slipped a polished fingernail under the flaps, projecting a radiance with which I was entirely unfamiliar.

I remember a shy smile, a quick glance in my direction, a brief hesitation before she removed the folded sheet of paper inside. I remember a map of the Soviet Union pinned to the wall behind our kitchen table, Magda's hands sweeping across the Urals, the Steppes, the highland plains of Asia as she gave substance to the words on the page.

Gregor's letters, right up to the end, were uniformly optimistic. Working from a list of relatives supplied by Magda, he developed various leads. The name Isidor Leibovits, for instance, Magda's brother, appeared in the wartime records of the Soviet Labor Ministry. A payment of the appropriate bribe to the appropriate KGB colonel revealed that after the war Isidor Leibovits had been moved east, to the oil fields of Kamchatka. A trip to the Kamchatka (for which, naturally, expense money was needed) yielded the sad fact that Isidor had moved again, to Leningrad, five thousand miles away.

Eventually, Isidor Leibovits, tracked to a lair in Minsk, disclaimed all knowledge of Magda's family. No big deal, however, because the trail of another Leibovits, an uncle, aunt, or cousin, had by this time already been crossed. By this time the chase was already in motion.

Oddly, my father reversed field, expressing, in the early months, a measure of respect for Gregor Glitzky. I remember him telling Magda that Gregor could neither move freely through the Soviet Union, nor freely correspond with an American, unless he had some clout. Later, he took a different tack. "For all I know," I heard him tell Grampa Itzy out of Magda's hearing, "this *gonif* never gets off his butt. For all I know, he mails letters to his buddies who mail them to us. I'm not writin' the bum another check."

I believe that my father recognized the terrible price Magda paid for Gregor's small-time con. Certainly, he kept writing checks long after he decided that Gregor was a hustler. But my father went off to work six days a week, busied himself with household chores on his one day off, while I, friendless even then, was left to watch Magda twist at the end of Gregor's line. Always quiet, over time she simply folded in on herself. Over time she became almost insubstantial, a vague, dreary presence hunched over the kitchen table, pen in hand, scratching away.

Dearest Gregor Glitzky.

* * *

I'll make this as simple as I can. At 4:30, Delaney sent the jury home and Priscilla came off the witness stand. As if expecting coronation, she strode, her chin high, across the well of the court before turning to embrace her mother. The trio of corrections officers assigned to escort her to the pens, though personal contact was expressly forbidden, made no attempt to interfere.

It was a beautiful moment, no doubt, a perfect moment, but what Sidney Kaplan did, out of a pressing need to redefine the aesthetics of that moment, was step up to his client, jam the barrel of his .32 beneath the base of her skull, and blow the top of her fucking head off.

Forty

Second day inside. I'm sitting on a bunk in an open housing area, an out of shape, middle-aged slice of Jewish whitebread, when Omar Skepps, his ebony skin humped with muscle, walks to within five feet of me and stops. Omar is the convict out of my worst nightmare. His eyes reflect a prison glare of such purity that it takes all the courage at my command to meet his gaze. Already I'm wondering if his cock will hurt a great deal more than a proctologist's gloved finger.

"Can I come in?"

Although I don't understand the question, the only conceivable answer is simple enough. Later, I will come to learn that a prisoner's bunk or cell is his home, that entry without permission is a deadly insult.

"Sure, c'mon in."

"I was wondrin' . . ." When Omar scratches the top of his freshly shaved head, the muscles on his shoulders rise to the tops of his ears. ". . . if you'd help me with my case."

Thus my new career begins. That night, over Styrofoam cups filled with muddy-black pruno, Omar and I cut a deal. For a price, I will work on any prisoner's case. (Not as an attorney, of course, but as a citizen adviser.) For a cut, Omar will screen clients, negotiate terms, collect debts, and protect his investment by watching my back.

Payment comes in many forms: cigarettes, of course, and cash, but also coke and smack, freshly pressed uniforms, smuggled legal forms, access to a typewriter, pork chop sandwiches from the Deputy Wardens' mess.

Business is at first desultory in the extreme. Everybody wants a free consultation, but only a desperate few are willing (and have the means) to pay for the service. Then Paul Blanchard, indicted for Possession 2, is released after his Legal Aid attorney, at Paul's insistence, files a motion for dismissal authored by yours truly. After that, success breeds success and my career takes off.

When Omar eventually cops to Rob 1 and is shipped off to Sing Sing, I find someone to replace him. When I, in turn, plead to Murder 2, and am transferred, first to Clinton, then to Attica, then to Green Haven, my reputation precedes me and I find cons with serious clout eager to become my partner. Even so, my incarceration is not without its negative moments. I have been attacked many times, and on one occasion beaten into unconsciousness.

A month after I enter the Clinton Correctional Facility I'm called to the office of Warden Thelonius Teagarden. Before he can threaten me, I vow that under no circumstances will I participate, now or ever, in a legal challenge to his or any other institution, that I am purely and simply a businessman. For this reason, and because I have done legal favors for dozens of corrections officers, I have never had my work confiscated, never been denied use of the law library or prison post office. It is also the reason, I am convinced, why I still possess the photographs gathered from my office three weeks after Priscilla's death by a newly impoverished Pat Hogan.

I keep the photos, of Caleb's and Magda's respective families, of Caleb, Julie, and myself, in a small wooden box made for me by a client in the Attica woodworking shop. The box is held together with dovetailed joints instead of nails or screws, thus allaying the fears of always nervous C.O.'s. The photos, of course, are far too precious to be displayed on a wall. No, like any other family treasure, they must be hidden away, protected from enemies and the elements, perused in secret like the fuck books that ignite the fantasies of my incarcerated brothers.

Priscilla died without making a sound. Her life's blood, mixed with pea-sized chunks of brain and shards of skull that had the feel of broken teeth, fell over Thelma Barrow and myself like an unexpected summer rain. Though I felt as if I might drown in blood, I was distinctly attracted to the heat and the wet, to the viscous feel of Priscilla's blood on my face, in my hair.

The atmosphere in the little courtroom was instantly saturated with the screams of innocent bystanders. I was yanked backward, slammed to the floor, rolled onto my face, and handcuffed. Still, they continued to scream and their screams blended in my ear like voices in a choir. As I was literally dragged from the courtroom to the pens, the blood flowing from my broken nose mixed with Priscilla's to fall sweetly on my tongue.

I think of Priscilla far less than I would have predicted, and of Magda far more. I've already said that I watched my mother twist in the wind. What I have not said, what I've only remembered since coming to prison, is that after Gregor's appearance (and before the nature of his scam grew too apparent to ignore) I became my mother's confidant, that we became closer than we'd ever been, closer than we'd ever be again. Not only did Magda read Gregor's letters aloud to me over lunch, but she spun little thumbnail sketches of this or that aunt or uncle or cousin, often keying her tales to whomever Gregor Glitzky was pursuing. These stories, as I remember them, had an impish quality, formed as they were in the mind of the child who'd left Budapest years before.

Of course, I was blind to the gravity of Magda's search, how much of her very life was at stake. All I knew was that my mother was happy and that she'd included me in her happiness as she'd never included me in her pain. When she pulled away from me, I became . . .

That's as far as I've gotten and as far I want to get: a little boy huddled over a bowl of potato soup, inhaling the blended fragrance of leeks, parsley, and dill, listening to his mother's voice, to the twin emotions of hope and happiness, accepting them as love.

About Priscilla Sweet's last moments, as has already been stated, I remember only bits and pieces. Still, I'm certain that I carried my .32 into Judge Delaney's courtroom that day as I'd carried it many times into many courtrooms. Like any other red-blooded American male, I loved the feel of a lethal weapon, the danger of it, the illusion of physical security generated by its mere presence. I'm also certain that if I'd been unarmed that afternoon, Priscilla would still be alive, that I lacked the courage to formulate the necessary intent to commit murder. Nevertheless, I was indicted for murder.

Though even Mary Immaculata Corvelli, the ADA assigned to prosecute me, agreed that my crime lacked the aggravating factors necessary for a sentence of death, I faced upon conviction two very ugly realities: life without parole or life with the possibility of parole after twenty-five years. Ever the positive and practical attorney, over the next two months I kept reminding myself that I would rejoin the free world at age 72, assuming I received the latter sentence and with time off for good behavior.

"Americans are living longer than ever," I explained to Omar Skepps over a game of chess. "Healthier, too." Around us, seventy-five merciless criminals howled, shouted, cursed, played a dozen radios tuned to a dozen stations. "What I have to do is plead it out."

"Why the man gonna give you a plea?" Institutional almost from birth, Omar had developed a practical side of his own. "Bein' as you got nothin' to give back."

"Because," I told him, "if they don't, I'm gonna plead not guilty by reason of mental defect and represent myself."

I'll be eligible for parole in a mere sixteen years.

Phoebe Morris will arrive to collect these last pages in a few hours and I have still not begun to approach the central issue. Phoebe has done extremely well over the last few years, jumping to the *New York Times*, then establishing a syndicated column that runs weekly in a hundred newspapers.

We've cut a deal, Phoebe and I. For a fee and the right to put her name on the cover and add chapters of her own, she will market the manuscript, see to collecting advances and royalties. In New York, according to a law that has already been once declared unconstitutional and rewritten, convicted felons are not allowed to profit from their crimes. We shall see.

About the killing of Priscilla Sweet let me say the following. On the one hand, I did not feel obligated to avenge Caleb and Julie. Not only had I not sent them to their deaths, I had insisted they remain home on the night in question. In so doing I had exercised, as they say in the legal biz, due diligence.

On the other hand, I must certainly have felt, on a level below pure (and mere) obligation, compelled to exact some measure of revenge. Why else would I have formulated so many truncated plans for revenge? True, I constructed a number of elaborate rationales in support of Priscilla's innocence before Hogan presented me with the proof positive. But I can argue that my rationales smacked of desperation precisely because I knew that something had to be done and I didn't want to do it. Viewed through that admittedly dark lens, Priscilla Sweet, when she stood up to her loss, when she bargained for her share of the blood money, when she refused to acknowledge the pain of any lesser punishment, invited her own death.

I was in residence at the very scenic Clinton Correctional Facility in northeastern New York State, maybe nine months into my sentence, teaching remedial English to a class of hardened cons who stood no chance of demonstrating their skills anytime in the near, or even distant, future, when a half dozen corrections officers barged into the room. The squad was led by a middle-aged, paunchy lieutenant named Harrelson who ordered us to undress for a search. There was nothing personal in this, certainly not on Harrelson's part. A CO had been stabbed in the mess hall a few hours before and the population was now paying the price.

Ever the good inmate, I stripped down without complaint, then lined up against the chalkboard to await developments. One by one, the other cons joined me, but it wasn't until the last man approached that I was jolted from my carefully cultivated air of indifference. Johnny Caitlin, the con in question, had two scars—two circular raised scars, each about the diameter of a cigarette—side by side in the center of his chest.

Later that night, I described the scars to my cell mate, a professional criminal who'd accumulated several decades of hard time, and asked him what they signified.

"You don't know?" Aureliano Aguirre loved to display incredulity in the face of my inexperience. "You never seen that before? Where you been all your life?"

I was tempted to reply that, unlike himself, I'd spent the major part of my years on the planet a free man, but settled for repeating the question.

Aureliano laid back on his bunk and shook his head. "You see scars like that," he told me, "you stay away. Them scars are the mark of a snitch."

As they say on the Rican side of the dining hall: *Chinga tu madre, maricon.*